Sarah N. (Sarah Nicholas) Randolph

The Life of Gen. Thomas J. Jackson

Sarah N. (Sarah Nicholas) Randolph

The Life of Gen. Thomas J. Jackson

ISBN/EAN: 9783337016395

Printed in Europe, USA, Canada, Australia, Japan

Cover: Foto ©Raphael Reischuk / pixelio.de

More available books at **www.hansebooks.com**

OF

GEN. THOMAS J. JACKSON.

("STONEWALL" JACKSON.)

BY

SARAH NICHOLAS RANDOLPH,

AUTHOR OF "THE DOMESTIC LIFE OF THOMAS JEFFERSON."

———

WITH ILLUSTRATIONS.

PHILADELPHIA:
J. B. LIPPINCOTT & CO.
1876.

TO

MY LITTLE FRIEND AND PUPIL,

WILLIAM CORCORAN EUSTIS,

I DEDICATE THIS BOOK,

HOPING THAT IN ITS SIMPLE STORY OF THE LIFE OF A GREAT
AND GOOD MAN HE MAY FIND INCENTIVES SO TO GUIDE AND
DIRECT HIS COURSE ON THE SMILING PATHWAY WHICH
LIFE OFFERS TO HIM, THAT DEVOTION TO TRUTH,
LOVE FOR GOD AND HIS FELLOW-MAN, AND HIGH
INTELLECTUAL ATTAINMENTS MAY MARK
HIM AS THE WORTHY HEIR OF THE
NOBLE GRANDSIRE WHOSE
NAME HE BEARS.

PREFACE.

It is with extreme diffidence that I appear before the public as the biographer of the great Captain whose name stands on the title-page of this little volume. I do not presume to rank my work with the great military biographies in which the young soldier studies the strategy of great leaders of great armies. Nor have I ventured to approach the discussion of the causes of the late war between the North and the South. I have merely attempted to write a popular life of Jackson by telling the simple story of his brief but brilliant career so that "he who runs may read." Awkwardly as I may have done this, the reader will find it a life, in its beginning, in its silent growth, and in its glorious sequel, full of instruction and of charm for the imagination.

The sifting events of years must pass, the unearthing of material in anecdotes and side-lights which the very appearance of different lives of Jackson will bring to light must be known, and the records of that army in whose achievements he played such a distinguished part must be published, before a really full and standard life of him can be written. But, until that time comes, the reader will find in the following unpretending pages the faithful record of the life of one of the most remarkable men this country has ever produced, and my task will indeed has been poorly executed if he does not rise from their perusal filled with admiration for Jackson's greatness, and with a reverence, almost approaching awe, for a purity of heart and an earnest simplicity of faith such as are rarely vouchsafed to the children of men.

I must here acknowledge the great assistance in the preparation of this volume received from the valuable "Life of Jackson," by Dr. Dabney, whom I have in one or two instances followed so closely that I might, but for this frank acknowledgment, almost be liable to the charge of plagiarism.

The vivid descriptions of battles found in the beautifully written "Histoire de la Guerre civile en Amérique," by the Comte de Paris, place me under obligations to their royal author, whose enlightened pages no Southerner can read without a sigh of regret that his materials at hand for the Southern view of the question were not as abundant as were those for the opposite side.

THE AUTHOR.

Edge Hill, January, 1876.

CONTENTS.

CHAPTER I.

EARLY LIFE.

CHAPTER II.

WEST POINT.

CHAPTER III.

LEXINGTON.

CHAPTER IV.

APPOINTED COLONEL.

CHAPTER V.

HARPER'S FERRY.

CHAPTER VI.

MANASSAS.

CHAPTER VII.

ROMNEY.

CHAPTER VIII.

KERNSTOWN.

CHAPTER IX.

WINCHESTER.

A*

CHAPTER X.

THE RETREAT DOWN THE VALLEY.

CHAPTER XI.

BATTLES AROUND RICHMOND.

CHAPTER XII.

SECOND BATTLE OF MANASSAS.

CHAPTER XIII.

SHARPSBURG.

CHAPTER XIV.

FREDERICKSBURG.

CHAPTER XV.

WINTER QUARTERS, 1863.

CHAPTER XVI.

CHANCELLORSVILLE.

CHAPTER XVII.

DEATH AND BURIAL.

CHAPTER XVIII.

CONCLUSION.

THE LIFE

OF

GENERAL THOMAS J. JACKSON.

CHAPTER I.

EARLY LIFE.

NOT quite half a century ago, a thoughtful-looking, rather slender, blue-eyed little boy, about eight years old, was seen walking along the road leading from Clarksburg to Lewis County, in Western Virginia. The sun was approaching the western horizon, and the boy moved along wearily and mayhap with aching feet, for he had walked eighteen miles that day. But the child is father to the man; a strong will and patient perseverance had borne him through the heat and toil of the day. A few more minutes, and he has reached the goal of his wishes, as, knocking at the door of a house at which he stops, the homeless little traveler announces himself to its owner as his nephew Thomas Jonathan Jackson, and, though an unexpected guest, receives from his kind-hearted uncle the affectionate welcome which assured him that here at last he had found a resting-place and a home which would be his as long as he needed one. This extraordinary display of daring and unyielding will and perseverance was indeed a fit opening of the career of one who was destined to command armies, make swift marches, win great victories, and to fall upon the field of battle with his name enrolled among those of the great captains of the earth, and his memory enshrined in the hearts of his countrymen.

The race from which this great man sprang were of a sturdy stock of pioneers in the New World, whose energies and great probity won for them the esteem of the early settlers with whom they lived. John Jackson, the great-grandfather of "Stonewall Jackson," landed with other British emigrants in 1748 in Maryland. There he married Elizabeth Cummins, of London, and moved at once with this estimable woman to the northern part of Virginia. They lived for a short time in a beautiful valley of the Potomac River where Moorfields is now found. Having remained here three years, they moved still farther west, and finally settled in a place in Upshur County, Virginia, which was once known as Fort Jackson, but is now called Buckhannon.

The couple are represented as being of very unequal stature, the wife towering above the husband, and being as remarkable for her quick energy and great daring as he was for his goodness, his industry, and his tranquil courage. Tradition has preserved many instances of the undaunted spirit which she displayed on different occasions when the safety of the colonists was endangered by the attacks—often formidable—of the Indians. We are told that she never quailed at the sound of the savage war-whoop, but when shut up in a stockade fort, to which the settlers fled in time of danger, her voice, more frequently than that of any other, was heard soothing the fears of the women and children, and exhorting the men to deeds of daring and self-sacrifice.

It is not now necessary to give a further account of this worthy couple, and I will only add that, when the American Revolution broke out, John Jackson fought in it with his elder sons, that he afterwards made quite a handsome fortune, and died in his eighty-sixth year. His stout-hearted wife survived him twenty-four years, and lived to the extreme old age of one hundred and five. This good couple had eight children,—five sons and three daughters. The second of these five sons, Edward Jackson, left fifteen children, one of whom, Jonathan Jackson, was the father of our hero.

Jonathan Jackson was a lawyer, and lived in Clarksburg. He married Julia Neale, of Parkersburg. She was a tall, graceful girl, whose sweet countenance and winning manners charmed all who met her, as in after-years her good sense and earnest piety commanded their respect. Her husband had inherited quite a snug little fortune from his father, which he might easily have increased by the labors of his profession, for he was quite an eminent lawyer. Unfortunately, however, in undertaking to assist some friends who were in trouble, he lost much of his own fortune in trying to rebuild theirs. The rest was lost at the card-table; and thus it happened that before he had reached the prime of life he had lost all of his property except the house in which he lived, and his family were dependent for their support on what he could make by his profession. Jonathan Jackson had four children: Elizabeth, Warren, Thomas Jonathan, and Laura,—of whom only the last is now living. He was a very devoted and affectionate father, and lost his life by a fever which he caught while nursing his daughter Elizabeth, who died of the same disease. He had nursed her day and night, and hoped on against hope as the progress of the disease showed too plainly what the result would be. At last the child died, and the heart-broken father, worn out by his fatigue, his distress, and the misfortunes accumulating upon him and his family, followed her to the grave two weeks later.

The little Thomas Jonathan was only three years old at the time of his father's death, and at that tender age the young child's troubles in life began. Happy it was for him that he was too young to appreciate his mother's desolate condition! Her husband left her penniless, and she found herself a widowed mother of three young children, without a home, and without any means of support. Kind friends were found who came to her relief. The Masons, of which order her husband had been an active member, gave her, soon after his death, a small house, containing only one room; and in this desolate little home, with her children around her, we behold this young mother commencing her widowed life.

To enable her to support herself and children, she took in sewing and taught a small school. The weight of troubles resting upon her was almost too great for one of her delicate health; and yet she bore up patiently and bravely, her bright and cheerful disposition only giving way occasionally to fits of gloom and despondency.

It is said, by those who knew him best, that General Jackson rarely spoke of his childhood, having so many painful recollections of its trials and heartaches; and when we think how many and how great these were, we can well understand how he should have shrunk from looking back on them. Three years after her husband's death, Mrs. Jackson, who was still young and beautiful, married again. Her second husband, a gentleman named Woodson, was, like her first, a lawyer. He was very poor, and her relations were violently opposed to her marrying him, and threatened, if she insisted on doing so, to take her children from her and support and educate them themselves. If, however, she would not marry him, they would aid her with all the money they could spare. But neither threats nor promises would make her give up her second marriage. She had, however, been married but a short time when she found that her husband was too poor to undertake the support of her children, and she was forced to divide them out among their father's brothers and sisters, who had offered to take charge of them.* We can easily appreciate the trial it was to her to give up her young children. She was particularly distressed at parting with little Thomas. He was then, it is said, a pretty, rosy-cheeked, blue-eyed little boy, just six years old. Young as he was, he never forgot his own nor his mother's distress at their parting. His father had owned several slaves, but there was now only one left, " Uncle Robinson," and he was to take the child behind him on horseback and carry him from his mother to his new home. The hour came for his departure; his poor mother, with an aching heart, put up with her own loving hands a lunch for the little boy to eat on the road. " Uncle Robinson"

* Since the above was written, I have learned that Mrs. Jackson gave up her children not on account of want of support for them, but because she went with her husband to Fayette County, and the journey was considered too trying for them. She herself had a presentiment of her own death when she left. Part of the time after her first husband's death she lived with her father.

rode to the door, and all was now ready for him to go. His mother bade him good-by, and the child was lifted up and placed on the horse behind the faithful slave. They had already started, when the poor mother —doubtless to have an excuse to fold her little son once more in her arms—called them back, to see whether she had omitted anything which could add to his comfort. But she had done all for him that her limited means would allow. . And it was perhaps some violent outburst of grief at this second farewell which so impressed the scene on the child's mind that as a man he looked back to it as the most painful of his life. The horse's head was once more turned away from the door; they again set out, and from that day his mother's home ceased to be his.

Mrs. Woodson did not live long after parting with her children. A son was born a year after her marriage, and two months later she died. Her children, Warren and Thomas and their little sister Laura, were summoned to their mother's bedside as soon as it was discovered how ill she was, and remained with her until her death. Thomas was seven years old when this took place. She talked a great deal to him as she lay on her death-bed; and those dying instructions and prayers of his mother were never effaced from his memory. She sank at last quietly and peacefully to rest. Young as he was when she died, General Jackson never forgot his mother, and to the day of his death he continued to think of her as of one who was beautiful, pious, and lovable in every respect.

Their father's sisters, Mrs. Brake and Mrs. White, took charge of the little orphan children after their mother's death. Thomas lived with Mrs. Brake, about four miles from Clarksburg. He was a quiet, grave, and thoughtful child, and had been living with his uncle and aunt Brake only a year when one day he left their house without any warning, walking, though only eight years old, alone to Clarksburg. There he went to the house of Judge Jackson, a cousin of his father, and asked Mrs. Jackson to give him his dinner. She kindly complied with his request, and while he was sitting eating at the table he said, very quietly, "Uncle Brake and I don't agree; I have quit him, and shall not go back any more."

Startled at this unexpected announcement, Mrs. Jackson tried to persuade him to return to his uncle Brake, who, it seemed, had offended him by his sternness. But he simply said, "No, he and I don't agree; I have quit him, and shall not go back any more." When he left Judge Jackson's house, he went to that of a lady cousin, to whom he was very much attached, and asked her to let him stay all night with her. She gladly consented; and he soon made to her the same remark he had made to Mrs. Jackson, and showed the same quiet determination never to return to live with the uncle he had just left.

It was the next morning that he left Clarksburg, and in that lonely walk of eighteen miles, already described, showed so remarkably that quiet self-reliance which characterized him in after-years, and which helped not a little to make him famous. The uncle to whom he went was Cummins Jackson, and from him, and two aunts who lived with their brother Cummins, he received the greatest kindness. In this new home he had the pleasure of living with his brother Warren, who had long been an inmate of his uncle's house.

To the two brothers Cummins Jackson fulfilled the duties of a father, and his house was always a happy home from the time he came to it, as we have seen, a forlorn little traveler, only eight years old, to the day when he left it, a stalwart youth, to enter the Military Academy of West Point. It would have been impossible for a child to lead a life better adapted to physical and moral development than the one Jackson led under his uncle's care. From him he learned all sorts of country games and occupations, and, associating with him more as a companion than as a child, became wonderfully independent and manly for his years.

Cummins Jackson gave to his two nephews every advantage of education which the country then afforded. Thomas was not quick in learning, but he was very industrious and devoted to study. His mind was clear and strong, and what he learned he learned thoroughly. His brother Warren did not like to study, and, disregarding his uncle's kindness, became impatient at being forced to attend school regularly, and finally refused to live any longer under his roof. His uncle, indignant at his ingratitude and rebellion against his authority, told him he might go; and the unhappy boy left, taking his younger brother with him.

Thomas, we are told, left his uncle's house with unfeigned sorrow; but such was his attachment to his brother that he could not bear to be separated from him.

The two boys accordingly, one fourteen and the other twelve years old, left their uncle's sheltering roof to seek their fortunes in the great world of which they knew so little. They went first to the house of a kind, maternal uncle; but he, like Cummins Jackson, insisted on their going to school. Warren again rebelled, and again persuaded Thomas to join him in leaving a home where they had found nothing but kindness.

The two children went down the Ohio River, and their friends lost sight of them. The fall months passed away, and the winter set in, and still there were no tidings of the young wanderers. At length, in February, they made their appearance. Their clothes were travel-stained and worn, and their faces showed the effects of sickness and hardship. Their relations, shocked at seeing their condition, heard with dismay the tale of their adventures. Their account was that they had floated in a boat down the Ohio, making their living by first one occupation and then another, until they reached its mouth. They then went down the Mississippi until they reached a lonely island opposite the southwestern corner of Kentucky. There they landed and made a bargain with some men to cut wood on this island for the Mississippi steamers. They lived in a cabin which barely protected them from the weather, and spent the summer cutting wood, at which they worked hard. The island was unhealthy, and they had chills and fever. At last, when they found they could stand it no longer, they asked a steamboat captain to take them back home. This he kindly consented to do, and thus, weary and worn, they were enabled to reach home once more.

Thomas Jackson returned to his uncle Cummins, and in his house he was tenderly cared for, and soon regained his health and strength. Warren, ashamed perhaps to return to the good uncle whom he had left so unceremoniously, went to live with his aunt, Mrs. Isaac Brake, from whom he received great kindness; but, never recovering from the effects of the hardships he had undergone, he died some years later, of consumption.

After his trip down the Mississippi, Thomas went back, as we have seen, to live with his uncle Cummins, nor did he ever again show any desire to leave him. He and his sister, after Warren's death, were the only two of their father's children left; the latter lived in Wood County, where her mother's relations took care of her. As soon as Thomas was separated from Warren, his desire to go to school was quite as great as his uncle could have wished. Cummins Jackson owned a mill, situated not far from his house, and close to it was the school-house in which Thomas Jackson spent his early school-days.

His mind, though clear and strong, was not a very quick one; but what he once learned was his forever. Nothing could induce him to attempt the recitation of a lesson which he did not understand. Of arithmetic he was very fond, and it was the one of his lessons which he learned and understood most quickly. His anxiety to learn and his fondness for study in no wise interfered with his devotion to boyish games and exercise. In games of base-ball he was generally chosen as captain of one side, which most frequently proved the winning party. He was not a fast runner, but was surpassed by none of his companions in jumping and climbing.

A quiet and peaceful boy, he was yet quick to resent an insult, and once, in a fight, preferred to receive a whipping rather than cry out, "Enough!"

Perhaps the most striking characteristic of Jackson as a child was his devotion to truth. From this neither threat nor temptation could induce him to swerve for an instant, and teachers and scholars alike admired and respected his courage, honesty, and truth. Industrious in and out of school, he was, however, always anxious to join his uncle whenever he went on a chase. Cummins Jackson, a fearless man and bold rider, enjoyed nothing more than a fox-hunt; and in this exciting sport he was joined by his young nephew as soon as he was old enough. We can easily picture to ourselves this uncle and nephew mounting their horses and sallying forth in the bracing air of a bright, frosty autumn morning, and being soon engaged in a wild ride over hill and dale, in which the boy was not surpassed by the man in boldness and daring. In such a school young Jackson could not fail to become a fine, fearless horseman, and to learn that disregard for fatigue and exposure which is so characteristic of the young men of the South. But it was no part of his uncle's training that he should partake only of his amusements; and he often had him to assist in his labors on his farm. To a lad as industrious as Thomas, this was no hardship, and his uncle found in him an able and willing assistant.

Though owning slaves, Cummins Jackson had not enough to perform all the work on his farm and at his mill. He and his nephew, therefore, put their own shoulders to the wheel. When Thomas was large enough to undertake such a task, it generally fell to his lot to take a team of oxen and haul logs from the woods to the mill, where they were to be sawed into planks. He soon learned to do this work so well, and showed so much resolution in the discharge of his duty, that whenever a particularly large log was to be brought to the mill he was sent to the woods with a party of men under his command, and the log always reached its destination safely. Thus he learned on his uncle's farm to work, to do well what he undertook, and to control himself and those under him.

An anecdote is told of him when he was quite a child, which shows that he had both courage and resolution even at that tender age.   When riding home late one evening, a tall, white, ghostly figure suddenly rose from the roadside.   The boy and horse were both frightened; the latter snorted and wheeled to run, but his young rider, recovering himself, pulled him back into the road, and, plying whip and spurs, galloped by the white figure, which a few minutes later proved to be one of his young uncles wrapped in a sheet.

In the school of such a life the boyhood of General Jackson was passed.   His love of independence led him to try to support himself when still very young, as he was anxious to be no longer dependent on his uncle.

His first occupation was that of a constable, a position whose stern duties could be fulfilled only by a brave and determined man, and Jackson was found to be well qualified for the post.   On one occasion he had to collect a sum which the person to whom it was owed had in vain tried to get.   Jackson, having failed in several attempts to get the money, finally made the man who owed it promise that he would meet him in the little village of Weston on a certain day and be ready to pay the money down. Having exacted this promise from the debtor, he pledged himself to the creditor to pay the money on that day.

The day came, and Jackson went to Weston.   The creditor was there, in readiness to receive his money, but not the man who was to pay it.   Jackson kept his promise with the former by paying him the required sum out of his own pocket.   Determined, however, that the other should be punished for failing to keep his word, he quietly waited for him to make his appearance in Weston, having made up his mind to seize and sell his horse if he could get the money in no other way.

As he expected, the man arrived the next day; but, it

being considered in that country improper, under any circumstances, to seize a man's horse while he was on him, the young constable waited until he saw him dismount. He then went to him, reproached him for his breach of faith, and, reminding him of how often he had played him false, tried to seize his horse. The rider resisted, and a violent fight and scuffle ensued, during which the man succeeded in jumping on his horse.

For a moment Jackson was disconcerted, but he was not to be outwitted by his cunning adversary. Holding the bridle firmly grasped, he looked around, and seeing the door of a stable near by open, he deliberately led the horse towards it. The door was too low for a man to pass through on horseback, and Jackson quietly told his adversary that he must dismount or be knocked off. He resisted and entreated, but the horse was led steadily on to the door, and as he reached it the man was forced to slip off in order to save himself, and thus Jackson was left in possession of the horse.

On the death of his brother Warren we find Jackson writing to his uncle, Mr. Neale, as follows: " I have received no answer to my last communication conveying the sad news of my brother's premature death. He died in hope of a bright immortality at the right hand of his Redeemer. His last hours were spent in admonishing his friends who wept around his bed to flee from the wrath to come. . . . As time is knowledge, I must hasten my pen forward. We have received the smiles of a bounteous Providence in a favorable spring. There is a volunteer company forming here to march for Texas in order to assist the noble cause of liberty."

Jackson's great devotion to his young sister has already been alluded to. As a pleasing proof of this, it is related that the first money he ever made was laid out in a silk dress for her.

During these days of his early youth, whether assisting his uncle on his farm or enjoying with him the exciting scenes of a fox-hunt,—of which sport there was danger of his becoming too fond,—or whether busily engaged in discharging the duties of a constable, there was one thought which possessed Jackson's mind above all others, one wish that was dearer to his heart than any other; and that was, to secure a good education. His heart was so full of this that every one who was thrown much with him saw how eager he was to learn, and, as we shall soon see, even a poor blacksmith living in his neighborhood found out his great desire to be well educated, and sympathized with him in his efforts to be so. But the difficulties to overcome were very great. He was poor, and began to earn his living long before it was time that he should have left school. The part of the country, too, in which he lived offered no educational advantages, the schools being few and not very good. But Jackson saw that no man could rise to great distinction without education, and next to his desire to be good was that of being great, and he determined to leave no stone unturned in his effort to secure an education which would enable him to attain honors for which his soul so early thirsted. But his days of trial on that subject were soon to have an end. His struggles and perseverance in overcoming the obstacles in his path had been witnessed by too many for some one not to be ready to give him a helping hand when the opportunity came, which it did at last, and unexpectedly he had the fond wish of his heart gratified in a manner which he had never dreamt of.

West Point, it is well known, has as many pupils or cadets as there are Congressional districts in the country. The expenses of this great military academy are paid by the United States Government with the money that the different States pay into its treasury. So that when a young man from Virginia is educated at West Point free of all cost to himself, it is no gift to him, but the payment of a just debt which the United States Government owes to his State.

In 1842 it happened that there was no cadet at West Point from the Congressional district in which Jackson lived. At the recommendation of Mr. Hays, the member of Congress from that district, a young man was appointed. He had a quick mind, but so little self-restraint and energy that, on seeing how hard the young men had to study at West Point, and under what strict rules they were obliged to live, he determined he could not stand such a life, and returned home in disgust, resigned his appointment, and left the place to be filled by one whose name and whose glory the world can never forget.

Just about this time, Cummins Jackson, going to the shop of a blacksmith, heard from him of this young man's ignoble conduct, the blacksmith concluding his remarks by saying, "Here now is a good chance for Thomas Jackson, as he is so anxious for an education." The thought struck Cummins Jackson as a happy one, and on returning home he told his nephew of the opportunity thus offered him of getting an appointment to West Point. Young Jackson began eagerly to take steps to secure this, and without a moment's delay went to his friends and asked them to sign a letter of recommendation for him to Mr. Hays. This they willingly did, as all were anxious to give him a helping hand. One gentleman to whom he applied asked him if he thought his education sufficiently advanced for him to enter West Point. For a moment his countenance fell, but was again lit up as he said, calmly, " At least I am determined to try, and I want you to help me do this."

As soon as the letters recommending his appointment were procured, they were forwarded to Washington. While awaiting the reply, Jackson made the most of his time by reviewing his studies. In this he was kindly assisted by a lawyer in Weston, who acted as his tutor but declined to receive any pay for his services. In due time the reply from Mr. Hays came, in which he said he would do all he could to secure the appointment for Jackson. The latter, in his eagerness to lose no time in entering West Point should he secure the appointment, determined to go at once to Washington in order to be ready to receive it. His plain and scanty wardrobe was accordingly packed in a pair of saddle-bags, and, dressed in a full suit of homespun, he mounted his horse and set out to make his entrance into the world, —that world which before his death was destined to resound with the fame of this now obscure youth.

He was accompanied by a servant, who was to return home with his horse when he took the stage, which he expected to do at Clarksburg. To that place he pushed forward, but found, on his arrival, that the stage had passed by. Nothing daunted, he galloped after it, overtook it, dismissed his servant with the horses, and continued his journey in the lumbering stage-coach.

On reaching Washington, he went directly to Mr. Hays, who, pleased with the energy he had shown, took him, all travel-stained as he was, to the Secretary of

War, from whom he was to receive his appointment. The Secretary, after a few minutes' conversation with him, was so well pleased with his manliness and quiet determination that he wrote the appointment out for him on the spot.

Mr. Hays wanted Jackson to stay several days with him in Washington and enjoy the sights and pleasures of the city; but the young man, who still thought only of that longed-for education which was now at length within his reach, said no; he only wanted to see the view from the top of the Capitol, and then hurry on to West Point.

To the top of the Capitol young Jackson accordingly went. In a long and silent gaze he looked down upon the city lying at his feet; upon the majestic river sweeping by, that like himself had its origin among the picturesque woods and rocks of Western Virginia; and farther on beyond its sparkling waters and dancing wavelets his eye rested on the territory of his own loved State. There, too, on a height overhanging the Potomac, he saw, embowered in trees and reflecting the light of the morning sun, the future home of the then modest but rising young officer whose twin brother in glory he was destined to be. Could his eye have seen a few miles farther into that loved land,—could he in prophetic vision have caught a glimpse of a not very distant future,—there, on the field of Manassas, he would have seen, amid the din and smoke of battle, the tall, calm figure of a Virginia commander, whose steadfastness under fire and against overwhelming odds caused a brother officer to point him out to his men as a shining example, and to shout out with his expiring breath the immortal name of STONE-WALL JACKSON.

3*

CHAPTER II.

An old friend and comrade of Jackson thus describes his arrival at West Point:

"In June, 1842, A. P. Hill, George C. Pickett, B. D. Fry, and the writer, having passed our first week at the Military Academy, were standing together on the south side of the south barracks at West Point, when a cadet-sergeant came by us, conducting a newly-arrived cadet to his quarters. He was apparently about twenty years of age, and was full grown; his figure was angular and clumsy; his gait was awkward; he was clad in old-fashioned Virginia homespun woolen cloth; he bore across his shoulders a pair of weather-stained saddle-bags; and his hat was one of those heavy, low-crowned, broad-brimmed wool hats usually worn in those days by county constables, etc. He tramped along by the side of the sergeant with an air of resolution, and his stolid look added to the inflexible determination of his whole aspect, so that one of us remarked, 'That fellow has come here to stay.' His name was Thomas J. Jackson.

"He had a rough time in the Academy at first, for his want of previous training placed him at a disadvantage, and it was all he could do to pass his first examination. We were studying algebra, and maybe analytical geometry, that winter, and Jackson was very low in his class standing. All lights were put out at 'taps,' but

30

just before the signal he would pile up his grate with anthracite coal, and, lying prone before it on the floor, would work away at his lessons by the glare of the fire, which scorched his very brain, till a late hour in the night. This evident determination to succeed not only aided his own efforts directly, but impressed his instructors in his favor, and he rose steadily, year by year, till we used to say, 'If we had to stay here another year, "old Jack" would be at the head of the class.'

" By the fourth year he attained a position in the first section ; but his lower standing during the early years in the course, and in drawing, French, and some other studies of a lighter and more ornamental character, brought his average below the point to which he had actually attained by the end of our course.

" In the riding-hall I think his sufferings must have been great ; he had a very rough horse, and when the order came to 'cross stirrups' and 'trot,' 'old Jack' swayed about and struggled hard to keep his horse. When he had advanced to riding at the heads, leaping the bars, etc., his equitation was truly fearful ; but he persevered through the most perilous trials, and no man in the riding-house would take more risks than he, and certainly no one had our good wishes for success and safety more than he.

" I believe he went through the very trying ordeal of the four years at West Point without ever having a hard word or a bad feeling from cadet or professor ; and while there were many who seemed to surpass him in the graces of intellect, in geniality, and in good fellowship, there was no one of our class who more absolutely possessed the respect and confidence of all than he did."

Knowing how badly prepared Jackson was, Mr. Hays wrote to the authorities and asked that his entrance examinations might be made as easy as possible. He also stated that young Jackson's opportunities for receiving an education had been very few, and that he was a most excellent and promising young man. Moved by these considerations, the authorities were very lenient in their examination of him; and he afterwards declared that if they had not been he could not have entered the Military Academy. As soon as he was numbered among the cadets at West Point, he devoted himself most earnestly to his studies. The older cadets, who were in the habit of playing tricks upon the new-comers, did not attempt anything of the sort with him, for he was so quiet and dignified that there were very few who would venture to take any liberties with him.

After working hard at his books all day, he generally went with some companion to take a ramble over the wild, beautiful hills around West Point, or spent an hour or two on the top of a bluff, watching the waters of the Hudson dancing at his feet. His countenance was grave when he was silent; but if he spoke on a subject which interested him his face became animated, and his eyes beamed with fire and intelligence. As the examinations at the end of the first term came on, he is said to have suffered great agony of mind, fearing he might be among those who, getting below a certain mark, would have to leave. Years afterwards he used to say that after entering West Point and finding what amount of study was required, and how many cadets were sent off annually, he fully expected to be dismissed, and in anticipation suffered all the shame of going home and being laughed at. He even prepared what he would say to his young friends and companions at home if he was sent back, and how he would tell them "if they had been there and found it as hard as he did, they would have failed too."

But, trying as this period of his life was, Jackson's patient perseverance and enduring courage enabled him to pass triumphantly through it, and, not allowing himself to be down-hearted, he never flagged at his work.

While at West Point, he wrote down for his own use certain rules of conduct and maxims by which he should be guided. Among the latter we find the chief one to be:

"*You May Be Whatever You Resolve To Be.*"

He had early determined to be great and good, and he never ceased striving to accomplish whatever he undertook.

In his intercourse with his fellow-students he was invariably kind and courteous in his manners, and was always ready to nurse and aid those who were sick and in trouble. The second year that he was at West Point he received seven demerits, which the bad conduct of others brought upon him. He remained silent and bore unjust blame, which he might have thrown on others had he not wished to shield them.

When he first entered West Point he was rather small, and one of his relations describes him as being "a slender lad, who walked rapidly, with his head bent forward. He had a grave, thoughtful face, which gave him a dull look usually; but when anything interested or excited him, his form became erect, his eyes flashed like steel, and his smile, as sweet as a woman's, would illumine his whole face."

The life he led at West Point, and the fine exercise which the drilling gave him, soon developed his frame,

B*

and he grew rapidly, and became a tall, fine-looking soldier. He was extremely erect, and while studying sat so bolt upright that he rarely touched the back of his chair.

As the time drew near for his final examinations at West Point, he became more and more anxious about his success, but more determined that if he failed it should be from no want of effort on his part. After they were over, his aunt, Mrs. Neale, with whom he was always very intimate, asked him how he felt about them. He looked up with a bright smile as he replied, "Aunt, I wept and studied and prayed."

His day of trial was passed successfully, and he graduated at West Point on June 30, 1846, and received the brevet rank of second lieutenant of artillery. He was then twenty-two years old.

He had only one personal difficulty while at West Point, which arose from a certain cadet taking Jackson's neatly polished musket and putting his own, uncleaned, in its place. Fortunately, Jackson had a private mark on his musket by which he could distinguish it from any other, and going directly to the captain of his company he told him of the trick which had been played upon him, and described to him the private mark on his gun. That evening, when the arms were all inspected, Jackson's musket was found in the hands of a cadet of bad standing both with professors and cadets, and who was the very person whom Jackson in his own mind had accused of taking his gun. When it was found actually in his possession, and he was accused of having taken it, he attempted to shield himself by a falsehood. Jackson, whose devotion to truth knew no bounds, had his indignation so aroused that for once he made no effort to control his anger, and, declaring that such a cadet was a disgrace to West Point, said he would ask to have him tried and dismissed; nor did he give up his determination to do so until moved by the entreaties and remonstrances of both cadets and professors. As it turned out, however, the young man's disgrace was only postponed, as a little later he was dismissed for breaking his parole. After knocking about the world for some time, and getting more and more steeped in crime, he finally wound up in the mountains of Mexico, where he became the chief of a band of roving and thieving Indians who robbed and murdered travelers. After being with them for some time, they quarrèled with him about a poor peddler whom they had murdered for his goods, and drove him from their band.

The war between Mexico and the United States had already broken out when Jackson graduated at West Point and received the brevet rank of second lieutenant of artillery. The young soldier was at once ordered to take the field, and from West Point went directly to New Orleans, from which place he sailed for Mexico. His company was with the little army of over thirteen thousand men which landed near Vera Cruz with colors flying, bands playing, and amid the enthusiastic shouts of the soldiers, on a lovely spring day (March 9) in the year 1847. The beauty and brilliancy of the scene were long remembered by young Jackson, and he often spoke of it in after-life.

Jackson first "smelt gunpowder" in the siege of Vera Cruz, which city having surrendered after a heavy bombardment on the 29th of March, the United States troops under the command of General Scott were led rapidly forward towards the city of Mexico. On this march they attacked and routed the Mexican army under Santa Anna at Cerro Gordo, where the plan of assault was made by Captain Robert E. Lee. In this battle Captain John Bankhead Magruder greatly distinguished himself as the commander of a battery of light field artillery. He was considered a very strict commanding officer, and the place of second lieutenant being vacant in his battery after the battle of Cerro Gordo, there were very few young officers who were anxious to fill it. But young Jackson, thinking it was a position which from exposure to danger and hardships offered great advantages for winning distinction, asked for and received it.

After the battle of Cerro Gordo, General Scott moved first upon La Puebla, and after a short stay at that city pushed on to the city of Mexico. He found the mountain-ridge which was between his army and the plain in the centre of which the city stood so well fortified that he would have lost nearly the whole of his army in attempting to force his way through its passes. There was, indeed, a route to the left, by following which the ridge could be avoided; but this was through a country so rough and broken up by ravines that the Mexican general, thinking it impassable, had not deemed it worth while to defend it either with troops or fortifications. He soon saw, however, that he had underrated the energy and courage of the army he had to deal with; for its young engineers, pointing out this circuitous route to their general, urged him to follow it, which he did; and after a rough and tedious march of several days the vanguard of the United States army was, by August 19, at San Augustin, a village only eight miles from the city of Mexico.

The Mexican general, alarmed at the sudden and un-expected appearance of his enemy so near the city, threw a force into and fortified the village of San Antonio, which lies between San Augustin and the city. Farther on to the west stands an isolated hill at Contreras; this he also fortified, and on its summit placed a heavy force of infantry and artillery. Most of his forces, however, he stationed in and around a village called Churubusco, just behind this hill, which was also fortified. Both positions, San Antonio and Contreras, were well chosen, but, unfortunately for the Mexicans, were too far apart to support each other. General Scott, seeing his advantage, marched around the hill of Contreras on the night of the 19th of August, and at daylight on the 20th attacked it in the rear, and after a fight of a few minutes' duration defeated and routed the force which held it. The Mexican force which was at San Antonio, being now in great danger of being cut off, fell back hastily, and reached Churubusco in great confusion. After a fierce battle of a few hours, this place was also taken by the United States troops, and the Mexicans drew in their lines closer to the city.

In the battle of Churubusco Jackson first won distinction. Magruder's battery was assigned to a post within nine hundred yards of the enemy's works. His first lieutenant, Mr. Johnstone, falling early in the action, Jackson took his place and became second in command. With what skill and courage he discharged his duty I leave Captain Magruder to describe. In his report he says,—

" In a few moments Lieutenant Jackson, commanding the second section of the battery, which had opened fire upon the enemy's works from a position on the right,

4

hearing our fire still farther in front, advanced in handsome style, and, being assigned by me to the post so gallantly filled by Lieutenant Johnstone, kept up the fire with great briskness and effect. His conduct was equally conspicuous during the whole day; and I cannot too highly commend him to the major-general's favorable consideration."

For his gallantry in the battle of Churubusco, Jackson received the brevet rank of captain. On the 8th of September the battle of Molino del Rey was fought, in which battle Jackson was only called upon to fire a few well-directed shots at the enemy's cavalry. The battle of Molino del Rey being another victory for the United States troops, and the Mexicans having been steadily pushed back upon their devoted city, there was only one obstacle left for the victors to overcome. This was the castle of Chapultepec, which was situated on a high hill, and commanded both roads by which the victors were to enter the city. Around this castle were assembled the wrecks of the Mexican army, and they were prepared to make a death-struggle for its defense. The fields around, being covered with corn and groves, besides being cut up by ditches, were almost impassable for infantry, and quite so for artillery; while behind every tree and hedge the Mexican sharpshooters held themselves in readiness to fire. Terrible as the assault of such a position would be, the officers of the United States army felt that it must be made, and that quickly, since, their troops being far from their ships and their supplies running low, it was absolutely necessary for them to enter the city of Mexico at once. Officers and men, therefore, braced themselves up to the coming conflict, which took place on the 13th of September. On the morning of that day, General Pillow, in whose command Magruder's battery was placed, was ordered to attack the castle on the west side, and General Worth was ordered to march around and attack it on the north.

Magruder was ordered to send one section of his battery, under Jackson, to attack the northwest angle, while he himself attacked in another direction. Jackson was sent forward with two regiments of infantry under Colonel Tronsdale. The latter ordering him to push steadily on, he suddenly found himself right under the enemy's guns. Instantly they opened fire upon him, killing or disabling nearly all his horses, while his men, for the most part, were shot down or driven from their guns. His rear was protected by a small party of infantry, who were already wavering under the murderous fire. Just at this moment, General Worth, who had been moving rapidly around to the north side of the castle, came up, and, seeing Jackson's danger, ordered him to fall back. Jackson replied that it would be more dangerous to withdraw than to stand his ground, and if the general would send him fifty brave soldiers he would prefer to make an attempt to take the enemy's battery in front of him which had so crippled his own. Magruder, in the mean while, having quickly accomplished the task which had been assigned to him, was moving rapidly forward to join his young lieutenant, when he was informed of his danger. With his usual gallantry, he dashed forward. His horse was killed and fell under him as he reached Jackson, who had just lifted, by hand, a single gun across a ditch and placed it in a position from which it could hurl death into the enemy's ranks. This gun, with the aid of a single sergeant, he was loading and firing rapidly, while his men were lying around him, either dead, dying, wounded, or skulking in the ditch. The indefatigable Magruder by his own exertions aided him in his efforts to silence the enemy's battery, and, another gun being brought over and placed in position, the Mexicans were soon driven from their guns. The other storming-parties having also succeeded in their assaults on the castle, the enemy were soon in full retreat upon the city. The order now was that the artillery should pursue and harass the enemy's disordered and flying columns. The horses attached to Jackson's guns were all killed or crippled, but, not wishing to be left behind in the pursuit, he quickly attached the guns to the limbers of his ammunition-box, and in a few minutes was dashing on in the headlong pursuit of the enemy, which stopped only at the very gates of the city. These were closed upon them only for the night, for the next morning (September 14) they were forced open by the exultant victors, and the American flag waved in triumph over the proud and beautiful city of the Montezumas.

In the assault on the castle of Chapultepec young Jackson covered himself with glory. He often expressed gratitude to General Pillow for having divided his battery and sent him off with a separate command, as he thus had an opportunity of distinguishing himself. For his gallant conduct he was rewarded with the brevet rank of major, and received compliments from all his superior officers in their reports of the battle. General Pillow says,—

"The advanced section of the battery, under command of the brave Lieutenant Jackson, was dreadfully cut up, and almost disabled. . . . Captain Magruder's battery, one section of which was served with great gallantry by himself, and the other by his brave lieutenant, Jackson, in face of a galling fire from the enemy's position, did invaluable service."

General Worth speaks of him as "the gallant Jackson, who, although he had lost most of his horses and many of his men, continued chivalrously at his post, combating with noble courage."

And Captain Magruder says,—

"I beg leave to call the attention of the major-general commanding the division to the conduct of Lieutenant Jackson, of the First Artillery. If devotion, industry, talent, and gallantry are the highest qualities of a soldier, then is he entitled to the distinction which their possession confers."

After the occupation of the city of Mexico, the American officers and soldiers mingled freely with the citizens, many of whom received them very gladly and treated them as guests. Jackson, not understanding Spanish, could not carry on a conversation with the natives. To overcome this drawback to the pleasure of his stay in the city of Mexico, he determined to study the language. He accordingly bought a grammar, and by dint of hard study soon learned to read and speak the Spanish sufficiently well to make himself understood. He devoted a great deal of his time to study, but enjoyed very much the delightful climate of Mexico and the beautiful scenery around him. Among the friends he made in Mexico there was a Spanish gentleman, at whose house he was a frequent and always a welcome guest. He had several daughters, who were so charming that the gallant major confessed he had to suspend his visits to their father's house for fear of leaving his heart behind him on his return home.

For the mere delight of living, Jackson considered that the city of Mexico excelled all others in the world. While there, he occupied one of the great chambers of the imperial palace. He made the acquaintance of the Archbishop of Mexico, and had several interviews with him, the subject discussed being generally the Roman Catholic religion. So little egotism had Jackson that he never spoke to his family of his achievements in Mexico. The only falsehood he ever remembered telling was when leading his men through a pass infested by Mexican guerillas. They became panic-stricken, and, when ordered to advance, refused to go. He stepped before them into the narrow pass, and, though he saw the broad leaves of the tropical plants around him riddled with balls, exclaimed, "Follow me, men! Don't you see there is no danger?" Knowing how rigid he was in after-life in his observance of the Sabbath, it sounds strange to hear of his joining, as we are assured that he did, in the Sunday evening dance in the gay capital of Mexico.

From Mexico, Major Jackson was sent with his command to Fort Hamilton, upon Long Island.

CHAPTER III.

At Fort Hamilton, Jackson remained two years. While there, his thoughts dwelt much on religious subjects. In his intimate friend and commanding officer, Colonel Taylor, he found an adviser, and one who sympathized with him in his anxiety to know what church it would be best for him to join. Having never been christened, he at last determined to have the rite administered by Mr. Parks, an Episcopal minister, in whose church he also took communion.

On leaving Fort Hamilton, Jackson was sent to Fort Meade, near Tampa Bay, on the coast of Florida. There he found the change from the harsh climate of New York to the milder one of Florida very beneficial to his health, which was far from strong. He had found at Fort Hamilton that the life of a soldier shut up in a fort is far different from what it is when he is in the midst of all the excitement and activity of war. At Fort Meade also his active and energetic spirit chafed under the tedium of the idle, inactive life he was forced to lead.

Jackson had not been many months at Fort Meade when he was relieved from the irksome life there by being elected Professor of Natural Philosophy and Artillery Tactics in the Virginia Military Institute at Lexington. Being weary of the idle life he was leading at the fort, he gladly accepted the appointment to a position where, besides the pleasure of instructing others, he would have an opportunity of continuing his own studies and increasing his knowledge. He resigned his position in the army, therefore, and went to Lexington in July, 1851. There he received a salary of twelve hundred dollars. He had had much bad health, which left his eye-sight very weak, and he made it a conscientious rule to take the best possible care of his eyes, and so long as they remained weak nothing could induce him to break the rule which he had laid down for himself, never to use them at night, not even to read a letter. As he had to study a great deal in order to fit himself for his duties as a professor, this was extremely inconvenient, and, to any one with a less determined will than his, would have been an obstacle not to be overcome.

Not being able to study at night, he read over during the day what he wished to study, and after tea moved his chair to one side, and, sitting apart from his family circle, at his desk, went over in his mind all that he had read. He thus fixed it in his memory, and had a clearer idea of it than if he had had the book before him. So strict was he in his observance of the Sabbath that he frequently did not read letters received on that day, for fear of their distracting his thoughts. A few months after going to Lexington to live, he joined the Presbyterian Church. In Lexington, as elsewhere, it was the custom for members of this church to meet in the middle of the week to join in a religious service, which was usually conducted by the pastor of the church. In these assemblages he often called upon individuals to lead in prayer. Jackson, though a constant attendant, from his extreme diffidence could only think with dread of being called on to pray before such a number of persons. But, feeling it to be his duty to do his part in carrying on these services, he asked his pastor not to allow any feeling for his modesty to prevent his calling on him to pray. A short time afterwards, the pastor called on him. He began his prayer with such embarrassment, and stammered through it with so much difficulty, that it was painful to hear him. After this attempt, several weeks passed without his being again called on. Feeling sure this was owing to his failure, he asked the pastor not to be deterred by this, but to call on him again. The minister did as requested, and Jackson's prayers in public were soon as good as any others made on similar occasions. Indeed, his stern sense of duty made him so far overcome his diffidence in public speaking that he once delivered a course of lectures on Christianity in the little village of Beverly, where he found the people very much given up to unbelief. He was zealous in discharging all the duties imposed on him as a member of his church. On one occasion, having to take up collections for the Bible Society, he succeeded even in getting some small contributions from free negroes, whom he persuaded to give their mite to the good work.

There was no gloom in Jackson's religion. It shed perpetual sunshine on his pathway through life, soothing his cares and enlivening his joys. His perfect and child-like faith in God's goodness made him think that nothing could happen except for the best. A friend, who knew how happy and contented his disposition was, once said to him, "Suppose, major, you should lose your health without any hope of recovering it: do you think you could be happy?" "Yes, I should be happy still," he replied. "But," continued his friend, "suppose you should lose your eye-sight and become perfectly blind: would not that be too much for you?" "No," he replied, calmly. His friend, still persisting, then said, "Suppose, though, that besides losing your health and becoming entirely blind you should lose all your property, and so be left lying in bed a helpless invalid, dependent for support on the charities of friends: would not that be too much for you?" Jackson was silent for a moment, and then said, in a reverent tone, "If it were the will of God to place me there, He would enable me to lie there peacefully a hundred years."

He had been in Lexington a little over two years, when he married Miss Eleanor Junkin, on the 4th of August, 1853. After spending fourteen months of uninterrupted happiness with his young wife, she was torn from him by death, in the autumn of 1854. His grief for her was so great that his friends were alarmed about him; yet in his moments of bitterest agony his resignation to God's will was unshaken. While still writhing under this sorrow, we find him writing to a friend (March, 1855), "Oh, do you not long to leave the flesh and mingle with the just made perfect?"

The summer after his wife's death, Jackson went to Western Virginia, to visit once more the scenes of his youth. There he spent some time with his uncle and aunt Neale, under whose hospitable roof some of the pleasantest days of his sad childhood had been passed. How tenderly he loved his mother's memory will be seen from the following extracts from a letter written to Mrs. Neale on his return from this trip. The letter is addressed to "Uncle and Aunt Neale."

" LEXINGTON, Sept. 4, 1855.

" I stopped on my way to see the Hawk's Nest, and the gentleman with whom I put up was at mother's burial, and accompanied me to the cemetery for the purpose of pointing out her grave to me. But I am not certain that he found it: there was no stone to mark the spot. Another gentleman who had the kindness to go with us stated that a wooden head- or footboard with her name on it had been put up; but it was no longer there. A depression in the earth only marked her resting-place. When standing by her grave, I experienced feelings with which I was until then a stranger. I was seeking the spot partly for the purpose of erecting something to her precious memory. . . . .

" On Saturday last I lost my porte-monnaie, and in it was the date of mother's birthday. Please give me its date in your next."

His friends, thinking change of scene might do him good,—for his health had given way under his continued grief,—suggested that he should take a trip to Europe; and he accordingly spent the summer of 1856 in traveling through England, France, Belgium, and Switzerland. From his boyhood he had longed to visit Europe and study the battle-fields of the great Napoleon, whom he admired more than any other great military leader the world had ever seen. He hastened to the field of Waterloo, and studied with all the zeal of an enthusiastic young soldier the positions of the armies there. When the time approached for his return to his post in Lexington, he sailed for America, leaving himself ample time to get back to his class at the opening of the session. The steamer being, however, unexpectedly delayed, he did not reach home for a week or two after the appointed time. His friends, knowing how exact and punctual to the minute he was, thought this would be a very great annoyance to him. On his reaching home, one of them said to him, "Why, major, how have you stood the delay in getting back to your post? As you are so particular in keeping all appointments, we have taken it for granted that you were beside yourself with impatience." "Not at all," he replied. "I set out to return at the proper time; I did my duty; the steamer was delayed by act of Providence, and I was perfectly satisfied."

The idea of becoming a missionary must have often occurred to so zealous a Christian as Jackson, and just before leaving for Europe we find him, early in the summer of 1856, writing to his aunt, Mrs. Neale, as follows:

"The subject of becoming a herald of the Cross, to which you alluded, has often seriously attracted my attention, and I regard it as the most noble of all professions. It was the profession of our Divine Redeemer, and I should not be surprised were I to die on a foreign field, clad in the ministerial armor, fighting under the banner of Jesus. What could be more glorious? But my present conviction is that I am doing some good, and for the present am where God would have me be. Within the last few days I have felt an unusual religious joy. I do rejoice to walk in the love of God."

It was his habit to select some one with whom at regular times he would join in prayer, in order to gain the full benefit of the promise, "that if two of you shall agree on earth, as touching anything that they shall ask, it shall be done for them of my Father which is in heaven." Some one complaining to him on one occasion of not being able to understand what was meant by the command to "pray always" and "without ceasing," he said, very modestly, that he would try to explain by showing how he understood and acted upon it. "For example," he said, "when we take our meals, there is the grace. When I take a draught of water, I always pause as my palate receives the refreshment, to lift up my heart to God in thanks and prayer for the water of life. Whenever I drop a letter into the box at the post-office, I send a petition along with it for God's blessing upon its mission and upon the person to whom it is sent. When I break the seal of a letter just received, I stop to pray to God that He may prepare me for its contents and make it a messenger of good. When I go to my class-room and await the arrangement of the cadets in their places, that is my time to intercede with God for them. And so of every other act of the day. I have made the practice habitual, and can no more forget to pray at these different times than to forget to drink when I am thirsty." One of the first things which he did after joining the church was to build up a Sunday-school for the negroes living in Lexington; and he was most untiring in his efforts to give them religious instruction. Those who have undertaken this task know how very disheartening it is; but Jackson's zeal in the good work never flagged, and he was rewarded by having a flourishing colored Sunday-school as long as he remained in Lexington.

On the 15th of July, 1857, Major Jackson was married a second time, to Mary Ann Morrison. Her father, Dr. R. H. Morrison, is a gentleman of the old school, and an eminent Presbyterian divine of North Carolina.

Jackson looked forward with inexpressible delight to

the time when he could have a home of his own. In writing to a friend, a short time after his marriage, he says, " We are still at the hotel, but expect on the 1st of January to remove to M——'s home as boarders. I hope that in the course of time we shall be able to call some house our home, where we may have the pleasure of receiving a long visit from you. . . . I shall never be content until I am at the head of an establishment in which my friends can feel at home in Lexington. I have taken the first important step by securing a wife capable of making a happy home. And the next thing is to give her an opportunity."

The opportunity was not long wanting. He soon became the happy possessor of a house and garden; and no man ever enjoyed the calm and sweet pleasures of home-life more than himself. As times prospered with him, he was enabled to gratify the desire which always seems to be chief in the heart of every Virginian,—that of having a farm. The purchase and cultivation of a few acres proved him to be a most successful farmer. His negro slaves were devoted to him, and were trained by him to be excellent servants.

Only those who saw Jackson at home, where he indulged freely in all the kind and tender feelings of his great and noble heart, can form a just idea of the love with which it was overflowing, or of the joyousness of his nature. There was nothing dark and gloomy in his disposition. The sunshine which dwelt in his heart shed its kindly light on all around him. He loved to use terms of endearment to those around him, and, as the sound of the Spanish language was more musical to his ears than that of the English, they were generally spoken by him in that tongue. So overflowing was his heart with love and tenderness for all, that the least unkind or cross word uttered in his household grated harshly on his ear and disturbed him not a little. On such occasions his usual gentle rebuke was, " Oh, that is not the way to be happy !"

He took the greatest delight in his garden and farm, and most of his leisure hours were spent in working with his own hands in the former. His vegetables were the earliest and best of the neighborhood, and his farm, which was a stony piece of land when it came into his possession, became under his skillful management a fertile spot, and he used to say that the bread made on it tasted sweeter to him than that which was bought. He gave a certain portion yearly of all he made to charitable objects.

His life at home was regular, and scarcely ever varied from its daily routine. He rose at dawn, devoted a certain length of time to secret prayer, and, if the weather was not bad, took a solitary walk. At seven o'clock he had family prayers, at which all his servants were expected to be present; but, with his usual punctuality, he never waited a minute for any one. He was engaged with his duties as professor from eight to eleven, at which hour he returned to his study. After reading his Bible attentively, he then prepared the lecture for his class on the following day, and gave up the rest of the time until dinner to his studies. From dinner until tea he usually gave himself to the rural pursuits of his garden and farm, which were so delightful to him. After tea his chair was pushed aside from the family circle, and he went over in his mind the studies of the morning. That task over, he spent the rest of the evening in conversation, which was frequently on literary subjects, or, when the state of his eyes permitted, in reading. He read generally on these occasions history or English poetry. Now and then when an interesting novel fell into his hands it was eagerly devoured by him, and, if suffering too much with his eyes to read it at night, some member of his family read to him, while he was all attention. He never allowed such reading, however, to take him from his regular studies, and the novel was quickly thrown aside when it came in the way of these.

We have a touching little anecdote preserved to us of Jackson, which shows him to have been tender-hearted and loving as a woman. A gentleman who once spent the night at his house was accompanied by his little daughter of four years. It was the first time that the child had ever been separated from its mother, and Jackson, fearing it might miss the tender watchfulness of a woman's heart, suggested that it should be placed under Mrs. Jackson's kind care for the night. But the father objecting, the little one was left to rest upon his pillow. After the whole household had sunk into slumber, the gentleman was aroused from his sleep by some one leaning over his little daughter and drawing the cover more closely around her. It was Jackson. Anxious lest his little guest should miss her mother's tender care under his roof, he could not rest quietly until he had assured himself that all was well with the little one.

The following extracts from his letters to Mrs. Jackson speak for themselves:

"April 25, 1857.

"It is a great comfort to me to know that though I am not with you, yet you are in the hands of One who will not permit any evil to come nigh you. What a consoling thought it is to know that we may with perfect confidence commit all our friends in Jesus to the care of our heavenly Father, with an assurance that all shall be well with them!

"I have been sorely disappointed at not hearing from you this morning; but these disappointments are all designed for our good. In my daily walks I think much of you. I love to stroll abroad after the labors of the day are over and indulge feelings of gratitude to God for all the sources of natural beauty with which He has adorned the earth. Some time since, my morning walks were rendered very delightful by the singing of the birds. The morning caroling of the birds, and their notes in the evening, awaken in me devotional feelings of praise and gratitude, though very different in their nature. In the morning, all animated nature (man excepted) appears to join in active expressions of gratitude to God; in the evening, all is hushing into silent slumber, and thus disposes the mind to meditation. And as my mind dwells on you, I love to give it a devotional turn, by thinking of you as a gift from our heavenly Father. How delightful it is thus to associate every pleasure and enjoyment with God the Giver! Thus will He bless us, and make us grow in grace, and in the knowledge of Him whom to know aright is life eternal."

"May 16, 1857.

"There is something very pleasant in the thought of your mailing me a letter every Monday, and such manifestations of regard for the Sabbath must be well-pleasing in the sight of God. Oh that all our people would manifest such regard for His holy day! If we would all strictly observe all His holy laws, what would not our country be!

5*

"When in prayer for you last Sabbath, the tears came to my eyes. . . . I felt that day as though it were a communion-day for myself."

In the following extracts we find him speaking to Mrs. Jackson of the different things about his house— the garden, fruits, horse, etc. — as "your garden," "your peaches." It was a favorite way he had of doing her a trifling honor.

"HOME, April 20, 1859.

"Our potatoes are coming up. . . . We have had very unusually dry weather for nearly a fortnight, and your garden had been thirsting for rain till last evening, when the weather commenced changing, and to-day we have had some rain. Through grace given me from above, I felt that rain would come at the right time; and I don't recollect having ever felt so grateful for a rain as for the present one.

"Last evening I sowed turnips between our peas.

"I was mistaken about your large garden-fruit being peaches. It turns out to be apricots, and I inclose you one which I found on the ground to-day. And, just think! my little —— has a tree full of them. You must come home before they get ripe."

So flowed by, peacefully and gently, the quiet life of our hero at Lexington. He rarely left home, except for a trip during the summer to the North or to the Virginia Springs. The time is now at hand when we are to see him go forth from the calm and happy retreat of his little home into the storms of battle and war, never to return, but to leave a name honored and loved by a grateful country, and one which all ages will revere.

CHAPTER IV.

MAJOR JACKSON spent the summer of 1860 in New England. On his return home he declared that he had seen enough to convince him that war between the States was inevitable; and from that time he braced himself up for the coming storm. He was a silent but close observer of the stirring events which succeeded one another so rapidly during the winter of 1860–61. He early discerned the signs of the times, and foresaw the fierce tempest which was to sweep over his own loved State.

South Carolina having, on the 20th of December, 1860, taken the lead in the solemn procession of States as one after another they withdrew their allegiance from the Union, others followed in rapid succession. On the 9th of February, 1861, a Provisional Government was formed at Montgomery, Alabama, for a Confederacy composed then of the States of South Carolina, Mississippi, Alabama, Georgia, Louisiana, and Texas. Jefferson Davis was chosen President, and Alexander H. Stephens Vice-President, of this Confederacy.

Virginia remained undecided but calm during the progress of these grave events. The oldest State in the Union, and one whose statesmen had done more than those of any other of her sisters to form the Constitution which drew all the States under one general government, she was loath to withdraw from it. Unwisely, perhaps, she delayed, hoping to heal the breach between the two sections. In the mean time, she drew upon herself the reproaches of her sister States in the South and the taunts and threats of those in the North. But, holding herself magnificently above both, she disregarded the reproaches of the one, as she held up a finger of warning at the threats of the other. Events, however, were hurrying on more rapidly than she thought.

After the secession of South Carolina, the United States troops that occupied Fort Sumter, in Charleston harbor, were not withdrawn. After many delays, the Governor of South Carolina was informed by the United States Government that the garrison of the fort would be reinforced, " peaceably if they could, forcibly if they must." The answer to this was the bombardment of Fort Sumter, which in a short time was battered to ruins. Then followed President Lincoln's proclamation declaring war against South Carolina and the Confederate Government, and calling upon the States for seventy-five thousand men to form an army of invasion.

Virginia now no longer saw her course darkly. At the first certainty of danger to her sister States of the South, all hesitation vanished, and like a lioness she leaped into the arena, ready to do battle in their defense and in that of what she considered right. She did not hesitate to bare her bosom to the invader and to offer her fair fields as the battle-ground of a fierce struggle which for four years was to rage within her borders. On the 17th of April she seceded, and immediately began her preparations for war. The enthusiasm with which men of all ages and classes flew to arms was only equaled by that with which they were urged on by the women at home. As company after company marched out to battle, the white arms of the maidens waved them on to victory, while mothers and wives invoked a blessing from above upon the defenders of a cause for whose success all prayed with religious fervor. Devoted to duty, and earnest in his love for his State, Jackson had been no indifferent spectator of the strange and rapid course of events. A month before the secession of Virginia, and while in the opinion of many there was yet a hope of averting from the land the fierce scourge of war, Major Jackson, while lamenting the bare chance of war, yet expressed the opinion that it was inevitable. After alluding to all its horrors, and his great desire that his people might be spared them, he said, "It seems to me that if they would unite in prayer, war might be averted and peace preserved." In his public prayers after this that was one of the chief subjects of his petitions. But Heaven decreed otherwise, and he was destined to act a conspicuous part in the war whose horrors his prayers were unable to avert from his country.

Having seceded, Virginia bent all her energies to make preparations for defense against the armies which were being rapidly enrolled to invade the South. As the news of her secession spread from one part of the country to the other, her sons belonging to either the army or the navy of the United States speedily resigned their commissions and hurried home to offer their services to their mother State, believing their first duty belonged to her. Thus in her hour of peril her children flocked into her borders from every clime, and she found willing hearts and wise heads to direct her preparations for defense. Foremost among her distinguished sons

was Colonel Robert E. Lee. When the news reached
Richmond that he had resigned his commission and had
declared his resolution never again to draw his sword
save in defense of his native State, men who were oppressed by the impending dangers breathed more freely.
They felt they had a great leader to direct their armies,
and from that moment until the day when he returned
a paroled prisoner from the ill-fated banks of the Appomattox he was the centre alike of the hopes and
the affections of his countrymen. Colonel Lee was appointed by his State major-general and made commander-
in-chief of her forces. In organizing the material for
her defense, one of his first steps was to form camps of
instruction, the chief of which was on the outskirts of
Richmond, and called after him Camp Lee. It was
decided to call to this camp from the Virginia Military
Institute the elder cadets, who could act as drill-masters
and assist in organizing into an army the patriotic but
untrained troops who poured in to offer their services in
the defense of the country. On Major Jackson devolved
the duty of taking the cadets to Richmond. In making
their preparations for sending their volunteer companies
into service, the people of Rockbridge had looked to
Major Jackson for aid and advice. Their unbounded
confidence in him as a man of sound practical sense, as
well as in his skill and experience as a soldier, made
them choose him as their counselor at this grave juncture. He had taken the deepest and most anxious
interest in the progress of events, and not without many
gloomy forebodings of the future. On one occasion,
about this time, having a friend as his guest, they sat
up late, discussing the news from Washington and the
South, which had become more and more exciting.

Both the host and guest retired depressed by the thought that war was inevitable. The guest arose the next morning with the same gloomy feelings, and was surprised on meeting Jackson to find him in his usual calm and tranquil state of mind, and on expressing his own fearful forebodings, Jackson replied, "Why should the peace of a true Christian be disturbed by anything which man can do unto him? Has not God promised to make all things work together for good to them that love Him?"

The meeting of the Presbyterian Synod in Lexington the week of the secession of Virginia had made the time unusually busy for Major Jackson, and on retiring to rest Saturday night he expressed the hope that the morrow (April 21) might prove a quiet Sabbath to him, which he could spend in undisturbed communion with his God. But how vain were his hopes! With the early dawn came the order from Richmond for the senior cadets to go at once to that place, and, as their commander, Major Jackson busied himself with preparations for their departure.

Having concluded these, he called on his pastor, and asked him to be at their rendezvous at twelve o'clock, in order to give them some parting Christian counsel and a prayer. He returned home at eleven o'clock, ate a hurried breakfast, and retired with Mrs. Jackson to his chamber, and there, taking his Bible, read the fifth chapter of Second Corinthians, the eloquent words of whose opening display such faith in that sublime promise of the resurrection: "For we know that if our earthly house of this tabernacle be dissolved, we have a building of God, an house not made with hands, eternal in the heavens." He then knelt in prayer, and in a voice choked with tears implored God, if it were His will, to avert the horrors of war from his country.

Thus breathing peace and good will towards all men, in close communion with h's God, and animated by an earnest devotion which could know no shadow of turning, he went forth from his peaceful little home, and its doors closed upon him forever!

All things being in readiness, at twelve o'clock the pastor, Dr. White, was asked by Major Jackson to have prayers, and also warned by him not to prolong them, by the remark, "Doctor, we march at one o'clock precisely." The religious services being ended before the hour for departure had arrived, one of the officers said to Major Jackson, "Major, everything is now ready; may we not set out?" The only reply was for the major to point to the dial-plate of the great clock; and not until the hand pointed to the hour of one did his voice ring out the order, "Forward, march!"

The cadets marched to Staunton, and went thence by rail to Richmond. From a depot east of the Blue Ridge, where their journey was interrupted for a short time, Major Jackson wrote to his wife, "Here, as well as at other points of the line, the war-spirit is intense. The cars had scarcely stopped here before a request was made that I would leave a cadet to drill a company."

Having reached Richmond, he wrote to Mrs. Jackson, April 23, "Colonel Lee, of the army, is here, and has been made major-general. His services I regard as of more value to us than General Scott could render as commander. . . . It is understood that General Lee is to be commander-in-chief. I regard him as a better officer than General Scott. . . . The cadets are encamped at the fair-grounds, which are about one and a half miles from the city. We have excellent quarters. So far as we can hear, God is crowning our cause with success; but I do not wish to send rumors to you. I will try to give facts as they become known, though I may not have time for more than a line or so. The Governor and others holding responsible offices have not enough time for their duties, they are so enormous at this date."

In the camp of instruction at Richmond, Major Jackson found no duties worthy of his experience as a soldier. He was eager for active employment, and anxious for promotion, which, however, he would not solicit. But it could not be long withheld from such a man, and while awaiting it he did not hesitate to act the part of drill-master towards all the raw soldiers and officers who thronged Camp Lee and who might ask his instruction. One day he was met by a man in the camp who told him he had just been assigned as corporal of the guard for the day; that the officer who had given him the order had left him without instructions as to his duties, of which he was entirely ignorant, and that, seeing from his uniform that he was an officer, he had stopped him to beg his aid. Major Jackson at once went with the soldier around the camp, and gave him all the necessary instructions, and that with such kindness and cheerfulness of manner that from that hour he was the object of the soldier's love and respect.

A few days after he reached Camp Lee, Major Jackson was chosen by the Executive War Council to receive an appointment in the engineer department, with the rank of major. The place was the one of all others most distasteful to him, offering as it did but little hope of promotion, and of that usefulness which he felt sure he could best render his country on the field of battle. At the urgent request of his friends, therefore, the appointment was withdrawn, and he received instead a commission as colonel of the Virginia forces, and was ordered to take command at Harper's Ferry. When, on the day following, his appointment was read out in the Convention for confirmation, a member from the floor asked, "Who is this Major Jackson, that we are asked to commit to him so responsible a post?" "He is one," replied the member from Rockbridge, "who, if you order him to hold a post, will never leave it alive to be occupied by the enemy." On the morning of Saturday, April 27, his commission as colonel was placed in his hands, and he at once set out for his command. After joining it, he wrote the following letter to his wife:

"Winchester, April 29.

"I expect to leave here about half-past two P.M. to-day for Harper's Ferry. I am thankful to say that an ever-kind Providence, who causeth all things to work together for good to them that love Him, has given me an independent command. To His name be all the praise. You must not expect to hear from me very often, as I expect to have more work than I ever had in the same length of time before ; but don't be concerned about me, as an ever-kind Father will give me all needful aid."

CHAPTER V.

HARPER'S FERRY.

Harper's Ferry is surrounded by scenery the beauty and magnificence of which must ever charm and awe the beholder. The village lies on the declivities of a ridge called Bolivar Heights, which runs along the neck of land that separates the Potomac and Shenandoah Rivers just before their junction. Standing on the Bolivar Heights, the spectator sees on his right the Shenandoah, which, having for a hundred miles hugged the Blue Ridge in search of an outlet, at last approaches one; on his left comes the Potomac; the two streams unite and rush through the mountains, which at some remote age has been cleft to its base by the rush of their waters. Through the cleft is seen, stretching far away into the distance, a broad, rich, and slightly undulating plain, whose pale, faintly-seen horizon is in striking contrast to the gigantic scenery of the foreground. The Potomac, having broken through the Blue Ridge, continues on its way to the ocean. The heights on the Virginia side at this point are called the Loudon Heights, and those on the opposite side the Maryland Heights. Both tower above Bolivar Heights, and the village at their feet. Harper's Ferry was selected by the Federal Government as a point at which to establish manufactures of fire-arms, and arsenals wherein to store them, and the banks of both streams were lined with factories, where thousands of arms were yearly turned out.   As soon as the war broke out, the possession of this place, with its arms and munitions of war, became of immense importance to Virginia, and the militia companies of the surrounding country flew to arms to effect its capture. But the officer in command of the Federal guard at the place, receiving timely notice of their designs, set fire to the arsenals and factories, and fled.   The Virginia troops entered the town to find the arms in the arsenals destroyed, with the exception of those which had been removed and secreted by patriotic citizens of the village; but the factories were saved.

Harper's Ferry now became the rendezvous of all the troops of the Valley of Virginia, and it was the command of these, and of others sent to reinforce them, that was given to Colonel Jackson when he received his commission in the Virginia service.   There were at Harper's Ferry twenty-five hundred men,—four hundred being Kentuckians and the rest Virginians.   This force consisted of eight companies of infantry, and four batteries of field-artillery, with fifteen light guns.   Three regiments of the infantry were partially organized; but the rest of these hastily-assembled troops presented pretty much a confused mass of men, many of whom had no arms.   To organize this force, to urge on the completion of arms at the factories, and to keep possession of all the roads leading to Washington, were the orders given to Colonel Jackson by General Lee when he was sent to Harper's Ferry.   He went, accompanied by Major Preston, Colonel Massie, and two young men whom he employed as drill-masters.

The new commander lost no time in executing the orders which he had received, and soon order prevailed where all had been chaos and confusion. The troops, who were raw recruits and were wearied with the confusion and want of discipline of an unorganized command, had been clamoring for leave to go home; but a few days after Jackson's arrival they found that a new man was in the saddle, and under his firm and wise rule soon became disciplined troops. The few who made any show of disobedience to orders were either so sternly rebuked or so swiftly punished that none dared follow their example.

The village of Harper's Ferry, being situated on the slope of Bolivar Heights, was completely commanded by the Maryland Heights, on the north side of the Potomac,—those heights towering far above both the village and Bolivar Heights. It was very important then to the Virginians for the Maryland Heights not to fall into the hands of the enemy. Maryland, however, had not yet seceded, and it was suggested that it would look too much like invasion for the Virginians to take possession of them. General Lee, with his usual dislike of anything approaching the violation of a country's laws, proposed that the Marylanders should be induced to enlist in the Southern army, and then they should be allowed to occupy and hold the important position; but that plan was soon abandoned. Colonel Jackson, feeling more and more the danger of his position so long as the Maryland Heights were not in his possession, quietly took the whole matter in his own hands and seized them. He placed a few companies of soldiers on the Heights, in block-houses which he had constructed for their quarters, and, acting as his own engineer, threw up a few intrenchments to aid in their defense should they be attacked.

On the 8th of May, he wrote to Mrs. Jackson, " I am living at present in an elegant mansion, with Major Preston in my room. Mr. Massie is on my staff, but left this morning for Richmond as bearer of dispatches, and is to return in a few days. I am strengthening my position, and, if attacked, shall, with the blessing of the kind providence of that God who has always been with me, and who, I firmly believe, will never forsake me, repel the enemy. I am in good health, considering the great labor which devolves on me and the loss of sleep to which I am subjected."

As matters then stood, Harper's Ferry was considered the most important position in Virginia. There it was thought blood would first be shed, as the handful of men whom Colonel Jackson commanded was constantly in danger of being attacked by a large number of United States troops that had been collected together and placed under command of Major-General Patterson. Colonel Jackson's spirits rose as the dangers of his position increased. In his dispatches to the Government he expressed his intention of making a Thermopylæ of his position, should it be necessary, and declared that it would be defended to the death. Like a true soldier, he spoke but little of his plans, and kept the number of troops under his command perfectly secret. On one occasion, while in command at Harper's Ferry, he was visited by a committee from the Legislature of Maryland. They came to inquire into his plans. He received them with perfect politeness and courtesy, but they could not discover anything from him. When they asked him how many troops he had, his reply was, " I should be glad if Lincoln thought I had fifteen thousand."

On the 20th of May the Confederate Congress adjourned from Columbia to Richmond, which place was henceforth the capital of the Confederate States, Virginia having adopted the Confederate Constitution and been received into the Confederacy. Thus the United States Government received as a reply to its declaration of war the removal of the seat of government of the Southern Confederacy to a place almost within hearing of the guns around its own capital.

All the Virginia forces and munitions of war were turned over to the Confederate Government. One of the first acts of this Government was to appoint as commander of Harper's Ferry General Joseph E. Johnston, a man whose skill and experience it was thought made him the most suitable commander for such an important post. But Colonel Jackson, having received no orders from the Virginia authorities to surrender his trust, declined to do so until he should receive an intimation to that effect from General Lee. For a short time it was feared that this determination on the part of Colonel Jackson might bring about a disagreeable feeling between General Johnston and himself; but, fortunately, a communication was received soon after General Johnston's arrival from General Lee, in which he referred to General Johnston as commander of Harper's Ferry. Colonel Jackson, considering this as a sufficient evidence that he was to surrender his trust, hastened to hand over the command to General Johnston, and in the campaigns which they afterwards fought together their intercourse was of the most agreeable and friendly character.

On being relieved from the command of Harper's Ferry, Jackson was put in command of a brigade composed of the 2d Virginia Regiment, commanded by Colonel Allen; the 4th, commanded by Colonel Preston; the 5th, commanded by Colonel Harper; the 27th, commanded by Colonel Gordon; and, later, the 33d, commanded by Colonel Cummings. This was the brigade which lives in history as the " Stonewall Brigade." Attached to it was a battery of light field-guns from Lexington, commanded by the Rev. Mr. Pendleton, an Episcopal clergyman, who had graduated at West Point before studying for the ministry. Colonel Jackson's brigade staff was composed of Major Frank Jones, Adjutant; Lieutenant-Colonel James W. Massie, Aide-de-Camp; Dr. Hunter McGuire, Medical Director; Major William Hawkes, Chief Commissary; Major John Harmon, Chief Quartermaster; and Lieutenant Alexander Pendleton.

In the mean time, the Federal general Patterson, who had been threatening Harper's Ferry, moved off from that point and approached the Potomac higher up, by the Pennsylvania Valley. Harper's Ferry then became useless as a point of defense against the Federal forces under his command. These, it was suspected, he intended to unite at Winchester with those under General McClellan, who was then advancing from Northwestern Virginia. General Johnston at once decided to take his army to Winchester. He therefore abandoned Harper's Ferry on Sunday, June 16, after having destroyed the railroad bridge and Government factories, and having removed all the heavy guns and stores.

This move was not made an hour too soon, for already the advance of the Federal army from the northwest was reported to be at Romney, only forty miles west of Winchester; while General Patterson with eighteen thousand men was crossing the Potomac at Williamsport, about the same distance to the north. General Johnston, after marching eight miles in the direction of Winchester, turned towards the west to oppose Patterson. With this view, he chose a wooded range of highlands between Winchester and Martinsburg, known as Bunker Hill; but General Patterson, hearing of his approach, hastily withdrew to the north bank of the Potomac. Concerning these movements Colonel Jackson thus wrote to his wife:

"Tuesday, June 18.

"On Sunday, by order of General Johnston, the entire force left Harper's Ferry, passed through Charlestown, and halted for the night about two miles this side. The next morning we moved towards the enemy, who were between Martinsburg and Williamsport, Maryland, and encamped for the night at Bunker Hill. The next morning we were to have marched at sunrise, and I hoped that in the evening or this morning we would have engaged the enemy; but, instead of doing so, General Johnston made some disposition for receiving the enemy if they should attack us, and thus we were kept until about twelve A.M., when he gave the order to return towards Winchester. At about sunrise we reached this place, which is about three miles north of Winchester, on the turnpike leading thence to Martinsburg. When our troops on Sunday were marching on the enemy, they were so inspirited as apparently to forget the fatigue of the march, and though some of them were suffering from hunger, this and all other privations appeared to be forgotten, and the march continued at the rate of three miles per hour; and when they were ordered to retire, their reluctance was manifested by their snail-like pace. I hope the general will do something soon. Since we have left Harper's Ferry, something of an active movement towards repelling the enemy is, of course, expected. I trust that through the blessing of God we will soon be given an opportunity of driving the invaders from this region."

His delight at having his brigade placed in the advance-guard of this little army of the Valley is shown in the following extract from a letter to Mrs. Jackson:

"The troops have been divided into brigades, and the Virginia forces under General Johnston constitute the first brigade, of which I am in command. I am very thankful to our kind heavenly Father for having given me such a fine brigade. He does bless me beyond my expectations, and infinitely beyond my deserts. I ought to be a devoted follower of the Redeemer."

The United States forces approaching from the north-west had about this time retired before Colonel A. P. Hill, who had been sent towards Romney with a small body of Confederate troops to oppose them. On the 19th of June, Colonel Jackson was ordered to move with his brigade north of Martinsburg, and there watch the enemy, who had regained courage enough to begin once more to cross the Potomac. But on the approach of Colonel Jackson they again beat a retreat.

At Martinsburg the Baltimore and Ohio Railroad Company had extensive workshops and depots, which contained forty of the finest locomotives, together with three hundred freight-cars. Instead of removing all these to Winchester, and thereby securing them for the use of the Confederate Government, Colonel Jackson received an order to destroy the whole. He had nothing to do but to obey, and he writes of it to Mrs. Jackson,—

"It was a sad work; but I had my orders, and my duty was to obey. If the cost of the property could have been expended in disseminating the gospel of the Prince of Peace, how much good might have been expected!"

Colonel Jackson remained with his brigade and with Colonel J. E. B. Stuart and his cavalry regiment, on his front north of Martinsburg, until July 2, when he first crossed swords with the enemy. The orders given him by his commander were to watch the enemy, and to fall back on the Confederate forces for support should he advance in full force. At length, on July 2, for the third time, General Patterson ventured to cross the Potomac, and advanced in the direction of Jackson's camp. This bold officer at once moved forward to meet him with the 5th Virginia Regiment, a few companies of cavalry, and a single light field-piece of Captain Pendleton's battery. He left orders to the rest of his command to move their baggage to the rear, and to be ready to march either forward or backward at a minute's warning.

Half-way between Martinsburg and the Potomac, near a little church called the "Falling Water Church," he met the van-guard of the enemy, which he attacked and drove back. Their reinforcements coming up, they again moved forward, and were again driven back. He had posted his infantry behind the buildings and in-closures of a farm-house and barn which stood on either side of the road, when he discovered that the enemy, having found out how small was his force, were pushing forward an extended line of infantry, with the intention of surrounding him.

His little force, from the houses which they occupied and from behind the fences, poured forth a galling fire until the enemy were about to close them in. Then, bringing up his little field-piece to cover their retreat, he withdrew his men and retired, skirmishing with the enemy until he met the army four miles south of Martinsburg hurrying to his support. This combat is known as that of Haines's Farm, and in it Colonel Jackson had only three hundred and eighty men engaged, and one piece of artillery. To push this little force out of their path occupied the enemy from nine o'clock in the morning until the middle of the day, with three thousand men and a full battery of artillery. In this engagement Colonel Jackson had two men killed and ten wounded. The enemy, besides losing forty-five prisoners, had many killed and wounded. It was the first time that Jackson's men had ever "smelt gunpowder;" yet he said that "both officers and men behaved beautifully." His skill in handling his troops, his coolness under fire, and his feeling for and kind attentions to the wounded, proved to his men that they had a commander who was as kind and unselfish as he was brave and skillful, and from that time he could never lead where they would not follow.

While these movements were going on, others of great importance were being made in other parts of Virginia, the chief of which was the organization of an army by General Beauregard at Manassas Junction. This point is about twenty-five miles southwest of Alexandria, where the Orange and Alexandria Railroad is met by the Manassas Gap Railroad, which runs west through the Blue Ridge into the Valley of Virginia. The gap through which this railroad passes, and from which it took its name, was called Manassas, after a poor Jew bearing that name who once lived there.

Manassas Junction was at once deemed a place of importance, as it commanded the road leading to Gordonsville, and thence south and west to Richmond and Charlottesville, and also the Manassas Gap Road, which led into the Valley. The United States troops which were assembled to assail this point were commanded by General McDowell, and to be in readiness for his attack now became the aim of the Confederate authorities, and to accomplish this all their energies were bent. General Johnston was then acting in concert with Beauregard at Manassas while directing the movements of his little army at the mouth of the Valley. It was his aim so to manœuvre as to prevent General Patterson from withdrawing his forces from the Upper Potomac and carrying them to join McDowell's army, which already far outnumbered the one under Beauregard. Besides General Patterson's army, there was another of equal size under the United States generals McClellan and Rosecrans in Northwestern Virginia, which was confronted by a small Confederate force under General Garnett. This force was enabled to hold its own until July, when it was utterly defeated, and its victors were left free to move their forces, if they chose, to swell the ranks of McDowell's army. But General Johnston's movements held these forces also in check. We have already seen how their van-guard was repulsed at Romney by General A. P. Hill. Had General Johnston remained at Harper's Ferry, he could only have reached General Beauregard by a circuitous route, while General Patterson could at any time have thrown his army into Washington by means of the Baltimore Railroad so long as he remained near Harper's Ferry. Once in Washington, he would have been at McDowell's back, ready to support him. By ascending the Potomac, he left General Johnston free to leave Harper's Ferry and to move in such a direction as to shorten and make more direct the distance between himself and Beauregard.

After the show of resistance made to the advance of Patterson's army by Colonel Jackson in the engagement at Haines's Farm, Jackson, as we have seen, retreated before him to a point four miles south of Martinsburg, where he was met by the rest of the Confederate forces. General Patterson then occupied Martinsburg. General Johnston was with his little army four miles distant, at the village of Darkesville, and daily offered him battle, which he daily declined. The skillful Johnston, however, as persistently refused to gratify the wishes of his men by attacking the enemy in Martinsburg. Thus passed four days; at the end of which time the Confederate commander fell back to Winchester.

On arriving in Winchester, Colonel Jackson received the following note:

"RICHMOND, 3d July, 1861.

"MY DEAR GENERAL,—I have the pleasure of sending you a commission of brigadier-general in the Provisional army, and to feel that you merit it. May your advancement increase your usefulness to the State.

"Very truly,   R. E. LEE."

His pleasure and agreeable surprise at this promotion are shown in the following extract from a letter to Mrs. Jackson: "I have been officially informed of my promotion to be a brigadier-general of the Provisional army of the Southern Confederacy. My promotion is beyond what I anticipated, as I only expected it to be in the volunteer forces. One of the greatest [grounds of] desires for advancement is the gratification it will give you, and of serving my country more efficiently. Through the blessing of God, I now have all that I ought to desire in the line of promotion. I would be very ungrateful if I were not contented and exceedingly thankful to our heavenly Father. May his blessing ever rest on you, is my fervent prayer."

General Johnston's withdrawal to Winchester served as a decoy to Patterson, who, on the 15th of July, advanced to Bunker Hill. As soon as he appeared, Johnston marched out and offered him battle. He again declined the challenge, and, pausing in his advance, stretched out his left wing eastward in the direction of the little village called Smithfield. This manœuvre at once unmasked his plans to General Johnston, who saw he was endeavoring to steal a march upon him and reach Manassas first. But the Federal commander little knew with whom he had to deal.

CHAPTER VI.

MANASSAS.

MANASSAS was now, alike for the North and for the South, the centre of hope and expectation. The day on which the two armies were first to meet in shock of battle was anxiously expected by both sides, but with far different feelings. The North looked forward to it with all the impatient arrogance of a nation who, under-rating the courage and resources of her adversary, and intoxicated with the sight of her own wealth in men and money, anticipated an easy triumph over an ill-disciplined rabble. By the South the long-expected day was awaited with calmness and confidence. Aware that the North had the whole world open to her whence to draw men and supplies, while the Southern ports were all closed, the people of the South, though cut off from all foreign aid, yet awaited with perfect self-reliance the issue. They felt that the result of the first combat must depend on the individual pluck of the men composing each army, and, such being the case, had no fear. But as the time for the struggle drew near, the feeling throughout the country became deeper and deeper, the pain of anxious suspense more and more intense, until at last, on the 16th of July, silently but swiftly the news ran through the South that the enemy had begun their advance.

Around Manassas Junction itself there was only a

simple circuit of earthworks mounted by a few cannon.
A few miles to the northeast is a high ridge, on which
lies the little village of Centreville; between it and
the Junction runs a little stream called Bull Run, and
along its banks and heights the battle was to be fought.
This stream runs from west to east, and flows into Occo-
quan River. The banks, as a general thing, are rocky
and steep, and are higher on the northern than on the
southern side, thus giving the advancing army the advantage of position. The little stream abounds in good
fords, which in summer are very shallow, so that it can
be easily crossed at that season.

General Beauregard's advance-guard, which was stationed at Fairfax Court-House, was driven in by General McDowell's advance on the 17th of July. The
United States army, sixty thousand strong, splendidly
equipped, and exultant over their anticipated success,
moved forward as if to an easy victory. The cry of
"On to Richmond!" rose from their ranks, and was re-
echoed by the people in their rear. Never did an army
rush into battle more hopeful of success than did that
under General McDowell. Never did a people wait
more impatiently to hear the shouts of triumph than did
those of the North. Everything had been arranged for
a grand entrance into Richmond when the city should
be captured. Too eager for the news of triumph to
wait for it to be brought to them, many persons, of both
sexes, left Washington and followed in the rear of the
advancing army, that they might be, if possible, eye-
witnesses of the battle.

The enemy, having driven in the advance-guard of
Beauregard's army and marched through Centreville,
were on the 18th of July repulsed at every point at

which they attempted to cross Bull Run. This fight, known as the battle of Bull Run, served to check their advance, and left time for the Southern army to receive reinforcements.

While watching General Patterson's movements, and ready to move with his little army in any direction on a minute's warning, General Johnston received at one o'clock on the morning of the 18th of July a telegraphic dispatch informing him of the advance of the enemy on General Beauregard, and calling on him to hasten to his aid. His tents were therefore struck early in the day on the 18th, and his army was ordered under arms,—as the men all thought, to attack the enemy in their front. Great, then, was their disappointment when they were ordered to turn their backs on Patterson, and were marched away from him. Colonel Stuart was left to watch the movements of the harmless Patterson, and, by presenting a bold front, to make him believe General Johnston was still present with the rest of the army. This was most successfully accomplished. Through Winchester the Southern troops marched. The inhabitants watched their departure with troubled hearts, and asked sadly if they were to be left to the mercy of the enemy. The soldiers shook their heads sorrowfully, and reluctantly continued their march. When, however, they had gone four miles beyond Winchester, General Johnston ordered a halt, and an order in the following stirring words was read: "Our gallant army under General Beauregard is now attacked by overwhelming numbers; the commanding general hopes that his troops will step out like men and make a forced march to save the country." Instantly the air was rent with shouts of joy. Men who had lagged back before

THE LONE SENTRY.

(Page 79.)

now pressed eagerly forward. All was animation and life where before there had only been sullen obedience. The Shenandoah had to be crossed, and into it the men rushed, though the water was waist-deep. On they hurried in their forced march, and, reaching the Blue Ridge, toiled up its sides where the road passes through Ashby's Gap. They did not pause in their march until they reached Paris, a little village on the crest of the mountain.

Arrived at Paris at two o'clock in the night, the whole command was halted to rest. Jackson's men were marched into a beautiful grove inclosed by a fence, and there, foot-sore and wearied with the long and hurried march, the men threw themselves on the ground and soon sank into profound sleep. In a little while one of the officers approached Jackson, and, telling him that no sentinels had been posted, asked if he should not waken some of the men and put them on guard. "No," replied Jackson; "let the poor fellows sleep. I will guard the camp myself." And during the rest of that quiet summer's night his tall figure was seen moving around the camp to see that all was well, or sitting on the fence calmly watching the peaceful slumber of the brave men lying at his feet. His aides offered several times to keep guard in his stead, but he would not give up his post until a short time before the dawn of day, when he lay down in a corner of the fence on a pile of leaves, and was soon enjoying that rest which he had so nobly secured to his wearied troops. At dawn he was again up and arousing his men to continue their march. They reached Piedmont Station, at the foot of the Blue Ridge, a point about midway between Winchester and Manassas, and thirty miles from each, when they were placed on trains to take them to Manassas on Friday morning (July 19). But for a collision, which was, perhaps rightly, attributed to treachery, the whole army would have reached Manassas Junction on Friday morning. As it was, however, General Jackson was fortunate enough to be among the first, and to arrive with his command at the Junction on Friday night.

After such a march, rest was absolutely necessary for the men, and accordingly Saturday was given up to that, they having been marched directly to Mitchell's Ford from the Junction on Friday night.

The enemy, in the mean while, after the repulse at Bull Run on the 18th, was rallying all his forces for the great battle of the 21st. General Johnston reached Manassas about noon on Saturday, the 20th, and, as senior officer, was entitled to the command of the army and the direction of all its movements; but the battle was too close at hand for him to make himself sufficiently acquainted with the nature of the ground and of the enemy's positions. He therefore intrusted all with perfect confidence to the skill and knowledge of General Beauregard. That intrepid and energetic officer had no intention of waiting for the enemy's attack. His army was divided into eight brigades, which occupied the southern banks of Bull Run, along which they were placed in the following positions: Brigadier-General Ewell's on the extreme right, at Union Mills Ford; Brigadier-General D. R. Jones's at McLean's Ford; Brigadier-General Longstreet's at Blackburn's Ford; Brigadier-General Bonham's at Mitchell's Ford; Colonel Cocke's at Ball's Ford, about three miles above; and Colonel Evans, with a regiment and battalion, held the extreme left at Stone Bridge. In the rear of the right were placed two brigades in reserve. The rest of the army of the Shenandoah was expected to arrive in the night of Saturday. It was feared that Patterson, having at length discovered that the bird had flown, might push forward and unite his troops with McDowell on the 22d. This made it of the utmost importance to the Confederates that the battle should be fought on the 21st.

General Beauregard proposed a plan of battle, which General Johnston approved. Beauregard then drew up the necessary order during the night, and it was submitted to General Johnston, and received his approval at half-past four in the morning of the 21st. But the remainder of the army of the Shenandoah did not arrive, and that, with some early movements of the enemy's troops on the Confederate left, prevented General Beauregard from carrying into execution his plan of attack. He then proposed to alter the plan, and let the Confederate left stand on the defensive, while the right made an attack. But the movements of the enemy's lines now became too active to render such an attack possible, and a battle followed different from any that had been planned by the Confederate commander.

The enemy began his firing upon the Confederate lines soon after sunrise, and, while making a show of attack upon their centre and right, marched the mass of his troops around through the woods on his right, and crossed Bull Run two miles above the Confederate left, and thus threw himself upon their flank and rear position. Fortunately for the Confederates, this move was discovered in time for them to swing their line of battle around and face the enemy, so that, instead of its running along the bank of Bull Run, the point on that

D*

stream held by the left became in reality their right, while the line was formed at right angles to the stream and made to extend to the south of it.

When Colonel Evans, who, as we have seen, held the extreme left of the Confederate line, found that the enemy had crossed Bull Run two miles above his position and was marching down upon his left flank, he moved to his left with eleven companies and two field-pieces, and, under cover of the woods, arranged his little force to receive the attack of the enemy, who rushed down upon him with overwhelming numbers.

Generals Johnston and Beauregard placed themselves, about eight o'clock, on a hill in the rear of General Bonham's position at Mitchell's Ford, and, seeing the enemy's forces coming down on the Confederate left, they at once ordered General Bee, who had been placed near Colonel Cocke's position, Colonel Hampton, and General Jackson, to move immediately to the left flank. General Bee, with a soldier's instinct, followed the sound of the firing and formed his troops near the Henry House. Finding, however, that Colonel Evans was sorely pressed by the enemy, he crossed a little valley which lay between his forces and those under Colonel Evans, and, forming on his right and a little in advance of his position, withstood with him the furious onslaught of the enemy. The Confederates were struggling against immense odds, their numbers at this point being only five regiments, with six howitzers, while those of the enemy were over fifteen thousand. The determined valor of the Confederates was beyond all praise, as they withstood one attack after another from the enemy, who threw regiment after regiment on the field in the hope of enveloping this gallant little band.

For one hour they stood their ground and held the United States army at bay. In that immortal struggle the 4th Alabama and the 8th Georgia covered themselves with glory. At last, shattered and broken, this gallant little band were forced to retreat, but not until so ordered by the heroic Bee. They then fell back to General Bee's original position on the plateau of the Henry House. General Jackson, in the mean time, had reached the scene of action and formed his brigade under the crest of this plateau. On the arrival of General Bee and his shattered forces, General Jackson proposed to him to form a new line, of which he should form the centre, and Bee, after rallying his men in his rear, should be on the right. The position chosen by General Jackson was one of great strength, being a long ridge running at right angles to Bull Run, the northern end commanding Stone Bridge, while the southern end and the eastern slope were covered with woods, and the western slope, which fronted the enemy, descended gently and commanded the valley and every approach from that side. On this plateau, in the space between the United States and the Confederate lines, were situated two farm-houses, now known in history as the Robinson and Henry Houses. With his flanks and rear protected by woods, General Jackson then formed his line of battle on this ridge. Two guns of Stanard's battery were hastily placed in position, and, through the skill and precision with which they were handled, served to keep the enemy's advance in check while the rest of the line was formed.

The artillery was placed a'ong the crest of the ridge in such a manner that while the guns swept the enemy's ranks the gunners were still protected. As they came up, the different pieces of artillery were placed in position, until at last seventeen guns were in line along the ridge.   On the left of the batteries were placed the 2d and 33d Virginia Regiments, in such a manner as to be concealed in the woods; on the right was posted the 5th Virginia Regiment, also partially protected by the woods.   Behind the line of the batteries were the 4th and 27th Virginia Regiments, the men lying on their breasts, to escape as much as possible the enemy's fire.   General Bee placed the fragments of his gallant band on the right of Jackson's brigade.

During these moments of extreme peril to the forces on the left, the two generals remained anxious spectators from a knoll near the Lewis House, in the rear of the centre; but by eleven o'clock the continuous sound of firing on the left fully revealed the enemy's plans, and the time for action had arrived.   General Johnston expressing to General Beauregard the conviction that the enemy was massing his troops on the left, and General Beauregard agreeing with him, they struck spurs into their horses, and, followed by their staffs, dashed off at full speed for the scene of battle.   They arrived not a moment too soon.   Worn out by the long contest, and beaten back by overwhelming numbers, the troops of Bee's and Evans's commands were shattered and discouraged; but, inspired by the presence and example of the generals, they turned upon the enemy with rekindled ardor.   It was at this moment that General Johnston, finding the 4th Alabama stripped of field-officers and much worsted, placed the color-bearer, who refused to give to another his colors, beside him, and led a charge to the front, followed by the devoted and heroic men, who eagerly rushed forward.   The two generals,

after thus cheering on the staggered troops and re-form-
ing their wavering lines, held a hurried consultation
and divided the duties of the field. Beauregard, as
the younger officer, claimed the field of action on the
left, while Johnston hastened back to the line of Bull
Run, to assume general direction of everything and to
hurry up reinforcements. These he met two miles off,
pushing eagerly forward to join their sorely-pressed
comrades.

The Confederate reserves and reinforcements being
several miles off, and those of the enemy right at his
back, he hurled his troops rapidly and fiercely against
the Confederate ranks. One line after another swept
across the valley and surged up against the hill held by
the invincible Southerners. For four hours, from eleven
A.M. until three P.M., Jackson's command lay motionless and exposed to the raking fire of the enemy, which
every now and then made sad havoc in their ranks;
but still they were calm and unyielding. Jackson rode
from one end of his line to the other,—his cheering cry
of "Steady, boys, steady," the calmness with which he
exposed himself to danger, and the glow of confidence
and animation on his countenance making his men look
to him as to a war-god.

But there is an end to endurance. The enemy press
forward; one fresh regiment after another is thrown on
the field and stretched out to the left, in the hope of
outflanking the Confederates. In the front his line
sweeps forward, and he takes the Robinson and Henry
Houses, in which his sharp-shooters lodge themselves.
On the Confederate left he moves forward a battery to
sweep the line of Jackson's guns; but the devoted 33d
Virginia, who have so long lain in concealment, wait

until this detachment is right upon them, when, spring-
ing to their feet, they fire, rush forward with a yell, and
capture the battery. The nature of the road, however,
and the hot fire of the enemy, force them to abandon it.

On the right, the enemy's crushing forces press down
upon the heroic band of Bee, who, feeling that he could
no longer bear up against them, rode up to General
Jackson, and exclaimed, in a tone of despair, "General,
they are beating us back!" "Then we will give them
the bayonet," replied Jackson. It was then that the
devoted Bee, turning his horse's head and dashing back
to his men, pointed to Jackson's command, and uttered
the memorable words, "There is Jackson standing like
a STONE WALL. Rally behind the Virginians. Let
us determine to die here and we will conquer. Follow
me!" To this appeal a few of the brave men who had
so long stood their ground replied by following his lead
as he headed a charge. It was his last : the next moment he dropped dead.

The struggle for the possession of the ridge held by
Jackson's command was now drawing to a close. Pressed
on each flank by the enemy, whose numbers still rolled
up on his front, his men wearied by the three hours'
action, and the ammunition running low, Jackson saw
that the time to bring his infantry into action had come.
The batteries in his front were divided, and, wheeling
to the left and right, passed to the rear, and left the
space in front of the infantry open. The men, who for
three hours had been under the ordeal of a murderous
fire without returning a shot, now hailed with delight
the hour of relief. Jackson rode up in front of the 2d
Virginia Regiment, and cried out to the men, "Reserve
your fire till they come within fifty yards; then fire and

The devoted Bee pointed to Jackson's command, and uttered the memorable words, " There is Jackson standing like a *stone wall*."

(Page 86.)

give them the bayonet; and when you charge, yell like
furies!" The general signal was given, the men sprang
to their feet, fired a volley, and dashed forward with a
loud and triumphant shout. Staggered by this furious
onslaught, the enemy's lines wavered, broke, and fled
from the field.

While Jackson thus pierced the enemy's centre, the
whole Confederate line was dashing forward and pushing the enemy back. Their reinforcements, however,
being right at their backs, their lines were again quickly
re-formed in a crescent shape, and, presenting a formidable array, they again moved forward to attack the Confederates, who, though worn down by incessant fighting
and hurried marches, gathered up the wrecks of shattered regiments and broken brigades to withstand once
more the shock of battle. The enemy again charged,
and again the Confederate lines were pushed back.

By this time, however, the Confederate reserves from
the right, which General Johnston had been pushing
up, began to arrive on the field of action, and were
rapidly thrown forward. Cheer after cheer broke from
the ranks of the weary but brave men who for so long
had borne up against such overwhelming odds, as they
saw that reinforcements had at last come up, and in time
to save the day. General Beauregard gave the order for
a second charge to be made, to attempt the recovery of
the plateau in front of the ridge which Jackson's men
had held so long. About this time—three o'clock—General Kirby Smith arrived from Manassas with three
regiments of Elzey's brigade, being part of the Army
of the Shenandoah which had been so long delayed. He
was ordered to fall on the right flank of the enemy, and,
following the sound of the firing, was successfully ex-

ecuting this move when he fell dangerously wounded. Colonel Elzey, being next in command, led the troops forward in a furious charge on the enemy's exposed flank. General Beauregard, seizing the opportunity to throw his whole line forward in the second charge, ordered the whole Confederate force, including every regiment on the field, to sweep onward. The charge was irresistible. The enemy was driven back from the long-contested hill, and victory was no longer doubtful. The persevering foe, however, made yet another attempt to retrieve the day. Again he extended his line with a wider sweep to the right, hoping to turn the Confederate left; again he was reinforced by his inexhaustible reserves. As he re-formed, however, Colonel Early, with three regiments from the right of the Confederate line, came upon the field of action. He threw himself upon the enemy's right, supported by Stuart's cavalry and Beckham's battery. General Beauregard at the same time once more moved forward his whole front, and this combined attack was too much for the Federals. Their lines broke under the charge. Their troops abandoned their artillery and fled disgracefully from the field, and victory perched upon the Confederate banners. Never was there a victory more complete than the Confederates',—never a rout more disgraceful than the enemy's. Their whole force, being seized with a panic, fled in the wildest dismay before a gallant little army numbering not half so many men as did their own. But there was no restraining them; all was confusion— all terror. An eye-witness of the scene on the Federal side thus describes the sight as the Confederate cavalry pursued the flying host:

"By the time I reached the top of the hill, the retreat, the panic, the heedless, headlong confusion was now beyond a hope. I was near the rear of the movement, with the brave Captain Alexander, who endeavored by the most gallant, but unavailing exertions, to check the onward tumult. It was difficult to believe in the reality of our sudden reverse. 'What does it all mean?' I asked of Alexander. 'It means defeat,' was his reply. 'We are beaten; it is a shameful, a cowardly retreat! Hold up, men!' he shouted; 'don't be such infernal cowards!' And he rode backward and forward, placing his horse across the road, and vainly trying to rally the running troops. The teams and wagons confused and dismembered every corps. . . . Meantime, I saw officers with leaves and eagles on their shoulder-straps, majors and colonels who had deserted their comrades, pass me, galloping as if for dear life. No enemy pursued just then; but I suppose all were afraid that his guns would be trained down the long, narrow avenue, and mow the retreating thousands, and batter to pieces army-wagons and everything else which crowded it.

"But what a scene! and how terrific the onset of that tumultuous retreat! For three miles, hosts of Federal troops—all detached from their regiments, all mingled in one disorderly rout—were fleeing along the road, but mostly through the lots on either side. Army-wagons, sutlers' teams, and private carriages choked the passage, tumbling against each other, amid clouds of dust, and sickening sights and sounds. Hacks containing unlucky spectators of the late affray were smashed like glass, and the occupants were lost sight of in the *débris*. Horses flying wildly from the battle-field, many of them in death-agony, galloped at random forward, joining in the stampede. Those on foot who could catch them rode them bareback, as much to save themselves from being run over as to make quicker time. Wounded men lying along the banks, the few either not left on the field or taken to the captured hospitals, appealed, with raised hands, to those who rode horses, begging to be lifted behind; but few regarded such petitions. Then the artillery, such as was saved, came thundering along, smashing and overpowering everything. The regular cavalry, I record it to their shame, joined in the *mêlée*, adding to its terrors, for they rode down footmen without mercy. One of the great guns was overturned, and lay amid the ruins of a caisson as I passed it. I saw an artilleryman running between the ponderous fore and after wheels of his gun-carriage, hanging on with both hands and vainly striving to jump upon the ordnance. The drivers were spurring the horses; he could not cling much longer, and a more agonizing expression never fixed the features of a drowning man. The carriage bounded from the roughness of a steep hill leading to a creek ; he lost his hold, fell, and in an instant the great wheels had crushed the life out of him. Who ever saw such a flight! . . . It did not slack in the least until Centreville was reached. There the sight of the reserve—Miles's brigade—formed in order on the hill, seemed somewhat to reassure the van. But still the teams and foot-soldiers pushed on, passing their own camp and heading swiftly for the distant Potomac, until for ten miles the road over which the Grand Army had so lately passed southward, gay with unstained banners, and flushed with surety of success, was covered with the fragments of its retreating forces, shattered and panic-stricken in a single day."

As a proof of how sure the enemy were of success, it

is recorded that a splendid dinner in honor of the victory had been prepared at Centreville for those who had gone over from Washington to witness the battle; but it remained uneaten. One of the ladies, in her haste to get into her carriage when the rout began, fell and broke her leg.

The Confederate troops followed the flying foe for a few miles, and then abandoned the pursuit. In the mean time, the Confederate wounded and dead were being tenderly cared for on the field which their valor had made so victorious and so glorious. The great fight had been fought and the battle won. For the first time in the history of America, the people of the North and South had confronted each other in battle-array, Northmen in overwhelming numbers; but Southern valor stood the terrible test, and the individual courage of the Confederates had proved more than a match for the skillful generalship and overwhelming odds of the enemy. This thought softened the sorrow felt for the brave men who had fallen in the Confederate ranks.

With the keen instincts of a soldier and the devoted enthusiasm of a patriot, it had been President Davis's fond wish to share with the soldiers of his army the danger and glory of that great day, and he accordingly left Richmond early Sunday morning, hoping to reach Manassas in time to witness the battle. On reaching the Manassas Junction, he mounted a horse and went at full gallop to the scene of action. The declining rays of the warm sun of July were lengthening the shadows across the now victorious and classic plains of Manassas ere his *cort'ge* swept over them. But he appeared then as the impersonation of the Confederate cause, and, as his slight, manly figure came in sight, cheer after cheer rose from the wrecks of the gallant army whose heroic efforts had been so gloriously crowned with success. The wounded forgot their pains as they raised their heads to join in the shout, and the dying spent their last breath in the cheer for him who represented the cause for which they had shed their life's blood.

But, in the mean time, where was Jackson? In the rear of the Confederate lines the wounded were the object of every attention, and the surgeons were busily engaged plying the knife and saw and binding up broken limbs or gaping wounds. On the cool and shady banks of a little stream in the rear, hundreds of the Confederate wounded were collected, and thither General Jackson made his way as soon as the rout of the enemy was seen to be complete. Those who had watched him closely during the fight had noticed him once shake his hand impatiently and then wrap it hastily in his handkerchief. It was when a rifle-ball struck it and broke the middle finger and lacerated one of the others. When he reached the spot where the surgeons were so hard at work on the wounded, one of them, Dr. McGuire, said, "General, are you much hurt?" "No," was the reply; "I believe it is a trifle." "How goes the day?" was Dr. McGuire's second question. "Oh," Jackson exclaimed, unable to restrain his delight at the success of our arms, "we have beat them! We have a glorious victory! My brigade made them run like dogs!" Two or three surgeons having come up to him to offer their services, he quietly declined them until those who were more seriously wounded were attended to, and, sitting down upon the grass to rest, he would not allow his wound to be dressed until he saw the surgeons had more leisure. Then they examined him, and, turning from one to the other, he found all but Dr. McGuire thought he should have at least one of the wounded fingers amputated at once. With an anxious look he then asked Dr. McGuire what his opinion was. "General," he replied, "if we attempt to save the finger, the cure will be more painful; but if this were my hand I should make the experiment." "Then, doctor, do you dress it," he said, as he laid his mangled hand in the doctor's. Dr. McGuire's advice proved judicious, as the hand was healed without removing the finger.

It was while at this place, among the wounded, that the President and his staff dashed by. Jackson arose, and, waving his cap, called upon those around him to give him a loud cheer,—which was quickly done. After describing the rout of the enemy, he said that "with ten thousand fresh troops he could enter the city of Washington."

So ended the day. By night the news of victory had flashed along the electric wires to every part of the South, carrying with it to many a home the sad tidings of the death of some dear one, who had fallen, as all the brave desire to fall, in defense of their homes and hearth-stones. With grateful but saddened hearts the people of the South retired to rest that night. In Richmond the scene was most impressive. The full moon shone down in undimmed splendor on the beautiful streets of this most beautiful Southern city. In front of the tele-graph- and newspaper-offices stood the silent crowd, fear-ing, yet anxious, to hear from the brave soldier that each had sent to the front. Before the private residences and on the sidewalks were seen mothers and wives and sis-ters, in anxious groups, or going from house to house to hear who had fallen or who survived that terrible day.

In the parlors of the hotels sat many an officer's wife, calmly and anxiously awaiting tidings from her husband, all unconscious that he was sleeping his last sleep and that the setting sun had left her a widow. The shouts of triumph which now and then burst from the crowd, as news confirming the completeness of the victory was received, were quickly repressed, as all felt the day had been dearly won. The cup of sorrows which war brings, even in its triumphs, had been pressed to their lips for the first time, and with grateful yet awed and subdued hearts they silently withdrew to their homes.

Twice during that memorable evening the writer of these lines was in the company of General Lee,—once to witness the bitterness of his regret as he announced to a few friends around him that the Secretary of War positively forbade him going to Manassas to offer his services in leading forward the victorious troops, and again, when a lady sitting opposite him asked if he would pursue, to see him lean forward, and say, in tones whose earnestness could never be forgotten, "Madam, I would follow them into their very dens." Nor could the tender sympathy be forgotten with which he spoke of the heart-broken wives and mothers whose loved ones had just fallen.

CHAPTER VII.

THE day after the battle of Manassas, Jackson's pastor, the Rev. Dr. White, was standing in a crowd assembled in front of the post-office in Lexington, anxiously awaiting the opening of the mail. A letter was handed to him as soon as this was done. He recognized Jackson's handwriting, and exclaimed to the anxious and expectant group around him, "Now we shall know all the facts." He opened it, and read:

"MY DEAR PASTOR,—In my tent last night, after a fatiguing day's service, I remembered that I had failed to send you my contribution for our colored Sunday-school. Inclosed you will find my check for that object, which please acknowledge at your earliest convenience, and oblige

"Yours faithfully,

"T. J. JACKSON."

What a picture of the Christian hero! As he sinks to rest after the fatigues of a "day's service" whose deeds had enrolled his name among the great captains of the earth, he does not think of himself, nor, ambitious as he was, of that fame which would follow,—he must, with the instincts of awakening genius, have felt how surely,—but of his colored Sunday-school scholars at home. Was he to be counted among the enemies of that ill-starred race? Yet how many in the world thought of the banner under which he fought, and on which his simple faith cast such lustre, as the emblem of their oppression!

Among the many touching incidents of the battle of Manassas, the death of two brothers—the two young Conrads*— deserves to be mentioned. They were the only sons of their parents, and both enlisted in the Confederate army as soon as the war broke out. Charming in their youthful enthusiasm, their amiable domestic virtues, and the singular purity of their lives, they were the idols of their home circle and the favorites of all who knew them. The eldest, Holmes, had enlisted and was in the field when the youngest, Tucker, came home from college to follow his example. In despair at the thought of both of his young masters rushing into the dangers of war, an old family slave remonstrated with him for joining the army, and said, "Suppose Master Holmes gets killed?" "Then," exclaimed his devoted brother, "I will be right there to fall with him!" They were members of the same company in the Stonewall Brigade, and in one of its magnificent charges both fell dead, killed by the same shot.

We find Jackson writing on the day after the battle of Manassas to Mrs. Jackson as follows:

"Yesterday we fought a great battle, and gained a great victory, for which all the glory is due to God alone. Though under a heavy fire for several continuous hours, I only received one wound, the breaking of the largest finger of the left hand; but the doctor says

---

* Holmes and Tucker Conrad, of Martinsburg, Virginia.

the finger can be saved. My horse was wounded, but not killed. My coat got an ugly wound near the hip. My preservation was entirely due, as was the glorious victory, to our God, to whom be all the glory, honor, and praise. Whilst great credit is due to other parts of our gallant army, God made my brigade more instrumental than any other in repulsing the main attack. This is for your information only; say nothing about it. Let another speak praise, not myself."

And again, on August 5, he wrote to her,—

"You think that the papers ought to say more about me? My brigade is not a brigade of newspaper correspondents. I know that the First Brigade was the first to meet and pass our retreating forces, to push on with no other aid than the smiles of God, to boldly take its position with the artillery that was under my command, to arrest the victorious foe in his onward progress, to hold him in check until reinforcements arrived, and, finally, to charge bayonets, and, thus advancing, pierce the enemy's centre. I am well satisfied with what it did, and so are my generals, Johnston and Beauregard. . . . I am thankful to our ever kind heavenly Father that He makes me content to await His own good time and pleasure for commendation, knowing that all good things work together for my good. Never distrust our God, who doeth all things well. In due time He will manifest all His pleasure, which is all His people should ever desire. If my brigade can always play as important and useful a part as in the last battle, I shall always be very grateful, I trust."

A few days after the battle of Manassas, General Jackson moved forward with his brigade to a point about a mile beyond Centreville, where he encamped, and set to work to perfect the discipline of his troops. The Confederate generals, having collected and re-organized their forces and being reinforced, moved forward, some weeks later, with an army of sixty thousand men. On reaching Mason's and Munson's Hills, they were within sight of Washington, and they hoped to tempt to battle the Federal general McClellan, who, after the defeat at Manassas, had replaced General McDowell in command of the Federal forces. But he declined every challenge to battle.

In writing to his wife on the 24th of September, General Jackson says,—

"This is a beautiful and lovely morning, beautiful emblem of the morning of eternity in heaven. I greatly enjoy it after our cold, chilly weather, which has made me feel doubtful of my capacity, humanly speaking, to endure the campaign, should we remain longer in tents. But God, our God, will do, and does, all things well, and if it is His pleasure that I should remain in the field, He will give me the ability to endure all its fatigues."

On the 7th of October, 1861, as a reward for his services in the battle of Manassas, Jackson was promoted to the rank of major-general. On receiving his commission, he wrote to his wife,—

"I am very thankful to that good God who withholds no good thing from me (though I am so utterly unworthy and so ungrateful), for making me a major-general of the Provisional army of the Confederate States."

In another letter to her he says,—

"I trust that you feel more gratitude to God than pride or elation at my promotion."

Shortly after being appointed major-general, he was

assigned to take command, under General Johnston, of the Valley district, and for that purpose was ordered to Winchester. His brigade, however, was to be left with the Army of the Potomac. His separation from this brigade, whose men had displayed such valor under his command, was a great grief to Jackson. When the day came for him to leave, he ordered the brigade to be paraded out under arms, and, riding down the line accompanied by his staff, he stopped in their front. Profound silence reigned through their ranks, their hearts being too sad to greet him with the accustomed cheer. Reining up his horse as he confronted them, he looked from one end of the line to the other, and in a few appropriate words expressed his attachment for the men of this brigade, his admiration for their brilliant conduct while under his command, and the hope that they might maintain the reputation which they had then won by the achievement of still nobler deeds in the future. Then, pausing, he seemed for a moment shaken with emotion, and, dropping the reins upon his horse's neck, extended his arms towards them and exclaimed, "In the Army of the Shenandoah you were the First Brigade, in the Army of the Potomac you were the First Brigade, in the Second Corps you are the First Brigade; you are the First Brigade in the affections of your general, and I hope by your future deeds and bearing you will be handed down to posterity as the First Brigade in this our second war of independence. Farewell!"

Gathering up the reins, he waved his hand and dashed off the field at full gallop, amid such cheers as only brave soldiers can give to a loved commander. His departure from the Army of the Potomac took place on the 4th of November, 1861.

Jackson had in the Valley district, though still under General Johnston, a command to a great degree independent. On reaching Winchester, he found the forces under his command consisting only of a few companies of badly-armed, half-organized cavalry and portions of three brigades of State militia. His first step was to issue immediately an order calling out at once from the adjoining counties militia to fill out these brigades. The people responded with the patriotic enthusiasm characteristic of that section of the country, and in a few weeks his force was raised to three thousand men. But before we proceed with an account of his movements we must glance at the advances of the enemy in Northwestern Virginia.

The command of the Baltimore and Ohio Railroad placed this region completely in the power of the Federal authorities, for by means of this road they could send troops thither and supply them with provisions or reinforcements, if needed. To penetrate into this district, however, the Confederates, after leaving the Central Railroad at a point west of Staunton, had to toil for many miles over rough, mountainous roads, and through a country which could afford them no provisions or supplies of any sort. These had to be carried after them, with great labor and expense, in wagons. Thus, in the contest in Northwestern Virginia, the odds were all against the Confederates, while fortune favored the success of the Federal arms.

Early in the season, after the first outbreak of the war, a United States army of about twenty thousand men was sent under McClellan to invade Virginia in the northwest. To meet this well-armed and finely-equipped army, a small force of five thousand men, under the command of General Garnett, was sent by the Confederate authorities. It advanced as far as Rich Mountain, where, on the 11th of July, being far away from all sources of supply, it was attacked by McClellan while, unfortunately, divided into two detachments, and utterly defeated. While still divided, the two portions of this gallant little band were forced to make a retreat, in which they lost their baggage and their heroic commander his life. McClellan's reward for this victory was to succeed McDowell in command of the Grand Army of the Potomac after its defeat at Manassas.

After the disastrous results of this expedition under Garnett, a second was sent out, under General Lee, to oppose Rosecrans, who had succeeded McClellan. General Lee's high reputation caused much to be hoped for from this expedition; but all such hopes were doomed to disappointment. This skillful commander found himself and his fine force locked in on all sides by high mountains, and an advance rendered impossible from the nature of the country and the condition of the roads. And so, after remaining powerless for some months, he was ordered to take command of the more important district of the Atlantic Coast.

The failure of these attempts to repel the invasion of the portion of his State to which he was deeply attached as the place of his birth and the home of his youth, was a source of great grief to General Jackson. He had been anxious to go with his men and join the Confederate force sent under Garnett, under whom, he said, he would cheerfully serve for the privilege of being allowed to join the expedition. And when General Lee—from whom he hoped much—went to take command in the northwest, he again expressed the wish to be sent there with his brigade, saying, "It is natural for one's affections to turn to the home of his boyhood and family."

General Loring succeeded General Lee in command of the Northwestern Department. Early in October, Brigadier-General Henry Jackson, of this command, sustained most successfully, with a force greatly inferior in numbers, an attack made by a force of the enemy which left their fastness at Cheat Mountain and attacked him at the head of Greenbrier River. On the 13th of December, Colonel Edward Johnson, of the same command, won a still more brilliant victory in resisting with only twelve hundred men an attack made upon him at Alleghany by five thousand of the enemy, who were not only defeated but driven some distance from the field.

These successes, so cheering as coming from a quarter where the Confederates had only known defeat, and so gratifying as proofs of the skill and heroism of the brave officers and men by whom they were accomplished, were destined to be fruitless, as the Confederate forces were too small for them to be followed up. This was too plainly proved a few weeks later, when the enemy, having occupied Hardy and Hampshire Counties, thus threatened the rear of the little Confederate army and forced it to fall back and take a position on Shenandoah Mountain, forty miles to the rear.

This was the state of affairs in the Northwestern Department when Jackson arrived in Winchester. He had long before predicted that the Confederates could not meet with success there as long as they continued to follow the plan of defense which had been adopted for that section, and even before reaching Winchester he wrote to Richmond proposing a different plan and urging its adoption. This plan was to organize a winter campaign, in which, starting from Winchester, he would move rapidly to the northwest, cut the Baltimore and Ohio Railroad, and thus, having cut the enemy off from supplies and reinforcements, he could fall upon his rear. To accomplish this, he urged that the forces under Loring and Johnston should at once be hurried to him.

The Confederate Government partly agreed to his plan, and to furnish him with sufficient force his old brigade—now known only as the Stonewall Brigade— was sent to him about the middle of November. With the brigade was also sent Pendleton's battery, under Captain McLoughlin. Early in December he also received other reinforcements, consisting of several regiments from the Army of the Northwest. He continued to urge that the remaining forces of that army which were now lying idle should be sent to him; but this was refused, and he did not hesitate to say that the absence of these troops would defeat his plan for a winter campaign in Northwest Virginia.

Though he had failed to secure troops enough to carry out his plan of a winter campaign in the northwest, yet with the force which he had assembled at Winchester, small as it was, he determined not to remain inactive, but at once commenced those brilliant movements in the Valley of Virginia which have rendered it so famous in history and made it seem enchanted ground to the enemy. This valley lies between the great North Mountain range on the west and the Blue Ridge on the east. Its width is at some points fifteen miles, at others thirty, but it is widest where the Potomac crosses it, and then spreads out from the sources of that stream away off in the Alleghanies to Harper's Ferry. The surface of the country lying between the two high mountain-ranges on each side of the valley is itself broken by hills and mountain-ranges. A mountain called Massanutten Mountain, which rises twenty miles southwest of Winchester, runs parallel with the Blue Ridge for fifty miles, and the valley lying between it and the Blue Ridge is watered by the Shenandoah River, and is known as the Luray Valley. The scenery of the Valley of Virginia, thus intersected by smaller valleys and mountain-ranges, is lovely beyond description. Its fertile fields, limpid streams, lofty mountains, waving woods, and smiling valleys form landscapes whose picturesque beauty is a constant source of delight and pleasure to the traveler passing through them. Nor is the race inhabiting the Valley unworthy of the bounties which, in fertile fields and beautiful scenery, nature has lavished on them. Noted for their hospitalities and the grace with which they were administered, they enjoyed in prosperity the easy lives natural to those living in a country which is the abode of plenty, and indulged in the manly sports and simple pleasures characteristic of country life. But it is in adversity that their noblest qualities shine forth. Loyal unto death, patient under hardship and toil, calm and undismayed amid the storms of war which devastated and desolated their country and homes, the first to rush to arms and the last to lay them down, the very air they breathed seemed to inspire with fresh courage and energy the forces sent to defend their beautiful country, and to render it for their foes the Valley of the Shadow of Death.

General Jackson determined to make with the small force under his command a move which he thought might be a serious annoyance to the enemy. This was to cut the Chesapeake and Ohio Canal, which ran down the Potomac from Cumberland, Maryland, to Washington, and thus break the enemy's communications by the river, as they had—by the burning of the bridge at Harper's Ferry—been broken by the railroad. The point he selected for attack was Dam No. 5, near Martinsburg; for if this dam could be broken it would let off the water which fed the canal.

With the Stonewall Brigade, his cavalry, and a part of the militia, he went to Martinsburg on December 10, and there completed his arrangements for carrying his plan into execution. Sending the militia to make a feint on Williamsport, he went with the rest of the troops to the dam. A working-party composed of men from Holliday's company, of the 33d Virginia Regiment, and from Robinson's, of the 27th, were assigned to the laborious task of breaking a gap through the dam. The Stonewall Brigade was placed near them, behind a hill, to prevent any attack upon them, while a mill near by was also filled with Confederate riflemen ready to fire upon any attacking party. There they worked from the 17th to the 21st of December, waist-deep in water, worn down with fatigue, almost overcome with sleep, and with the enemy's cannon-balls booming over their heads. But still they labored on through the cold winter days and the colder winter nights. The Federal general Banks, at the head of a large force on the other side of the Potomac, thundered away with his cannon in the vain attempt to drive the brave fellows from their task. On the 21st the breach through the dam was finished, and the waters of the Potomac rushed through and left the canal drained to its bottom. In this affair only one man was killed by the enemy. But who can describe the sufferings of the men on such an expedition? Who can

E*

sufficiently admire the heroism and patriotic devotion which prompted the men who volunteered to enter the chill waters of the Potomac on such a laborious work?

When General Jackson returned to Winchester on the 25th of December, he found awaiting him the remainder of Loring's force. This increased the number of men in his command to eleven thousand, including three thousand militia. By order of the Government, Loring was to retain command of the troops which had been under him, but was to act under Jackson's orders. An unfortunate jealousy which afterwards sprang up between these two commands was a source of infinite trouble to General Jackson, and in more than one instance served to cripple movements which might otherwise have Leen successful.

Had Loring's forces arrived earlier, and been only accompanied by those under Colonel Edward Johnson, Jackson would have been able to carry out his fondly-cherished plan of invading Northwestern Virginia. As it was, with such a fine body of men under his command, and tempted by the mildness of the weather, he determined to start on an expedition which might accomplish a part of what he had hoped to achieve could he have succeeded in sooner assembling a sufficient number of troops. This expedition was to sweep away three separate detachments stationed in the counties west of Winchester, where they were ruling the people with a rod of iron. These three detachments were stationed,— one at Bath, in Morgan County, forty miles north of Winchester; one at the little town of Hancock, on the opposite side of the Potomac; and one at Romney, on the south branch of the same river. The detachments at the first two places were small, but the one at Romney numbered ten thousand men, and the enemy had also intrenched himself there. Jackson's plan was to move swiftly upon Bath and Hancock, capturing the detachment at each place, and then to attack Romney. The success of this well-planned movement was destined, however, to be marred by the jealousy which now broke out between the two commands, and the disinclination of the men and officers under Loring to enter upon a winter campaign.

The morning of New Year's day of 1862 was as mild and balmy as if it were in the month of May, and, with a bright sky over his head, Jackson started from Winchester with his little army of eight thousand five hundred men, with five batteries. But the weather, which was so auspicious in the morning, became lowering and threatening as the day advanced, and with the night came a cold rain or sleet, and the balmy air of the morning was exchanged for weather so intensely cold as to be scarcely endurable for either man or beast. To avoid betraying the movement to the enemy, the march was conducted over roads but rarely used, and consequently rough and in no order for traveling. Matters grew worse as the march advanced, and the hardships of the troops moving under a driving sleet or snow over frozen roads were very great, and their sufferings intense. Many of the men fell in their tracks, unable to go on. For several nights they slept out under the cold winter skies without blankets or tents. General Jackson shared all these hardships with his troops, and by his patient endurance encouraged them to bear up and push on.

At last, at the end of a three days' hard march, this little band reached Bath, and drove in the enemy's pickets on January 3. General Jackson arranged his forces so as to capture the enemy the next day and enter the town. But here his plan was frustrated by the sluggish movements of the troops, and his cavalry dashed into the town just in time to see the enemy escape, leaving behind him all his stores and provisions. The indefatigable Jackson at once ordered a pursuit, and for this purpose divided his force and sent a body down each of two roads by which the enemy had taken flight for the river. He was soon overtaken on the road leading to Hancock, and his forces driven into that town. The Confederate body moving down the other road also came up with the enemy, but, not pressing the pursuit as closely as they ought to have done, he was allowed to cross the Potomac but little damaged, and to find refuge in Hancock. A Confederate force had been sent by Jackson down a third road leading to the railroad bridge across the Capon, which they were ordered to destroy. This they did, and thus Romney was cut off from Banks, who was in command of a considerable force lower down the river.

On the morning of the 5th, General Jackson sent Colonel Ashby to summon the town of Hancock to surrender. He was led blindfolded through the streets into the presence of the Federal commander. Ashby's heroic deeds had already spread his fame abroad, and, as he was led through the streets, a crowd, curious to catch a glimpse of the dashing cavalryman, followed close after him, and he heard it whispered from mouth to mouth, "That is the famous Ashby!" The Federal commander having refused to surrender the town, General Jackson cannonaded it and drove the Federal forces out. After this he hurried off on the 7th towards Romney. Late that day, his van-guard falling in with a detachment of the enemy at Hanging Rock, fifteen miles from Romney, a skirmish took place, in which the Confederates lost two guns. At this point Jackson was forced to halt to rest his jaded troops, and to have his horses re-shod with rough shoes to enable them to keep their footing on roads covered with ice. This caused a delay of several days, and the march was not resumed until the 13th.

On the 14th of January, Jackson entered Romney to find the bird flown. Though having a greatly superior force, the Federal commander, on hearing of Jackson's approach with his little band, fled before him on the 14th, and in such haste that he left his tents standing. Had the Confederates come up in time to attack the enemy, they would have rushed into battle with an eagerness and a spirit of revenge never felt by them before, for from Hanging Rock to Romney the country presented a pitiable scene of desolation. The enemy had spread fire and ruin everywhere. Not a house was left, and only smoking ruins now marked the spot where they had stood. The peasant's cot and the rich man's mansion had shared the same fate. The widow and the orphan had been driven out from their homes as the torch was applied to them. Old men were shot down in wanton cruelty; and even the domestic animals, horses, mules, sheep, and hogs, were alike butchered. On that dreary march of fifteen miles not one thing was seen moving through fields that had so lately teemed with life and given every mark of the highest rural prosperity. Now all was ruin and desolation; the country was like a smoking charnel-house, the ashes of burnt houses and the bodies of dead animals being mingled together. One scene of ruin following another, the Confederate forces moved on in this march, the sad silence being only broken now and then as some scene of ruin more horrible than the preceding came to view, or by some fierce vows of vengeance as a soldier who had come from that section came in sight of the ruins of his once happy home. No wonder that men who had committed such atrocities should be frightened at the approach of the brave soldiers before whom they fled.

On finding the enemy gone, General Jackson ordered an advance movement to destroy a very important railroad bridge; but so greatly had his troops been demoralized by the hardships of their march, and so averse were they to this move, that he was obliged reluctantly to abandon it.

Leaving General Loring with three brigades and thirteen pieces of artillery at Romney, where he had made all necessary arrangements for his defense should he be attacked, General Jackson returned to Winchester on the 24th of January, taking with him the Stonewall Brigade, that he might be in readiness for any move of Banks.

On this expedition General Jackson had had much to contend with in the disaffection among both the officers and men of Loring's command, but his unbending authority and iron will had held it all in check, and in the face of almost every kind of obstacle he had succeeded with a handful of men in driving the enemy from each of his positions which he attacked, and in chasing him from a district in which he had been a scourge to the unhappy people placed in his power. Having accomplished all this with but little or no aid from the Government, he was astounded by the receipt of the following telegram from the Secretary of War on the 31st of January:

"Our news indicates that a movement is making to cut off General Loring's command; order him back to Winchester immediately."

Jackson was too good a soldier to hesitate in carrying out this order, but too independent a man to retain a position where he would be responsible for success or failure and yet be liable to have his plans and arrangements for a campaign interfered with by orders sent from the remote office of an official who could not judge of what should or should not be done, and he accordingly wrote at once to the Secretary of War as follows:

"HEADQUARTERS VALLEY DISTRICT,
"January 31, 1862.

"HON. J. P. BENJAMIN, *Secretary of War.*

"SIR,—Your order requiring me to direct General Loring to return with his command to Winchester immediately has been received and promptly complied with.

"With such interference in my command I cannot expect to be of much service in the field, and accordingly respectfully request to be ordered to report for duty to the Superintendent of the Virginia Military Institute at Lexington, as has been done in the case of other professors. Should this application not be granted, I respectfully request that the President will accept my resignation from the army.

"Respectfully, etc., your obedient servant,
"T. J. JACKSON."

When it became known that Jackson had resigned,

he was besieged by letters and entreaties to withdraw his resignation, from persons of all ranks in public and private life, which showed plainly the hold he already had on the hearts and imagination of his countrymen. The Governor wrote a letter to him begging him to reconsider, and sent one of the most influential men of the State as a special messenger to urge him to withdraw his resignation. But Jackson was firm. In his reply to the Governor's letter he wrote, "The order was given without consulting me; it is abandoning to the enemy what has cost much preparation, expense, and exposure to secure; it is in direct conflict with my military plans; it implies a want of confidence in my capacity to judge when General Loring's troops should fall back; and it is an attempt to control military operations in detail from the Secretary's desk at a distance."

He remained inexorable until he heard that the Governor had withdrawn his letter of resignation in the name of Virginia, and a few days later received assurances that the Government did not intend to interfere with his military plans.

During this period of trial to him, Jackson preserved his calm outward demeanor, and went frequently to dine with a friend in Winchester whose young family afforded him the pleasure he always enjoyed in playing with children. Only once did he give vent to his feelings, and then it was in an outburst of passion which awed and impressed those around him, as he strode up and down the room and expressed all he had suffered in having his plans destroyed.

CHAPTER VIII.

KERNSTOWN.

THE first two or three months of the year 1862 were marked by a succession of disasters to the Confederate arms which plunged the whole South into gloom and depression. The first of these disasters was the loss of the battle of Somerset, in Kentucky. In this battle fell the noble-hearted Zollicoffer, who was so beloved by his troops that their grief and terror at his death cost them the victory which his skill and courage had almost completely secured. The defeat at Somerset was followed by that off the North Carolina coast, on Roanoke Island, in which a handful of Confederate troops were utterly overpowered by a superior Federal force. This defeat, which occurred on the 8th of February, was one of the causes which later led to the evacuation of Norfolk. Again, in Kentucky, one disaster followed quickly upon the heels of another during this month of February. The noble Albert Sidney Johnston was making there the most heroic efforts to organize a force sufficiently large to cope with the thousands which the Northwestern States were pouring down the Mississippi, and which were destined, for the most part, for Kentucky and Tennessee. This skillful general was indeed one of the lofty spirits of the earth, for while he worked day after day with indefatigable energy and unflagging ardor, resting at night on a bundle of straw, as did his lowest soldiers, an impatient and ignorant country was taunting him with sluggishness and want of skill. Yet so earnest was he in his efforts, so devoted in his patriotism, that he received these reproaches as part of the trials which a soldier must expect in discharging the duties of his profession. " I observed silence, as it seemed to be the best way to serve the cause and the country," he nobly wrote in a letter to President Davis,—a calm, manly, but touching letter, which was read by many of his country-men after his death with tears.

To prevent the Federal forces from penetrating to the heart of the country included in his command, it was necessary for Johnston to keep them out of the Missis-sippi, Tennessee, and Cumberland Rivers. To do this he attempted to close the Mississippi by batteries at Co-lumbus, the Tennessee by Fort Henry, and the Cumber-land by Fort Donelson. Fort Henry was attacked on the 6th of February, and surrendered after a defense of but little more than an hour. On the 15th of the same month Fort Donelson, after a heroic resistance, fell, many Confederate soldiers being captured with it. After the fall of these two forts came the necessary evacuation of Columbus, followed by that of Nashville and Mem-phis. Generals Albert Sidney Johnston and Beauregard, who had been sent to join his command, were thus forced to fall back and assume a line of defense south of the Tennessee River.

So much for affairs in the West. In Virginia they were but little more promising.

McClellan, we have seen, was commanding and di-recting the movements of the troops in front of John-ston at Manassas. He was now just completing the organization of the immense force—over two hundred thousand men—with which he expected to overcome the thinned Confederate ranks and capture Richmond at an early day.

General Johnston, with a greatly inferior force, had to defend a long line extending from Evansport on the Potomac, on his right, to Winchester, beyond the Blue Ridge, on his left. Thus Jackson's little force held the extreme left of this line. A strong force was ascending the Peninsula from Fortress Monroe, and was only kept in check by the audacity of General Magruder. This dashing officer, by hurrying his little force from one point to another, appearing first at one place and then at another, and always ready for a fight, confounded the Federal commanders by his boldness, and made them think by this skillful handling of his troops that his force was four times as numerous as it really was.

While the odds were thus fearfully against the Confederates on land, the Federal Government was sending out from its ports immense armaments to ascend the navigable streams and throw invading armies into the very heart of the country. The North had the whole world open to her. The eagerness of her people to invade the South threw open to her Government inexhaustible wealth with which to get men and material to equip and sustain immense armies and extensive navies. The South, on the other hand, being shut out from the rest of the world, had to look to her own resources for help. Her people, brave and high-spirited, patient and enduring under toil, hardship, and suffering, were yet impatient under that restraint so necessary for the discipline of an efficient army. The most domestic people in the world, loving their homes with a love rarely surpassed, it required the greatest self-denial and sacrifice on their part to lie idle in camp. Hence the difficulty of retaining the men in hand after a battle, and the consequent impossibility of reaping the full benefit of a victory. With such material for armies, and with limited resources and blockaded ports, it behooved the rulers of the South to push the war vigorously forward. But they failed to seize the propitious moment of their early success, when the Southern people, animated by the loftiest spirit of liberty and devotion to country which ever swelled the breast of man, and flushed with victory, would have rushed into battle with an *élan* which few armies could resist. The precious time employed by the Federal authorities in organizing immense forces was spent in listless inactivity by those of the South. The inferior forces that she already had were rapidly melting away. No steps had been taken for the re-enlistment of the men, most of whom had enlisted for only a year, and they insisted on returning home, if only for a short visit; there seemed every probability of the whole army being disorganized. It was this condition of affairs, even more than the actual reverses to Confederate arms, which made the situation of the South seem most appalling.

When it became evident that General Johnston had to fall back from Manassas, it also became evident that his retreat would have to be accomplished with thinned if not disorganized ranks; for, by an almost fatal law of the Confederate Congress, the old officers in the army were on the eve of being dropped and new ones elected by the soldiers, and this in the face of a greatly superior force and one enjoying every advantage both in numbers and in equipments. No wonder that men's hearts sank within them when they thought of the coming campaign, and no wonder that they trusted as earnestly as they did to Providence alone to crown a just cause with success.

But, amid all this gloom and depression, where was Jackson? At Winchester, undaunted and unshaken; heading a forlorn hope as it were, and defying with six thousand men the united forces of Lander and Banks, —consisting of forty-six thousand men,—one thirty-five miles north of him, and the other at Harper's Ferry. He had orders from General Johnston by no means to allow the enemy to ascend the Valley and, slipping through one of the gaps in the Blue Ridge, fall upon his flank on his retreat from Manassas. He was to handle his faithful little band of veterans in such a manner as to keep the enemy in the Valley. This was the task set before him; and most nobly and heroically did he accomplish it.

As Jackson had foreseen, on the retreat of Loring from Romney the Federal forces pressed forward, and advanced so far as again to threaten the rear of Colonel Edward Johnson's command. This forced him to fall back, and he withdrew his force to Shenandoah Mountain, within twenty-five miles of Staunton. Winchester was now threatened on all sides, and, to make matters worse for Jackson, Loring being ordered to another command, part of his troops were sent east of the Blue Ridge, and thus at the moment of the most imminent danger Jackson's force was cut down to six thousand men. But he was so far from despairing that he boldly declared that should Lander with his eleven thousand or Banks with his thirty-five thousand men move on him, he would instantly march out and attack him.

Banks crossed the Potomac at Harper's Ferry on the

25th of February with four thousand men, and early in March had his headquarters established at Charlestown, twenty miles from Winchester. General Shields was now in his command, and these two generals very soon had assembled an army of thirty-six thousand men.

As Johnston fell back on the eastern side of the Blue Ridge, it became necessary for Jackson to fall back on the western side, but the question was whether he should retire to Front Royal, a village lying at the mouth of the Luray Valley, which, as we have seen, stretches for fifty miles between the Massanutten Mountain and the Blue Ridge; or whether he should fall back to Strasburg, which village is situated at the head of the main valley running down to Staunton. In their communications on the subject, General Johnston, while leaving General Jackson to act as he thought best, was in favor of his falling back down the Luray Valley, as he would there be next to the Blue Ridge and in a better position to prevent Banks from crossing that ridge to fall upon his flank than if he retreated down the main valley. But Jackson said that Banks would never cross over the Blue Ridge and leave him in the main valley, while by staying there he would be in a good position to prevent the Central Railroad, leading to Richmond, from being cut at Staunton. He accordingly determined to take the main valley as his line of retreat, and to fall back first to Strasburg. In the mean time, he freed himself of all unnecessary incumbrances and got his little army in light marching order by sending all his sick and stores to Mount Jackson, forty-five miles above Winchester. This was accomplished by the 11th of March.

The good people of Winchester saw with dismay the departure from their town of the stores and sick of Jackson's army, for they knew too well that it betokened the withdrawal at no distant day of the army itself, and the relinquishment of their section of the country to the invasion of the Northern troops. Gloom and depression now filled hearts which had lately beat high with hope and patriotic enthusiasm.

But it was no part of Jackson's plan to leave these loyal people without striking a blow in their defense. His force consisted now of only three Virginia brigades, six batteries of field-artillery, and Colonel Ashby's cavalry regiment; yet on the 11th of March, when Banks with a force four times as large marched within four miles of Winchester, he did not hesitate to march out of the town with his troops to meet him and offer him battle. This the Federal commander declined, and Jackson, after thus flaunting the Confederate colors in his face, led his troops back to the town. But, still eager for a fight, he was in no wise discouraged by this failure to force one from the enemy, and he conceived the bold idea of becoming the attacking party himself. His plan was to allow his men time to refresh themselves after the morning's march, and to lead them back under cover of the night to the enemy's front, and, having silently arranged his forces for the attack, to fall unexpectedly upon him before dawn of day on the 12th. This attack he was the more anxious to make as Shields had not yet joined Banks with his reinforcements. He summoned to a council of war the commander and the colonels of the Stonewall Brigade to lay his plan before them. In the mean time, while they were assembling, he went, all booted and spurred, with his haversack swung across his shoulders and ready for the march, to the house of a friend whose hospitality he had frequently enjoyed while Winchester was his head-quarters. He found his friend and his family oppressed by the gloom which overspread the whole town. His countenance radiant with hope, his eyes flashing with the fire of genius and patriotic devotion, full-armed and ready for the fray he appeared in their midst, his whole bearing breathing the spirit of a war-god. His cheering words and hopeful predictions that all would yet be well soon dispelled the gloom which had settled on this family circle, and after supping with them he asked his host to have family prayers as usual, after which, having first requested to have his haversack filled, he bade them good-night, saying that he would perhaps return the next day to dinner. The family, doubtless to share with a neighbor the hopes with which his visit had cheered them, went out to make a call. In an hour, with anxious looks and rapid steps, Jackson returned. The servant who answered his loud ring at the bell was told to ask his master to come at once to his headquar-ters. The gentleman on going there found Jackson pacing his room in great agitation, and he quickly learned from him the cause. He told him of his plan of attack on the enemy, and that on laying it before his officers they had disapproved of it, saying that the men, already wearied with the ten miles' marching to and fro of the day, were in no condition to make the march back to the enemy's front and then fight a battle, and that, in addition to this, the chance that the enemy's re-inforcements might come up at a critical time during the fight made the plan too hazardous to be undertaken. Jackson then in rapidly-spoken words was revealing to his friend, as he continued to pace the room, his deep disappointment and the anguish it cost him to be forced to leave Winchester without striking a blow, when, stopping suddenly, with his head thrown back and the light falling full upon his countenance, which again became animated with an expression of hope, he grasped the hilt of his sword, and said, in the slow tones of desperate determination, "But—let me think—can I not yet carry my plan into execution?" During the momentary pause which followed, his friend, who was unused to seeing him with his battle-look upon him, trembled, as he afterwards confessed, before the fire which now glared from his eyes, as, peering into space, he vainly sought some expedient to avoid a speedy retreat. The next moment the loftily-raised head dropped, and to his fiery looks succeeded those of regret, as he said, sadly, "No, I must not do it; it may cost the lives of too many brave men. I must retreat, and wait for a better time."

Jackson, after thus giving way for a moment to the feelings which agitated him, recovered his usual calmness, and proposed to return with his friend and bid adieu to his family. His altered looks revealed too plainly the change in his plans, and his farewell to these kind friends was a sad one, though he expressed the firm hope that a kind Providence would soon enable him to return and free them from the rule of the foe.

The dawn of the 12th found the Confederate army leaving Winchester for Strasburg, instead of attacking the Federals, as its general had fondly hoped to do. When General Banks found that he had now no foe to dread, he entered Winchester slowly at nine o'clock the same morning. The Confederate force had been so carefully withdrawn that he did not make a single capture, though Colonel Ashby withdrew his troops deliberately before his advance, and did not himself leave the town until the enemy were close at hand, when, giving a parting shout of defiance, he turned his horse's head and dashed after his bold troopers. General Shields, with his part of the Federal forces, did not reach Winchester until the afternoon of the 12th. General Banks, having occupied Winchester, and having no fear of Jackson's returning, left Shields in command of his army, and returned to Washington, fondly hoping that his troops could be sent across the Blue Ridge to fall on Johnston's flank, or at least that he would hear no more from Jackson until he should advance to beat him up himself.

The night of the 12th found Jackson and his little army at Strasburg, twenty miles from Winchester. Retiring slowly up the Valley, he arrived at Mount Jackson on the 17th, where he halted. Two days after reaching this place, he received a dispatch from General Johnston, dated the 19th. That commander was just at the most critical point of his withdrawal from before McClellan, who, with his immensely superior force, was trying to cut him off, and for this purpose had already issued orders calling the troops of Banks across the Blue Ridge to attack Johnston's left. The latter general in his dispatch to Jackson urged upon him the importance of keeping the enemy in the Valley and away from him, and for this purpose ordered Jackson to march back down the Valley and hang as closely upon the enemy as he could without risking the capture or destruction of his little army. The Federals had already begun their march from the Valley to Manassas, and were moving in the direction of Snicker's Gap, where they were to cross the Blue Ridge.

The morning of the third day after this dispatch was received found the indefatigable Jackson again on the road and leading his little army back on the line of his late retreat. A rapid and hard day's march of twenty-six miles brought him on the night of that day, March 22, to Strasburg. Colonel Ashby, who was sent ahead with his cavalry and a light battery, drove the enemy's pickets into Winchester. The movement had been so rapid on the part of the Confederates that they were upon the Federals before they knew anything of their approach. Shields, who was in command at Winchester, had most of his troops encamped on the side of the town opposite to that from which Ashby approached. This officer, not seeing many in that neighborhood, and hearing through his scouts, who entered the town secretly, that many regiments had been sent off in the direction of Snicker's Gap, was deceived as to the true size of their force. He accordingly sent a courier to General Jackson to tell him that there were only four regiments in Winchester, and that they were on the eve of leaving for Harper's Ferry.

On receiving this intelligence from Ashby, General Jackson determined to push forward, and did so on the morning of the 23d. The enemy, however, having heard of his approach, drew out all of his forces, which were encamped below the town, and recalled by couriers the troops already on their way to Manassas. Thus, Jackson, on reaching Barton's Mills, five miles distant from Winchester, found Colonel Ashby driven back by the advancing columns of the enemy, and himself and his little army in an open, rolling country, not offering him any favorable position, and in the presence of troops numbering more than four times as many men

as he had in his own command; for, many furloughs
having been given to officers and men after the late
retreat, when it had been thought a period of repose
would follow, and many being either sick or foot-sore
after the rapid marches which they had made, the little
army was reduced to two thousand seven hundred men,
while that of the enemy numbered eleven thousand.

With no favorable position which he could reach
within many miles, and yet too far advanced to retreat
in the face of such a superior force without almost certain destruction; with only a handful of foot-sore and
wearied men, half of whose officers were absent, to meet
fresh troops so greatly outnumbering them, never was a
command in a more perilous situation than Jackson's.
But his energy and courage were equal to the emergency.
His spirits rose as the dangers of the situation thick-
ened around him, and he determined to attack the enemy
rather than to await an attack from him.

Running parallel with the turnpike leading to Winchester, and west of it, was a wooded ridge. Around
the southwestern end of this ridge sweeps the Opequon
Creek, which is at that point dammed up to form a mill-
pond. The ridge runs in a northeastern direction for
two miles, and then slopes down into the plain. On this
northeastern slope the enemy rested his right wing, while
his left rested upon the little village of Kernstown. As
his infantry and artillery were massed on his centre,
Jackson saw that an attack made there would be the
certain destruction of his little band, and his soldier's
eye rested on the northeastern slope of the wooded ridge
as the only point at which he should begin the attack.
But being prevented by the mill-pond from ascending the
ridge at its southwestern end and marching along its crest,

as would have been the safest approach for him, he was obliged to march his force under fire of the enemy's guns in an oblique direction from the turnpike to the northeastern slope. This movement was executed speedily and in good order.

It was towards the close of the Sabbath-day—about four o'clock in the afternoon—when the necessary arrangements for the attack were completed. Jackson's force—with the exception of a few Marylanders—consisted entirely of Virginians. On his right, and fronting Kernstown, he placed Ashby, with most of his cavalry, a battery of three guns, and four companies of infantry; the 5th Virginia fronted the enemy's centre, and a mile to its left were collected the rest of the troops; and there, in an oblique line across and down the western slope of the wooded ridge, was formed the main line of battle. On a hill beyond the meadows at the base of the hill were stationed four companies of cavalry.

The battle was opened by a brisk cannonade from the Confederate batteries which silenced several of the enemy's. Then the infantry attack was begun by the 27th Virginia, and fighting at close quarters was soon raging along the whole line. The Confederate troops engaged were, for the most part, men from the Valley; they were fighting, many of them, in sight of their own homes; and never did men rush into battle with greater enthusiasm or sustain the shock with more heroic valor. Twice did two of the regiments rout their assailants and hold the entire Federal line in check until reinforcements could be brought to them. As regiment after regiment was led into the fight, the tall, commanding figure of General Jackson was seen leading them on, and his voice was heard ringing out in cheers to his men where the fire was hottest. The cannonade was raging fiercely, and told the good people of Winchester the fierce combat in which their friends were engaged, and they knew too well the odds that were against them. On the right the gallant Ashby thundered upon the enemy with his three guns, and drove them steadily back. A body of the enemy, moving around, attempted to outflank his position and capture the guns, but the four companies of Virginia infantry, under Ashby, dashed into the woods through which they were advancing, and, cheering enthusiastically, drove them back while the guns were being moved to a safer position.

On the left the battle still raged with unmitigated fury. The enemy, feeling secure in his numbers, led one regiment up after another as they were driven back by the deadly fire of the Virginians, who three times drove their line down the hill. The Federal officers were seen in the rear of their men, driving them on to the fight with the free use of their sabres. The regiments of the two armies fired into each other often at a distance of only a hundred paces. Colonel Fulkerson, who commanded the Third Virginia Brigade, being engaged in a hot contest with a body of the enemy, perceived a stone fence between himself and the foe. Both adversaries made a rush for it, each hoping to use it as a breastwork, but the superior dash of the Virginians enabled them to reach it first, when, throwing themselves on their knees behind it, they fired just as the enemy's line was almost at the muzzles of their guns. So deadly was this volley that the enemy's line seemed, it is said, almost "to sink into the earth." Many of their men threw themselves upon their faces to escape the fire, while others tried to crawl back to their lines; but the unerring Virginia marksmen picked them off. The regiment which was thus almost annihilated proved to be the 5th Ohio, which more than any other had been engaged in the outrages committed in the country around Romney.

The Virginians availed themselves of every tree and ravine as a shelter from which to fire upon the enemy. At length the ammunition began to give out, and as each man fired his last round his officer permitted him to go to the rear, until at last the thinned Confederate ranks offered but a shadow of resistance to the fresh troops which were constantly being brought up to attack them. Finally, General Garnett, of the Stonewall Brigade, finding his ammunition all gone, and his right wing pierced, took upon himself the responsibility of ordering the retreat of his command without orders from General Jackson.

The retreat of the whole force now began, and the gallant little band fell back from the well-contested field, each man taking care of himself, and those who were fortunate enough to have a round of ammunition left taking advantage of the shelter afforded by every tree or bush to reload and give a farewell shot to the foe.

The retreat began at about nightfall. The two companies of Confederate cavalry which Jackson had placed on his extreme left now did good service in keeping the enemy's cavalry in check, and finally put them to flight. On the eastern side of the Opequon, the night found a number of Confederate soldiers between the mill-pond and the enemy, by whom they were captured. The rest of the infantry, broken and shattered, but elated at the glorious stand which they had made against the foe, retreated a few miles that night to Newtown, where, wearied and worn, they halted for the night. General

Jackson, having made good his retreat and gathered his heroic little band around him, begged some food from a party of his soldiers bivouacking around a fire, after partaking of which he threw himself on the ground a little in the rear of his outposts, and was soon lost in profound slumber.

The gallant Ashby, who had been left to cover the retreat, made a stand a mile in the rear of Barton's Mills, and so annoyed the enemy that he held him in check until ten o'clock the next day. The Federals then, after pursuing Jackson cautiously for a few miles, returned to their quarters. Jackson ordered his medical director to send all his wounded to the rear; and when his surgeon said, "But that requires time. Can you stay to protect us?" "Make yourself easy about that," he replied; "this army stays here until the last wounded man is removed." And then, in tones betraying deep feeling, he added, "Before I will leave them to the enemy I will lose many men more."

In the mean time, the agony of the people of Winchester about the result of the battle, and their anxiety to know who had friends among the dead or the wounded, were indescribable. As the Confederate prisoners taken in the fight passed through the streets, the inhabitants turned out almost *en masse*, and made their passage through the town to the depot, where they were to take the cars for Baltimore, almost a triumphal march. When leave was given to the mayor to send out and bury the Confederate dead on the battle-field, persons of all ages and all sexes flocked thither. An eye-witness says of the scene,—

"This was Tuesday. The fight had taken place on Sunday, and now, on the third day, preparations were made for the burial of the Confederate killed. Under the directions of the mayor of Winchester, some fifty citizens collected the dead, dug a great pit on the battle-field, and gently laid the poor fellows in their last rest-ing-place. It was a sad sight, and sadder still to see women looking carefully at every corpse to try and iden-tify the bodies of their friends. Scarcely a family in the county but had a relative there; and what torture of anxiety must have been suffered, knowing only that their friends were in the fight, and ignorant whether they were prisoners at Baltimore, suffering in the hospitals, or lying unburied on the sand!"

The attentions lavished by the women of Winchester on the Confederate wounded brought there knew no bounds, and, to their own honor be it said, and that of the cause they loved so well, their attentions were not withheld from the enemy's wounded.

Such was the glorious little battle of Kernstown, than which there was no nobler fight during the war. General Jackson himself said of the gallant men in it that each man acted the part of a hero. The losses by the fight were two guns, three or four caissons, and in killed, wounded, and captured a little over seven hundred men, or more than one-fourth of the force engaged, while the enemy's losses, perhaps, were fully equal to the whole number of men that Jackson had in the fight.

But, whatever were the losses on Jackson's side, this battle secured for him what he had made the move to get, namely, the recall of the troops sent to join those under McClellan, and gave the enemy a proof of Virginian valor which he could not soon forget.

On the 1st of April, Jackson fell back leisurely five miles from New Market to a hill called Reede's Hill,

F*

where, taking position, he began to reorganize and recruit his force. Banks soon followed him, and, taking position on the opposite range of hills, cannonaded the Confederates, without doing them any harm.

Ashby's fame was now so great that his name had become a watchword in the Valley, and so many recruits were added to his cavalry companies that they numbered two thousand men. But this body of men, which might have been such a powerful addition to General Jackson's force, was hardly of any use except as scouts, or for a raid. Their gallant commander had no talent for organization, and there was so little discipline among them that they could never be held well in hand and ready to strike a decisive blow. This state of affairs was rendered still worse by the Government making the cavalry in the Valley an independent command under Ashby, who was thus, with the exception of a major, the only field-officer of a regiment which contained eleven companies of cavalry. Ashby—a man of singular purity and amiability of character, brave and generous to a fault—had a greater reputation for military talent than he was able to support. His dash and coolness, and the enthusiasm with which he inspired his men, made him invaluable as the leader of a charge, or to make a bold front in covering the retreat of a column. But his discipline was too lax for him to have his command always well in hand; and hence the inefficiency of the cavalry attached to General Jackson's little army.

Jackson having received a small reinforcement, and his men and officers who were on furlough returning, he now had, including Ashby's force, eleven thousand men.

After the battle of Kernstown, he wrote to Mrs. Jackson, March 24,—

"Our God was my shield. His protecting care is an additional cause for gratitude. . . . My little army is in excellent spirits; it feels that it inflicted a severe blow on the enemy."

And again, on April 7,—

"Our gallant little army is increasing in numbers, and my prayer is that it may be an army of the living God as well as of its country. Yesterday was a lovely Sabbath-day. Though I had not the privilege of hearing the word of life, yet it felt like a holy Sabbath-day, beautiful, serene, holy, and lovely. All it wanted was the church-bell and God's services in the sanctuary to make it complete. . . . After God, our God, again blesses us with peace, I hope to visit this country with you and enjoy its beauty and loveliness."

CHAPTER IX.

WINCHESTER.

By the middle of April a general change was made in the disposition of troops on both sides. General McClellan, with a single eye to the good of his country, and with consummate ability, had perfected early in the spring the organization of the magnificent army with which he was so soon to take the field. His plan was to move on Richmond up the peninsula between the York and James Rivers; and for this purpose he left eighteen thousand men at Manassas, and embarked with the rest of his army for Fortress Monroe. So perfect was the organization of this immense force that he handled over a hundred thousand men with the same ease that he would have moved a regiment. The embarkation of his troops began on the 17th of March, at Alexandria, where he had assembled four hundred vessels of all kinds to take them down to Fortress Monroe. By the 6th of April he had landed on the Peninsula one hundred and nine thousand four hundred and nineteen men, fourteen thousand five hundred and ninety-two animals, forty-four batteries, and all the material for such an army, having lost in the embarkation only eight mules drowned, and nine caissons that had been crushed. But, magnificent as this army was, it fell far short in numbers of what he had intended it to be. Yielding to Mr. Lincoln's timidity, which was kept alive by the constant

132

representations of the exposed condition in which Washington would be left, made to him by McClellan's rivals and enemies, the young commander-in-chief reduced his force to its minimum to leave a strong guard of eighteen thousand men at Manassas, where they were to face the deserted camps of a departed foe. In the works around Washington he had left a strong garrison, and other divisions, as we shall see, were strung out in a line reaching to the Alleghanies. Patiently submitting to the useless withdrawal of so much material from his army, McClellan left for Fortress Monroe on the 1st of April, with the promise from Mr. Lincoln that all the remaining forces waiting for transportation at Alexandria should be sent after. His disappointment, then, was great and bitter when it was announced to him that McDowell's corps, the finest of his army, being thirty-eight thousand strong and splendidly equipped, would not be allowed to embark; and this announcement was followed by a short note from Mr. Lincoln simply stating that this corps had been withdrawn from his command. Later McDowell was sent to Fredericksburg, and there confronted the Confederate general Anderson.

Upon the Rappahannock was stationed a division of the Confederates under General Ewell, to check any advance of the Federals on the Orange and Alexandria Railroad.

West of the Blue Ridge was Jackson, with eleven thousand men, at Reede's Hill. Banks confronted him with twenty-five thousand men, and a reserve at Strasburg of eleven thousand. He had orders from McClellan to push on and capture Staunton as soon as he could make an advance. Twenty miles west of Staunton, General Edward Johnson was strongly posted at Shenandoah

Mountain with six regiments. In front of him stood the Federal general Milroy, who was backed by a force under General Schenck in the Valley of the South Branch of the Potomac. The two last-named generals were acting under General Fremont, who was organizing a large force in Northwestern Virginia at Wheeling. So stood the different commands of the two armies on both sides of the Blue Ridge.

Johnston having left Manassas, there was now no need for Jackson to watch the mountain-gaps through which the Federals might slip; and, not expecting any sudden call from Johnston to join him, he was enabled to be freer and more independent in his movements.

By the 17th of April the fords of the North Fork of the Shenandoah, which lay between Jackson and Banks, were so far passable as to make it unsafe for the former to remain with his small force so close to an enemy superior to him in everything but valor. He therefore gave orders for his little band to strike their tent-pins. Leaving Reede's Hill on the 17th, he reached Harrisonburg after a leisurely march of two days, General Banks in the mean while pursuing him so slowly as to prove that he dreaded nothing more than to overtake him. At Harrisonburg Jackson turned to the east, and, crossing the southern end of Massanutten Mountain, left the road open before his adversary, and no obstacle between him and Staunton. But he dared not continue his march to that place, for fear of Jackson falling in some unexpected way on his rear. Jackson continued his march, and, having crossed the South Fork of the Shenandoah, halted at last in Swift Run Gap.

In that gap he rested for a fortnight, and during that time corresponded with General Lee as to the plans for the movements in the Valley. General Lee leaving him to act as he thought best, he suggested and adopted the following plan. General Ewell should be called with his force to Swift Run Gap, and there remain, while Jackson going to Staunton should from there move on Shenandoah Mountain and join General Edward Johnson. They would then capture or put to flight Milroy, and with their united forces return to join Ewell. The three combined would then clear the Valley of Banks and his forces.

General Ewell was accordingly ordered to Swift Run Gap, which he entered on the afternoon of the 30th of April, just after Jackson had moved out. Ewell's force consisted of eight thousand picked men. They were filled with all the impatience for active service which is felt by troops in fine condition and good heart who have been long lying idle in camp; they were therefore eager for the fray.

Jackson, since his departure from Harrisonburg, had been lost to Banks, who on the 20th telegraphed to McClellan that Jackson's "flight from the Valley" had been confirmed by scouts, and it was believed he had gone by the mountain road to Gordonsville. Jackson, wishing to conceal his march to Staunton, and to mystify the Federal commander still more as to his movements, did not march directly across the South Fork of the Shenandoah to Staunton. He moved quietly up the eastern bank of that little stream until he reached the small village of Port Republic, when, facing to the east, he ascended the Blue Ridge, and, passing through Brown's Gap, dropped unexpectedly with his command down into Albemarle County. He then moved rapidly southward for a few miles along the eastern base of the

Blue Ridge until he reached the Central Railroad. Here his troops were placed on trains and taken to Staunton. In the march from the Valley into Albemarle, before reaching the western slope of the Blue Ridge, the little army had to cross a broad plain. The incessant rains had rendered the roads traversing these flats almost impassable, and so great was the difficulty of moving the wagons across these beds of mud—for they were nothing more—that to a less determined and energetic commander it would have been an insurmountable obstacle. For a day and a half the wagons were floundering along through the mud, and before they could be moved the roads had sometimes to be paved. In this laborious work no one took a more active part than Jackson himself. His uniform was bespattered with mud, as in his eagerness to push the work forward he carried timber and stones on his shoulders. After the last wagon had crossed the muddy level and struck the firm stony roads of the mountain-sides the troops had no further hinderance in their circuitous march to Staunton.

If an angel had dropped down in their midst, the good people of Staunton could not have been more astonished or delighted than they were by General Jackson's arrival. Like Banks, they thought he had withdrawn from the Valley and left them to fall into the hands of the enemy. The rumor of his evacuation of the Valley had even reached the Confederate commander at Shenandoah. The officer in command during a temporary absence of General Johnson thought it necessary to fall back before an enemy who was already sorely pressing him. He accordingly retreated to West View, a point within six miles of Staunton. Jackson, hearing of this move on his arrival at Staunton, was impatient to join Johnson's command, which he successfully accomplished.

He allowed his troops one day's rest, and on Wednesday, the 7th of May, the army marched forward to attack the Federal forces under Milroy. A march of a few miles brought the hostile armies face to face. A slight collision occurred, and the enemy fell back before the Confederate advance. He abandoned the position on Shenandoah Mountain, and continued to retreat to the village of McDowell. The Confederates slept that night upon the sides of Shenandoah Mountain, and early the next morning resumed their march and began to ascend Bull Pasture Mountain, beyond which the enemy lay. This mountain spreads out on its summit into a breadth of two miles, which is studded by steep, precipitous hills. The two Confederate generals rode ahead of the troops, and, ascending this mountain, viewed the enemy's position from its summit. Jackson's eye discovered a point in the enemy's rear by gaining possession of which he could cut off his retreat and make good his capture. He accordingly gave orders for the artillery to be moved forward to that point, and declined to have any of it brought up on the summit of the mountain, from whence he was making his observations. Not expecting any engagement that day, he dismissed most of his staff.

Milroy, however, having been reinforced by the arrival of General Schenck with three thousand men, determined to attack the Confederates and drive them from their strong position. The engagement began at four o'clock in the afternoon, and raged furiously until eight, when the enemy, having been unable to make any impression on the Confederates, ceased firing. In this fight the Confederates used no artillery. They lost in killed and wounded four hundred and sixty men.

The troops behaved with great gallantry, the 12th Georgia being conspicuous for the daring bravery of its men and officers. At one time during the fight they stood on the crest of a hill, and their figures, being thrown out in bold relief against the sky, offered good marks to the enemy, who poured their fire mercilessly into their ranks. Order after order was given by their officers for them to retire below the crest of the hill, but they obstinately refused to yield an inch. At length one of the officers succeeded in forcing back one wing of the regiment; but as he moved along the line to force the whole of it back, this wing swung back into its former position, and was as much exposed as ever. The losses in this regiment were more than one-third of the whole loss sustained in the fight.

By nine o'clock that night the men, wearied by their march and fight, began to bivouack and to seek that repose so sweet to the wearied soldier. Jackson did not leave the field until the last wounded man had been removed. Having gazed long down the valley leading to McDowell, and watched the enemy's camp-fires in a full blaze of light, he at last retired to his headquarters an hour after midnight, and threw himself on a bed. He was so overcome by fatigue that, though he had eaten nothing since morning, he exclaimed, "I want nothing, —nothing but sleep," when his servant offered him food.

By early dawn he was again in the saddle, and the first thing which greeted his sight was the smoking ruins of Milroy's stores and provisions. That general, becoming alarmed at the repulse he had met, had quietly withdrawn his forces in the night, and was in full retreat.

His plan was to move west for a few miles, and then turn north and march down the valley of the South Branch of the Potomac towards Franklin and Romney, in the hope of meeting Fremont with his forces.

As soon as he found that the bird was flown, Jackson determined to give him chase; but before he left he sent to Richmond the following simple announcement of his victory:

"God blessed our arms with victory at McDowell yesterday."

The army was collected in the valley leading west from McDowell, and the pursuit began. All the mountain-passes on the east through which Banks might send aid to the flying foe were obstructed, and the people of the country were exhorted to cut the bridges in front of him, and to do everything to obstruct his path. Milroy was soon so hard pressed by the Confederates that his rear-guard had to turn and make a stand. General Jackson saw this with delight, and immediately gave orders for a battle; but before they could be executed the enemy was again on the wing. He was now pressed so hard by his eager pursuers that to impede their march and conceal his own movement he fell upon the expedient of setting fire to the woods. It proved a most fortunate thing for him, for the country was soon so overclouded with smoke that the pursuing army could not see whither they were going nor what forces might be hanging unseen on their flanks. But still the cry was "Forward!" and the line of skirmishers on each side of the road pushed their way through the smoking forests, closely followed by the army. Jackson himself, in his eagerness to catch the enemy, was at times far ahead of his command. Finally, seeing that he could not gain upon him at all, and having driven him into the village of Franklin, by Sunday night he determined to abandon the pursuit and return to the Valley, whence he hoped to drive Banks. He had, moreover, received a message from General Lee calling him to him.

Before beginning his march on his return, he allowed his soldiers to rest for half a day on Monday, and issued the following order:

"Soldiers of the Army of the Valley and Northwest, —I congratulate you on your recent victory at McDowell. I request you to unite with me this morning in thanksgiving to Almighty God for thus having crowned your arms with success, and in praying that He will continue to lead you on from victory to victory, until our independence shall be established, and make us that people whose God is the Lord.

"The chaplains will hold divine service at ten o'clock A.M. this day, in their respective regiments."

The early rays of the morning sun found the men reposing in cool pastures covered with the richest verdure of spring, and the heavy dews of morning had scarcely disappeared before their voices were heard singing hymns of praise and thanksgiving to the Lord of Hosts and God of Battles. The last sounds of these had scarcely died away when the order was given to march, and, the little army getting into motion, the picturesque scenes of these mountains were once more left to silence and solitude. The command reached McDowell on Wednesday. As soon as Jackson abandoned the pursuit of Milroy he had sent a courier to General Ewell to inform him that he was on his way back.

While Milroy and his army were thus being chased like a flock of frightened sheep through the mountains of Virginia, where was Banks? When he discovered that Ewell was occupying Swift Run Gap, and that Jackson was gone, no one knew whither, filled with alarm lest some mysterious move was designed on him, he determined to save himself by flight. With his twenty thousand men—more than Jackson and Ewell had together—he beat a retreat, and fell back from Harrisonburg to Strasburg, closely pursued by Ashby and his dashing troopers, leaving, however, in the neighborhood of New Market a heavy rear-guard.

When this unlucky general heard of Milroy's retreat, he hurried off to his assistance with Blenker's division, which reached him just too late to be of any use. By another fatal mistake, he sent his two best brigades—Shields's and Kimball's, which together contained seven thousand men—across the Blue Ridge to join the Federal forces on the Rappahannock. This was particularly unfortunate for him, as Shields held the New Market Gap in Massanutten Mountain, the only pass from the Great Valley into the Luray Valley, which lies between Massanutten Mountain and the Blue Ridge. At the moment, then, when Jackson was about to pounce upon him like an eagle on his prey, his forces were scattered, and by the evacuation of New Market Gap he left the Confederate chief free to attack him in front and on his flank.

Ewell had just received the message from Jackson telling him to hold himself in readiness to join him at Harrisonburg and with their united forces move upon the enemy, when an order came from the commander-in-chief calling him with his force back to Gordonsville. Knowing what a blow this would be to Jackson, destroying, as it would do, his plans, he determined to have an interview with him before obeying the order.

He therefore mounted his horse, and, setting out without an escort, rode night and day until he reached Mossy Creek, where he found Jackson on Sunday, the 18th of May. He told him of the order he had received, and the grief it gave him to be compelled to withdraw his force at a time when, of all others, it would be most useful and necessary to him. As Jackson listened, the vision of the brilliant moves and splendid successes which he had planned vanished, but, with characteristic resignation, and casting no blame upon any one, he said, sadly, "Then Providence denies me the privilege of striking a decisive blow for my country, and I must be satisfied with the humble task of hiding my little army among these mountains to watch a superior force." Ewell, seeing how keenly he felt the disappointment, said that if Jackson, as his ranking officer, would take the responsibility, he would remain until the commander-in-chief could at least hear the reasons for his detention. This Jackson promptly consented to do, and it was then hurriedly arranged between them that they should join their forces at New Market, a day's march below Harrisonburg. In a short time Ewell was again in the saddle and riding post-haste back to his division.

Ashby, in the mean time, was hovering on the enemy's front, and his troopers scoured the country, and thus cut him off from all news of Jackson's movements, so that he was ignorant of the toils prepared to entrap him. All was now ready for the advance; and never was an army in better heart for a fight. The forces under Jackson had returned from their pursuit of Milroy, flushed with victory and well trained for swift marches and sharp fighting. In Ewell's command they found men chafing with impatience at their prolonged inactivity, and eager to cross swords with the foe. The two commands rushed forward with delight to meet each other, and, having joined forces, were ready to sweep down the Valley with all the impetuosity of men confident of success. This was particularly the case with the Louisianians of this command in Taylor's brigade. The fall of New Orleans, Butler's outrages, and the published appeal from the defenseless women against whom he was warring, all conspired to fire their hearts and give them such incentives to march upon the foe as happily for mankind, rarely occur in civilized warfare.

Banks was lying in fancied security in his intrenchments at Strasburg in the main valley, while silently and swiftly Jackson and Ewell were moving upon him down the Luray Valley.

The little village of Front Royal lies, as we have seen, at the mouth of the Luray Valley. On a line with this place, and west of the northern termination of Massanutten Mountain, lies Strasburg. Jackson's object was to capture the Federal force at Front Royal, and throw a part of his force forward on the road to Winchester, while with the rest he would march westward, and, striking the large Valley turnpike at some point between Strasburg and Winchester, cut off Banks's retreat to this last place, or fall upon his flank should he already have begun his march.

The advance-guard of the Confederate army, consisting of the 1st Maryland Regiment and Wheat's battalion, under command of General Stewart, pushed rapidly forward for Front Royal. In order to make the surprise of that place more complete, they turned off from the turnpike, moving from the south, and, marching to the right, approached the town from the east along a rugged path leading over the hills. They arrived about two o'clock in the afternoon of May 23; and so unexpected was their arrival that the Confederate volley fired into the town was the first information the enemy had of their approach. Strangely enough, it happened that the 1st Maryland Regiment of the United States army was one of those which occupied the town, and when the 1st Maryland of the Confederate army rushed in they found themselves encountering in combat their acquaintances and, in many instances, relatives. Two brothers being on opposite sides, one was captured by the other, each thinking himself the patriot and his brother the traitor. So great are the horrors of civil war! The Federal forces were driven quickly through the town, but on reaching a hill overlooking it on the side next to Winchester they halted and made a stand. They began at once to cannonade the Confederates, who, disregarding their fire, ran across the fields to attack them. The main body of the army having now come up, the advance-guard were well supported; but the enemy were driven from the hill by the skirmishers before the support could get into action. General Jackson dashed forward to the summit of the hill, from whence he got a full view of the enemy. Beyond the hill flowed the South Branch of the Shenandoah, and along its nearer bank were the tents of the enemy's camp, which, having been fired by them, were now in full blaze. Stretching along the road leading up from the opposite bank was the column of the enemy's infantry in full retreat. As Jackson beheld their closely-serried ranks, he exclaimed, in a tone of impatient regret, "Oh, what an opportunity for artillery! Oh that my guns were but here!" He knew that they were almost too far behind for it to be possible to get them up in time, but, hoping against hope, he turned quickly to one of his aides and ordered him to dash to the rear and " order up every rifled gun and every brigade in the army." The guns were hurried forward, but before they could be placed in position the enemy were out of range and the Confederates were in hot pursuit.

General Jackson had sent a courier back from Front Royal to order the rest of the army to come up by the turnpike leading directly to the town, and not to follow the rough, circuitous route which the advance-guard had taken. But the courier, being a timid boy unused to war's alarms, became frightened at the roar of the cannon, and slunk off into the mountains out of hearing, and the rear brigades of the army toiled along without guides over the track which had been followed by the advance-guard, so that they did not reach the town until nightfall, and were then too weary and foot-sore to join in the pursuit.

After crossing the South Branch of the Shenandoah, the enemy had to pass the North Branch. The Confederate cavalry crossed the South Branch above the point where they had crossed in order to cut off their communications with Strasburg, and now pressed down upon the enemy retreating on the Winchester road. The latter crossed the North Branch safely, and tried to burn the bridge after them. The Confederates, however, extinguished the flames, though not before they had burnt a span of the bridge. Colonel Flournoy, of the Confederate cavalry, succeeded with great difficulty in getting four companies of his regiment across the stream. With them General Jackson crossed, and, leaving orders for the rest of the cavalry to hurry on, with this small force he thundered along in pursuit of the flying foe. They overtook them at Cedarville, five miles from Front Royal. The enemy, numbering about a thousand, fell into line and formed in order of battle. "Charge!" shouted Jackson as he saw this. The word thrilled through the little Confederate band of two hundred and fifty men like an electric shock. Their commander, Colonel Flournoy, instantly dashed his force in a column against the serried ranks of the enemy and broke their centre. They soon re-formed, however, but were again charged by the Confederate troopers, and again broken. Now, panic-stricken, their cavalry fled, the gunners abandoned their guns, and the infantry threw down their arms and were scattered. By this time the rest of the Confederate force was arriving, and the enemy were captured, giving the Confederates seven hundred prisoners and two guns. General Jackson was enthusiastic in his expression of admiration of the gallant conduct of the Confederate cavalry in this engagement.

In the mean while, General Ewell, who had been advancing on the road to Winchester, arrived within four miles of that town. General Jackson determined to move from Cedarville with the rest of his force still farther across the Valley, to Middletown, a village between Strasburg and Winchester, six miles from the former place and thirteen from the latter.

The force moved forward for Middletown early on Saturday morning, May 24. Ashby, with his cavalry, and Chew's battery, led the van. About midway between Cedarville and Middletown they were confronted by a force of Federal cavalry, which a few shots from a section of artillery scattered and caused to disappear. The army now advanced rapidly to Middletown, General

Jackson hurrying everything forward. At length, when he came in sight of the town, he saw the long line of Banks's army filling the streets and the road beyond, in full retreat. Away dashed Ashby and his men, with loud shouts, right down upon their flank, breaking through their line, while the artillery poured shot and shell into their ranks. Then came the infantry at a double-quick, cheering as they ran, and firing deadly volleys into the mass of terrified men and horses that thronged the main street of the village. It is impossible to describe the scene of confusion and carnage that followed. Numbers of the enemy's cavalrymen threw themselves from their horses and sought protection behind the stone fences, where they promptly surrendered when summoned to do so.

In this encounter the Confederates captured two hundred prisoners and horses, with their arms and equipments. Upon inquiry, Jackson learned from the inhabitants of the village, that the enemy had been passing through it since early in the morning. He could not discover, however, what force was still left at Strasburg. That the enemy still had some troops there soon became apparent, for they began to shell Middletown from that direction. General Jackson ordered a force to advance and meet their attack; but the enemy made no stand, and, retreating hastily, burned the bridge over Cedar Creek, which flowed between them and the Confederates; and so ended all further pursuit towards Strasburg. This force left at Strasburg, which was probably small, afterwards made good its escape towards the North.

All the Confederate forces were now pushing forward and centring on Winchester. The enemy's wagon-trains were here and there found deserted, and standing with the horses attached to them. Everything betokened a disgraceful flight on their part. Jackson began now to feel cruelly the inefficiency of the cavalry, and to see the success of his movements marred by the want of horsemen to press the retreating foe. After the first engagement, the fine body of horse which Ashby had around him melted away like mist before the sun. Every man had turned aside from the pursuit to plunder and secure booty for himself out of the abundant stores left by the enemy. So little was the enemy harassed by them that, on reaching Newtown, a few miles from Winchester, they were encouraged to make a stand, and, planting a battery on each side of the village, once more presented a show of resistance. Nor could they again be put to flight until sunset, by which time they had burned many of their wagons and valuable stores.

Saturday night came, and found the enemy again on the wing, and Jackson in pursuit. The stone fences along each side of the road formed a good protection, behind which their sharp-shooters fired on the Confederate advance and retarded their pursuit. General Jackson, being always in advance, was in great danger, but in his eagerness rode ahead all night, surrounded by a small cavalry escort. Once or twice they were surprised by a fire from a concealed party of the enemy. The first time this occurred, General Jackson called out to the cavalrymen, "Charge them! charge them!" and his indignation knew no bounds when, after a timid advance, they turned and fled at the second volley from the Federals. Skirmishers were now ordered to be thrown out on each side of the road and sweep away the enemy's riflemen, who lined the fences. Thus the advance continued all night, the skirmishers untiringly pushing their way through the rank grass-fields, reeking with dew, which stretched out on either side of the road. At Barton's Mill the Federals made another stand, and a sharp fight ensued before they could be dislodged. At length, when they were within a mile or two of Winchester, Jackson ordered a halt for a short rest, and the wearied men threw themselves on the ground where they stood, and slept on their arms, while their untiring and vigilant commander stood as a sentinel at the head of the column, in the chill night air, straining his ear to catch every sound which might betoken an unusual move on the front.

At dawn, Jackson gave in an undertone the command, "Forward, march," which roused the men from their deep slumbers, as one sentinel after another took it up and passed it down the line. Dripping with the dews of the night, they arose, and as every man took his place in the ranks the first dim light of early dawn disclosed the heights of Winchester, and on them the indistinct forms of the enemy's skirmishers. A salvo of artillery and the rattle of musketry resounded through the hills and vales of this lovely region as the sun rose and ushered in a Sabbath May morn. The enemy made a fierce attack with their artillery, and Jackson, as he rode forward to reconnoitre their position, had an officer shot down on each side of him.

General Ewell's command, on the right, had slept that night within two miles of Winchester, and they, too, began with the dawn to move forward, and their guns were soon re-echoing the sound of those of their comrades in arms on the left. All was now ready to give the enemy a finishing blow. General Jackson, fearing that they might seize a wooded height on the left, which commanded his position, sent a messenger to order the Louisiana Brigade, held in reserve, under General Taylor, to move forward in that direction. Since the sound of the first gun, that officer and his command had waited impatiently for the order to advance, and as he saw the messenger approaching he spurred his horse forward to meet him. His fine brigade rushed forward as soon as the command to advance was given, and under the hottest fire of shot and shell wheeled into line. Seeing them fairly under way, Jackson rode again to the brow of the hill to reconnoitre the enemy's position, and as he reached its crest beheld Ewell's forces sweeping around on the right, and the enemy, beaten out of their lurking-places, flying frantically towards the town. "Forward after the enemy!" shouted Jackson; and the whole line dashed ahead in the wildest enthusiasm. Into the streets of the town rushed friend and foe. The surging mass rolled on; but as the inhabitants of the town caught the first glimpse of the Confederate uniform and saw the Confederate banners borne so proudly aloft, they rushed into the streets in the wildest joy and enthusiasm to welcome their countrymen and deliverers. All ages and all sexes mingled together, and for a time the chase after the enemy was impeded by the overjoyed inhabitants, who rushed from their houses utterly regardless of the shots that now and then rattled along the streets. Indeed, the women of the town, running out, pushed aside the bayonets of the gallant pursuers and pressed into the ranks to welcome their friends. Thus the whole mass, friend and foe, footmen and horsemen, surged along, until, reaching at last the open fields north of the town, the column spread out over the country. Heading the pursuit and cheering on his men towered the tall form of Jackson, who, carried away by the enthusiasm of success and the wild joy of their reception in Winchester, his face flushed by the excitement of the scene, dashed wildly forward, the impersonation of valor and patriotic devotion. "What shall we do now, general?" said one of his staff, as they reached the summit of a hill, whence they saw the dense masses of the enemy flying across the fields in front of them. "Let us hurrah!" said the general, with the enthusiasm of a boy, as, reining up his horse, he waved his hat over his head. The shout which followed rent the air. But the next moment Jackson was the soldier again, and, as he watched the black masses of the enemy rolling over the fields out of the reach of his faint yet pursuing infantry, he exclaimed, in a tone of bitter regret, "Oh that my cavalry were in place! Never was there such a chance for cavalry!" Alas! where was that recreant cavalry? In the rear, plundering the enemy's deserted train, or, loaded with booty, on their way to their mountain homes. So inefficient is undisciplined valor! An officer, standing by, suggested that the light field-batteries should be brought up to bear upon the flying foe. "Yes," he replied, eagerly; "go back and order up the nearest batteries you find." And again, in a few minutes, turning quickly to a member of his staff, he ordered him, in a tone whose sternness amounted almost to fierceness, to "go to the rear and order every battery and brigade forward to the Potomac." Then, as his longing eyes were turned back towards the fast-retreating ranks of the Federals, again the sight wrung from him the exclamation, "Oh, for the cavalry! Never was it in the power of cavalry to reap a richer harvest of the fruits of victory!"

The 2d and 6th Regiments of cavalry, which were intact, and might have been hurled upon the enemy, did not receive orders to join in the pursuit until the enemy were far advanced in their rush for the Potomac. After pursuing them with infantry and artillery until near noon, and seeing his wearied soldiers sinking exhausted beneath the warm rays of the noonday sun, General Jackson was obliged to abandon the pursuit. The cavalry, as they came up, continued it until they drove the enemy into Martinsburg or across the Potomac. Among the first fugitives who entered Martinsburg was the Federal general Banks.

General Jackson, as soon as he saw that his presence was no longer needed on the field, turned his horse's head towards Winchester. On reaching the town, he went directly to a hotel, and, refusing to stop to partake of a repast, asked only for a room, into which he was no sooner ushered than, throwing himself on his face on a bed, all booted and spurred as he was, he had in a moment sunk into profound slumber.

On the next day, May 26, he wrote to Mrs. Jackson from Winchester,—

"An ever-kind Providence blessed us with success at Front Royal on Friday, between Strasburg and Winchester on Saturday, and here with a successful engagement yesterday. . . . I do not remember having ever seen such rejoicing as was manifested by the people of Winchester as our army yesterday passed through the town in pursuit of the enemy. The town was nearly frantic with joy. Our entrance into Winchester was one of the most stirring scenes of my life. Such joy as the inhabitants manifested cannot easily be described."

The confusion caused by the rush of the pursued and

pursuers through the town was increased by the burning of some buildings which the enemy fired as they left. The whole town might have been soon wrapped in flames, but for the energy of some of the older inhabitants, who, recovering from the excitement of the scene, began to take steps to subdue the flames. The women joined in the efforts, and, it is pleasing to record, were among the foremost of those who, at the risk of their lives, rushed into the burning buildings and dragged out some sick and wounded Federal soldiers, who had been left by their comrades to perish in the flames or save themselves as best they might.

The following is a description of the flight of the Federal troops through Winchester, by one who witnessed the scene and favored the success of the Federal army:

"During breakfast I heard the tramping of horses upon the road and the heavy rolling of artillery over the pavements. Certainly, I thought, there can be no haste; we shall not be compelled to leave Winchester.

"Presently there was a commotion, a sobbing among the women, and a running to and fro, which brought me to my feet in time to find our forces were started on a hasty retreat; and, as I saw flames rising from the burning buildings not far off, and heavy volumes of smoke roll upward from them, I began to realize that we were to abandon Winchester. The enemy were in the other end of the town, as the rattle and echo of the musketry up the streets and between the houses most plainly indicated. All the streets were in commotion. Cavalry were rushing disorderly away, and infantry, frightened by the rapidity of their mounted companions, were in consternation. All were trying to escape faster than their neighbors, dreading most of all to be the last.

G*

" Presently the enemy's cannon boomed in the rear, and a small cloud of smoke in the sky, suddenly appearing and then dissolving, showed where the ball had exploded. Some shell fell among our men, and the panic was quite general for a short time. Guns, knapsacks, cartridge-boxes, bayonets, and bayonet-cases lay scattered upon the ground in great confusion, thrown away by the panic-stricken soldiers."

CHAPTER X.

THE RETREAT DOWN THE VALLEY.

On abandoning the retreat of Banks, General Jackson ordered his army to go into camp at a point three miles north of Winchester. Monday, the day after the engagements around Winchester, was spent in repose and religious services, the following general order being issued by the commanding general on the morning of that day:

"Within four weeks this army has made long and rapid marches, fought six combats and two battles, signally defeating the enemy in each one, captured several stands of colors and pieces of artillery, with numerous prisoners, and vast medical, ordnance, and army stores; and, finally, driven the boastful host which was ravaging our beautiful country into utter rout. The general commanding would warmly express to the officers and men under his command his joy in their achievements, and his thanks for their brilliant gallantry in action and their patient obedience under the hardships of forced marches; often more painful to the brave soldier than the dangers of battle. The explanation of the severe exertions to which the commanding general called the army, which were endured by them with such cheerful confidence in him, is now given in the victory of yesterday. He receives this proof of their confidence in the past with pride and gratitude, and asks only a similar confidence in the future.

"But his chief duty to-day, and that of the army, is to recognize devoutly the hand of a protecting Providence in the brilliant successes of the last three days (which have given us the results of a great victory without great losses), and to make the oblation of our thanks to God for his mercies to us and our country in heartfelt acts of religious worship. For this purpose the troops will remain in camp to-day, suspending as far as practicable all military exercises, and the chaplains of regiments will hold divine service in their several charges at four o'clock P.M."

After allowing his army a rest of two days, Jackson, eager to reap the fruits of his victories, ordered the advance to be continued, and on the 28th of May the army started for Charlestown, eight miles from Harper's Ferry. When within a mile of the town, the Confederate advance on emerging from a wood found the force of the enemy, about fifteen hundred strong, drawn up in line of battle. The gallant Winder, in command of the advance, without waiting for the rest of the army to come up, made an immediate attack. A few well-directed shots fired at the Federals from a field-battery broke their lines, and, abandoning their arms and baggage, they fled from the field in disorder. The Confederates pursued them closely to within two miles of the Potomac, when, giving up the chase, they returned to the neighborhood of Charlestown. The next day the whole army advanced to Halltown, a mile or two from the Potomac.

Thus Jackson in one week swept the Valley clear of the enemy who had so plundered and outraged its peaceful inhabitants, and now stood, as it were, with his little thundering at the gateway of the avenue leading to the Federal capital. For his plan was to threaten an invasion of Maryland, and, by making the feint of a move on Washington, to force the enemy to recall some of his forces which were now assembled in such formidable numbers around Richmond. He hurried a trusty messenger off to Richmond to ask the authorities for reinforcements, and to point out to them that the best and surest way of breaking up the formidable lines with which the enemy was now enveloping Richmond was to give him a force with which he could attack the Federal capital. "Tell them," he said, "that I have now but fifteen thousand effective men. If the present opening is improved as it should be, I must have forty thousand." But, as in the case of so many other Confederate victories, the fruits of his brilliant successes were to be partially lost from want of force with which to reap them, for the reinforcements so much needed by him could not be withdrawn from the defense of Richmond.

On the 29th of May, just after General Jackson had begun to make the movements necessary for an attack on Harper's Ferry, he received the startling intelligence that Fremont was moving with a heavy force from the northwest down to Strasburg, while Shields, having been ordered to retrace his steps, was moving back from the east for the Valley, and the two, forming a union at Strasburg, were to fall upon his rear and cut off his retreat. Already the advance-guard of Shields's force had entered Front Royal, and, driving out the 12th Georgia, which had been left as a guard, had recaptured the prisoners left there, and forced the Confederates to fire the captured stores to prevent their being also retaken.

With a full appreciation of the perils of his situation, General Jackson confronted them with an undaunted spirit, and with his characteristic energy and skill at once took steps to insure his escape from the trap which had been laid for him. Orders were immediately given for a speedy but orderly retreat, and by the afternoon of the 30th the whole army was on the march. General Jackson, going in advance, found on reaching Winchester that the enemy were so close upon Strasburg, and bearing down upon it so rapidly, that in order to save himself from being cut off he must get his army safely through that place by noon of the next day,—May 31. Orders for moving rapidly forward were again given, and the little band moved swiftly but steadily ahead. The energy and enthusiasm inspired by their confidence in their leader enabled the men to make marches scarcely surpassed in the annals of war for their celerity. The faithful Stonewall Brigade marched thirty-five miles over muddy roads and under spring showers without pausing, while the 2d Virginia Regiment, which was farther in the rear, marched forty miles without rations. In so orderly a manner was this skillful retreat begun that not a man nor a gun was left behind. The 21st Virginia started from Winchester on the 31st, in charge of twenty-three hundred prisoners. The seven hundred of the enemy's sick and wounded who were left in the town were paroled not to fight until exchanged.

On reaching Strasburg, Jackson found that Fremont had already arrived on his right flank, for his troops had poured through the gap leading across North Mountain and were ready to fall upon him. Ewell was at once ordered to face about to the west and offer him battle, which he did; but, after a skirmish in the mountain-gorge, it was declined, and the Confederate retreat was continued steadily but leisurely up the Valley. Jackson knew that Shields had been for two days at Front Royal, where he was east of the South Fork of the Shenandoah, and, to prevent his crossing the Massanutten Mountain by New Market Gap and falling upon his left flank while Fremont threatened his rear, he sent a detachment of cavalry to burn the bridges across the South Fork of the Shenandoah. This having been accomplished, he continued his retreat with less anxiety, and its steady, orderly pace was a perpetual challenge to the tardy Fremont on his rear, but one which he dared not accept. The rear of Jackson's army left Strasburg on June 1. It was covered by the cavalry and Chew's light battery, under the command of the untiring Ashby, who had just received his commission as brigadier-general. Fremont's cavalry followed the retreating army, and under cover of the darkness drew so near at night that the men in the Confederate rear, hailing them, asked who they were. They replied, "Ashby's cavalry," and were thus allowed to draw closer, when they charged a cavalry regiment and threw it into disorder. It was, however, re-formed, and, charging the enemy, repulsed them and took some prisoners. On the 2d of June the Confederate rear was again thrown into disorder by a cannonade from the enemy's guns, which were brought to bear upon them, followed by a charge of their cavalry. Ashby, seeing this, threw himself from his horse, and, collecting a few riflemen who were lagging behind, stationed them in a wood beside the road, and as the enemy in their charge drew near he ordered them to fire, which they did with such unerring aim that many riders fell from their saddles, and a part, turning their horses' heads, retreated in confusion, while those in advance, being carried forward into the Confederate rear, were all, with one exception, captured or killed. That night, when this adventure was related to the general, one of the officers who had witnessed it remarking that the men had charged so gallantly he hated to kill them, Jackson said, quietly, "No; shoot them all; *I* do not wish them to be brave." It was by such occasional remarks that he betrayed the intensity of his feeling towards those who fought against the cause so dear to him and his countrymen.

By the 3d of June the retreating army had safely crossed the North Fork of the Shenandoah. General Ashby was left to burn the bridge over which it had passed. ·This he successfully accomplished; but so close were the enemy upon him that they were on the opposite bank before he could get out of their reach. His horse was shot dead under him, while he himself barely escaped the same fate.

The rebuilding of this bridge by Fremont consumed a whole day, and thus the foot-sore Confederates could continue more leisurely their retreat, and without attack, to Harrisonburg.

All during the retreat, while Fremont was pressing down on his rear, Jackson knew that east of the Massanutten Mountain Shields was pushing up the Luray Valley. The race was hot and close between them which should get up the Valley and be able to turn the southern extremity of the Massanutten Mountain first. If Shields arrived first, he would be able to turn round the base of the mountain, and, meeting Jackson, attack him on the front while Fremont fell upon his rear. Jackson's soldiers knew of the trap that had been set for them, and as they moved up the Valley before crossing the road leading across from the Luray Valley through New Market Gap, they watched with intense anxiety the summit of the mountain at that point, expecting every moment to see the road leading down from the gap darkened with the blue coats of the enemy moving upon their flank. The prisoners with whom the Confederate army was encumbered were exultant at the prospect of a speedy release, and tauntingly told their captors that the tables would soon be turned, and that Shields would be down upon them and bag Jackson's army. But the Confederates, confident in their leader's ability to save them from the lines with which the enemy was endeavoring to envelop them, replied defiantly, and urged them forward as they attempted to retard the retreat by lagging sullenly behind.

A mile south of Harrisonburg, Jackson having reached the southern terminus of the Massanutten Mountain, and Shields not having yet appeared, he turned the head of his advancing column eastward on the road to Port Republic, a small village situated at the southern end of the Luray Valley, upon the South Fork of the Shenandoah, near the foot of the Blue Ridge. It was not until the 6th that Fremont's cavalry were again upon Jackson's rear. About two miles south of Harrisonburg it was overtaken by a regiment of their cavalry, led by Sir Percy Wyndham, an English adventurer, who, having joined the Federal army, had expressed a great desire to meet Ashby and overcome him in combat. In the sharp encounter which now took place between his regiment and Ashby's cavalry, the Federals were signally repulsed, and among the prisoners captured was Sir Percy Wyndham himself. The sound of the firing in this engagement made General Ewell turn back to aid with reinforcements if necessary. The gallant Ashby told him he was sure the enemy would return in a short time to the attack, and asked for a small infantry force to aid in repelling them. General Ewell accordingly sent him the 58th Virginia and the 1st Maryland Regiments. Ashby placed the Maryland regiment in a wood on the roadside, from which they were to fire upon the flank of the enemy as they approached, while at the head of the 58th Virginia he prepared to receive their attack in front. Elated by the chase after the enemy and by his late brilliant success, his countenance flushed with excitement, his eyes flashing fire, and the tones of his voice ringing out in unwonted clearness, Ashby had scarcely arranged his force to receive the Federals when they came in sight. They advanced across the open fields, and, sheltering themselves behind a fence, fired into the exposed ranks of the 58th Virginia. Ashby dashed to the front and ordered the regiment to advance and dislodge the enemy from their advantageous position. Scarcely had he given the order when his horse was shot and fell dead beneath him. Disentangling himself, he sprang to his feet, and, seeing the regiment falter, exclaimed, as he waved his sword over his head, "Charge, men! for God's sake, charge!" The words had scarcely died on his lips when he fell dead, struck by a bullet which pierced his breast. His men, seeing him fall, rushed frantically forward and poured a galling fire into the enemy's front, while the Marylanders rushed upon their flank. They broke and fled,—the Confederates firing upon them as long as they were within musket-range.

But Ashby was dead. His name alone was worth ten

thousand men to the Confederate cause in the Valley, so great was the dread with which he inspired his foes, and the confidence his presence kindled in the breasts of his friends. No braver or more chivalrous knight ever drew sword in defense of a noble cause. His comrades in arms carried his body from the battle-field, and, as it was borne through the country which he had so nobly defended, the people flocked to see the face— now still in death—of him they called the savior of the Valley. Gentle women came to kiss his dead hands, and young children were held up to gaze with love and awe upon the beautiful countenance of the hero whose simple Christian faith sheds such lustre on his heroic deeds.

The sad and sorrowing little group of horsemen who carried the body of their gallant leader swept swiftly past the retreating army, and "Ashby is dead!" were the sad words which ran along the lines in the subdued tones in which men are wont to speak when in the presence of the mighty dead. To Port Republic his body was taken, and there shrouded in his soldier's dress. To the heart of no one did the news of his fall carry a bitterer pang than to that of Jackson, for to no one were the virtues of the man and the untiring energy and skill of the soldier better known. On hearing of Ashby's death, and of his removal to Port Republic, he hastened to the house where the body lay, and, asking to see it, entered the room and shut himself up alone with it. There the young warrior lay, his slightly-built and graceful figure now stiff in the rigidity of death, his flashing gray eyes closed forever, and his thick black hair and heavy raven beard looking darker than ever in the contrast with the pallor of death which overspread his noble countenance. Over this still figure bent the war-god of the Valley. Who can tell what thoughts passed through his great soul, or what prayers ascended from his lips, as he paused thus on the eve of the brilliant close of the most daring and skillful manœuvring to devote a few precious moments to silent communion with the dead?

The news of the fall of her second son in defense of the cause so dear to every noble Southern heart quickly reached the home of Ashby's widowed mother. With a sickened heart and wearied longing she watched for the return home of his body; but, the enemy being in possession of her county, even that boon was denied her, and his comrades bore it across the Blue Ridge to Albemarle, where it found an appropriate resting-place in the grave-yard at the University of Virginia. From that spot it has since been removed to be placed beside that of the brave brother whose untimely death he avenged so well. The tomb of these two brothers—models, as they were, of all that is brave and knightly—is a monument to be pointed out by their mother-State with pride and gratitude through all succeeding generations.

After the skirmish in which Ashby was killed, the prisoners, and those of the wounded Confederates who could bear the march, were quickly carried forward, there being no time to lose, for the enemy were pressing steadily on. To those of the wounded who could not be moved, General Ewell was seen giving a few parting words of cheer, and supplying them from his own purse with money.

The repulse given the enemy in this last fatal attack was so severe as to make them more cautious as to how they pressed too closely upon the rear of a retreating Confederate army. When Ashby fell, the main body of the army had reached Port Republic. This village is situated at the western base of the Blue Ridge, and lies in a triangle formed by the junction of the North and South Rivers, whose union forms the South Fork of the Shenandoah. On the eastern side of this stream, it will be remembered, Shields was marching up the Valley, while Fremont was dogging the steps of the retreating army. In the triangle formed by the junction of the North and South Rivers, Jackson was safe from both his pursuers. The South River could be crossed by means of a passable ford, while a wooden bridge connected the village with the Harrisonburg road on the other side of the North River,—the deeper and larger of the two. At Conrad's Store, fifteen miles below Port Republic, there was a bridge over the Shenandoah by which Shields might have crossed the river and joined Fremont. Aware of its importance, Generals Shields and Jackson each sent a detachment of cavalry, the one to destroy and the other to hold it. The Federal cavalry reached the bridge first, but, instead of remaining to guard it, dashed off to capture some Confederate stores which they heard were near by and but poorly guarded. In the mean time, Jackson's cavalry came up and fired the bridge, so that when Shields arrived in sight of it at the head of his column it was a sheet of flame, and already too far gone to be saved. With this bridge vanished his last hope of joining Fremont. The game was now in Jackson's hands, and he made his arrangements to attack and defeat separately his two opponents.

Shields was at Conrad's Store, some fifteen miles from Port Republic, while Fremont, with his army in the neighborhood of Harrisonburg, was at about the same distance. Thus Jackson was equidistant between the two. His plan was to attack Shields—who was on the opposite bank of the South River—first, and then cross the North River and crush Fremont. On the north side of this river, and near the Harrisonburg road, he left General Ewell to guard against the advance of Fremont. Jackson had his headquarters at Port Republic, and connection between him and Ewell was kept up by means of the bridge across North River. On the night of the 7th, a company of cavalry was sent down the Shenandoah to reconnoitre the position of Shields, who was reported to be advancing. Early the next day the Sabbath stillness of a lovely morning was broken by the noise and clatter of this company of Confederate cavalry dashing pell-mell into the town with the Federal cavalry close upon their heels, accompanied by artillery. The Federals dashed across South River, and so unexpected was their arrival that General Jackson came near being captured, and just had time to gallop off towards the bridge and escape. Several Confederate officers were captured in this dash, and one who could not get over the bridge collected a handful of stragglers and poured a volley into the Federal cavalry as they were dashing out of the village to capture Jackson's ordnance-train. This check gave the Confederates time to open upon them with two guns and increase their discomfiture.

General Jackson, in the mean while, had dashed across the bridge and up the hill on which his troops were encamped. He ordered the long roll to be beaten and the men to be under arms, and the batteries to take position on the hills which commanded the town. Then, placing himself at the head of the 37th Virginia Regiment, he started back to the bridge, the possession of which was of such vital importance to him, but which had now fallen into the hands of the enemy. He saw with dismay that they had placed a gun at its farther end and were prepared to sweep it with their fire. Seeing that there was not a minute to be lost, he dashed down to the bridge at the head of the regiment, and there ordered them to fire upon the enemy at the other end of it, and then, rushing across, sweep them away with the bayonet. Their fire proved a murderous one, sweeping the threatening gun of its cannoneers. Then, with a yell, the gallant Virginians burst over the bridge, and it was theirs. Jackson had no sooner given the order to the regiment to fire than, throwing the reins upon his horse's neck, he raised his hands to heaven and prayed as he had never prayed before; and never was prayer more gloriously answered. Other troops dashed over after the 37th Virginia, and, rushing upon the enemy, captured their gun and drove their cavalry through the town and across the village, while the batteries played upon them from the hills north of the North River. The flying cavalry met a body of infantry coming up to their support, but the spirited fire from the batteries made them soon face about and follow in the tracks of their discomfited horse down the eastern bank of the Shenandoah. The light field-batteries of the Confederates dashed along the heights on the west rn side for about a mile, and poured shot and shell into their ranks until they disappeared in a wood round the bend of a road.

In the mean time, the sound of Shields's guns roused Fremont to activity, and the enemy had scarcely been driven out of Port Republic before he was advancing upon Ewell's front, down the Harrisonburg road. The Confederate picket on that road, the 15th Alabama, disputed their advance so stubbornly that General Ewell had leisure to select his own position. This was well chosen, being on a commanding ridge, a rivulet and large open field in front, a wood on each flank, and the road leading to Port Republic passing through the centre of his line. The batteries were placed in the centre, and Trimble's brigade, which was destined to take the most active part in the fight, was on the right, just under the crest of the hill. At ten o'clock the enemy threw out his skirmishers, and, placing his batteries in position, began an animated and spirited fire, which lasted for several hours on both sides. Under cover of this fire a Federal brigade advanced on the Confederate right, when General Trimble, holding his men well in hand and making them reserve their fire until the enemy, reaching the crest of the hill, were in full musket-range, gave the order to fire. The volley was a withering one. The enemy staggered, and fell back in confusion. The order to charge with the bayonet was immediately given to the Confederates, who, advancing with a shout and a bound, drove the yielding enemy down the hill and across the open meadow into the woods opposite. Then, per-ceiving a battery about to be placed in position on the enemy's left, General Trimble pushed forward to capture it; but it was withdrawn before he reached the spot. The enemy did not renew the attack, and later in the day Ewell advanced, driving in the Federal skirmishers, and that night his troops slept on their arms on ground which had been held by the enemy in the morning. So ended the battle of Cross Keys, a fight in which the enemy's movements were so timid that General Ewell remarked that he felt all day as if he were fighting the feeble, semi-civilized armies of Mexico.

The Confederates had only six thousand men on the field in this fight, and only thirty-five hundred actually engaged. Their losses were forty-two killed and two hundred and thirty-one wounded.

Having thus severely chastised Fremont, General Jackson turned quickly to Shields. The echoes of the guns of Cross Keys had scarcely died away on the mountain-sides when Jackson, under cover of the night, began to make a foot-bridge over the South River, by which he could pass his infantry across and go in search of Shields. The bridge was formed by driving wagons into the stream until a line across was completed, and on these planks were placed. Unfortunately, however, just in the middle of the stream there was some bad arrangement of the planks leading from one wagon to another, and only one plank was found firm enough to serve as a bridge, so that the whole army at that point had to go over in single file, instead of two or three abreast. This caused serious delay in the passage of the whole force.

It was no part of Jackson's plan to allow Fremont to escape with only the defeat at Cross Keys. He intended to attack and defeat Shields early enough in the day to enable him to turn back on Fremont and crush him. In giving his orders to Colonel Patton, commanding the Second Virginia Brigade, and who was to conceal Ewell's withdrawal from Fremont's front while he joined in attacking Shields, he told him to hold his position as long as possible, and concluded by saying, " I will be back to join you in the morning." This was spoken at two o'clock in the morning of the 9th, while he was busy making the necessary arrangements for the battle with Shields. When Colonel Patton asked how long he would be expected to hold Fremont at bay, he replied, " By the blessing of Providence, I hope to be back by ten o'clock."

General Ewell was ordered to move at an early hour on the morning of the 9th, and cross the bridge leading to Port Republic, while the troops left to confront Fremont were ordered, if hard pressed by him, to retire across the North River and burn the bridge in their rear. All things were now in readiness for the advance, and by five o'clock in the morning of the 9th the Stonewall Brigade had crossed the South River; but the unfortunate defect in the hastily-constructed foot-bridge so delayed the crossing of the other troops that the hour at which Jackson had hoped to whip Shields and be ready for a second brush with Fremont passed by before all the troops had crossed South River. By ten o'clock the last of the Confederate forces had crossed North River, and the bridge was burnt, thus leaving Fremont a helpless spectator of the coming fight.

In the mean time, the Stonewall Brigade, commanded by the knightly Winder, had advanced far on its way to attack the enemy. The latter was judiciously posted near Lewiston, a mile or two down the Shenandoah, his right resting upon the river, his left upon a thick wood, while the inclosures and buildings of Lewiston sheltered his centre. Near the edge of the wood, on his left, on a rising ground near the Lewis house, he had planted a battery of six guns, which commanded the level field extending in front and the road to Port Republic.

Against this formidable position General Jackson led the Stonewall Brigade and the gallant Louisiana Brigade, under General Taylor. The Confederate batteries directed their fire against those of the Federals, but with little effect. Winder, being reinforced by a Louisiana regiment, determined to charge the enemy and capture his battery, as the only means of silencing it ; but as his gallant brigade swept across the field fronting the batteries, they were met by such a furious fire from both artillery and small arms that they were thrown into confusion and fell back in disorder. The enemy, seeing this, dashed forward with their infantry, and pushed the Confederate infantry so far back that their artillery had to retire. At this critical juncture, General Taylor, who had moved to the right along the mountain acclivity, through a rough and tangled forest, emerged from the woods on the enemy's left. With loud cheers his brigade dashed forward to seize the battery, and, though the enemy in vastly superior numbers attacked them in front and flank, they captured it.

This diversion made by Taylor enabled Winder to reorganize his scattered force, while the Confederate batteries were again placed in position. The Confederate line being thus re-formed, they advanced and drove the Federals steadily back to their original position. But the struggle over the battery captured by Taylor was long and fierce. A fresh Federal brigade advanced under cover of a wood and fell upon his flank, while a galling fire of canister was poured into his ranks from a piece placed in position at a distance of three or four hundred yards. Under this fiery tempest the gallant Louisianians had to abandon the battery and fall back to the edge of the wood near which it was stationed. Two of General Ewell's regiments now coming up to their aid, the attack was again renewed. Never was there a severer contest than over this battery. Twice the enemy lost it, and twice re-took it ; but when it was captured for the third time by the undaunted Confederates, the enemy began to withdraw. Fresh troops coming up to the Confederates, they made a general advance and swept the Federals from the field. The cavalry now dashed forward and converted their retreat into a disorderly flight.

The Confederates continued the pursuit for eight miles, and returned with several hundred prisoners. The losses of the Confederates in this battle were ninety-one killed and six hundred and eighty-six wounded. As the gallant little army assembled its shattered ranks after the fight and marched off the field of battle towards the mouth of Brown's Gap, they beheld, on the heights on the opposite bank of the river, Fremont, who, in consequence of the burning of the bridge, could now only watch as an idle spectator the flight of the Federals and the triumphant march of the Confederates from the field which their courage had won.

Enraged at being outgeneraled and forced thus to witness the defeat of his friends, General Fremont was guilty of an act of barbarity as outrageous as any that ever disgraced the records of civil warfare. Many of the wounded had been borne from the battle-field and placed in a house, over which the yellow flag was floating, as a signal to friend and foe that for the time being the building was a hospital. There the surgeons were busily engaged binding up broken limbs and staunching the ghastly wounds of the gallant soldiers, while the chaplains were soothing the last moments of the dying. On this hospital General Fremont directed his guns to be turned, and poured upon it such a heavy fire that those of the wounded who could move fled in dismay from their cots, while others more disabled had to stay and undergo the terrible ordeal of lying helpless under fire.

To add to the suffering caused by this cruel act, those who were thus driven from shelter were exposed to a cold rain which was just beginning to fall. Not only the house, but the field in which many wounded were still lying, was cannonaded, and many a poor fellow who had escaped with his life from the storm and tempest of the morning's battle was thus murdered ere the close of the day.

The day after the battle of Port Republic, General Fremont withdrew his forces and retreated down the Valley. The Confederate cavalry, under Colonel Munford, entered Harrisonburg on the 12th, where they captured about two hundred of the enemy's sick and wounded, besides medical stores, wagons, camp-equipage, and two hundred small arms. The prisoners captured here and at Port Republic numbered nine hundred and seventy-five, the small arms about one thousand, and the artillery seven pieces.

From the hard-contested but gloriously-won field of Port Republic Jackson led his gallant troops into Brown's Gap, where they bivouacked for two days. Early in the morning of the 12th they were led down to the pleasant green meadows on the banks of the Shenandoah, where they rested for five days under bright skies and safe from the fear of any approaching foe. On Saturday, the 14th, divine service was held in the army, to render thanks to the God of battles for the brilliant success with which He had crowned their arms. The services were held in a wood, overarched by serene skies, and the sound of hymns of praise and thanksgiving rose from amidst mountains on whose sides the echoes of the clash of arms and the cries of battle had scarcely died away. The services were rendered more solemn by the administration of the holy communion. Among those who on this occasion received the sacrament with the lowly humility of a child was the chief of the little army assembled around him,—he who so lately had fallen like a thunderbolt upon one foe after another, crushing all who crossed his war-path.

The jaded troops were now encamped in grassy fields on the beautiful banks of the Shenandoah, near Weyer's Cave. During this short period of sweet repose from the din of arms, General Jackson wrote to Mrs. Jackson:

"Near Weyer's Cave, June 14.

"Our God has thrown his shield over me in the various apparent dangers to which I have been exposed. This evening we have religious services in the army, for the purpose of rendering thanks to the Most High for the victories with which He has crowned our arms; and my earnest prayer is that our ever-kind heavenly Father will continue to crown our arms with success until our independence shall, through his divine blessing, be established."

While Jackson's army was on one occasion resting after one of his forced marches, two sentinels who were on duty in a steady fall of rain were complaining of the hardships of a soldier's life, when one of them exclaimed, "I wish the Yankees were all in h—l!" "I do not," said the other, quietly. "Why not?" asked his companion, impatiently. "Because, if they were, 'old Jack' would have his pickets at the gates before breakfast to-morrow morning," was the reply.

CHAPTER XI.

BATTLES AROUND RICHMOND.

BEFORE we again take up the line of march with General Jackson's little army, which we left reposing amid the peaceful meadows and green pastures of the Shenandoah Valley, it will be necessary to glance at the operations of the two contending armies in the neighborhood of Richmond.

General Johnston had succeeded in transferring his army safely from Manassas to the peninsula between the York and James Rivers, and was early in April confronting McClellan. With his greatly inferior force he was compelled to fall back before the advances of the able Federal commander, but not without contesting his approach. On the 5th of May took place the battle of Williamsburg, in which the Confederates were believed to have inflicted heavy losses upon the Federals. This check was not sufficient, however, to delay their advance long, and the inhabitants of Richmond saw the theatre of war transferred to the very gates of their city.

On all the approaches to the city the Confederates fell back before the steady advance of the Federals, who, having now perfected their plans and arrangements, seemed to have everything in their own grasp; and indeed the Confederates appeared everywhere to be yielding to their onward move. On the 11th of May, the Virginia, which by her exploits in the mouth of the

James had been rendered so famous, was run ashore in the vicinity of Crancy Island and fired. After burning fiercely for upwards of an hour, she blew up before five o'clock in the morning. The destruction of this vessel left the river open to the Federal gunboats as far up as Drewry's Bluff, a few miles below Richmond, where the Confederates had powerful batteries commanding the river. The Federals were not long in feeling their way up the stream. Their gunboats appeared in sight on the 15th of May, but the batteries at Drewry's Bluff prevented their passage up the river, and so signally repulsed them that they had to drop down the stream.

But, in spite of this repulse, McClellan at once saw that the proper approach for attack on Richmond would be by the James, now that the destruction of the Virginia had opened that river to the ascent of Federal vessels and transports. To this idea he clung, and was only prevented from changing his base at an early day by the promise held out to him by Mr. Lincoln that McDowell would be sent from Fredericksburg to join him. This general and his fine corps were within sixty miles of McClellan's right when that was established on the north bank of the Chickahominy. Deluded by the hope of soon joining hands with this able lieutenant, the young commander-in-chief left this part of the army on this side of that stream, and delayed taking the initiatory steps for his change of base longer than he would have done but for the false promises held out to him.

Johnston, in the mean time, continuing to fall back before the Federal advances, finally settled down with his army between Richmond and the Chickahominy. As the Federals began to cross that stream, however, he watched his chances to give them battle, and was not long in finding one. Having learned that General Keyes of the Federal army was encamped with his corps on the Richmond side of the Chickahominy, he determined to attack him, and did so, on May 31, with the divisions of Major-Generals Longstreet, D. H. Hill, and G. W. Smith. Major-General Huger was to have assisted in this attack, but his division failed to get into position. The Confederate advance was begun at two o'clock in the afternoon, and by three the fighting was hot and fierce. "The principal attack was made by Major-General Longstreet, with his own and Major-General D. H. Hill's division,—the latter mostly in advance. Hill's brave troops, admirably commanded and most gallantly led, forced their way through the abatis which formed the enemy's external defenses and stormed their intrenchments by a determined and irresistible rush. Such was the manner in which the enemy's first line was carried. The operation was repeated with the same gallantry and success as our troops pursued their victorious career through the enemy's successive camps and intrenchments. At each new position they encountered fresh troops belonging to it and reinforcements brought on from the rear. Thus they had to repel repeated efforts to retake works which they had carried. But their advance was never successfully resisted.

"Their onward movement was only stayed by the coming of night. By nightfall they had forced their way to the 'Seven Pines,' having driven the enemy back more than two miles through their own camps, and from a series of intrenchments, and repelled every attempt to recapture them with great slaughter."*

---

* Johnston's Report.

11*

The next morning, June 1, the Federals were found too strongly intrenched for the attack to be renewed, and, after gathering up all the arms, the Confederates returned that evening to their camps.

In this battle the Confederates captured ten pieces of artillery, six thousand muskets, one garrison flag, and four regimental colors. Their own losses in killed and wounded were over four thousand, while the Federal losses were estimated by their own papers at more than ten thousand.

The great valor displayed by the Confederates in this battle called forth the applause of the whole South. General Johnston, having received a serious wound in the battle, was unable to resume command of the armies around Richmond, and his post was filled by General Lee.

General McClellan's forces were extended from the James River on the south to Mechanicsville and its neighborhood on the north. His lines were pierced by the Chickahominy, so that his army lay on both sides of that stream, and he drew his supplies from a point on the York River, with which he was connected by the Richmond and York River Railroad. In order to ascertain the exact positions of the enemy, General Lee ordered General J. E. B. Stuart—called from his initials "Jeb Stuart"—to make a raid in the rear of the enemy and find out how his troops were stationed. This dashing officer set out at the head of a fine cavalry force, numbering twelve hundred men, with a section of light field-artillery, to make the required reconnoissance. He started out from a point north of Richmond, and, riding round the rear of the whole Federal army, re-entered the city by the road running along the James, having made a complete circuit of the enemy's lines. His march extended as far to their rear as the White House, where his men fired three transports lying in the Pamunkey, and destroyed other Federal property and stores. When they reached the Chickahominy on their way back, they found the bridge by which it was to be crossed destroyed. This made their position most perilous, and it was a life-and-death matter to restore the bridge as speedily as possible, for its destruction told too surely that the enemy were on their track and laying toils with which to entrap them. With the enthusiastic energy of men who felt that but one more effort had to be made to secure success, they fell to work, and in a short time the bridge was up, and soon a cloud of dust marked the disappearance from sight of the troop as it clattered along. The success of this brilliant exploit was now secured, and General Stuart left his command and pushed forward to report in person to the commander-in-chief the brilliant result of his expedition. In a few days the whole country was resounding with the news of this daring feat, friend and foe alike awarding praise to the skillful leader and the brave men under his command. History, indeed, shows few exploits which can equal this, and Stuart and his troopers will live in its pages as bold and dashing soldiers.

Among the many interesting incidents occurring on this expedition was the death and burial of Captain Latané. A body of the enemy being encountered near Hanover Court-House, a squadron of the 9th Virginia cavalry, commanded by young Latané, was ordered to charge them, which they did in gallant style. Down the road they dashed, the brave Latané ten paces ahead. "Cut and thrust!" shouted the Federal commander, as he led his troops boldly up. "On to them, boys!" yelled Latané, and the meeting squadrons rushed together in full shock. The front men of each column were unhorsed, and the fight became instantly hot and bloody. Captain Latané singled out the Federal commander, aimed a blow at his head, and cut off his hat close to his head, but the Federal, dodging the cut, rode past, and as he did so discharged his revolver at Latané, who fell dead from his saddle. The enemy soon broke and scattered, when a private, dashing after the Federal commander, clove his skull in twain. This short but fierce and sanguinary fight being over, the victorious Confederates dashed on in their exciting ride through the enemy's lines. The body of their gallant comrade in arms was left behind. It was carried to the house of Mrs. Brockenbrough, where preparations were made for its burial, but a Federal officer coming up ordered the minister not to read the funeral service over the dead soldier. Feeling deeply the insult thus intended for her dead countryman, Mrs. Brockenbrough herself presided over the touching scene of his burial, and in clear, soft tones read the beautiful words of the Episcopal service for the burial of the dead. This scene— the dead soldier lying before the calm Virginia matron, the sorrowing group around, consisting of the old and young members of the family, from the little girl with flowers for the young officer's body to the faithful slave who had dug his grave, the whole illumined by the last rays of the setting sun—has been the subject of a picture to be found in many a Southern home and cottage, and which has made this touching incident one of the most familiar of the war.

It was General Lee's intention to make no move against

McClellan until reinforced by Jackson, yet he knew that if the Federal commander discovered that Jackson was marching to Richmond, the authorities in Washington could no longer refuse his oft-repeated request to have McDowell—who was lying idle before Fredericksburg —sent to him. With this heavy reinforcement to the Federals, the odds against the Confederates would be as great after Jackson's arrival as they had been before. In order, therefore, to blind the Federals as to his real movements, he sent to Staunton by Lynchburg and Charlottesville seven thousand men, consisting of Hood's, Lawton's, and Whiting's brigades, to make the Federals believe that these reinforcements were sent to Jackson to enable him to sweep once more down the Valley. This movement had the desired effect, for when McClellan next applied for McDowell's forces, President Lincoln replied that they could not now be needed by him, since Lee's army had been so much weakened by the reinforcements which he had just sent Jackson.

This last officer seconded General Lee's efforts by deceiving the enemy in the Valley as to his movements. He ordered Colonel Munford, who, as we have seen, had advanced to Harrisonburg, to arrest all persons going up and down the Valley, and to press so closely upon Fremont's outposts as to make him believe that the whole Confederate army was close at hand. Colonel Munford in moving forward met a flag of truce twelve miles north of Harrisonburg, brought by a major, accompanied by a number of surgeons and ambulances, to take back the Federal wounded, whose release they demanded. Colonel Munford, stopping this long train at his outposts, returned to Harrisonburg, accompanied by the major and surgeon, who enjoyed his hospitality until he could get

General Jackson's reply to their demand. In the mean time, the general having sent him word to do all he could to make the Federals believe he was returning down the Valley, he communicated this message to one of his troopers, and told him to slip out of the village and return as a pretended bearer of dispatches from Jackson. The two Federal officers were very boastful, and tauntingly told their host that Fremont and Shields would soon unite and come back to sweep Jackson from the Valley; but they were soon to have their pride lowered. The trooper returned in a short time disguised as an orderly, and Colonel Munford received him purposely in a room adjoining one in which the Federal officers were. "What answer do you bring, orderly, from General Jackson?" he said, in a loud voice. "Why, the general laughed at the demand for the surrender of the wounded prisoners," was the reply; "he has no notion of it." "Do you bring any good news?" asked Colonel Munford. "Glorious news!" he answered; "the road from Staunton this way is chock-full of soldiers, cannon, and wagons come to reinforce Jackson in his march down the Valley. There is General Whiting, General Hood, General Lawton, and General I don't know who. I never saw so many soldiers and cannon together in my life. People say there are thirty thousand of them."

Colonel Munford, after listening to this, went out to relate it to the citizens, in order to deceive more surely the Federal officers. The town was thrown into a delirium of joy by this news, and when the colonel dismissed the two officers with a refusal of their demand, they returned rather dejected. Colonel Munford pushed after them with his advance as far as New Market, and as soon as they reached their own camp General Fremont withdrew immediately to Strasburg, where he began to fortify his position.

General Jackson, having taken these prompt measures to deceive the enemy as to his real movements, was now ready to act on General Lee's orders, which were to move quickly, and without letting any one know where he was going, across the Blue Ridge and down to Richmond. So strict was he in keeping secret this move that he did not reveal it even to General Ewell, his second in command, who was simply directed to move to Charlottesville, while the rest were ordered to follow him. They began to move on the 17th of June, and in two days' march arrived in the neighborhood of Charlottesville. The men, elated by the brilliant success of their late campaign, stepped out to begin this march with the alacrity of soldiers who are sure of being led to victory by a beloved chief, and their march through the country was a perfect ovation. Their grateful countrymen, anxious to see the men who had achieved such prodigies of valor, and anxious, too, to show their appreciation of their brilliant achievements, thronged the line of their march. This uprising of the country increased the enthusiasm of the troops, and as they moved swiftly along they answered with cheers the blessings invoked upon them by old men and old women, while from the hill-tops the white arms of maidens waved them on to deeds of greater valor and scenes of more fearful contest than any they had yet witnessed.

"Where are you going?" was the oft-repeated question of the citizens to these travel-stained and foot-sore soldiers. "We don't know, but old Jack does," was the cheery reply, as regiment after regiment disappeared from the sight of the admiring eyes of their countrymen. The scenes witnessed on this march, the enthusiasm of the troops, the outbursts of patriotism of the citizens, and the rush of the inhabitants of all ages and each sex to the highways to see and to cheer the troops as they passed by, every heart filled with patriotic devotion, every face radiant with hope for the future and with the pride of success in the past, and every thought directed to the great events the certainty of whose near approach pervaded all ranks, the effect of the whole heightened by the loveliness of the landscape and the surpassing beauty of the country through which they moved,—these scenes will form a brilliant page in the history of this civil war, and the historian will have no more enthusiastic or joyous march to describe than that of this little band from the mountains to the sea.

After a day's delay at Gordonsville, caused by a rumor of the approach of Shields, Jackson arrived on June 22 at Frederickshall, a point fifty miles from Richmond. Here the army halted to rest. At Charlottesville, under the strictest injunction of secrecy, Jackson had confided to his chief of staff the destination of his command. An advance-guard of cavalry preceded the army to forbid all persons from going before it to Richmond. Thus the appearance of the van-guard of the army was the first notice the people of the country through which it passed had of its approach.

After a day's rest, General Jackson rose at one o'clock in the morning of June 23, and started with a courier to ride express to Richmond, to have a private interview with General Lee. He wished to keep this visit to Richmond a profound secret, and few knew of his departure. When he reached his outposts, the guard, not recognizing him, refused positively to let him pass. The general, eager to push forward, but anxious not to make himself known, tried to pass first as an officer on military business, and then as one bearing important intelligence to General Lee; but the faithful guard refused, saying his orders were that he should allow neither officers nor citizens to go through the lines. After some persuasion, he finally agreed to send for the captain of the guard and let him decide the question. When this officer came up, he recognized the general, and at once let him pass; but Jackson did not go on without praising the faithful guard with great warmth for his strict obedience of orders. After meeting General Lee and receiving from him a full explanation of his plan of battle, Jackson returned the next day to his command, with which he arrived safely at Ashland, twelve miles from Richmond, on the evening of the 25th of June.

Thus silently, swiftly, and secretly this little army swept down from the mountains to the plains of Richmond, to join there in the fierce contests which were to rage at the very gates of that devoted city. Through the information gained by Stuart in his rapid raid round McClellan's camp, General Lee learned the exact position of his forces, and speedily perfected his plans for driving them from their intrenchments. To understand this plan, the reader must have an idea of the direction in which the Chickahominy flows, and also of the roads entering the city.

The Fredericksburg and Potomac Railroad starts from Richmond on the western side of the city, the Central Railroad from the northern, and the York River Railroad from the eastern. The first of these roads bends towards the north and northeast and crosses the Central

Railroad at Hanover Junction, twenty-five miles from Richmond. The Chickahominy rises west of the Fredericksburg Railroad, and flows in an easterly direction. It is crossed successively by the Meadow Bridge road and the Mechanicsville road, and farther down still by Grapevine Bridge. A short distance below this bridge it turns more to the south, and crosses the line of the York River Railroad. It continues for a few miles to flow in a southerly direction, and south of the railroad is crossed first by Bottom's Bridge and then by Long Bridge, just above which latter point it bends back towards the east, and, flowing sluggishly along in that direction, empties into the James many miles lower down. The country immediately on the course of this river is more or less swampy, but this is particularly the case between Mechanicsville and Long Bridge, which was destined to be the theatre of the struggle between the two contending armies.

McClellan had the right wing of his army resting on the north side of the Chickahominy and the left on the south side; several bridges and causeways erected by him connected the two. His whole front was strongly fortified by intrenchments, heavy guns, and abatis. The approaches to his front were further impeded by felled trees, so that an attack on him in that direction would have resulted in a useless and cruel loss of life for the Confederates, with little hope of success. To avoid this, General Lee conceived the brilliant plan of crossing the Chickahominy high up, and, after turning McClellan's left, sweep down the north side of that stream, clearing it of the Federal forces until he reached the point where the stream bends more to the south, when, still keeping along its northern, or rather at that point its eastern, bank, he would seize all the bridges in McClellan's rear, and thus cut off his retreat down the peninsula, while Huger and Magruder, who confronted his left wing, were to push down and attack his flanks should he attempt to escape to the James, and thus effect the capture of his whole command.

Everything being in readiness to carry this great plan into execution, the commander-in-chief issued his general order, giving a clear but short and simple statement of what he wished the different leaders and divisions of his army to accomplish. The reader will remember that the Meadow Bridge road crossed the Chickahominy high up the stream, and that then came the Mechanicsville road. The extreme left of the Confederate army was held by General Branch, of A. P. Hill's division, which was stationed south of the Chickahominy, within a few miles of Ashland, where, as we have already seen, Jackson arrived on the evening of June 25.

In his general order, General Lee directed the movements of the army as follows. Jackson was to move forward from Ashland on the 25th and encamp for the night at some point west of the Central Railroad. At three o'clock on Thursday morning, the 26th, he was to resume his line of march across the Central Railroad, and in a line bearing to the left of Mechanicsville. He was to communicate his march to General Branch, who would immediately cross the Chickahominy and move down the road leading to Mechanicsville. As soon as General A. P. Hill heard that these two columns were in motion, he was to cross the Chickahominy with the rest of his division and march directly upon Mechanicsville. As he approached that point, the heavy Confederate batteries on the Chickahominy were to open upon it to aid his advance. The Federals being driven from Mechanicsville, and the passage across the bridge there being thus opened, Generals Longstreet and D. H. Hill, the heads of whose columns were to be in readiness at that point, would cross the stream and push forward, Longstreet to support General A. P. Hill, and D. H. Hill to support Jackson,—the four divisions to keep in communication with one another, General Jackson bearing well to the left, turning Beaver Dam Creek, which flowed into the Chickahominy below Mechanicsville, and then to march towards Cold Harbor. They were to press forward towards York River Railroad, closing upon the enemy's rear and forcing him down the Chickahominy.

The divisions under Generals Huger and Magruder, on the Confederate right, were to confront the Federals there and hold their positions against attack. General Jackson's left was covered by General Stuart and his cavalry.

While these plans were being rapidly developed, and the orders for their execution issued at the Confederate headquarters, was McClellan ignorant of the toils that were spreading for him? Not entirely; for on the morning of the 24th a deserter informed him that Jackson had left Gordonsville and was advancing to attack him. Thinking it impossible that he should have escaped through the seventy thousand men who, under pretense of capturing him, had been withheld from his own army, McClellan could not give this report full credence. But the next day, in the hot engagement at Oak Grove, he learned that the cavalry, which he knew was only clearing Jackson's way before him, had arrived at Hanover Court-House. The meaning of the Confederate movements now became only too apparent to him, and at this supreme moment, in preparation for which he had toiled so many months in perfecting the discipline and organization of his fine army, he found himself still deprived of the portion of his forces which he deemed necessary for his success. This moment was one of great bitterness to him, recognizing, as he did, the fact that his defeat was certain.

He had to suffer what so many other generals have had to suffer when there has been a weak or timid civil power above them, able with a single stroke of the pen to destroy all the hopes of a whole campaign. It must be acknowledged that he met the trial with the manly resignation of a brave soldier and true patriot. Seeing now that instead of conquering there was left to him only the humbler task of withdrawing his army safely from the toils which had been spread for it, he set himself to work with skillful celerity to accomplish this. Clinging to his fond hope of changing his base to the James, already the initiatory steps for that move had been taken, and the combat at Oak Grove was but to beat up the Confederate forces and see how the change could be best effected. Orders were given on the night of the 25th, and with astounding audacity he cut himself off from his base of supplies on the York and provisioned his army for its march across to the James. All that it could need was supplied, herds of cattle being in readiness to accompany the army on its line of march, and vessels with supplies ordered to the mouth of the James.

The night of the 25th General Jackson devoted to prayer and to contemplation of the work before him. Laboring under a deep sense of the responsibilities resting on him, feeling how much hung upon the success of the coming struggle, and yet knowing too well how many accidents might occur, any one of which would thwart the execution of the plan of attack adopted by General Lee, the thought of sleep did not enter his mind. To one general officer after another he gave the necessary directions for their early advance in the morning, and every moment of solitude was devoted by him to prayer.

An hour or two after midnight, while he was alone and pacing his room anxiously, two of his generals came to propose to him to move his army in two columns and by two different roads instead of by one. He listened to them calmly, and told them he would decide by the morning. The two officers left, and when they were alone one said to the other, " Do you know why General Jackson would not decide upon our suggestion at once? It was because he has to pray over it before he makes up his mind." The next minute, the other officer, finding that he had left his sword in General Jackson's room, returned to get it, and when he entered found his great leader upon his knees, engaged in prayer.

Jackson, as we have seen, was to have begun his march by three o'clock in the morning; and he made every effort to start at the appointed hour; but in vain. The sun had risen before the march began, and, with its early rays shining full in their faces, the men moved quickly forward. At each cross-road which they reached was a detachment of Stuart's cavalry, which silently swung into line on their left and moved on, until at last Stuart's whole command covered Jackson's left. At four o'clock in the afternoon Jackson's command had reached the neighborhood of Pole-Green Church, which stands on a line with Mechanicsville, a few miles to the north of it.

General A. P. Hill had already been in position before the enemy's works at this last place for several hours, and was only waiting the sound of General Jackson's guns on the north to make the attack. This welcome sound now reached his ears, as Jackson had the woods in front of him shelled in order to drive out McClellan's pickets, and to enable the Confederates to repair the bridge across the Tottopottamoy Creek, which lay in front of them.

At the sound of the longed-for firing, General A. P. Hill dashed forward, and soon carried the Federal works and swept the enemy from the little village and down the Chickahominy across Beaver Dam Creek, where they went into their strong intrenchments on its eastern bank. The Confederates, impatient to drive them from this position, would not wait until General Jackson's advance could turn their flank and force them to retreat, but attacked them that evening on their left. After severe fighting, however, not being able to dislodge the Federals, the firing ceased, and the Confederates slept that night on their arms.

Expecting Jackson to arrive on the enemy's right and turn it, at early dawn on the morning of the 27th A. P. Hill renewed the attack, and it was sustained with great animation for two hours, when, Jackson having crossed Beaver Dam above, the Federals abandoned their intrenchments and retired rapidly down the river, destroying a great deal of property, but leaving much in their deserted camps. The bridges over Beaver Dam being repaired, the Confederates moved quickly forward, A. P. Hill and Longstreet keeping near the Chickahominy, and Jackson and D. H. Hill still bearing to the left.

Longstreet and Hill reached the neighborhood of New Bridge about noon, the line of the Federal retreat having been marked by the conflagrations of wagons and stores. It was now discovered that the Federals had taken position behind Powhite Creek, which flows into the Chickahominy just below New Bridge, and were prepared to make a desperate stand; and certainly never did an army have a better position for such a purpose. "He [McClellan] occupied a range of hills, with his right resting in the vicinity of McGeehee's house, and his left near that of Dr. Gaines, on a wooded bluff which rose abruptly from a deep ravine. The ravine was filled with sharp-shooters, to whom its banks gave protection. A second line of infantry was stationed on the side of the hill, behind a breastwork of trees, above the first. A third occupied the crest, strengthened with rifle-trenches and crowned with artillery. The approach to this position was over an open plain about a quarter of a mile wide, commanded by this triple line of fire, and swept by the heavy batteries south of the Chickahominy. In front of his centre and right the ground was generally open, bounded on the side of our approach by a wood with dense and tangled undergrowth, and traversed by a sluggish stream which converted the soil into a deep morass. The woods on the farther side of the swamp were occupied by sharp-shooters, and trees had been felled to increase the difficulty of its passage and detain our advancing columns under the fire of infantry, massed on the slopes of the opposite hills, and of the batteries on their crests. Pressing on towards the York River Railroad, A. P. Hill, who was in advance, reached the vicinity of New Cold Harbor about two P.M., where he encountered the enemy. He immediately formed his line nearly parallel to the road leading from that place towards McGeehee's house, and soon became hotly engaged. The arrival of Jackson on our left was momentarily expected. Under this impression, Longstreet was held back until this movement should commence. The principal part of the Federal army was now on the north side of the Chickahominy. Hill's single division met this large force with the impetuous courage for which that officer and his troops are distinguished. They drove the enemy back, and assailed him in his strong position on the ridge. The battle raged fiercely, and with varying fortune, more than two hours. Three regiments pierced the enemy's line, and forced their way to the crest of the hill on his left, but were compelled to fall back before overwhelming numbers. The superior force of the enemy, assisted by the fire of his batteries south of the Chickahominy, which played incessantly on our columns as they pressed through the difficulties that obstructed their way, caused them to recoil. Though most of the men had never been under fire until the day before, they were rallied, and in turn repelled the advance of the enemy. Some brigades were broken, others stubbornly maintained their positions, but it became apparent that the enemy was gradually gaining ground." *

But where was Jackson during these hours of deadly struggle between his friends and his foes? After turning the enemy's right on Beaver Dam Creek, he continued his advance, and, meeting General Lee, had an interview with that chief, who instructed him to march on towards Cold Harbor, still bearing to the left, so as to let the approach to that place be on his right. Jack-

---

* Lee's Report.

son continued his march, having for guides young men who lived in the neighborhood and were acquainted with the roads of the country. He told them he wished to go to Cold Harbor; and they, supposing he wished to get there by the shortest road, on coming to a fork in the road, took the one on the right hand, which, going by Gaines's Mill, approached Cold Harbor on Jackson's left instead of on his right. After moving along this road for a mile and a half, General Jackson was startled by hearing the sound of cannon directly in front of him. Turning quickly to the guide near him, he asked, sharply, "Where is that firing?" The guide replied that it came from the direction of Gaines's Mill. "Does this road lead there?" the general asked, in a startled voice. The guide told him that it led by Gaines's Mill to Cold Harbor. "But," exclaimed he, "I do not wish to go to Gaines's Mill; I wish to go to Cold Harbor, leaving that place on the right." "Then," said the guide, "the left-hand road was the one which should have been taken; and had you let me know what you desired, I could have directed you aright at first." Thus, as he had feared, from his want of knowledge of the country a blunder had been committed, and at a crisis when no man knew what it might cost. General Jackson, however, bore himself with his accustomed equanimity, and allowed no one to see the anxiety he felt. The column was reversed with as little delay as possible and marched back to the right road. When it was suggested to him that this mistake might prevent him from reaching the field of action in time to save the day, he said, "No, let us trust that the providence of our God will so over-rule it that no mischief shall result." As it turned out, the delay did not result in any serious mischief. Jackson continued his march, and reached the point north of Cold Harbor in time to form a junction with General D. H. Hill; after which he pushed forward to the right, and, passing Cold Harbor, they saw the enemy about half a mile to the south, drawn up in battle-array. General Jackson rode forward, accompanied by many of his officers, to reconnoitre the enemy's position, but very soon, a heavy fire being opened upon them, they had to retire.

Here again the want of good maps of the country, which ought to have been made when the Confederates were in undisturbed possession of it, was cruelly felt by General Jackson. The thundering cannonade coming from west of Cold Harbor told him that A. P. Hill was engaged in fierce combat with the Federals; but if he led his troops forward to him, he feared, from the apparent position of the enemy, that his own men might be taken for the foe, and be fired into by their friends. There was no time to make a reconnoissance, and the forests prevented an extensive view of the country. There was nothing then left but to advance cautiously and fight the enemy wherever found. When he did come in contact with him, General Jackson drew up his line of battle on a road which formed an angle with the enemy's position, so that the brigades on his left (held by D. H. Hill) were near the enemy, while those on the right were farther off, and had to sweep around the arc of a circle to reach him, and thus had some distance to traverse in striking his line.

The brigades on Jackson's left were soon hotly engaged with the enemy, and, like the men under A. P. Hill, they advanced to the charge with undaunted valor. Pushing their way through the morass, they ascended the hill and engaged the enemy in the forest. Never did soldiers move forward under a hotter fire; line after line withered away under the storm of shot and shell and bullets poured into their ranks; but the unfaltering officers rallied their shattered troops, and the battered regiments pressed on with undying courage.

While this deadly struggle was going on on Jackson's left, the brigades which were on his right, being, as we have seen, farther from the line of the enemy, were kept idle there by a misconception of General Jackson's order, —one which, but for the great intelligence and patriotic devotion of his chief of staff, Colonel Dabney, might have been a fatal error. That officer having been sick, General Jackson was anxious to relieve him from the arduous duties of that perilous day; but, finding that he could not be persuaded to leave the field of action on the plea of health, he ordered him to go to the rear and look for a brother whom he knew to be there. Colonel Dabney obeyed reluctantly, and as he moved off from the general was heard to say, " I am obliged to go, but he will see I won't stay."

Colonel Dabney, a short while before, had wished to carry an important message from the general to the brigades in the rear, but the general, in his tender care of him, refused to let him go, and the colonel heard him give the order to another officer, who, it was apparent, misunderstood the general. Colonel Dabney, after making some pretense of looking up his brother, turned his horse's head in the direction of the rear brigades. He found, as he had suspected, that the order had been given them to await further orders before moving forward, instead of an order, as the general intended, to go at once into action. There was not a moment to be lost. One part of Jackson's force was engaged in a life-and-death struggle with the enemy, while the other was lying idle on the roadside. Colonel Dabney acted in this emergency with a promptness and decision worthy of his beloved chief. Going at full gallop to one after another of the brigade commanders, he laid the state of the case before them, and urged that without delay they should move rapidly forward to the aid of their comrades, for there was not a moment to be lost. The commanders, comprehending instantly the situation of affairs, got their troops into motion, and one after another disappeared from sight as they moved into the pine thickets or pierced the dense forests with no other guide to the foe than the sound of the firing. Such was the nature of the country, and so dense were the tangled forests and thickets, that the different brigades soon lost sight of one another, and, indeed, crossed one another's track to the field of action.

In the mean time, the struggle on the field of battle was raging with unmitigated fury. The Confederate ranks were being rapidly thinned away, and their ammunition, even, was running low. General Jackson, unconscious that his order for the rear brigades to be brought into action had been misunderstood, thought his whole force was on the battle-field, and, seeing how slight the impression they were making on the enemy, his heart sank within him, and his whole bearing manifested more agitation than he had ever before been seen to betray. An eye-witness of the scene says of him,—

"He was in a state of excitement such as I never saw him in, which transfigured his whole nature. His usual self-possessed, business-like air in battle had given place to a concentrated rage, by which his faculties were not confused, but braced. His face was crimson, the nerves of his chin and cheeks twitching convulsively, his lips purple from sucking a piece of lemon which he held in his hand and applied to his mouth unconsciously, his blue eyes blazing with a species of glare. He was riding hither and thither as if almost carried away with an uncontrollable impulse to dash into one or another part of his line of battle, but after a career of twenty or thirty yards he arrested his horse with a sudden jerk which almost threw him upon his haunches. His voice especially had undergone a peculiar change. Always rather curt, it had now become actually savage, like the bark of some beast of prey in furious combat: the very tones made my blood tingle. Yet let not the reader misunderstand me; still there was no rant, no scolding or declamation, no forgetfulness even of his ordinary courtesy, and not a superfluous word or a shade of confusion in his orders. There seemed to be in his single body the energies of a volcano or a tempest, curbed by his iron will. I thought then, and still think, that I could conceive the cause of this unwonted excitement: he believed that his last brigade had been engaged for an hour, or possibly for hours, and that the enemy's force was unbroken: hence his anxiety and anger. . . . Captain Pendleton, the assistant adjutant, and a favorite aid of the general, came from the direction of the fight and reported something. I surmised a message from General Lee. Jackson's answer was, ' Very well.' After a few moments he wheeled his horse upon him, and said, in a tone of inexpressible sharpness and authority, ' Captain Pendleton, go to the line and see all the commanders. Tell them this thing has hung in suspense too long. Sweep the field with the bayonet!' . . . Before he had gotten out of our sight, however, a rolling cheer ran like a wave along the line for more than a mile, and told us that the day was won. As was apparent afterwards, the six reserve brigades had now gotten well into action at various points, and their overtasked comrades, with their assistance, were enabled to drive in the enemy at almost every point. The sun was now near the tree-tops."

Chief among the brilliant charges of the day was that of the Texan Brigade, under General Hood, and of a Mississippi brigade under Colonel Law, of Whiting's division, on the Federal left. General Jackson in his report thus describes it:

"Advancing thence through a number of retreating and disordered regiments, he came within range of the enemy's fire, who, concealed in an open wood, and protected by breastworks, poured a destructive fire, for a quarter of a mile, into his advancing line, under which many brave officers fell. Dashing on with unfaltering steps in the face of these murderous discharges of canister and musketry, General Hood and Colonel Law, at the head of their respective brigades, rushed to the charge with a yell. Moving down a precipitous ravine, clambering up a difficult ascent, and exposed to an incessant and deadly fire from the intrenchments, these brave and determined men pressed forward, driving the enemy from his well-selected and fortified position.

"In this charge, in which upwards of a thousand men fell, killed and wounded, before the fire of the enemy, and in which fourteen pieces of artillery and nearly a regiment were captured, the Fourth Texas, under the lead of General Hood, was the first to pierce these strongholds and seize these guns. . . . The shouts of triumph which rose from our brave men as they, unaided by artillery, had stormed this citadel of their strength, were promptly carried from line to line, and the triumphant issue of this assault, with the well-directed fire of the batteries, and successful charges of Hill and Winder upon the enemy's right, determined the fortunes of the day."

An extract from General Lee's report will close the account of this fierce battle:

"The arrival of these fresh troops [Jackson's] enabled A. P. Hill to withdraw some of his brigades, wearied and reduced by their long and arduous conflict. The line being now complete, a general advance from right to left was ordered. On the right the troops moved forward with steadiness, unchecked by the terrible fire from the triple lines of infantry on the hill, and the cannon on both sides of the river, which burst upon them as they emerged upon the plain. The dead and wounded marked the way of their intrepid advance, the brave Texans leading, closely followed by their no less daring comrades. The enemy were driven from the ravine to the first line of breastworks, over which our impetuous column dashed up to the intrenchments on the crest. These were quickly stormed, fourteen pieces of artillery captured, and the enemy driven into the field beyond. Fresh troops came to his support, and he endeavored repeatedly to rally; but in vain. He was forced back with great slaughter, until he reached the woods on the banks of the Chickahominy, and night put an end to the pursuit. Long lines of dead and wounded marked each stand made by the enemy in his stubborn resistance, and the field over which he retreated was strewn with the slain. On the left the attack was no less vigorous and successful. D. H. Hill charged across the

open ground in his front, one of his regiments having
first bravely carried a battery whose fire enfiladed his
advance. Gallantly supported by his troops on his right,
who pressed forward with unfaltering resolution, he
reached the crest of the ridge, and, after a sanguinary
struggle, broke the enemy's line, captured several of his
batteries, and drove him in confusion towards the Chickahominy, until darkness rendered further pursuit impossible. Our troops remained in undisturbed possession
of the field, covered with the Federal dead and wounded,
and their broken forces fled to the river or wandered
through the woods."

Thus ended, amid smoke and darkness, the shouts of
the victors and the flight of the conquered, the battle of
the Chickahominy. The following description of General Jackson's condition and appearance at the close of
this anxious day is from the pen of the eye-witness from
whom I have already quoted:

"The task was now to find the general again; no
easy one in the confusion of the closing battle and gathering darkness. The roads, the fields, were thronged
with bodies of infantry, trains of ambulances, stragglers,
cavalry, artillery, and wagons. As we struggled hopelessly along, a voice was heard ten yards in front of us,
which we recognized as that of General Jackson, but
calm and subdued. On joining him, we found him
leaning forward on the pommel of his saddle, his head
drooping, and his whole form relaxed with languor.
The fire of battle had burned out in him, and nature
asserted her rights to repose. After the exchange of
greetings and congratulations, he said, 'I must rest;
please find out a house where I can get some food and
sleep.' He then rode wearily towards the west, and

I*

ultimately found a resting-place in the house of Mr. Sydnor, above Gaines's Mill."

On the morning of the next day, the 28th, it was ascertained that none of McClellan's troops were confronting the Confederates north of the Chickahominy. It was not certain, however, in which direction he would push his retreat,—whether down the peninsula or across to the James.

To provide against the former course, a regiment of Confederate cavalry, supported by Ewell's division, was ordered to seize the York River Railroad. When the cavalry reached Dispatch Station, on that road, the Federals who were there withdrew to the southern side of the Chickahominy and burnt the railroad bridge. Ewell was ordered to proceed down the river to Bottom's Bridge, to guard that point, while the cavalry were to guard the bridges lower down the stream.

Thus far General Lee's admirable plan for defeating and capturing McClellan's army had been well executed. He had been swept from the northern bank of the Chickahominy, and his retreat down the peninsula was cut off. It now only remained for the Confederate right wing to get between him and the James to complete the success by the capture of the whole Federal army. Magruder and Huger were therefore ordered to use the utmost vigilance, and attack the enemy should they discover that his forces in front of their commands were retreating. But now came obstacles which human skill could not overcome, and which were destined to thwart, in part, plans that were so ably conceived, and whose execution had been so brilliantly begun. Chief among these was the nature of the country, which rendered it impossible to obtain any certain intelligence of the movements of the Federals, covered as they were by dense forests and impassable swamps. The bridges across the Chickahominy were burnt by the Federals as soon as they had crossed them. Late in the day of the 28th, clouds of dust showed that the Federal army was in motion, and later still it became apparent that their line of retreat was towards the James River. By Sunday morning they had burnt the bridges and gone. The Confederate generals were now eager to pursue. Longstreet and A. P. Hill were ordered to cross the Chickahominy at New Bridge early on the morning of the 29th. The Grapevine Bridge on Jackson's front was so broken down that there was necessarily considerable delay in having it repaired, but it was sufficiently repaired by a late hour on Sunday afternoon to enable General Jackson and his staff, accompanied by the Stonewall Brigade, to cross. He passed through the wrecks of the camp which had been so hastily abandoned. The whole country was strewn with deserted wagons, heaps of half-destroyed meat and grain, ambulances, medicine-wagons, axes, picks, torn clothing, vegetable-cans, and every thing which an army could need,—all more or less destroyed or injured. As he advanced, General Jackson came up with the forces of Magruder, with whom General Lee was present, watching the movements of the enemy. It was decided upon consultation that it was too late for General Jackson to bring his troops over the Chickahominy that night and make an advance, and that he should return to them and renew the pursuit early in the morning.

On reaching the northern bank of the Chickahominy, Jackson soon heard the sound of guns, which betokened the engagement between Magruder and the Federals.

Had Jackson been able to carry out General Lee's original plan and cross the Chickahominy sooner, his route would have brought him at this time to the rear and flank of the Federal army, which by this joint attack would have received a severe if not fatal blow. The fight was severe, but not decisive, and the Federals continued their retreat under cover of darkness, leaving behind many hundred prisoners, and their dead and wounded. Jackson, chafing at being idle when such activity was needed, gave orders for all to be in readiness to move forward at early dawn, and lay down in the open air to rest for a short time, but was awakened at midnight by a shower of rain, which wetted him through and through. Feeling that there would be no more rest for his men that night, he ordered them to move at once, while he himself rode forward; and when his forces reached the battle-field near Savage Station early on Monday, the 30th, they found him standing before a camp-fire drying his clothes.

Not stopping to get any food, he moved on, capturing at Savage Station a field-hospital containing twenty-five hundred sick and wounded. Other prisoners fell into his hands at every step, until at last he sent a thousand to the rear, saying, in reply to some one who remarked that the maintenance of such a number would be a great expense, " It is cheaper to feed than to fight them."

In the mean time, Longstreet and A. P. Hill were advancing on the Darbytown road, followed by Magruder, while Jackson followed the road taken by the enemy. Longstreet and A. P. Hill, continuing their advance on the 30th, soon came upon the enemy strongly posted on Frazier's farm, across the Long Bridge road. Huger's route led to the right of this position, and Jackson's to the rear. General Holmes had crossed from the south side of James River the day before, and was moving down the river road and coming upon the line of the retreat. He was ordered to attack the column with artillery. Finding that the batteries placed on Malvern Hill, supported by a heavy force of artillery and aided by the gun-boats in the river, commanded this point of the line, he sent for reinforcements. Magruder was ordered to him, but could not reach him in time to make the attack that night. Huger, in the mean while, reported that the roads were so obstructed that he could not make his way to Longstreet and Hill. Jackson, who was also to have been up in time to aid these two generals, was delayed by having his passage of White Oak Swamp disputed, and they were left to engage the enemy alone. The fierce battle of Frazier's Farm ensued, and raged furiously until nine o'clock at night. Here, again, a serious but not fatal blow was given the Federal army. Under cover of darkness it continued its retreat, and again was lost an opportunity of annihilating it.

General Jackson, having found the bridge across White Oak Swamp destroyed, could not push across, as we have seen, on the 30th, for the men could not be induced to repair the bridge, exposed as they were to the Federal fire. Perhaps if General Jackson had not been so prostrated as he was by fatigue, he would have led his forces across by two fords which were found not far from the bridge. But flesh and blood could stand no more than his had done, and, after an ineffectual effort to cross, he gave it up, saying that night, as he dropped asleep, exhausted and worn out, "Now, gentlemen, let us at once to bed, and rise with the dawn, and see if to-morrow we cannot *do something.*" During the day he had written a note to Mrs. Jackson, expressing his gratitude to Providence for the successful defense of Richmond, and venturing the hope that an honorable peace would soon enable them to be together at home once more.

During that night the Federal forces were skillfully and silently withdrawn from Jackson's front and moved to Malvern Hill, which was destined to be on the morrow the scene of another fierce and bloody, but to the Confederates fruitless, contest. Jackson crossed the Chickahominy early on the morning of July 1. The wearied and shattered troops of Longstreet and Hill had been withdrawn, and replaced by Magruder's. Moving forward for Malvern Hill, Jackson passed by these last, by whom he was loudly cheered, and hastened on after the enemy. He was not long in finding him, for he was posted on a high and commanding ridge in front of Malvern Hill. It would have been impossible for McClellan to secure a better position to make a stand than the one he there had, or for him to post his troops more skillfully than he did on this ridge, which towered above all the surrounding country and was also under the protection of the gun-boats in the James River. He had collected the remnants of his defeated but well-disciplined army, and had there a hundred pieces of artillery. With these guns and his whole force, he was prepared to stand at bay and once more confront his assailants. Facing the Confederates, this ridge sloped gently down to a plain; but to reach this plain they had to make their way through a swampy wood. They then had to charge across the plain exposed to the galling fire of McClellan's powerful artillery, and, as they neared his formidable intrenchments and position, that of his equally deadly musketry. The line of battle was formed by Jackson with Whiting's division on his left, D. H. Hill's on his right, and in the interval one of Ewell's brigades. On Jackson's right two of Huger's brigades were placed, and on the right of these Magruder's forces later took position. So ignorant were the Confederate leaders of the country, and so greatly were their communications with one another impeded by the density of the forests, that the whole line was not formed until late in the afternoon. The same causes prevented a general advance at a given signal, so that General Hill, after dashing forward in gallant style, sweeping the plain and breaking and driving back the enemy's first line, found himself unsupported, and was forced to yield the ground so gallantly won. After several determined efforts to storm the hill, brigade after brigade advancing over a plain swept by a hundred guns, night put an end to the conflict, and left the Federals still holding their position and with the safety of their retreat now secured.

After the battle was over, General Jackson went to the rear to rest. He found a pallet prepared for him on the ground by his faithful servant in the midst of wagons and ambulances. After taking some food, he threw himself upon it, and was soon wrapped in profound slumber. About one o'clock Generals Ewell and Hill tried to rouse him to get orders for the coming day. So sound asleep was he that it seemed almost impossible to do so, and, turning away from General Hill, he said, in an impatient tone, "Go away; the Yankees are all gone; you will find none of them to-morrow." His words were prophetic. The 2d of July opened with a steady, pouring rain, and all that was to be seen of the Federal army, but a few days before so dazzling in the splendor of its equipments and the magnificent array of its serried battalions, were the wrecks that marked the precipitate retreat of a vanquished host. They had retreated during the night, and in the morning the people living in the neighborhood of Haxall's saw spreading over the open fields a multitude of wearied and hungry soldiers, who, without any organization, thought only of reaching the shelter of their gun-boats. This they found at Harrison's Landing, where, their position being flanked on both sides by a creek and defended in front by intrenchments, they were safe from pursuit of the wearied Confederates.

The 2d of July was spent by the Confederates in resting, and orders were given that the whole army should set out next day in pursuit of the enemy. General Jackson was anxious to make an early start, but could not rouse his staff: they were all wearied out. Finally the general, out of all patience, ordered his servant to pack up everything, and to throw away all the coffee, which, having been captured from the enemy, was considered a great luxury; and he further declared that he would arrest the whole staff if they did not rise at once. This threat effectually awakened them.

This move of the Confederate army proved to be useless; the enemy was safe under the protection of his gun-boats, the opportunity of effecting his capture was gone, and, after spending a few days in gathering up arms, the army was marched back on the 8th of July to the vicinity of Richmond.

General Lee, in the close of his report of these engagements, says,—

"Under ordinary circumstances the Federal army should have been destroyed. Its escape was due to the causes already stated. Prominent among these is the want of correct and timely information. This fact, attributable chiefly to the character of the country, enabled General McClellan skillfully to conceal his retreat and to add much to the obstructions with which nature had beset the way of our pursuing columns. But regret that not more was accomplished gives way to gratitude to the Sovereign Ruler of the Universe for the results achieved. The siege of Richmond was raised, and the object of a campaign which had been prosecuted, after months of preparation, at an enormous expenditure of men and money, completely frustrated. More than ten thousand prisoners, including officers of rank, fifty-two pieces of artillery, and upwards of thirty-five thousand stand of arms, were captured. The stores and supplies of every description which fell into our hands were great in amount and value, but small in comparison with those destroyed by the enemy. His losses in battle exceeded our own, as attested by the thousands of dead and wounded left on every field; while his subsequent inaction shows in what condition the survivors reached the protection to which they fled."

An extract from an account of this retreat, written by one who was with McClellan's army, will close this chapter:

"Huddled among the wagons were ten thousand stragglers: for the credit of the nation be it said that four-fifths of them were wounded, sick, or utterly exhausted, and could not have stirred but for the dread of the tobacco-warehouses (used as prisons) of the South. The confusion of this herd of men and mules, wagons and wounded, men on horses, men on foot, men by the roadside, men perched on wagons, men searching for water, men famishing for food, men lame and bleeding, men with ghostly eyes looking out between bloody bandages that hid the face,—turn to some vivid account of the most pitiful part of Napoleon's retreat from Russia, and fill out the picture, the grim, gaunt, bloody picture, of war in its most terrible features.

"It was determined to move on during the night. The distance to Turkey Island Bridge, the point on James River which was to be reached by the direct road, was six miles. Commencing at dusk, the march continued until daylight. The night was dark and fearful. Heavy thunder rolled in turn along each point of the horizon, and dark clouds spread the entire canopy. We were forbidden to speak aloud, and, lest the light of a cigar should present a target for an ambushed rifle, we were cautioned not to smoke. Ten miles of weary marching, with frequent halts, as some one of the hundred vehicles of the artillery-train in our centre, by a slight deviation, crashed against a tree, wore away the hours till dawn, when we debouched into a magnificent wheat-field, and the smoke-stack of the Galena was in sight. Xenophon's ten thousand greeting 'The sea! the sea!' were not more glad than we.

"On reaching the river, General McClellan immediately proceeded on board one of the vessels. He appeared greatly perturbed. General McClellan met General Patterson as he stepped on board, laid his hand on his shoulder, and took him in a hurried manner into the aft cabin or ladies' saloon. As he went in, he beat the air with his right hand clinched, from which all present inferred there was bad news. To the astonishment of all, it was explained 'that the whole Army of the Potomac lay stretched along the banks of the river.'"

CHAPTER XII.

SECOND BATTLE OF MANASSAS.

GENERAL JACKSON always remained so closely in camp that he was never seen by the citizens, except those who happened to be near his war-path. They never, however, missed an opportunity of showing their devotion for him, and the host who could number him among his guests considered his house blessed by his presence. In the movements of the troops around Richmond, Jackson and his staff were, on one occasion, forced to ride through a field of uncut oats. The owner, seeing them, rushed up in great anger, and, addressing the general, vented all his rage on him, and wound up by asking his name, that he might report him. To this demand the general replied by saying, quietly, "Jackson is my name, sir." "What Jackson?" asked the farmer. "General Jackson," was the answer. "What!" exclaimed the man, after a pause, seeming dumfounded as the truth dawned upon him,—"what! Stonewall Jackson?" "That is what they call me," Jackson replied. "General," said the man, taking off his hat, and evincing in the tones of his voice the deepest love and veneration, "ride over my whole field ; do whatever you like with it, sir."

After the battles around Richmond, General Jackson, seeing that McClellan's army was so crippled that several weeks must elapse before it could be re-organized and again ready for service, was anxious that the Confedcrate forces should be moved northwards and threaten Washington City. He urged this plan upon General Lee, and, through a friend, it was also submitted to President Davis. Events now took a turn which rendered it necessary for the Confederate army to move in the direction he desired.

After his defeat around Richmond, McClellan lay inactive for a month at Westover. In the mean time, however, the Government at Washington formed a force called the "Army of Virginia," out of the wrecks of the commands of Shields, Fremont, and the troops of Banks and McDowell. The army thus formed numbered about sixty thousand men, and, being placed under the command of Major-General Pope, was ordered to march from Alexandria upon Gordonsville, in order to seize there the junction of the Orange and Alexandria and the Central Railroads. General Pope, on taking command, issued an order in which he boastfully declared that he had never seen anything of his enemies but their backs, that his headquarters should be in the saddle, and that his army should be fed from the country through which it passed. He also gave permission to his troops to plunder the citizens of the country, and announced that those who would not take the oath of allegiance to the United States Government should be driven from his lines. After this order the counties through which this army marched were of course subjected to indiscriminate plunder and pillage.

To check the advance and the atrocities of this army, General Lee ordered General Jackson, who had returned to the vicinity of Richmond on the 10th of July, to proceed with his command to Gordonsville.

While the command was preparing for this march, on

Sunday, the 13th, there entered Mr. Hoge's church in Richmond an officer, who was alone and apparently a stranger to the place. He was dressed in a sunburnt uniform, and, coming quietly into the church, took his seat modestly near the door. He seemed absorbed in his devotions and in attention to the services. As these closed, it was whispered around that the stranger was no other than General Jackson; but he, not giving the eager congregation an opportunity to feast their gaze upon his warlike figure, passed quickly through the crowd as he bowed to one or two acquaintances. He called on a mother who had lost a son in his command, and then returned to his tent. This was the only occasion upon which the living hero was seen on the streets of the Confederate capital.

The next day he wrote to Mrs. Jackson,—

" RICHMOND, July 14.

" Yesterday I heard Dr. M. D. Hoge preach in his church, and also in the camp of the Stonewall Brigade. It is a great comfort to have the privilege of spending a quiet Sabbath within the walls of a house dedicated to the service of God. . . . People are very kind to me. How God, our God, does shower blessings upon me, an unworthy sinner!"

Jackson arrived at Gordonsville with his command on the 19th of July. The change from the heavy, unhealthy atmosphere of the Chickahominy marshes to the light, bracing air of Piedmont was very necessary to him, for he reached Gordonsville jaded and worn out, and seemed just to be feeling in their full force the effects of the extraordinary fatigues and labors which he had undergone in the Valley campaign and in the battles around Richmond. At Gordonsville he found repose under the hospitable roof of the Rev. Mr. Ewing, with whose family he spent his leisure moments after the duties of the day were over. The children of the household afforded him much pleasure, and he delighted to take notice of them. One of them in particular—a little girl—was often caressed by him. She was frequently found sitting on his knee, and took such pleasure in playing with and admiring the bright buttons of his uniform that she made him promise to give her one for a keepsake when the coat was worn out. Nor did he forget this promise to his little pet; for, months afterwards, when the coat was laid aside, though burdened with all the cares and anxieties of a great military leader in the midst of a fierce war, he remembered her desire to have the button, and sent it to her. It is needless to add that she carefully preserved it among her most highly-prized treasures.

While an inmate of Mr. Ewing's house, General Jackson was a constant attendant at family prayers, and sometimes conducted them himself. Mr. Ewing says of his prayers, "There was something very striking in his prayers. He did not pray to men, but to God. His tones were deep, solemn, tremulous. He seemed to realize that he was speaking to heaven's King. I never heard any one pray who seemed to be pervaded more fully by a spirit of self-abnegation. He seemed to feel more than any man I ever knew the danger of robbing God of the glory due for our success."

Having spent a few days in Gordonsville, he went with his command into Louisa County, near by, where his horses were refreshed by the abundant pastures he found there. Fully appreciating the toil and anxiety of the coming campaign, Jackson seemed weighed down by the load of care and responsibility resting upon him; but, though he alludes to this in his letters to Mrs. Jackson, he at the same time administers a reproof to himself for his repining spirit by recalling the toils of St. Paul, who "gloried in tribulation," and also by saying how unlike a Christian it was in him to murmur at any toil for his Redeemer.

Having received information that Pope's force was very large, Jackson applied to General Lee for reinforcements. General Lee sent him immediately A. P. Hill's division. With this accession to his command he had no intention of lying idle near Gordonsville while Pope should collect his troops and perfect his plans for the capture of that place. This latter general was now at Culpeper Court-House, with only a part of his army, and Jackson determined to strike him a blow before his reinforcements should arrive. For this purpose he gave orders for an advance in the direction of the enemy on the 7th of August. Now, as on the eve of every other move, Jackson devoted all his spare moments to prayer and to petitions to the God of battles for guidance and support. His servant, Jim, had observed this, and when on this occasion some gentleman asked him if he knew when a battle was coming off, he replied, "Oh, yes, sir. The general is a great man for praying,—night and morning, and all times. But when I see him get up several times in the night besides to go off and pray, then I know *there is going to be something to pay;* and I go straight and pack his haversack, because I know he will call for it in the morning."

The result of this advance of Jackson's was the battle

of Cedar Run, which took place eight miles from Cul-peper Court-House. Ewell's division, which formed the advance, crossed the Rapidan on the 8th. Through some misconception of orders, however, A. P. Hill did not cross the river until the next morning, and the attack on the enemy could not be made until that day. On the morning of the 9th, therefore, Jackson was early in motion, and when within eight miles of Culpeper Court-House a body of Federal cavalry was seen drawn up on a ridge in his front. This body was soon found to have a heavy force at its back, and Jackson at once made his dispositions for battle.

On the right of the road leading to Culpeper Court-House stands Slaughter's Mountain. On the north-eastern side of this ridge Jackson stationed Ewell, with Lattimer's and Johnson's batteries. These batteries, being by their position elevated about two hundred feet above the plains below, had full sweep at the enemy, and kept these plains free from them. Thus the Con-federate right was secure. The centre was held by General Early in advance, on the right of the road to Culpeper, with Taliaferro on his left. The left extended to the left of the road and along the edge of a wood. This part of the line was held by the Second Virginia Brigade, with the Stonewall Brigade in reserve as a sup-port. In front of the Confederate left lay a stubble-field, the shocks of wheat still standing, and beyond this field was a wood. In General Early's front there was a field of corn.

After a furious cannonade of two hours, the battle began in good earnest at five o'clock in the afternoon. At that hour, the Federals, pushing their skirmishers through the cornfield in Early's front, advanced their infantry to the attack, while another body of infantry moved forward on his right. He thus was soon warmly engaged on his right and front. Upon his calling for reinforcements, Thomas's brigade of A. P. Hill's division came to his aid, and he stubbornly maintained his position. In the mean while, the main body of the Federal infantry moved suddenly out of the wood in front of the Confederate left, and, rushing across the intervening stubble-field, fell in superior numbers and with irresistible fury upon that part of the line. The battalion holding the extreme left of the line, finding that that of the enemy was overlapping theirs, fired a few shots and gave way. The left regiments of the Second Brigade, which stood next, now found the Federals on their flank, and in the wood in their rear. Thus beset on all sides, they fought like madmen ; but in vain. The Federals fell on them in front and rear. Surely, but not without desperate hand-to-hand fighting, the Confederate line was doubled back. The whole Second Brigade fell back in disorder ; and the left of Taliaferro's brigade, being exposed, yielded also to the impetuous attack of the enemy, as did the left of Early's. The Federals seemed to be sweeping everything before them. It was now one of those moments in battle when an appeal has to be made by the commanding general to the devotion of his soldiers to follow his lead and save the fortunes of the day. Jackson saw it, and, having delivered a few necessary orders, rushed forward, his countenance flashing with the fires of undying courage and patriotic devotion. For the first time during the war, he was seen to draw his sword. Waving it around his head, he cried out, in a voice whose ringing tones rose above the roar of battle, " Rally, brave men, and press forward ! Your general will lead you! Jackson will lead you! Follow me!" His cry was not in vain. His shattered veterans rallied round his noble figure, which towered like that of a war-god above them. With a handful of men, he rushed forward to the fence which ran along the road, and from behind it they poured a volley into the advancing column of the enemy. Startled by this unexpected rally, the Federals staggered back. The Confederates, who had now all rallied at their general's command, followed this blow by another, and, their reserves coming up, the Federals found themselves in their turn attacked both in flank and in rear. The Confederates pressed forward with loud shouts, and drove back their lately victorious adversaries. The Federal commander, in his maddened attempts to retrieve the fortunes of a day which he had so nearly won, threw forward a splendid body of cavalry. On they rushed, men and heavy war-steeds, jarring the earth beneath as they thundered along. The heavy mass fell upon the Confederate front, and by its very weight swayed it back. But the Confederates closed in on either flank; those in front rallied. On all sides a murderous fire was poured into the splendid array of men and horses. Volley followed volley. Baffled and beaten, enveloped in the pitiless fire of foes eager to avenge their late repulse, they soon became a mangled, mutilated mass, and were pushed off the field. The Confederates now rushed forward with shouts of victory on the left and centre, while Ewell's brigades swooped down from their lofty stand on Slaughter's Mountain and fell with irresistible force on the Federal left, and their retreat became a rout. Night closed on the victorious Confederates two miles in advance of the field of battle. Jackson was eager to push on to Culpeper

"JACKSON WILL LEAD YOU! FOLLOW ME!"

(Page 218.)

Court-House, and continued his advance after nightfall, until the reply of the Federal batteries showed him that Pope had been reinforced. He then ordered a halt, and his soldiers bivouacked for the night.

After every battle, the excitement and fatigues of the day for Jackson seemed to be followed by a weariness and prostration which in more than one instance wrung from him the cry of "Rest; nothing but rest." The night was clear, but there was no moon, and he rode back to the houses in the starlight, seeking a house where he could repose. Finding, however, that every one which he approached was filled with wounded men, he refused to enter, saying that his place might be given to some sufferer needing it more than he did. Just after turning away from one of these houses, he came to a little grass-plot, whose soft, inviting turf he could not resist, and, saying that this must be his resting-place, he dismounted. One of his staff spread a cloak on the grass for him, and the weary chief threw himself on his face upon it. There, beneath the stars, he slept; the din of battle faded from his ears, and he dreamt, perhaps, of the distant wife, and of the home-joys, so much longed for, which he was destined never again to experience. In his heart rested the heavenly peace of a God-fearing man, and over his head hovered the angel-blessings invoked upon him by a grateful and loving country.

In this battle Jackson lost, in the fall of the knightly Winder, one of his ablest lieutenants. While standing near a battery whose position he was directing, this lamented officer was struck by a shell, which knocked his field-glasses from his hand and inflicted a wound from the effects of which he expired in a few hours.

Singularly gifted with graces of both mind and person, Heaven seemed to have made him to captivate the hearts of the brave men whom he so ably and so nobly led. It was characteristic of the man, and a nobler song in his praise than poet could sing, that when on the occasion of this battle he was ordered by his surgeon, on account of the state of his health, not to go into action, his only reply was to buckle on his sword and place himself at the head of his command. It is said that he never looked so handsome as when borne, dying, on a litter from the field of battle; and the living still remember with what regret the news of his death was received by his countrymen.

Two days after the battle, General Jackson wrote to Mrs. Jackson,—

"On last Saturday God again crowned our arms with victory, about six miles from Culpeper Court-House. All glory be to God for his unnumbered blessings!

"I can hardly think of the fall of Brigadier-General C. S. Winder without tearful eyes. Let us all unite more earnestly in imploring God's aid in fighting our battles for us. The thought that there are so many of God's people praying for his blessing upon the army which in his providence is with me, greatly strengthens me. If God be for us, who can be against us?"

On the 11th of August, General Pope sent a flag of truce to ask permission to bury his dead. The request was granted; and during this day of truce the burial-parties of the two armies, so lately engaged in deadly combat, mingled in friendly converse while engaged in the discharge of their pious duty to their fallen comrades.

In this battle the Confederates had eighteen or twenty thousand men engaged, and the Federals, according to their own account, thirty thousand. Their loss greatly exceeded that of the Confederates, which, in killed, wounded, and missing, was a little over thirteen hundred. They captured from the Federals one piece of artillery and three colors, and several thousand small arms.

By this victory they inflicted such a blow upon Pope that his farther advance was hindered until Lee could bring up the remaining Confederate forces from around Richmond, where they were now no longer needed. Having been informed that Pope had been heavily reinforced, General Jackson sent his wounded and the captured arms to the rear, and on the night of the 11th of August quietly withdrew to Gordonsville.

After the battle of Cedar Run, Burnside's corps, which had been brought from North Carolina by the Federals, was marched to reinforce Pope at Culpeper Court House. It was also believed that McClellan's remaining forces were to be recalled from James River and sent to Pope. General Lee accordingly began to move his troops from Richmond to Gordonsville. General Longstreet left Richmond on the 13th of August, and marched directly to Gordonsville.

In the mean time, Pope had his forces along the line of the Orange and Alexandria Railroad; but, in the hope of turning Jackson's left, he moved his right up towards Madison. This exposed his flank and rear, and General Jackson was anxious to attack him while thus exposed. As soon, therefore, as the troops began to arrive from Richmond, he left Gordonsville, in obedience to orders from General Lee, and, passing Orange Court-House, halted near the eastern base of Clarke's Mountain, where he massed his forces near the fords of the Rapidan. General Lee, who was now on the ground, was as impatient as Jackson to throw the Confederate column forward and dash it against the exposed flank and rear of his adversary, and accordingly he determined that the troops should advance across the Rapidan at early dawn on the morning of the 18th. Could he move before Pope suspected his design, he felt certain of his capture or annihilation; for, shut up between the Rapidan on the south, the Rappahannock on the north, and the mountains on the west, and attacked suddenly on flanks and rear by troops flushed with victory, his escape would have been beyond the skill of man. But here, as so often before and afterwards, General Lee's plan, owing to the laggard movements of some of his subordinates, could not be fully executed. It was found on the 18th that the troops were not all in readiness to move forward. Jackson, chafing like a caged lion in sight of his unconscious prey, was eager to dash forward with such troops as he had in hand. He saw that every moment's delay involved the risk of the enemy's gaining information of the intended move, the success of which would thus be thwarted. But General Lee, restraining both his own and Jackson's impatience, put off the advance until the 20th, to give time for all the troops to be in readiness.

This delay, as Jackson had foreseen, was fatal to the success of the design of capturing the whole Federal army, for on that night—the 18th—a party of negroes made their escape to Pope's camp and gave information of the movement of Confederate troops. The ill-starred Federal commander instantly took the alarm, and on the morning of the next day General Lee, from the summit of Clarke's Mountain, whence could be seen the whole Federal encampment across the Rapidan noticed that their tents which were farthest west were gradually disappearing. One by one the different commands there were seen to be striking their tents and silently stealing away. Pope, aroused to a full sense of his danger, was in full retreat for the northern side of the Rappahannock.

General Lee started at once in eager pursuit of his retreating adversary, and early on the morning of the 20th the whole Confederate army was in motion. General Longstreet crossed the Rapidan at Raccoon Ford, while Jackson crossed it higher up, at Somerville Ford, and moved rapidly on Brandy Station, on the Orange and Alexandria Railroad. He encamped that night near Stevensburg, and early on the morning of the 21st again took up his line of march in the direction of Beverly's Ford. On approaching the ford, the Federals were seen on the opposite bank. A Confederate battery was immediately placed in position, and, opening fire upon them, soon silenced their guns. General Stuart, who, with his fine cavalry division, was now co-operating with Jackson, dashed over the Rappahannock, and, after skirmishing with the enemy a few hours and capturing some prisoners, returned with the information that the Federals were moving in large force upon his position there. Pope, as was to be expected, was in full force on the northern bank of the Rappahannock and ready to dispute its passage with General Lee.

The Confederate commander-in-chief now ordered Jackson to move up the Rappahannock, cross the stream high up, and then, after moving north a short distance, turn to the right and by a forced march reach Manassas Junction, where he would be in Pope's rear. Longstreet was to follow in the same path, but in the mean time he was to tarry in Pope's front until that general, having heard of Jackson's move, should fall back to face him, to whose aid Longstreet would then march in all haste.

In carrying out this plan, Longstreet dragged his march out along the southern bank of the Rappahannock until the 26th. Pope, with his army, kept pace with him on the northern bank,—the two armies opening fire upon each other with their artillery whenever the opportunity occurred, and now and then a body of the Federals dashing across the river, and, after a skirmish with the Confederates, again retiring to the north bank.

With his men in light marching order, three days' rations in their haversacks, their hearts full of eagerness for the fray, and reposing unbounded confidence in their beloved leader, Jackson was far advanced on his brilliant march.

On the morning of the 22d he resumed his line of march up the south side of the Rappahannock, a force of the enemy moving abreast with him on the north side. After crossing the Hazel River, a tributary of the Rappahannock, his wagon-train was surprised by a small party of the enemy, who captured a few ambulances and mules, which, however, were soon recaptured. Continuing the march up the stream, the command passed by Freeman's Ford, which was found to be heavily guarded by the enemy, and halted at a point opposite Warrenton Springs. There he found the bridge destroyed, and every evidence that the Federals were close at hand. In the afternoon, Early crossed with his brigade and took possession of the Springs. Before other troops could be passed over to his support, a heavy fall of rain suddenly raised the river so as to make it impassable.

Cut off from his friends, and surrounded by the enemy, the darkness of the night rendering every move uncertain, and the rain pouring down in torrents, Early's situation was extremely critical. But, with admirable skill and coolness, he concealed his troops from the Federals, whom he kept at bay with his artillery during the 23d, while General Jackson on his side of the stream hurried up the construction of a temporary bridge, and before dawn on the morning of the 24th, Early had safely recrossed the Rappahannock, without the loss of a single man.

While a heavy cannonade was going on between A. P. Hill's artillery and the Federals, Jackson bent his line of march away from the river to the village of Jeffersonton, a few miles off. He was thus lost sight of by the enemy, who, through Longstreet's presence at that point, was led to believe that the Confederate army would attempt the passage of the river at Warrenton Springs.

Disembarrassed of the enemy, Jackson's path was cleared before him, and he girded himself up for the race. Leaving his wagons and taking only his ambulances, he started from Jeffersonton early in the morning of August 25. He was to move swiftly and silently with his command across the Rappahannock, and then northward for a short distance between the Blue Ridge and the Bull Run range of mountains, when, turning eastward, he would cross the latter range through Thoroughfare Gap and strike the Orange and Alexandria Railroad behind Pope, between whom and Washington he would thus be with his whole command. His men, forgetting the fatigues which they had undergone in fighting and marching since the 20th, pressed eagerly

K*

forward. Many of them were without rations, and the green corn which they had hastily gleaned from the fields along their route was the only food they had. Having crossed the Rappahannock, after a march of twenty-five miles they approached the village of Salem about sunset on the evening of the 25th.

It was at the close of this day's march that Jackson's men paid him as touching a tribute of devotion as general ever received from his soldiers. He had gone in advance of his column, and, dismounting, stood upon a large stone by the roadside, his cap in his hand, and the last rays of the setting sun playing around his noble head and brow. His position, the magnificent repose of his figure in the midst of such stirring scenes, and the glow of his countenance already beaming with the assured hope of victory, made him the impersonation of patriotic devotion and military zeal. No wonder that when the advancing column caught sight of him an outburst of cheers rose from his devoted soldiers. By a gesture to the officers, he at once tried to suppress it, as to observe silence was one of the most necessary means to conceal their movements from the enemy. When the officers made his wishes known to the men, instantly the words ran along the line, " No cheering, men; the general requests it." The noisy outburst ceased, but the far more touching silent cheer followed, for, amidst a silence broken only by the dull sound of the soldiers' weary tread, their heads were uncovered and their caps waved in the air as they passed their beloved commander. As regiment after regiment and brigade after brigade made this unwonted display of devotion, Jackson turned to his staff, and exclaimed, with emotion, " Who could not conquer with such troops as these?"

THE SILENT CHEER.

(Page 226.)

With the early dawn the line of march was again taken up on the 26th, and, turning to the right on leaving Salem, Jackson led his troops through Thoroughfare Gap and down to Bristol Station, on the Orange and Alexandria Railroad, which place he reached after sunset. He was now between Pope and Washington, and cut off from his friends in front by the whole Federal army. General Stuart was protecting his right. This gallant officer had attacked the enemy on the night of the 22d at Catlett's Station, and, in spite of darkness and a heavy storm of rain, captured several hundred prisoners. Pope barely escaped capture, losing not only his uniform and money-chest, but also, what was of far more value, his dispatch-book, which revealed to General Lee the strength of his army, its position and movements.

On reaching Bristol Station, General Jackson's first thought was to effect the capture of Manassas Junction, and he gladly accepted General Trimble's offer to move on it that night, in spite of the lateness of the hour and the fatigues of the day's long march. Trimble accordingly advanced to the work. General Jackson sent General Stuart to his support, who, being ranking officer, thus took command of an expedition which was entirely successful, and resulted in the dispersion of the force at the Junction, and the capture of several hundred prisoners, eight guns, and immense supplies of commissary and quartermaster stores.

On the morning of the 27th, Jackson arrived at Manassas with two of his divisions,—the third, Ewell's, being left at Bristol to watch Pope, with orders to resist him as long as he could if attacked, but when too closely pressed to fall back to Manassas.

Soon after reaching Manassas, having in the mean

time driven off a Federal battery which had fired into his troops, Jackson perceived a body of the enemy advancing on him with great spirit along the railroad leading from Alexandria. They had just arrived in all haste by a train from that place, having been sent, with the gallant General Taylor at their head, to clear Pope's rear of the Confederate force which was now upon it. They were ignorant that the said force was Jackson's whole corps, and, thinking it to be only a light body of horse, they dashed forward with all the impetuosity of men sure of an easy victory. The hot fire which greeted them both in front and in flank showed them the toils in which they were now hopelessly entangled. Volley after volley was poured into their ranks, until General Jackson, moved by their pitiable situation, rode towards them alone and at the risk of his life and waved his handkerchief as a sign that he wished to save them from slaughter. Their reply was a volley of musketry. His advances of mercy thus repulsed, he returned quickly to his men and ordered them to finish their bloody work. The enemy were instantly routed and pursued from the field, on which they left their commander mortally wounded.

After this brief engagement, the weary Confederate troops had leisure to refresh themselves out of the vast captured stores. The two days' subsistence on green corn was now followed by a feast on the spoils of the enemy. The troops, after bountifully supplying their wants, destroyed the remaining supplies and stores, to prevent their recapture by the enemy.

In the mean time, Ewell, who had been left at Bristol Station with orders to fall back to Manassas should he be too heavily pressed by the Federals, had been attacked by them in full force on the afternoon of the 27th. Finding from the fresh troops constantly arriving that their whole army was upon him, he fell back as ordered, General Early bringing up his rear, and with consummate skill withdrawing the infantry and artillery in perfect order from the engagement.

That night Jackson sent one of his divisions across the Warrenton and Alexandria turnpike, which it crossed near Groveton, and then halted near the battle-field of the first Manassas. This division was joined by the remaining two divisions of Jackson's corps on the morning of the 28th. His whole command, together with Stuart's cavalry, was now concentrated north of the Warrenton turnpike; his left wing rested on Bull Run; his right extended towards the road leading from Thoroughfare Gap, to which point his eyes were now anxiously turned, hoping every hour to see the head of Longstreet's column coming in sight. Jackson's position was becoming more and more critical, for, although he had been brilliantly successful in the execution of the movement intrusted to him by General Lee, yet by it he had roused the Federal commander to a sense of the dangers thickening around him, and had placed himself with the whole Federal army between him and his friends. Should Longstreet's march be seriously delayed by any unforeseen danger, Jackson would be crushed by the sheer weight of superior numbers.

He had scarcely placed his troops in position north of the Warrenton turnpike before the enemy were seen advancing in full force down that road. Jackson, fearing that they were in full march for Alexandria in order to escape a battle, did not hesitate to risk his own safety by attacking them. He could not see the game slip thus easily from the toils so skillfully spread for it, and he instantly prepared to attack the Federal column on the flank as it passed. It was soon seen, however, that its line was bending southward away from the Warrenton turnpike towards Manassas Junction. Jackson lost not a moment in ordering an advance on his right, and, having gained a commanding position, opened fire upon the enemy. They returned the fire very fiercely, and a bloody conflict ensued. The Federals obstinately held their ground until about nine o'clock, when, having succeeded in protecting the exposed flank of their column as it passed slowly, they fell back and left the field to the Confederates. In this engagement two of Jackson's three major-generals—Ewell and Taliaferro—were wounded. Under cover of darkness the Federal army moved that night farther to the east and to Jackson's left, placing itself between him and Washington.

The morning of the 29th dawned and revealed to Jackson the enemy's position and his design, which was manifestly to give him battle and crush him, if possible, before the arrival of succor. The danger of their situation was plain now to both officers and men of the Confederate army. Once more, and with increased anxiety, all eyes were turned in the direction of Thoroughfare Gap; but there were still no signs of the approaching reinforcements. Early in the day, clouds of dust along the Thoroughfare road excited hopes of their near approach; but these passed away with the clouds of dust, from which emerged the dark lines of a body of Federal troops. At ten o'clock the Federals opened fire from their batteries on Jackson's right, whence his replied with spirit. A general and fierce engagement was threatened every minute. But now once more high and dense columns of dust rose along the road, towards which all Confederate eyes were turned, and couriers dashed up out of breath to announce the near approach of Longstreet. His men, wearied by a long forced march, pressed forward with revived energies as their ears caught the sound of Jackson's guns. Men and officers saw that the race was now to the swift, and all dashed forward. Stuart's horse met them and cleared their path to Jackson: the union of the two corps was complete, and the game was won.

After Longstreet's arrival on Jackson's right, the Federals changed the face of their attack to his left. Jackson's troops were formed along the line of an unfinished railroad, whose cuts and embankments thus gave him an admirable line of defense. About two o'clock in the afternoon the enemy hurled his dense masses against Jackson's left, which was held by A. P. Hill's division. In spite of a withering fire, the Federals pressed forward with great valor. Again and again they were repulsed, and again and again they returned to the charge. At one time they dashed over a deep cut in the railroad and penetrated a gap in the Confederate line between two brigades; but from this point they were soon driven back. To meet these furious assaults the Confederates fought with unsurpassed bravery. Six times the enemy charged; six times he was driven back, the combatants firing into one another sometimes at a distance of not more than ten paces. The Confederates stood firm. Along the embankments and in the cuts they fought until their ammunition was exhausted; they fought with the bayonet, and they fought with stones, which they found in the cuts where they stood. Now and then a soldier would volunteer to carry from a staff-officer in the rear a small supply of ammunition, and, running through a heavy fire, would drop down like an angel into the midst of some party whose ammunition was exhausted.

These brave men, after being under fire for seven hours, were now yielding, and were replaced by Early's brigade, who, finding the enemy occupying the railroad, dislodged them and drove them across the field, pursuing for a short distance, when the Confederate troops were recalled, and the combat ceased for the day on that end of the line.

In the mean time, Longstreet, whose line, being at right angles to Jackson's, fronted eastward, was informed by General Stuart that the enemy was approaching from Bristol in heavy columns on his right. This proved to be a corps of McClellan's army which was being hurried to Pope's support. Longstreet immediately disposed his troops to meet them, while the indefatigable Stuart made his troopers dash up and down the Thoroughfare road, dragging brush and raising such clouds of dust that the enemy, thinking a large body was coming to Longstreet's aid, fired a few ineffectual shots at him, and, moving around to the east, joined the forces in front of Jackson.

Longstreet now moved forward, and was engaged in combat until nine o'clock at night, capturing many prisoners, a piece of artillery, and several regimental standards. Finding the enemy heavily massed on his front, he withdrew to his original lines at one o'clock in the morning; and it was this withdrawal which made Pope telegraph to his Government that the day had been victorious for the Federal arms.

The combat at length died away along the whole line,

and the wearied but heroic Confederates sank to sleep, arms in hand, along the lines which they had so bravely held. But, before the whole army was lost in slumber, small groups of soldiers and officers were seen scattered here and there through the woods, and the solemn tones of the chaplains in their midst showed that they were reporting to that great Captain into whose presence many of them would have entered and found the heavenly rest before the next day's sun had set.

Wearied and worn, travel-stained and begrimed with the smoke and dust of battle, Jackson and his officers, as they assembled around him that night, presented a group whose pale and stern countenances betokened too well the fatigues and anxieties of the past week and their appreciation of the fierce struggle of the morrow. The dead and the dying surrounded their bivouac in the open air, and little was said beyond inquiries and remarks about the events of the day which had been so dearly won. Jackson's surgeon, Dr. McGuire, in speaking to him of the fierce struggle, said, "General, this day has been won by nothing but stark and stern fighting." "No," said Jackson, earnestly; "it has been won by nothing but the blessing and protection of Providence."

General Lee, who had arrived upon the scene of action with Longstreet, now had his foe in his iron grasp, for he could not retreat in safety in front of the Confederate army, and the Southern leader knew well that in a battle victory must perch on his banners. The morning of the 30th, therefore, found Lee calmly awaiting in the lines of the previous day the enemy's attack. The Federals now had Bull Run at their backs and the Confederate army confronting them. The Confederate line of battle was concave,—Jackson, as we have seen, holding the left and Longstreet the right. The artillery was placed on a fine position in the centre. Thus, with its arms spread out, it was prepared to receive the Federals in a deadly grasp.

The Federals did not begin their regular attack upon the Confederate lines until about four o'clock in the afternoon, when, moving from under the cover of a wood, they dashed gallantly forward to the charge. Line after line, brigade after brigade, swept up to the Confederate lines. But the brave troops who defended them held them against the repeated and determined assaults of the enemy. As on the previous day, the fiercest fighting was in and around the cuts,—the Federals obstinately endeavoring to dislodge the Confederates from them, and the Confederates holding them gallantly against fearful odds.

In front of one of these cuts, where the struggle was intensely fierce, and at times almost hand to hand, a Federal flag was seen to hold its position for half an hour within ten yards of a Confederate regimental flag. It went down six or eight times, but was as often raised and waved aloft. · The Confederates again supplied the want of ammunition by stones, with which they fought furiously and effectively. A Confederate officer, in his report of this battle, mentions having seen a Federal soldier killed by a stone thrown by one of his lieutenants. The battle raged with this intense fury on Jackson's lines for about half an hour, when, finding that they were giving way at several points, Longstreet was ordered to reinforce him. But, before he received this order, that able commander, finding that the enemy's advancing lines were exposed to his artillery fire, thundered away at them, and by the slaughter which he made relieved Jackson's men from the pressure upon them. The enemy now began to yield, and a general advance was ordered. The two wings of the Confederate army began to close in upon the Federals, who were now literally in the jaws of death, while the artillery poured an unrelenting fire into their ranks. Their retreat soon became a rout, and their magnificent regiments and brigades dissolved into a horde of men seeking safety in the shelter of the woods to which they were fleeing. Inclosed as they were between Bull Run and the Confederate lines, the slaughter was immense, and ceased only when night put an end to it. Under cover of darkness the Federals escaped across the stream, and a storm which had been gathering for hours and overhanging the scene of carnage burst with pitiless force upon the heads of friend and foe. The day which had been spent by the wearied soldier in a fearful struggle was followed by a night in which but little rest could be found beneath the fierce pelting of the storm.

Jackson's men rose from the ground on the morning of the 1st of September drenched with rain and stiff with cold. They soon had orders to march, and in a few hours were under way. The enemy having reformed their lines on the heights of Centreville, and presenting once more a front, Jackson was ordered to turn their position. As soon, however, as they found that he was moving for that purpose, they resumed their line of march; but when they approached Fairfax Court-House the indefatigable Jackson was found ready to fall on them. A sharp engagement, known as that of Ox Hill, followed, in which the Federals, though successful for a few moments, were finally repulsed, and they resumed their line of retreat. Here, as upon the bloody field of the evening before, the roar of a thunder-storm succeeded that of the battle, and once more the soldiers slept upon the wet earth.

The Confederates lost in this succession of battles over seven thousand men, of which number nearly five thousand belonged to Jackson's corps. On the 1st of September he wrote to Mrs. Jackson,—

"God in his providence has again placed us across Bull Run; and I pray that He will make our arms entirely successful, and that the glory will be given to his holy name, and none of it to man.

"God has blessed and preserved me through his great mercy."

One of Jackson's officers, being at home on furlough, applied for an extension of his leave of absence. A member of his family had just died, and another was dangerously ill, and it seemed almost cruel for him to leave just then his home, so darkened by domestic affliction. Jackson felt for him keenly, and there could be no more striking proof of the warmth of his affections, and of his high sense of duty, than is given in the following admirable letter written in reply to this officer, asking, under such painful circumstances, for an extension of his furlough:

"My dear Major,—I have received your sad letter, and wish I could relieve your sorrowing heart; but human aid cannot heal the wound. From me you have a friend's sympathy, and I wish the suffering condition of our country permitted me to show it. But we must think of the living, and of those who are to come after us, and see that, with God's blessing, we transmit to them the freedom we have enjoyed.   What is life without honor? Degradation is worse than death. It is necessary that you should be at your post immediately. Join me to-morrow morning.

"Your sympathizing friend,

"THOMAS J. JACKSON."

CHAPTER XIII.

SHARPSBURG.

On the morning after the battle of Ox Hill the Federal army had entirely disappeared from sight, and was reported to have passed Fairfax Court-House in full retreat for Washington. Thus the two armies of McClellan and Pope returned broken and shattered to the shelter of the fortified Federal capital, which they had so lately left great in numbers, splendid in equipment, and believing that they could easily sweep every obstacle from their path. The theatre of war was now removed from the interior of the State to the frontier; and in order to prolong this state of affairs, in every way so desirable to the Confederates, General Lee determined to cross the Potomac and draw the enemy away from his base of supplies. Lee's troops, feeble in transportation, lacking clothing, and thousands of them destitute of shoes, with but a scanty supply of the matériel of war, were poorly equipped for an invasion. But their commander had such confidence in their fortitude, energy, and courage that he determined to carry the war, even under these disadvantageous circumstances, across the Potomac, his hope being that the Federals might at least be detained on the frontier until the approach of winter should make their advance into Virginia difficult, if not impossible.

The Confederate army was then put in motion for the

Potomac, and on the morning of the second day after the fight at Ox Hill General Jackson and his braves—who were now jestingly called "foot-cavalry," from the rapidity of their marches—moved forward, without having stopped for more than a day's rest after their long forced marches and hard-fought battles. The first day's march brought them to Dranesville, the second to Leesburg. The whole country now resounded with Jackson's fame, and to gain a glimpse of him was the great desire of all those within whose reach he passed. Old and young vied with one another in doing him honor. The glory which his brilliant achievements had shed upon the Confederate arms, his devoted patriotism, and the singular piety and purity of his character, made him the darling of the nation. The devotion of his countrymen for him was shown in the many touching attentions which he received whenever his line of march led him near their homes. On the occasion of this march through Leesburg he passed a house in the doorway of which stood a lady. Hearing who he was, in her enthusiasm she ran down the steps and out into the middle of the street, where, hastily taking off her scarf, she cast it before the general's horse. Not understanding her motive, and too modest to think that it was to honor him, the general reined up his dun war-horse and looked in amazement from the lady, who had now retreated to the side-walk, to the scarf spread in front of his horse's feet. One of the young officers attached to his staff, and close behind him, seeing his bewilderment, said to him, in a stage whisper, "She means you to ride over it, general." A sweet smile at once overspread his face as he comprehended the honor intended him, and, spurring his horse forward, he gracefully took off his hat as his steed bounded over the scarf. In more than one instance, on his march through parts of the country where he was known only by fame, people rushed forward and threw their arms around his horse's neck.

Jackson's command bivouacked on the 4th of September near the Big Spring, between Leesburg and the Potomac, and on the 5th they crossed that river at White's Ford. At this point the Potomac is about half a mile wide, and flows over a level, pebbly bottom; and here for hours the troops were to be seen crossing the stream. The whole army rushed forward as they came in sight of the river; the infantry waded cheerfully through its waters, and the northern bank resounded with enthusiastic cheers as one detachment after another planted their feet on the Maryland shore. That night they bivouacked near the Three Springs, and the next day reached the vicinity of Frederick City, in Maryland. General Jackson was met by a committee of citizens, who presented him with a horse. At Frederick City he rested from the 6th to the 10th of September. As soon as he had crossed the Potomac, the most stringent orders against straggling from the ranks and against the depredation of property were issued; and so excellent was the discipline in his command that the people of the country suffered in no way from the presence of the Confederate troops. The day after his arrival in Frederick City being Sunday, Jackson attended services held in the German Reformed Church; and the citizens of the place attended their various churches with as perfect a feeling of security as if there had been no invading army in their midst.

In the mean time, the Government at Washington had

been filled with alarm at the passage of the Potomac by the Confederate army, and General Halleck, the commander-in-chief, trembled for the safety of the capital. President Lincoln was no less alarmed, and, at his verbal request, General McClellan was at once placed in command of the Federal army. As General Lee had foreseen, this commander immediately withdrew all of his troops to the north bank of the Potomac. General Lee had also taken for granted that the Federal troops at Harper's Ferry would at once be recalled to Washington upon his advance into Maryland becoming known. And indeed McClellan urged that they should be, but General Halleck declined; and now, with the Confederate army between Washington and Harper's Ferry, all communication between the two places was interrupted.

The whole Confederate army having assembled around Frederick, General Lee called a council of war in which to consult his generals as to the next step to be taken. It had been his intention to carry his army to Western Maryland, establish his communications with Richmond through the Valley of the Shenandoah, and, by threatening Pennsylvania, induce the Federal commander to follow, and thus draw him from his base of supplies. He had supposed that the advance upon Frederick would lead to the evacuation of Martinsburg and Harper's Ferry, thus opening the line of communication through the Valley. This not having occurred, two plans were left to the Confederates: one, to disregard Harper's Ferry for the present, and, choosing a good position, attack McClellan as he advanced; the second, to move the army by different routes through the mountains into Western Maryland, one part of the army to reduce Harper's Ferry, and then the different corps to concentrate and join battle with McClellan. General Jackson was in favor of the first plan, but General Lee of the second, which it was determined to follow. To accomplish the capture of Harper's Ferry with the least possible delay, General Jackson was ordered to proceed with his command to Martinsburg, and, after driving the enemy from that place, to move down the south side of the Potomac upon Harper's Ferry.

To carry out this plan, Jackson left Frederick on the 10th of September, and, passing rapidly through Middletown, Boonsboro', and Williamsport, recrossed the Potomac into Virginia on the 11th. The Federal commander in Martinsburg, on hearing of Jackson's approach, evacuated the town on the night of the 11th, and, retreating to Harper's Ferry, fell into the trap which the Confederate commander-in-chief had set for him. Jackson's cavalry entered the town on the morning of the 12th.

Thus in three summer months he had swept down the Valley, winning the battles of Cross Keys and Port Republic, had fought through the seven days' fighting around Richmond, had turned north to win the battle of Cedar Mountain and to see victory perch once more on the Confederate banners in the second battle of Manassas, and now completed the circuit by entering Harper's Ferry at the mouth of the Valley.

In that loved Valley the trumpet of his fame had given forth no uncertain sound; in its defense his most glorious victories had been achieved, and now, when he returned with fresh laurels interwoven with those won there, he was welcomed back by its grateful people with the wildest enthusiasm. A party of ladies, moved by their admiration for him and their desire to see him, visited him at his headquarters and extended to him the most cordial greetings. One of them begged for one of his uniform buttons. His crimsoned face showed his embarrassment, and, saying, "Really, ladies, this is the first time I was ever surrounded by the enemy," he slipped from their midst.

Jackson paused but a short time in Martinsburg, and, pressing forward the same day, the head of his column came in sight of the enemy about eleven o'clock the next morning (13th), and found them drawn up in force upon Bolivar Heights. These heights, extending from near the Shenandoah to the Potomac, shut Harper's Ferry up in the triangle formed by the union of these two rivers.

General Lee, in his admirable plan for the capture of the Federal force at Harper's Ferry, had ordered General McLaws to advance and seize the Maryland Heights, on the northern side of the Potomac, and General Walker to cross the river and seize the Loudon Heights, on the Virginia side. These movements would shut the Federals up in Harper's Ferry, with no chance of escape. General Jackson, having completed the circuit of sixty miles round by Martinsburg from Frederick to Harper's Ferry, was anxious to know whether Generals McLaws and Walker had arrived at their respective posts, to reach which required only one day's march. He accordingly signaled the Loudon and Maryland Heights, and, receiving no reply, found that he had reached the post assigned him before they had attained theirs. He sent couriers at once to the Maryland and Loudon Heights to report the arrival of Confederate troops there. They returned during the night with the intelligence that McLaws, having swept the enemy from the Maryland Heights, had taken possession of that point about half-past four o'clock in the afternoon (13th), and that General Walker had seized Loudon Heights the same evening. The Federals were now beset on all sides. The night of the 13th, and part of the day of the 14th, were spent by General McLaws in cutting a road by which artillery could be taken up to the Maryland Heights. By two o'clock in the afternoon he had four pieces in position, and he and Walker poured shot and shell into Harper's Ferry and the enemy's camp, spreading great consternation among them. The batteries from the heights, however, could not reach the Federals in their works along Bolivar Heights. On the extreme left of the enemy's line General Jackson observed an eminence held only by infantry. He ordered General Pender, of Hill's division, to seize this position, while Branch and Gregg were directed to march along the river under cover of the night, taking advantage of the ravines cutting the banks of the stream, and establish themselves on the plain to the left and rear of the enemy's position. Both moves were successfully accomplished, and the dawn of day found the Confederates in rear of the Federal line of defense.

At daybreak, General Lawton, who was to support General Hill's advance, moved forward and attacked in front and flank, while McLaws and Walker thundered down upon them from their lofty positions. After an hour's resistance, the Federals hoisted the white flag, and in a short time the Confederates on the Loudon Heights had the extreme satisfaction of seeing the head of General A. P. Hill's column approach the town to take possession of it.

By the capture of Harper's Ferry, eleven thousand prisoners, seventy-three pieces of artillery, and thirteen thousand small arms fell into the hands of the Confederates, besides stores of different kinds.

Most liberal terms of surrender were allowed the prisoners by General Jackson. The officers were permitted to retain their side-arms and all their personal effects on giving parole. They also had wagons and horses lent them to carry their baggage into the Federal lines. The privates were released on parole.

In the mean time, grave events for the Confederate army had occurred in Maryland, which it is necessary now to notice.

When Jackson began his march from Frederick on the 10th, Longstreet and D. H. Hill started the same day, and, crossing the South Mountain, moved towards Boonsboro'. General Stuart was left east of the Blue Ridge, to watch the movements of the enemy. General Hill halted near Boonsboro', to prevent the enemy from escaping from Harper's Ferry by Pleasant Valley, and also to be in supporting distance of the cavalry; while General Longstreet continued his march to Hagerstown. When the Confederates left Fredericktown, the advance of the Federals had been so slow that it was thought that Harper's Ferry could be reduced and the Confederate army again concentrated before it would be called on to confront the Federals. But an unfortunate accident hurried up McClellan's advance and endangered the very existence of the victorious Confederate army. A copy of General Lee's order directing the movements of his army from Fredericktown was dropped in the streets of that town, and fell into McClellan's hands. This paper revealing to him General Lee's plans and the disposition of his troops, he at once determined to disregard the timid orders from Washington urging caution, and, pressing forward with vigor, to fall on his adversaries before they could concentrate and present to him a solid front. The situation of the Confederate army was now one of extreme peril, but not too great, however, for the skill of its heroic commander or for the courage of its brave troops. McClellan began at once to push forward, and on the afternoon of the 13th was reported to be approaching the pass in South Mountain on the Boonsboro' and Fredericktown road. The Confederate cavalry fell back slowly before him, constantly retarding his advance, and thus securing time to the Confederates for preparations to oppose him. Should he succeed in penetrating the mountains here, he would be able to march down Pleasant Valley, fall upon Mc-Laws's rear, and relieve the garrison of Harper's Ferry. General D. H. Hill, being, as we have seen, near Boonsboro', sent back, on the 13th, the brigades of Garland and Colquitt to defend the pass, and advanced later with the rest of his division on hearing that the enemy was near in full force. Early on the morning of the 14th, the enemy, by a road south of the Boonsboro' and Fredericktown road, attempted to force their way to the rear of Hill's position. A fierce conflict ensued, in which the enemy were repulsed, but the gallant Garland fell.

For five hours Hill's small force repelled the repeated assaults of the Federals and checked their advance. In the mean time, Longstreet, hearing of his danger, hurried from Hagerstown, and arrived on the scene of action, with his troops much exhausted, at between three and four P.M. The fighting continued to be spirited until night. On the south of the turnpike the Federals were driven back some distance, and their attack on the centre was repulsed with loss. Their greatly superior numbers, however, enabled them to stretch beyond both the Confederate flanks, and, ascending the mountain, to press down upon their left, which was gradually forced back; while beyond their right a body of the enemy entered Pleasant Valley through Crampton's Gap, where they were only five miles in rear of McLaws.

General Lee now determined to withdraw to Sharpsburg, where he would be on McClellan's flank and rear should he attack McLaws, and in a position, too, to concentrate his own army. The move was effected safely and without interference on the part of the enemy, who were so harassed in their advance by Fitz-Hugh Lee's cavalry that they did not appear on the west side of the pass at Boonsboro' until about eight o'clock in the morning of the 15th. In the mean time, McLaws, with untiring energy, held the Federals in check at Crampton's Gap, while from the Maryland Heights his artillery thundered down upon Harper's Ferry. The surrender of that place was received at nine o'clock on the morning of the 15th of September. General Jackson, having been informed by General Lee of the grave aspect which affairs had assumed, and having been ordered by him to hasten with all speed to Sharpsburg, left General A. P. Hill to receive the surrender of the Federal troops, and set out with the rest of his command for that place by Shepherdstown, leaving orders for Walker and McLaws to follow.

Soon after the arrival of Longstreet and D. H. Hill at Sharpsburg on the morning of the 15th, the welcome news of the fall of Harper's Ferry was received there, and reanimated the courage of the troops. Early on the 16th General Jackson arrived, and General Walker came on the evening of the same day. General Mc-

Laws's movements were embarrassed by the presence of the enemy at Crampton's Gap, so that he did not reach Sharpsburg until the 17th, at a most critical hour of the battle.

Sharpsburg is a village situated two and a half miles east of the Potomac, and one mile west of Antietam Creek. When they reached this place on the morning of the 15th, Longstreet and Hill were placed in position on a range of hills lying between the town and the creek, and nearly parallel to the course of the stream,—Longstreet on the right of the road leading across the creek to Boonsboro', and Hill on the left. McClellan followed the Confederates so slowly, and was so harassed in his advance by Fitz-Hugh Lee's cavalry, that he did not appear on the opposite side of the Antietam until about two in the afternoon of the 15th. During the rest of the day the batteries on each side were slightly engaged.

On the 16th the artillery fire began in earnest, and was kept up with animation the whole day. The Federals crossed the Antietam and threatened the Confederate left. In anticipation of this move, General Lee had ordered Hood to take position on Hill's left, and now General Jackson on his arrival on this day was ordered to place himself on Hood's left,—his own left extending towards the Potomac,—while General Walker went to Longstreet's right. As evening approached, the enemy bore down heavily with his infantry upon Hood, while his artillery thundered away most vigorously. His attack was, however, gallantly repulsed, and the two armies, confronting each other, slept upon their arms that night, to renew the bloody contest with the coming day.

At early dawn on the 17th the Federal artillery opened with great spirit from both sides of the Antietam, the heaviest fire being directed against the Confederate left, which, as we have seen, was held by Jackson. By sunrise the Confederate skirmishers were driven in, and the enemy appeared in immense numbers on Jackson's front. His little band, foot-sore and wearied out by long marches and hard fighting, now numbered only seven thousand men. Against these McClellan hurled the forces under Hooker, Mansfield, and Sumner, numbering, by his own statement, forty-four thousand men, and supported by five or six batteries of rifled guns. This terrible onslaught was sustained by Jackson's veterans with the utmost resolution and gallantry, and for several hours the battle raged with great fury and varying fortune. The murderous fire of the Federals made sad havoc in the Confederate ranks. Three brigadiers, one after the other, were placed *hors du combat*. The gallant General Starke was killed. Officer after officer fell. Yet the Federal lines were repeatedly broken; but, fresh troops being brought up to replace those who were defeated, Jackson's troops were in turn forced back. His shattered lines, reduced to a shadow, sullenly fell back, turning to make a stand wherever the ground offered a good position.

Jackson ordered Early to replace with his brigade a division which, its ammunition being exhausted, had to be withdrawn. Fragments of other commands attached themselves to his brigade and went into action. Hood and Early now held their ground against overwhelming odds. The enemy's lines were broken; but, being reinforced, he again pressed forward, forced back the Confederates, and began to gain ground. But the stubborn resistance of the Confederates retarded their advance until General McLaws arrived on the scene of action,

I.*

and until General Walker could be hurried from the right to the support of the sorely-pressed left. Hood's brigade, diminished in numbers and out of ammunition, withdrew, and was replaced by that of General Walker, who rushed into the attack with spirit, and drove the Federals back with great slaughter. General Early, having in the mean time seen reinforcements arrive under McLaws, dashed forward at the same time, and the enemy were driven back in confusion, closely followed by the Confederates, beyond the position occupied at the beginning of the engagement.

Assault after assault was made by the Federals on the Confederate left, but they were finally repulsed with loss, and, abandoning the attack with infantry, they for several hours kept up an artillery fire, which was sustained with the same coolness and spirit.

The attack on the left was followed by one on the centre, in which the Federals were repulsed, and retired behind the crest of a hill, whence they kept up a desultory fire. At this part of the field, through an unhappy mistake, a Confederate brigade was withdrawn from its position. The enemy, seeing this, pressed forward, and, pouring through the gap thus caused, pierced the Confederate lines. In trying to make a stand against this rush, Generals R. H. Anderson, G. B. Anderson, and Wright were wounded,—the second mortally,—and borne from the field.

General D. H. Hill and other officers rallied a few hundred men to the support of four pieces of artillery, and with these the heavy masses of the enemy were resisted. So firm a front did this small force present (Colonel Cooke, with the 27th North Carolina Regiment of Walker's brigade, standing boldly in line without a cartridge) that, with the assistance of two other batteries, the advance of the Federals was checked, and in an hour and a half they retired.

While the attacks on the left and centre were going on, the Federals were making every effort to force the passage of a bridge across the Antietam, opposite the right wing of General Longstreet, which General D. R. Jones commanded. The bridge was defended by General Toombs with two regiments, and with this small force he repulsed five different assaults of the Federals. In the afternoon the Federals began to extend their line, as if to cross the Antietam below the bridge, and at four P.M. Toombs's regiments retired from the bridge. The enemy immediately crossed over in great numbers, and advanced upon General Jones, who held the crest of the hill with less than two thousand men, and forced him to retire.

In the mean time, General A. P. Hill, who had, as we have seen, been left at Harper's Ferry, received orders from General Lee early in the morning of the 17th to hurry forward to Sharpsburg. By half-past seven his division was in motion, and at half-past two P.M. he reported in person at its head to General Lee on the battle-field of Sharpsburg, having by that hour completed the march of seventeen miles from Harper's Ferry. Never was the arrival of reinforcements to a sorely-pressed army more opportune. Hill was at once ordered to the right. He moved forward to the post assigned him, and threw his troops rapidly into position. He reached the field not a moment too soon. The enemy, advancing from the bridge in three lines, had broken through D. R. Jones's division, captured a battery, and were in the full tide of success. Hill's batteries united their fire with those of General Jones, and one of D. H. Hill's, on the left of the Boonsboro' road. The effect of this concentrated fire was marked: the Federal advance was immediately arrested, and their line wavered. The Confederates saw the happy moment, and eagerly seized it. Toombs was ordered to attack the Federal flank, while Archer, of A. P. Hill's division, with a yell of defiance, charged them in front, recaptured the lost battery, and drove them back pell-mell. A destructive fire was now poured into their ranks by the brigades of Branch and Gregg, of Hill's division. The gallant Branch fell, but the Federals surged back, broke, and retreated in confusion, closely pursued by the troops of Hill and Jones, until they reached the protection of their batteries on the opposite side of the creek. And so ended the struggle.

The shades of night were now gathering over the scene, and the approaches to the stream were swept by a number of batteries massed for that purpose by the enemy. On the opposite shore, too, stood the Federal general Porter, with his corps of fresh troops, ready to dispute the advance of the Confederates. These, exhausted by long marches and the fatigues of the hard-fought battle, had performed prodigies of valor in repelling successfully the attack of so powerful a foe. An advance under these circumstances, in the face of fresh troops, was not to be thought of, and the pursuing troops were recalled and formed on the line held by them in the morning, with the exception of the centre, where it was drawn in about two hundred yards. In this engagement General McClellan's army numbered ninety thousand splendidly-equipped men. General Lee, in his report, gives the following picture of his gallant little band of veterans:

" The arduous service in which our troops had been engaged, their great privations of rest and food, and the long marches, without shoes, over mountain roads, had greatly reduced our ranks before the action began. These causes had compelled thousands of brave men to absent themselves, and many more had done so from unworthy motives. This great battle was fought by less than forty thousand men on our side, all of whom had undergone the greatest labors and hardships in the field and on the march. Nothing could surpass the determined valor with which they met the large army of the enemy, fully supplied and equipped, and the result reflects the highest credit on the officers and men engaged."

The Confederates slept upon their arms on the night of the battle on the field the possession of which they had so determinedly held. The 18th was spent by both armies in burying their dead and removing their wounded. General Lee, finding on that day that McClellan was about to receive fresh troops, determined, in view of the exhausted state of his army, that it would be best not to risk another battle, and accordingly, on the night of the 18th, quietly withdrew his forces to the Virginia side of the Potomac, leaving not a man or a gun behind him, and taking with him all of his wounded except those who could not bear the removal. General Jackson brought up the rear-guard, and for hours he was seen sitting on his horse in the middle of the river watching the passage of his troops across the Potomac; nor did he cross over himself until he had seen the last man and the last gun safely landed on the Virginia shore.

After crossing the Potomac, General Jackson marched his troops four miles up the road towards Martinsburg, and there encamped. On the heights overlooking the

Potomac, General Pendleton was placed with thirty pieces of artillery, with which to defend the passage of the river should the Federals attempt it. They in the mean time had advanced and planted seventy guns on the northern bank, and one of their army corps was soon on the same shore. Under cover of night a detachment crossed the river, surprised the Confederates, and captured most of their guns, their infantry support being seized with a panic and deserting them. General Pendleton went at once to General Jackson's headquarters and reported this disaster, which he believed to be greater than it even was, for he reported the loss of every gun. It is said that General Jackson never during the war betrayed so much anxiety as he did on this occasion, hearing, as he did, that the army had been thus stripped of its artillery. He at once gave orders to effect the recovery of the lost guns. A. P. Hill, with his usual activity, was first on the scene of action, and, forming his troops into two lines, he charged the enemy with great gallantry, and with utter disregard of the shot and shell which were poured into their ranks from the seventy guns on the opposite shore. The Federals tried to resist this sweeping charge, and bore heavily on Hill's left. Upon this, his second line, marching by the left flank, moved from behind the first. The two now charged at the same time, converging upon the Federal troops. Down the hill the Confederates rushed, with a defiant yell, sweeping all before them. Into the river they drove the Federals pell-mell, and then from the bank poured a murderous fire into the confused mass of human beings struggling in the stream. In vain the Federal batteries directed their fire with redoubled fury on the Confederates. They coolly held their ground, and dealt

ASLEEP IN THE SADDLE.

(Page 255.)

death to the unhappy force they had just swept into the river.

The news of the temporary success of the Federals having reached General Lee had excited his alarm for his artillery quite as much as it had roused General Jackson, and he had dispatched two messengers to him to take steps for its recovery, which he had already adopted. The second messenger reached him just as he was watching the repulse of the enemy, and he only remarked, " With the blessing of Providence they will soon be driven back."

In this brilliant engagement, known as that of Boteler's Ford, the Confederate loss was not quite three hundred, while the Federals admitted a loss, in killed, drowned, and prisoners, of over three thousand.

The Confederate army, worn out by long marches and hard fighting, now enjoyed a few days' repose on the banks of the Opequan, near Martinsburg, after which time it was marched to the vicinity of Winchester.

No private or officer had felt the fatigues of this arduous campaign more than Jackson. In the forced marches which were so frequent towards its close, more than once he was so completely overcome with sleep that members of his staff rode beside him and held him on his horse as he rode along half asleep. Several times he stopped, and, dismounting, leaned his head on a fence, and, stretching his arms out on it, slept for five or ten minutes, having ordered his staff to rouse him at the end of that time. He was afraid to lie down, lest he should drop into a slumber so profound as to make it difficult to awaken him.

It was at the end of this campaign that an incident occurred which illustrates his extreme amiability and kindness of heart. An old woman made her way to his headquarters and annoyed the young officers on his staff excessively by saying she had come to see her son John, who was with "Jackson's company." She thought it strange that they could not tell her where "John" was, for he had been with "Jackson's company" in all the battles. The young men were disposed to laugh at her, —when the general appeared, and, hearing her simple story, rebuked them for their manner to her, and had the regiments in his whole corps searched through and John found and restored to the loving arms of his simple-hearted old mother.

CHAPTER XIV.

FREDERICKSBURG.

NEVER were the enchanting days of a Virginia autumn more intensely enjoyed than by the veterans of the army of Northern Virginia as they reposed amid the pleasant fields of the lovely Valley of Virginia. Never had the sweets of rest been so grateful to wearied soldiers as they were to these heroes after an arduous and honorable campaign of several months. General Jackson's fame was now at its height. The love his soldiers bore him knew no bounds, and the enthusiastic cheers which arose from their ranks always announced his appearance. He was affectionately and familiarly spoken of by them as "Old Jack."

This lull in the activities of war was not spent by Jackson in idleness. He busied himself in reorganizing his shattered battalions after the ravages of the terrible campaign through which they had just passed, and he bent all his energies towards having his troops properly armed and clothed. In this he partially succeeded; but, after every effort had been exhausted, many of the men were left barefooted, and in this condition were forced to meet the inclemencies of the approaching winter season.

On the 11th of October the Confederate Government conferred on General Jackson the rank of lieutenant-general. It must be borne in mind that this rank was given to Jackson after the most brilliant achievements of his extraordinary career,—achievements which had placed his name among those of the world's great captains,—and that in this war the splendor of his military career was second only to that of his beloved commander-in-chief; and yet in spite of this brilliant record the authorities placed his name fourth on the list of lieutenant-generals, all of whom were appointed at the same time. Both Jackson's ambition and his sense of justice were wounded by this, and, though too far above all paltry jealousies to complain, yet he felt it keenly, and never forgot it.

After this appointment of lieutenant-generals, General Lee's army was divided into two corps,—Longstreet commanding one, and Jackson the other. Jackson's corps consisted of his old division, commanded by Brigadier-General Taliaferro; Ewell's division, commanded by Brigadier-General Early, who was soon raised to the rank of major-general; A. P. Hill's and D. H. Hill's divisions. There were, besides, a number of batteries thrown into battalions, and placed under the general charge of Colonel Crutchfield, a young officer whose merits General Jackson had quickly discerned, and whose promotion to the responsible position of colonel of artillery he had urged and obtained. With these four fine divisions, and a skillful set of artillerists, his corps was complete, and formed as fine a body of soldiers as any nation could produce.

But, in the midst of reorganization, promotions, and all the absorbing duties of army life during war, his thoughts still turned more devoutly and more enthusiastically to religion than to any other subject. The following letter to Mrs. Jackson affords ample proof of this:

"Bunker Hill, October 13.

"Mr. G—— invited me to be present at communion in his church yesterday, but I was prevented from enjoying the privilege. But I heard an excellent sermon from the Rev. Dr. S——. His text was 1 Timothy, chap. ii., 5th and 6th verses: 'For there is one God, and one mediator between God and men, the man Christ Jesus; who gave himself a ransom for all, to be testified in due time.' It was a powerful exposition of the word of God. He is a great revival minister; and when he came to the word '*himself*,' he placed an emphasis on it, and gave to it, through God's blessing, a power that I never before felt. . . . And I felt, with an intensity that I never before recollect having realized, that truly the sinner who does not, under gospel privileges, turn to God, deserves the agonies of perdition. The doctor several times, in appealing to the sinner, repeated the 6th verse: 'Who gave *himself* a ransom for all, to be testified in due time.' What more could God do than give *himself* a ransom? . . . He is laboring in a revival in General Ewell's division. Oh, it is a glorious privilege to be a minister of the gospel of the Prince of Peace! There is no equal position in this world."

With such deep devotional feelings, General Jackson, of course, took the greatest interest in the labors and success of the army chaplains in their professional duties; and for those chaplains who shirked these duties he had no patience whatever, and was even for bringing them under strict military discipline and forcing them up to the mark.

History tells, perhaps, of no more touching scenes than those given us in the descriptions of the nightly services held in the Confederate army, both on the march and in the camp. In the days of the second battle of Manassas we have seen these nightly services carried on in the lull afforded by night between two hard days' struggle. At the close of this campaign these meetings were attended by unusual numbers. While resting in the Valley of Virginia on their well-earned laurels, officers and men seemed alike to feel that, having been borne safely through such an ordeal as the bloody campaign just ended, they at least owed their Maker daily worship and praise. Thus, night after night, a hymn rising from a little group that the chaplain had assembled around him was the signal that the hour of evening worship was at hand. Then from the different brigades and regiments groups were seen approaching to join this little company, officers of every grade and rank mingling with the privates, until, at last, the mellow light of the October moon shone down on an assemblage of several hundred men, who thus in the midst of all the pomp and pageant of war, surrounded as they were by its grim realities, sat with the meekness of little children at the feet of the Prince of Peace. By the flickering light of a torch the chaplain read the Bible to his numerous and silent hearers, and as the torchlight was reflected upon their uplifted grave and thoughtful faces, —faces in whose stern lines might be read the victories of the Valley, the severer but equally glorious successes around Richmond, the hard-fought field of Manassas, and the stubborn resistance at Sharpsburg,—what inspiration must he not have drawn from the solemnity of the scene, and with what earnestness must he not have uttered the words of truth, of hope, and of consolation!

In promoting the success of the chaplains in their

labors in his corps, General Jackson never stopped to inquire of what denomination they were. It was only necessary for him to know that they were sincere Christians and earnest laborers in the calling which they had undertaken. On one occasion a Roman Catholic priest who visited Jackson's corps wished to have a tent in which to carry on the services of his Church for the benefit of the men in this corps belonging to it. He made application to Jackson for the tent. The general saw no objection to his having it, but, before granting the application, made inquiries concerning the priest and satisfied himself that he was a man of good character. When his attention was again called to the matter, he at once agreed that the priest should have the tent, and added, with some warmth, as if to suppress any objection which might be made to it, "He shall have it, I care not what may be said on the subject."

On the 18th of October General Jackson went to Martinsburg to superintend the destruction of the Baltimore and Ohio Railroad, which afforded the enemy such facilities for the transportation of men and supplies. From a point west of Martinsburg to the neighborhood of Harper's Ferry the track was torn up and destroyed. Bridges were burnt and culverts blown up; and the iron rails after being torn from the track were thrown on heaps of burning logs. Becoming red-hot in the middle, the heavy ends soon dropped, and bent and warped them out of all shape. The soldiers, moreover, seized them by the ends and wrapped them around trees and posts. For thirty miles the track was thus effectually broken up; and, to assure himself that the destruction was complete, General Jackson rode along the whole line.

About this time, in writing to Mrs. Jackson, after

mentioning several presents that he had received, he says,—

"Our God makes me so many friends! I mention these things in order that you may see how much kindness has been shown me, and to express thanks for blessings for which I should be more grateful, and to give you renewed cause for gratitude. . . .

"Don't trouble yourself about representations that are made about me. These things are earthly and transitory. There are real and glorious blessings, I trust, in reserve for us beyond this life. It is best for us to keep our eyes fixed upon the throne of God, and the realities of a more glorious existence beyond the verge of time. It is gratifying to be beloved and to have our conduct approved by our fellow-men; but this is not worthy to be compared with the glory that is in reservation for us in the presence of the glorified Redeemer."

About this time he had an interview with one of his officers with whom he was very intimate, which reveals more even than the above letter the strength and depth of his faith. After having transacted the business on which he had come, the officer was pressed very kindly by the general to resume his seat and spend a few minutes with him, as the evening was dark and rainy and the camp unusually dull. The officer willingly assented, and the conversation soon turned on the subject of religion. The general said, in reply to some remark of the officer, that a man was probably first moved to seek heavenly things both by fear and by love, but that as he was drawn into closer communion with his Lord and Saviour perfect love cast out fear. For his part, he continued, so perfect was his assurance of his own salvation through Christ, so secure was he in his trust in

Him, that he had no dread of the wrath of God, although he felt himself a great sinner, and love of God and Christ was now the motive which led him to a religious life. After this he rose, and, with great humility but solemn elation, said,—

"'Nothing earthly can mar my happiness. I know that heaven is in store for me, and I should rejoice in the prospect of going there to-morrow. Understand me: I am not sick; I am not sad; God has greatly blessed me, and I have as much to love here as any man, and life is very bright to me. But still I am ready to leave it any day, without trepidation or regret, for that heaven which I know awaits me through the mercy of my heavenly Father. And I would not agree to the slightest diminution of one shade of my glory there —' (here he paused, as though to consider what terrestrial measure he might best select to express the largeness of his joys)—'no; not for all the fame which I have acquired, or shall ever win in this world.' With these words he sank into his chair, and his friend retired,— awe-struck, as though he had seen the face of an angel. But he did not fail to notice the revelation made of Jackson's master-passion by nature, in the object he had chosen to express the value of his heavenly inheritance. It was fame! Not wealth, nor domestic joys, nor literature,—but well-earned fame. Let the young aspirant consider, also, how even this passion, which the world calls the most honorable of all, was chastened and crucified in him by a nobler longing."*

So flowed by the tranquil hours of relaxation spent by General Jackson in the lovely region of his beloved

---

* Dabney's Life of Jackson.

Valley of Virginia. But they were drawing rapidly to an end. His tent-pins were soon to be struck, and he to leave forever the country so dear to him, and to move to scenes which are now hallowed to every Southern heart as being those which witnessed the closing acts and the closing hours of his eventful, but, alas! too brief career.

The following extract from General Lee's report best describes the change in the position of the two armies:

"The enemy seemed to be concentrating in and near Harper's Ferry, but made no forward movement. During this time the Baltimore and Ohio Railroad was destroyed for several miles, and that from Winchester to Harper's Ferry broken up to within a short distance of the latter place, in order to render the occupation of the Valley by the enemy after our withdrawal more difficult.

"On the 18th October, General Stuart was ordered to cross the Potomac above Williamsport with twelve or fifteen hundred cavalry, and endeavor to ascertain the position and designs of the enemy. He was directed, if practicable, to enter Pennsylvania, and do all in his power to impede and embarrass the military operations of the enemy. This order was executed with skill, address, and courage. General Stuart passed through Maryland, occupied Chambersburg, and destroyed a large amount of public property; making the entire circuit of General McClellan's army, he crossed the Potomac below Harper's Ferry without loss.

"The enemy soon afterwards crossed the Potomac east of the Blue Ridge, and advanced southward, seizing the passes of the mountains as he progressed. General Jackson's corps was ordered to take position on the road between Berryville and Charlestown, to be prepared to oppose an advance from Harper's Ferry or a movement into the Shenandoah Valley from the east side of the mountains, while at the same time he would threaten the flank of the enemy should he continue his march along the eastern base of the Blue Ridge. One division of Longstreet's corps was sent to the vicinity of Upperville, to observe the enemy's movements in front.

"About the last of October the Federal army began to incline easterly from the mountains, moving in the direction of Warrenton. As soon as this intention developed itself, Longstreet's corps was moved across the Blue Ridge, and, about the 3d of November, took position at Culpeper Court-House, while Jackson advanced one of his divisions to the east side of the Blue Ridge.

"The enemy gradually concentrated about Warrenton, his cavalry being thrown forward beyond the Rappahannock, in the direction of Culpeper Court-House, and occasionally skirmishing with our own, which was closely observing his movements.

"This situation of affairs continued without material change until about the middle of November, when the movements began which resulted in the winter campaign on the Lower Rappahannock."

About this time the Federal Government, having become thoroughly dissatisfied with McClellan, removed him from the chief command of their army, and thus relieved General Lee of the ablest general with whom he had to contend during the war. He was replaced by General Burnside, who was destined to hold his arduous position for but a brief time.

I again quote from General Lee's report to carry on the description of the movements of both armies:

"On the 15th of November it was known that the

enemy was in motion towards the Orange and Alexandria Railroad, and one regiment of infantry, with a battery of light artillery, was sent to reinforce the garrison at Fredericksburg. On the 17th it was ascertained that Sumner's corps had marched from Catlett's Station in the direction of Falmouth (the town on the north side of the Rappahannock opposite Fredericksburg), and information was also received that on the 15th some Federal gun-boats and transports had entered Aquia Creek. This looked as if Fredericksburg was again to be occupied, and McLaws's and Ransom's divisions, accompanied by W. H. F. Lee's brigade of cavalry and Lane's battery, were ordered to proceed to that city. To ascertain more fully the movements of the enemy, General Stuart was directed to cross the Rappahannock. On the morning of the 18th he forced a passage at Warrenton Springs, in face of a regiment of cavalry and three pieces of artillery guarding the ford, and reached Warrenton soon after the last of the enemy's columns had left. The information he obtained confirmed the previous reports, and it was clear that the whole Federal army, under Major-General Burnside, was moving towards Fredericksburg. On the morning of the 19th, therefore, the remainder of Longstreet's corps was put in motion for that point. The advance of General Sumner reached Falmouth on the afternoon of the 17th, and attempted to cross the Rappahannock, but was driven back by Colonel Ball, with the 15th Virginia cavalry, four companies of Mississippi infantry, and Lewis's light battery.

" On the 21st it became apparent that General Burnside was concentrating his whole army on the north side of the Rappahannock. On the same day General Sumner summoned the corporate authorities of Fredericksburg to surrender the place by five P.M., and threatened, in case of refusal, to bombard the city at nine o'clock next morning. The weather had been tempestuous for two days, and a storm was raging at the time of the summons. It was impossible to prevent the execution of the threat to shell the city, as it was completely exposed to the batteries on the Stafford hills, which were beyond our reach. The city authorities were informed that, while our forces would not use the place for military purposes, its occupation by the enemy would be resisted, and directions were given for the removal of the women and children as rapidly as possible. The threatened bombardment did not take place; but, in view of the imminence of a collision between the two armies, the inhabitants were advised to leave the city, and almost the entire population, without a murmur, abandoned their homes. History presents no instance of a people exhibiting a purer and more unselfish patriotism, or a higher spirit of fortitude and courage, than was evinced by the citizens of Fredericksburg. They cheerfully incurred great hardships and privations, and surrendered their homes and property to destruction rather than yield them into the hands of the enemies of their country. General Burnside now commenced his preparations to force the passage of the Rappahannock and advance upon Richmond. When his army first began to move towards Fredericksburg, General Jackson, in pursuance of instructions, crossed the Blue Ridge, and placed his corps in the vicinity of Orange Court-House, to enable him more promptly to co-operate with Longstreet. About the 26th of November he was directed to advance towards Fredericksburg." . . .

Since early in August the Confederate army had

fought, besides minor engagements, the battles of Cedar Mountain, Manassas, and Sharpsburg, and had effected the capture of Harper's Ferry. During that time this army had made a circuit of over three hundred miles, and now found itself once more facing a Federal army whose cry was still "On to Richmond!" from which place they were only sixty miles distant. So vast were the numbers and so complicated the machinery of war of the Federal army that it took six days to effect the passage of the Potomac at Harper's Ferry, at the beginning of this new move on Richmond.

General Jackson transferred his corps from Winchester to Fredericksburg in eight days, two of which were spent in resting the troops on the march. In spite of his strenuous exertions to perfect the equipment of his corps, many of his men were still without shoes, which rendered the march over mountainous roads painful in the extreme. The naked feet, cut and stone-bruised, and in many cases cracked open, rendered marching impossible for many a poor soldier, who was thus compelled to fall from the ranks and be left behind, while the blood left in the tracks of those who pushed on showed with what pain and toil it was done.

Longstreet, as we have seen, had gone before Jackson to Fredericksburg. His corps constituted the left of General Lee's line. Anderson's division rested upon the river at Fredericksburg, with those of McLaws, Pickett, and Hood extending to the right in the order named. General Ransom with his division had charge of Marye's Hill, which was destined to be the object of the enemy's most furious assaults, though it was itself commanded by heights on each side, which the Confederates held. At the foot of Marye's Hill, behind a stone wall, Cobb's brigade and the 24th North Carolina Regiment were stationed.

Jackson's corps formed the right of the Confederate line. Next to Hood, of Longstreet's corps, came A. P. Hill, of Jackson's. His first line, consisting of the brigades of Pender, Lane, and Archer, occupied the edge of a wood. Lane's brigade, thrown forward in advance of the general line, held the woods which here projected into the open ground. Thomas's brigade was stationed behind the interval between Pender and Lane, and Gregg's behind that between Lane and Archer. On the right, on an eminence, General Jackson placed fourteen picked guns, under Colonel Walker. Early's and Taliaferro's divisions formed Jackson's second line,— D. H. Hill's his reserve.

On the north side of the Rappahannock the Stafford Heights command the plain of Fredericksburg. On the south side of the river the low grounds below Fredericksburg spread out into a plain some miles in width, bounded by a range of low wooded hills, which terminate on the lower side in the low grounds of the Massaponax, a creek flowing into the Rappahannock, and on the upper side in a series of bluffs. The plain of Fredericksburg being completely commanded by the Stafford Heights, which were black with Federal artillery, no effectual opposition could be made by the Confederates to the construction of bridges and the passage of the river, which was here very narrow.

General Lee determined, therefore, to guard the river by a force merely sufficient to impede the enemy's advance until his army could be concentrated. Before dawn on the 11th of December the Confederate signal-guns announced that the enemy was in motion, and the troops were instantly at their different posts and the whole army on the *qui vive.* The Federals had begun preparations to throw two bridges across the Rappahannock,—one opposite Fredericksburg, the other a mile below. The Confederates, sheltered in the cellars of houses overlooking the stream, and in trenches, repelled the repeated efforts of the enemy to lay his bridges from daybreak till four P.M., driving his working-parties back with great slaughter. At the lower point, the Confederates, not having the same protection, resisted the enemy until nearly noon, when they were withdrawn, and by about one P.M. the bridge was completed. In a short time one hundred and fifty pieces of artillery from the opposite heights opened a furious fire upon the city, forcing the Confederates to retire from the river-bank at four P.M. They bravely resisted the advance of the enemy into the town until dark, and then were withdrawn.

Throughout the night of the 11th and the day of the 12th the Federals crossed over in great numbers, took possession of the town, and formed on the plain below; but a dense fog which overhung the scene hid their movements from view, and an occasional boom from their cannon alone gave token of their presence. The morning of Saturday, December 13, came, and with it the same dense fog as on the day before. The two armies, though invisible to each other, could hear distinctly the sounds along their separate lines. As the hours of the morning advanced, it became apparent that the mist would soon roll away, and the different generals went to their respective posts. On this day General Jackson rode forth from his head-quarters mounted on his favorite horse,—a large, powerfully-built dun,—and clad in a new suit of uniform, wearing, for the first time since his promotion, the lieutenant-general's hat. He moved down his lines accompanied by his staff, and the group attracted the fire of the Federal sharp-shooters. He pointed out to his staff the point in his line—Lane's position—which the enemy would first attack, as they in reality did, and then passed on to the summit of a commanding hill whence General Lee was watching the movements of the enemy on the plain below. Mr. Dabney, Jackson's biographer, thus describes the scene:

"It was now past nine o'clock, and the sun, mounting up the eastern sky with almost a summer power, was rapidly exhaling the mist. As the white folds dissolved and rolled away, disclosing the whole plain to view, such a spectacle met the eyes of the generals as the pomps of earth can seldom rival. Marshaled upon the vast arena beneath them stood the hundred and twenty-five thousand foes, with countless batteries of field-guns blackening the ground. Long triple lines of infantry crossed the field from right to left, and hid their western extreme in the streets of the little city; while down the valleys descending from the Stafford Heights to the bridges were pouring in vast avalanches of men, the huge reserves. For once, war unmasked its terrible proportions to the view with a distinctness hitherto unknown in the forest-clad landscapes of America; and the plain of Fredericksburg presented a panorama that was dreadful in its grandeur. . . . Lee stood upon his chosen hill of observation, inspiring every spectator by his calm heroism, with his two great lieutenants beside him, and reviewed every quarter of the field with his glass. It was then that Longstreet, to whose sturdy breast the approach of battle seemed to bring gayety, said to Jackson, 'General, do not all these multitudes of Federals frighten you?' He replied, 'We shall see very soon whether I shall not frighten them.'"

The generals soon parted to go to their posts, and the battle opened with a thunderous outburst from the three hundred guns on the opposing hills. Heaven and earth seemed to be at war with each other, so continuous was the boom of the cannon. A young Confederate officer engaged in the battle thus describes it in a letter written a few days after it was fought:

"The whole battle-field was the most dramatic and imposing tableau I have ever witnessed; and indeed the whole spectacle seemed gotten up for our special amusement. The low grounds of the Rappahannock below Fredericksburg spread out into a plain of some miles in width, bounded by a range of low wooded hills, which terminate on the lower side in the Massaponax low grounds, and on the upper in a series of rather high and abrupt bluffs next to the river and above the town. At one point in this line of hills a wooded marsh projects far into the plain.

"Imagine now this long line of wooded hills peopled with men who have inducements, physical or mental, to fight desperately; every little promontory bristling with artillery; the whole line of the railway (which runs at the foot of the hills) and every hedge-row and ditch gleaming with bayonets; and you have what must have been the impressions of the Yankees of our position. Again, stand with me upon one of the same little promontories and look out upon the Yankee lines, and see what we saw. Far upon the left the smoke from the smouldering ruins of the town and Longstreet's camp-fires seem to blend together; while in front, and almost as far as the eye can reach to the right and left, you see the blue-coated Federal lines extended, well armed, well equipped, and seemingly assured of success. Behind them the hills seem crowded with artillery, which can hurl its missiles to the very foot of the hills upon which we stand. The word is given to advance. How gallantly they come on! Not a sound is heard from our side except the sharp cracking of our skirmishers as they fall back slowly before this overwhelming advance. The air seems alive with the whistling shot and shell which the enemy send as precursors to their infantry charge. Suddenly a battery (Walker's) of thirty guns, from just where we are standing, opens upon the column of attack. They falter, and reel, and stagger; they rally, and break, and rally again; but in vain: flesh and blood cannot stand it; they retire routed and confused. At that moment an officer gallops wildly up to General Jackson, and exclaims, in almost breathless haste, 'General, the enemy have broken through Archer's left, and General Gregg says he must have help, or he and General Archer will both lose their position.' The general turned as quietly round and ordered Early's division up to support the centre as if nothing extraordinary had happened. Yet every one said afterwards that this was the turning-point of the day. In about an hour the footing which the enemy had gained in the wood was recovered from them by Trimble and Thomas, and they pursued far into the plain. This was all I saw of the fight."

So eager were the Confederate troops to pursue the retiring Federals that it was difficult to restrain them from rushing madly down to the banks of the Rappahannock itself, and when recalled from the pursuit and

M*

ordered back to their original position, some of the men were seen actually to shed tears of bitter disappointment.

While the enemy were so gallantly repulsed by Jackson on the right, they dashed even more furiously against the unshaken front presented by Longstreet's corps, only to meet, however, with an even more disastrous repulse, and as the shades of evening approached it was seen that another "On to Richmond!" had been most gloriously defeated, and once more victory perched on the Confederate banners.

During a lull in the battle, early in the action, General Jackson, wishing to get a good view of the enemy's position, rode to his extreme right, dismounted, and, followed by his aide, Mr. Smith, advanced on foot far out into the field. Suddenly a sharp-shooter rose out of the tall weeds at about two hundred yards from him, and, deliberately taking aim at him, fired. The ball whistled between the heads of the general and his aide, for they were standing only two paces apart. The general turned to Mr. Smith, and, with his face beaming with humor, said, smiling as he spoke, "Mr. Smith, had you not better go to the rear? they may shoot you."

As the last struggles of the battle were dying away, late in the afternoon, General Jackson was seen sitting silently on his horse, with his watch in hand, counting the minutes before the sun should set, and noting the effect of General Stuart's artillery fire upon the enemy. He was revolving in his mind an advance on the beaten foe. He chafed at seeing them hurled back battered and bruised and yet no effort made to follow up the victory. At length his resolution was taken. He would follow up the day's work with a crushing blow. He instantly gave orders for every piece of artillery to be advanced to the front, and at sunset to move together across the plain, the infantry following in line of battle, and at the first sign of confusion caused in the enemy's lines by the cannonade, the infantry were to charge with fixed bayonets and sweep them into the river. Already the batteries had advanced and were opening fire, while the infantry were forming in their rear, when the general saw that his plan would be impracticable and must be abandoned. The different batteries could not act in concert, and the troops, jaded by the day's fighting, were not fresh enough to renew the action; while the enemy's artillery still swept the field with a terrible fire. Reluctantly, therefore, he countermanded his orders, and the troops slept that night on their arms without further disturbance.

In this battle General Lee had not quite twenty-five thousand men engaged, and his loss was a little over four thousand. The Federals acknowledged a loss of twelve thousand in killed and wounded, and one thousand prisoners.

When the fatigues and duties of the day were finally over, General Jackson went to his tent. There he found his friend Colonel Boteler, who had rendered him such efficient aid in his campaign in the Valley in carrying his dispatches to the Government and there using every effort to have his demands and wishes for his department granted. He offered to share his pallet with the colonel, but did not retire himself until almost midnight, being busily engaged in writing and sending dispatches. He threw himself on his soldier's couch, all uniformed as he still was, and slept soundly for two or three hours, when he rose, lighted his candle, and went back to his writing. The light from the candle shone full in the face of Colonel Boteler, whom he supposed to be asleep, and, noticing this, he rose, and, with all the thoughtfulness of a woman, placed a book in front of the candle, so that his friend's face was shaded from its light.

Jackson was much troubled at the condition of General Gregg, who, lying in a house near by, was rapidly sinking from the effects of a mortal wound received in the battle of the previous day. No one appreciated better than Jackson the noble qualities, both as a man and as a soldier, of this gallant officer, and he felt his fall particularly, for high words had passed between them, and he did not wish the heroic Gregg to die thinking he had any but the kindest feelings towards him. After rising, as we have seen, from a few hours' rest, he sent for his surgeon, Dr. McGuire, and asked if nothing could be done for the dying man. Dr. McGuire replied that, though receiving every attention which medical aid could give, he was beyond the reach of human skill; but that if General Jackson wished him to take a message to him he would carry it. The general said he did not wish to send a message to him, but he would be very much obliged if the doctor would go and see how he was, and satisfy himself that he had everything he could desire. Dr. McGuire went at once to the dying man's bedside and told him that he had been sent by General Jackson to ask how he was. As he spoke, some one entered the room behind him. He looked up, and there in the doorway, in full uniform, stood the tall figure of General Jackson. Carried away by his feelings, he had followed close on Dr. McGuire's footsteps, and entered, unannounced, the chamber of death. The dying soldier was sinking rapidly, but as in the storm of battle, so at the approach of death, his heroic spirit was unshaken by fear, and he calmly awaited his end. Jackson took a touching farewell of him, and then, leaving the house, rode back with Dr. McGuire in silence to his tent.

In ordering his horse to follow Dr. McGuire, the general had wished to mount the same horse which he had ridden the day before, but his servant, Jim, objected positively to the animal being ridden again so soon; and, though the general was as positive in his wish to ride this horse, Jim succeeded in mounting him, in spite of himself, and much to his amusement, on another.

So easily had the Federal army been repulsed that the Confederate generals expected a renewal of the attack on the next day; but, though they could see the Federal line drawn up in battle-array on the plain below, they waited in vain for their advance. Their general-in-chief, Burnside, indeed, wished to renew the attack; but this was so violently opposed by his three leading generals that he had to abandon all thought of doing so.

On Monday, the 15th, a flag of truce was sent by the Federals, asking a few hours' truce between their left and the Confederate right, that they might take care of their wounded, many of whom had been lying on the frozen ground since the day of the battle. The note asking for the truce being signed by a subordinate general, General Jackson refused to grant it unless the demand came authorized by Burnside, that *he* might not, as McClellan had done at Sharpsburg, deny having asked for a truce after having received and enjoyed the benefits of one. The demand soon coming back with the proper authority, it was granted, and then men and officers of the two armies mingled together and discussed amicably the scenes of the late battle.

The Confederates now became more and more impatient for the advance of the Federals, and the different commands were eager to be ordered to the front that they might be ready to meet them. Indeed, so great was the enthusiasm among the troops that D. H. Hill's division, whose turn it was to be relieved from duty on the 15th, sent a written request to General Jackson to be allowed to remain on the front another night, that they might be ready to meet the enemy in the morning. The request was granted, and the morning came; but at their feet lay the plain without a foe, and the town of Fredericksburg abandoned by the enemy, while their regiments were seen once more blackening the Stafford Heights and lying there in security. During the darkness of the night, while a fierce storm was raging, they had abandoned their lines and stolen away across the river. Their retreat was managed with great skill and secrecy, —so silently, indeed, that not one of the hundreds of Confederate sentinels who were on duty that night was aware that there was any unusual move going on along the enemy's lines. Dead men with muskets in their hands were propped up to occupy the vacancies left by the sentinels, to whom the orders for withdrawal were given in whispers by officers who moved from post to post. In such perfect silence did they march through the streets of Fredericksburg that the citizens in their houses did not know what was going on in the streets. A few who opened their doors, candles in hand, to see what was the cause of the muffled sounds outside, were amazed to see the army which had so lately passed through their streets in all the pomp and pride of war, now hurrying along, a bedraggled procession, to reach the banks of the river and cross it in safety. So fearful were they of pursuit that the sight of the citizens standing in their doors with candles in hand alarmed them, and instantly the command, "Put out that light! put out that light!" was whispered by a hundred voices. In their feverish impatience, some of the officers sprang from their ranks, and, rushing forward, snatched away the candles and pushed the citizens back into their houses.

Thus again the fruits of victory slipped from the hands of the Confederates. The town was found to be greatly battered and defaced, but not seriously injured, by the bombardment, and the number of buildings destroyed by it was small. But the pillage committed by the Federal soldiers during the two days which they occupied the city was fearful. Private houses were sacked and private property destroyed in the most wanton manner. Handsomely-furnished houses were, under the hands of the licensed soldiers, speedily disgorged of their contents; mirrors were hurled out upon the pavements; pianos, wardrobes, and other costly pieces of furniture were cut to pieces with axes; while the handsomely-bound volumes which filled the shelves of the libraries were heaped into baskets and thrown into the river.

With the battle of Fredericksburg ended the arduous and, to the Confederates, glorious campaign of 1862. Both armies now prepared to go into winter quarters, the Federals on the northern, and the Confederates on the southern, bank of the Rappahannock. Burnside paid for his defeat by the loss of his position as commander-in-chief of the Federal army, and was soon replaced by General Hooker.

CHAPTER XV.

WINTER QUARTERS, 1863.

AFTER the battle of Fredericksburg there was no
danger of another advance of the enemy for some months
to come. With this battle had closed the campaign of
1862, which had been so glorious for the Confederates,
so disastrous for the Federals. General Lee spent the
interval of rest which followed in perfecting the discipline of his army, and in taking steps to diminish the
number of desertions from its ranks. As far as possible
he had his brave soldiers re-clothed and re-equipped.
Resting upon their dearly-won laurels at the close of a
brilliant and arduous campaign, the Confederate soldiers
found enjoyment even in camp-life in the comfortable
winter quarters with which their ever-watchful chief
had provided them. The rigor of the winter prevented
the enemy from making any move serious enough to
call them from their encampment. The monotony of
camp-life was occasionally broken after a fall of snow
by mock battles between the different regiments, and
even brigades, of the same corps. They attacked one
another's camps with snow-balls, and fought like school-
boys, in companies and regiments, led on by their regular
officers. On one such occasion an officer commanding a
regiment, and not engaged in the sport, which he was
watching, saw an aide galloping towards him at full
speed, and the next moment was greeted by him with

280

the words, " Colonel, to the rescue! —— Regiment has surprised and captured our camp! Camp-kettles and frying-pans are all lost! The officer in command calls for reinforcements!" It is needless to say that the colonel responded to the call in the spirit in which it was made, and, ordering out his officers and men, they were all soon engaged in the snow-ball fight with the wild spirits of school-boys, and gallantly recovered for their sorely-pressed comrades the captured kettles and frying-pans.

Thus merrily for the soldiers the hours of camp-life passed by. To the commanding general they brought, as we have seen, duties which were as faithfully discharged as those of the campaign and field of battle.

To General Jackson, too, this season of repose offered an opportunity, which he eagerly seized, of perfecting the discipline of his own command. The winter quarters for his troops extended from near Guinea's Station towards Port Royal. Moss Neck, the residence of Mr. Corbin, and situated in the midst of his troops, half-way between Fredericksburg and Port Royal, was offered to him for his headquarters, and, after a few days' hesitation, accepted. But he declined to have rooms in the house, for fear of inconveniencing the hospitable family occupying it, and accepted in its stead the use of a cottage on the edge of the lawn. The room on the first floor he occupied as his office, and in the second story his military bed was spread. Near the cottage, which had been used as a hunting-lodge, a large tent was pitched, and served as a dining-room for his military family.

General Jackson's first labor, after seeing that his troops were all comfortably lodged for the winter in huts built by themselves, was to write the reports of his battles, which he had been unable to do during the hurry and fatigues of his arduous campaigns and rapid marches. These reports are written in the calm, simple, soldier-like style of a great captain who needs not words, but the simple statement of facts, to perpetuate his own glory and that of the brave men he so skillfully led. Not a word of exaggeration, not the least deviation from truth, can be detected in them. He had just finished the report of his last battle when he was called to take the field in the execution of the most brilliant move, perhaps, of his marvelous career, whence he rose to report in heavenly spheres to the Captain of Hosts.

One of the first evils which he endeavored to correct in his corps was that of absence from the army without leave. This prevailed to an alarming extent, as may be seen from the fact that one of his brigades reported twelve hundred absentees! He urged that the Committee on Military Affairs should take some steps to put a stop to this evil.

So rigid was he in adherence to duty that he never once left his command during the war. Towards the close of this year he was made happy by the birth of a little daughter. But not even the temptation of meeting Mrs. Jackson and the dear little stranger at the house of a friend could induce him to ask for a furlough. We find him writing to Mrs. Jackson about this time as follows:

"CHRISTMAS, 1862.

"I do earnestly pray for peace. Oh that our country was such a Christian, God-fearing people as it should be! Then might we very speedily look for peace.

"It appears to me that it is better for me to remain

with my command so long as the war continues, if our ever-gracious heavenly Father permits. The army suffers immensely by absentees. If all our troops, officers and men, were at their posts, we might, through God's blessing, expect a more speedy termination of the war. The temporal affairs of some are so deranged as to make a strong plea for their returning home for a short time; but *our* God has greatly blessed me and mine during my absence; and whilst it would be a great comfort to see you and our darling little daughter, and others in whom I take special interest, yet duty appears to require me to remain with my command. It is important that those at headquarters set an example by remaining at the post of duty.

"Dr. —— writes, 'Our little prayer-meeting is still meeting daily to pray for our army and leaders.' This prayer-meeting may be the means of accomplishing more than an army. I wish that such existed everywhere. How it does cheer my heart to hear of God's people praying for our cause, and for me! I greatly prize the prayers of the pious."

With the new year came the news of the occupation again of Winchester by the Federals. The following extract from a letter written to his friend Colonel Boteler, January 21, 1863, will show the deep interest which he took in the Valley and its inhabitants:

"Though I have been relieved from command there, and may never again be assigned to that important trust, yet I feel deeply when I see the patriotic people of that region again under the heel of a hateful military despotism. There are all the homes of those who have been with me from the commencement of the war in Virginia;

who have repeatedly left their families and property in the hands of the enemy, and braved the dangers of battle and disease; and there are those who have so devotedly labored for the relief of our suffering sick and wounded."

And again, in another letter to the same gentleman, he says,—

"It is but natural that I should feel a deep and abiding interest in the people of the Valley, where are the homes of so many of my brave soldiers who have been with me so long, and whose self-sacrificing patriotism has been so long tested."

But though his interest in the Valley, which had been the scene of his brilliant campaigns, was unflagging, yet he felt the relief of not having the responsibility of a separate command, and it was observed that he was much freer from care and in much brighter spirits than he had been when at the head of a separate army.

His reputation attracted many, both of the curious and the patriotic, to visit him, and his countrymen were enthusiastic in their love and admiration for him. Foreigners visiting the Confederacy were always anxious to see the great soldier whose short but brilliant career had invested his name with such a charm for both friend and foe. His visitors always received a courteous welcome from him. They found him a tall, soldierly-looking man, a little grave, perhaps, in his address, but polite and affable, and dispensing with quiet ease and dignity the hospitalities of his plain, soldier's lodgings. He showed great anxiety to contribute to his guests' comfort, and not the smallest thing which could add to it escaped his attention. He always enjoyed a jest, and for this reason found great pleasure in the visits of his comrade-in-arms, General **J. E. B.** Stuart, whose bright, happy temper and unchanging flow of spirits carried mirth wherever he went.

An Englishman who visited Jackson at this time wrote of his visit as follows:

"I brought from Nassau a box of goods for General Stonewall Jackson, and he asked me when I was at Richmond to come to his camp and see him. I left the city one morning about seven o'clock, and about ten landed at a station distant some eight or nine miles from Jackson's, or, as his men call him, 'Old Jack's' camp. A heavy fall of snow had covered the country for some time before to the depth of a foot, and formed a crust over the Virginia mud, which is quite as villainous as that of Balaklava. The day before had been mild and wet, and my journey was made in a drenching shower, which soon cleared away the white mantle of snow. You cannot imagine the Slough of Despond I had to pass through. Wet to the skin, I stumbled through mud, I waded through creeks, I passed through pine woods, and at last got into camp about two o'clock. I then made my way to a small house occupied by the general as his headquarters. I wrote down my name and gave it to the orderly, and I was immediately told to walk in.

"The general rose and greeted me warmly. I expected to see an old untidy man, and was most agreeably surprised and pleased with his appearance. He is tall, handsome, and powerfully built, but thin. He has brown hair and a brown beard. His mouth expresses great determination. The lips are thin and compressed firmly together; his eyes are blue and dark, with keen and searching expression. I was told that his age was thirty-eight; and he looks about forty. The general, who is indescribably simple and unaffected in all his ways, took off my wet overcoat with his own hands, made up the fire, brought wood for me to put my feet on to keep them warm while my boots were drying, and then began to ask me questions on various subjects. At the dinner-hour we went out and joined the members of his staff. At this meal the general said grace in a fervent, quiet manner, which struck me much. After dinner I returned to his room, and he again talked for a long time. The servant came in and took his mattress out of a cupboard and laid it on the floor.

"As I rose to retire, the general said, 'Captain, there is plenty of room on my bed; I hope you will share it with me.' I thanked him very much for his courtesy, but said, 'Good-night,' and slept in a tent, sharing the blankets of one of his aides-de-camp. In the morning, at breakfast-time, I noticed that the general said grace before the meal with the same fervor I had remarked before. An hour or two afterwards it was time for me to return to the station; on this occasion, however, I had a horse, and I returned up to the general's headquarters to bid him adieu. His little room was vacant, so I stepped in and stood before the fire. I then noticed my great-coat stretched before it on a chair. Shortly afterward the general entered the room. He said, 'Captain, I have been trying to dry your great-coat, but I am afraid I have not succeeded very well.' That little act illustrates the man's character. With the care and responsibilities of a vast army on his shoulders, he finds time to do little acts of kindness and thoughtfulness which make him the darling of his men, who never seem to tire talking of him.

"General Jackson is a man of great endurance; he drinks nothing stronger than water, and never uses tobacco or any stimulant. He has been known to ride for three days and nights at a time, and if there is any labor to be undergone he never fails to take his share of it."

General Jackson found himself so situated in his headquarters at Moss Neck that he could indulge the domestic tastes of his nature, and particularly his fondness for children, in a way which he had not done since he had left his quiet little home in Lexington. The children in Mr. Corbin's family soon became his pets, and on one of them particularly, little Jane Corbin, he lavished his attentions and caresses. The child—who was only six years old—soon became such a pet that the general begged her mother to send her to him every evening after the labors of the day were ended, and thus his hours of relaxation were spent in playing with this fair young child. They romped, played, or talked together, and often the general's laughter was heard mingled with that of the little girl. Whenever she went to him she found him with some little present ready for her,—a cake, an orange, a bit of candy, or a toy. One evening she arrived, and he had no present ready for her. While looking around to see what his scanty quarters contained that he might offer her, the gilt band on a new cap which Mrs. Jackson had just sent him caught his eye. With his knife he ripped it off, and, placing it around her head, said, as he stood off and admired her, "This shall be your coronet!"

Thus the great captain, whose fame was now wafted upon every gale, danced this little girl upon his knee, while unconsciously the sands of both were running low, for just before he went into that battle from which he was to return to die, she fell a victim to scarlet fever, and passed to the realms of the blessed, too soon to be joined by her loving hero. The gilt band with which he had crowned her young head is now prized by her widowed mother as a memento alike of her child and of her country's great soldier.

From the letters which he wrote during the winter to Mrs. Jackson I make the following extracts:

"Our ever-gracious heavenly Father is exceedingly kind to me, and strikingly manifests it by the kindness with which He disposes people to treat me." (After mentioning a number of presents which he had received, he says,) "And so God, my exceeding great joy, is continually showering his blessings upon me, an unworthy creature.

"I hope to have the privilege of joining in prayer for peace at the time you name, and hope that all our Christian people will; but peace should not be the chief object of prayer in our country. It should aim more specially at imploring God's forgiveness of our sins, and praying that He will make our people a holy people. If we are but his, all things shall work together for the good of our country, and no good thing will He withhold from it." . . .

"If I know my unworthy self, my desire is to live entirely and unreservedly to God's glory. Pray that I may so live." . . .

"January 17, 1863.

"I derive an additional pleasure in reading a letter, resulting from a conviction that it has not been traveling on the Sabbath. How delightful will be our heavenly home, where everything is sanctified!"

" January 22.

" I regret to see our Winchester friends again in the hands of the enemy. I trust that, in answer to prayer, our country will soon be blessed with peace." . . .

" Our heavenly Father is continually blessing me with presents. He withholds no good thing from me."

" February 3.

" I trust that in answer to the prayers of *God's people* He will soon give us peace. I haven't seen my wife for nearly a year, and my home for nearly two years ; and I never have seen my sweet little daughter. . . . My old brigade has built a log church ; as yet I have not been in it."

After an allusion to some presents which he had received from London, he says,—

" Our ever-kind heavenly Father gives me friends among strangers. He is the source of every blessing, and I desire to be more grateful to Him.

" To-morrow is the Sabbath. My Sabbaths are looked forward to with pleasure. I don't know that I ever enjoyed Sabbaths as I do this winter. I do hope, trust, and pray that our people will religiously observe the 27th day of next month as a day of humiliation, prayer, and fasting, as the President has designated in his proclamation."

General Jackson interested himself greatly this winter in getting chaplains for regiments which had none, and also in trying to arouse more zeal in those chaplains who were with the army, for while there were many who stood to their posts like men, and faithfully discharged their duty, there were others who often shirked it, and frequently left the army without sufficient cause. At his invitation, a Presbyterian clergyman, Mr. Lacy, became General Jackson's chaplain, and came to his headquarters the 1st of March. About the middle of this month General Jackson moved his quarters to Hamilton's Crossing, near which place the chaplain preached in an open field every Sunday. A rude pulpit had been there prepared for him, and around it seats were placed. Here every Sunday General Jackson came to attend worship, and here, too, was often seen the majestic figure of General Lee. Other distinguished generals and officers in the Confederate army soon followed their example, until from a few hundred the number of these worshipers in the open air was swelled to thousands. There the private's plain gray jacket was seen beside the brilliant staff uniform of a major- or lieutenant-general, —all ranks being leveled while adoring the great Father of all.

General Jackson established the custom in his corps of having a weekly meeting of the chaplains to consult over their duties and report the progress of the good work they were engaged in. Whenever his chaplain returned from one of these meetings, the general would summon him to his presence, and greet him, as he entered, with the words, "Now come and report." He listened with the deepest interest, and often with tears in his eyes, to the account of the interest in religion which the men in the army showed.

The soldiers soon began to erect log chapels in which these services were held. The Stonewall Brigade first built such a chapel, and its example was soon followed by others. In these rude little chapels prayer-meetings were held during the week; here the men were taught, in the weary hours of camp-life, to study the Bible, and here they frequently met to sing hymns. The chapel of the Stonewall Brigade being near his quarters, General Jackson often went to attend the services held there. On such occasions, taking his seat among his war-worn veterans, he would refuse to sit higher up in the little chapel, insisting that the men should crowd around him as they did around one another in their eagerness to hear the preacher's words.

After establishing his headquarters at Hamilton's Crossing, he had prayers with his mess every morning, conducting these himself when his chaplain was not present. The members of his staff knew too well how much pleasure their attendance on such occasions gave him for any of them to be often absent. At his headquarters also a prayer-meeting was held every Wednesday and Sunday night. Several members of his staff, being fond of sacred music, gratified him by singing hymns on Sunday afternoons, and often he would say, as they were ceasing, "Now let us have the hymn,—

> "'How happy are they
> Who their Saviour obey.'"

Just before moving to Hamilton's Crossing, he wrote to Mrs. Jackson as follows:

"March 14, 1863.

"The time is about come for campaigning, and I hope early next week to leave my room and go into a tent near Hamilton's Crossing, which is on the railroad, about five miles from Fredericksburg. It is rather a relief to get where there will be less comfort than in a room; as I hope thereby persons will be prevented from encroaching so much on my time. I am greatly behind in my reports, and am very desirous of getting through with them before another campaign commences."

To a cousin he wrote on the 2d of April,—

"I have a daughter, and have named her Julia, after mother. I don't suppose you have any recollection of mother, as she has been dead nearly thirty years. In the summer of 1855 I visited her grave in Fayette County. My wife and daughter are staying in North Carolina.

"I hope that you are a Christian: there is no happiness like that experienced by a child of God."

About the middle of April his heart was gladdened by a visit from the wife whom he had not seen for nearly a year, and the "sweet little daughter" whom he had never seen, and for whom his heart was filled with such tender yearnings. Mrs. Jackson, who had been awaiting in Richmond his permission to visit him, at length received the joyful summons to do so. A cold rain was falling as the train neared Hamilton's Crossing. It had scarcely come to a stand-still when, quietly entering and moving through the crowd assembled at the door, was seen the tall, commanding figure of General Jackson. Cap and cape were both dripping with the rain through which he had ridden. His eager eye soon found the mother and child whom he was so fondly expecting, and in a second he was beside them. The child he had expected to find a frail, delicate little fledgling; for more than once since its birth he had been made anxious by hearing of its sickness, and the mother, as if to prepare a surprise for him, had refrained from telling him into what a rosy cherub she had bloomed. His delight and admiration, then, knew no bounds when she looked up at

him with the fresh and bright countenance which infants
wear when just awakened, as she then was, from a long
and refreshing slumber. An eye-witness says it would
be impossible to imagine a picture of greater delight than
he presented as he gazed in astonishment and admiration
at her, but fearing to take her in his wet but loving
arms.

" His first care, after the accustomed salutation, was to
get the mother and child safely through the crowd and
rain into the carriage which was to convey them to their
temporary home (a gentleman's house near Hamilton's
Crossing). Arrived there, he divested himself of his
wet overcoat, and, taking his baby in his arms, caressed
it with tender delight, exclaiming upon its beauty and
size. Henceforth his chief pleasure was in caressing
her, and he was several times seen, while she was sleeping, kneeling long over her cradle, watching her with a
face beaming with admiration and happiness." *

But, though his devotion for the little one knew no
bounds, yet, with the true soldier's ideas of discipline, he
had no notion of her escaping her share of military restraint. Of this we have ample proof in the following
amusing and characteristic incident, which I have from
the child's mother.

Being one day present when the child was having—as
infants so often do—a fit of passionate crying, he looked
on in amazement at its being considered by both nurse
and mother as one of the ills of babyhood, for which
there was no remedy, and which was to be regarded as
a matter of course. The child had begun to scream because it wished to be taken from the bed on which it

---

* Dabney's Life of Jackson.

was lying, and once under way it continued to cry. The astonished general watched the scene in silence for a few minutes, and then, rising, said, in a quick, rather annoyed tone, " Oh, this will never do!" and, taking the child, laid her back on the bed, and would not take her up until she ceased crying. If she began again on being taken up, he placed her back on the bed, where she remained until again quiet. And thus, when only five months old, the little Julia was taught her first lesson in self-control, and for the first and last time was the object of paternal discipline. What a picture this offers us! The great captain, whose thoughts and time were devoted to the discipline and guidance of thousands of gallant soldiers, stooping in the midst of his cares and responsibilities to train an infant a few months old!

It was during these happy days, when he was enjoying this visit from his wife and child, that he sat for the last picture which was taken of him. The photographer came and asked permission to take his picture. He at first objected, but, the artist pressing his request, and Mrs. Jackson urging him to grant it, he at length yielded. Mrs. Jackson hastily smoothed his hair while t' e artist placed his instrument in position in the hall of the house where they were staying, and the result was the fine three-quarters face and head with whose classic outlines every Southerner is now so familiar, and which adorns the walls alike of the cottage and of the palace, of friend and of foe. A stream of light falling on the general's face during this sitting caused a slight contraction of the brow, which gives to the picture a rather sterner look than was natural to him.

The general's devotion to his child was remarked upon by all who saw them together, and an officer's wife who saw him often during this time, in a letter to a friend in Richmond, says, "The general spends all his leisure in playing with the baby."

But these last happy, peaceful days were rapidly passing away. The hour was near when the warrior was to leave the caresses of his infant daughter to rush into battle and for the last time lead his gallant little band to victory. It was the giant's last struggle; but, as he fell, the evening breeze bore the shouts of victory to his ears, which—alas for his country!—were so soon to be filled with the sweeter strains of celestial music.

CHAPTER XVI.

CHANCELLORSVILLE.

WITH the first warm days of early spring the enemy began to move in his winter camps and fortifications, and the Confederate leaders knew that the Federal general would soon lead his powerful army across the Rappahannock, to repeat the oft-renewed attempt to break through the Confederate lines and march on to Richmond.

Ever since the battle of Fredericksburg, a thorough system of scouts had enabled General Lee to know, in a few hours after its occurrence, every change in the Federal army. Moreover, the alphabet of the Federal signals having been discovered, the Confederate signal-officers could read every order and message sent from the Federal general's headquarters, and near General Lee's headquarters at Moss Neck a signal-party was kept constantly on duty to take down the messages transmitted through a signal-station on the other side of the river.

How well General Lee employed the inactivity of the winter months to get his army in fine fighting order for the spring campaign is seen from the following extract : *

---

* This is taken from " The Battle-Fields of Virginia—Chancellorsville," a most valuable and interesting historical tract, by two able officers of the Army of Northern Virginia, Captain

"A long interval of quiet now intervened. For more than two months the condition of the roads rendered any important movement impracticable. Both leaders devoted this time to improving the discipline, perfecting the organization, and filling up the ranks of their armies. Lee addressed himself assiduously to his task. His attention was first turned to supplies and equipment. All the available means for the purpose were put into requisition. Agents were sent out through the country drained by his army, and, in conjunction with the authorities at Richmond, gathered supplies in every quarter. These were collected at various depots convenient to his troops. And when the usual method of procuring supplies by purchase and the tithe failed, General Lee issued an appeal to the people, which soon filled his commissariat. The reserve artillery and all the surplus transportation of the army were sent to the rear, where it was more easy to forage them. The arsenals at Richmond were kept constantly at work to re-equip his army and arm the men coming in. Much of his field-artillery was replaced by new and improved guns. Careful attention was bestowed upon discipline. Many regulations were introduced to promote that system and order which is the life of armies. When the weather permitted, the troops were constantly engaged in field exercises. Prompt measures were taken to prevent desertion, and those who had deserted were brought back in large numbers. The number of absentees from various causes was very great in the beginning of the year. By the spring it was re-

---

Hotchkiss, late Topographical Engineer of the Second Corps, and Colonel William Allan, late Lieutenant-Colonel and Chief of Ordnance of the Second Corps.

N*

duced more than half. The Conscription Act, now fairly put into operation, increased the strength of the army daily. Jackson's corps grew in three months from twenty-five to thirty-three thousand muskets. . . .

"The splendid *morale* of this army did not need improvement, but it enabled it to bear without injury the privations and hardships of the winter. Insufficient clothing and scanty rations produced no effect upon it. When the spring opened, General Lee found himself at the head of an army unsurpassed in discipline, and all the hardy virtues of the soldier, strengthened by the additions of the winter, reinvigorated by the compactness and order which had been given to its organization, with an enthusiasm acquired by a long series of victories, and ready to add to that series a triumph more remarkable and illustrious than any of its predecessors."

The Federal general was equally assiduous during this period of rest in re-organizing and disciplining his army. Its condition when General Hooker took command may be easily imagined from the fact that he found absent nearly three thousand commissioned officers, and over *eighty* thousand non-commissioned officers and privates. He saw at once the need of an effective cavalry force, and succeeded in having one organized. To try their mettle, a cavalry division, under General Averill, was sent to cross the Rappahannock at Kelly's Ford on March 17. They there found a small Confederate picket of twenty men, which they easily drove in, and, crossing the river in safety, moved on in the direction of Culpeper Court-House. General Fitz-Hugh Lee, who was near the railroad bridge with the greater part of his brigade, marched to meet the advancing column. He came up with General Averill a mile from the ford. A sharp and severely-contested struggle followed, in which, owing chiefly to the skillful handling of the artillery under that accomplished young officer Major Pelham, the Confederates were victorious, and the Federals withdrew and re-crossed the river. In this fight fell young Pelham, deplored alike by his comrades-in-arms and his country. In history he will live under the title of "the gallant Pelham," given him by General Lee after the battle of Fredericksburg, while by his countrymen he will be ever remembered with the tender love and gratitude which made them give him, while living, the appellation of "the boy hero."

After the fight at Kelly's Ford, no further demonstration was made by the Federals until the great struggle around Chancellorsville, with which they opened the campaign. General Lee, knowing early in April that Hooker was ready and anxious to move, hurried up his preparations to meet him.

So stood matters on the eve of the opening of the campaign. Both sides were braced up for the struggle, and both were eager for it to begin. The Federal army numbered one hundred and twenty-three thousand men and four hundred pieces of artillery; the Confederate army, one hundred and seventy pieces of artillery and fifty-eight thousand men, being decreased in numbers about one-fourth by the absence of Longstreet with two of his divisions, he having been sent to Suffolk.

General Jackson grew more impatient for the hour of combat to come as the time for it drew near. On one occasion, after listening to an account given by one of his officers of the gigantic scale of the enemy's preparations for the coming campaign, and of the eagerness of the Confederate soldiers for it to begin, he sprang to his feet, and, showing more excitement than was his wont, exclaimed, " I wish the enemy would come on !" Then, raising his eyes to heaven, he said, in a subdued tone, " My trust is in God."

In speaking of the campaign, he would say that the Confederates ought to make it a very active one; that it was only in that way that they could make up for their want of strength; and he would add that Napoleon never waited for his adversary to become fully prepared, but struck him the first blow.

Early on the morning of the 29th of April an officer came to the house where the general was staying, and asked for him. The general, on being aroused, said, as he was preparing to go down, " That sounds as if something stirring were afoot." In a few minutes he returned, and told Mrs. Jackson that General Early had sent his adjutant to inform him that Hooker was crossing the river in force. He then told her that they were on the eve of great events, and he would have to go at once and watch the enemy's movements; if they were threatening, the house where she then was would be no place for herself and child, and she must be prepared to leave for Richmond should he send word to her to do so. If possible, he would come back and see her off; but if he could not do this, he would send one of his aides. Fearing that he might not be able to return, he bade her and the little Julia adieu, and, mounting his horse, rode to the front. Finding on his arrival there that he could not return to Mrs. Jackson, he sent her brother, his aide, Lieutenant Morrison, to take her to Guinea's Station, where she would leave for Richmond. This young officer, impatient to return to the front, placed Mrs. Jackson under the care of Mr. Lacy, the chaplain, and hurried back to the lines. Mrs. Jackson left for Richmond filled with anxiety and gloomy apprehensions about the general, knowing so well as she did the terrible nature of the storm and struggle over which he was to be, under his great chief, the presiding spirit.

As soon as General Jackson found that the Federals were crossing the river, he sent one of his aides to inform General Lee of the move. The officer sent found General Lee sitting in his tent, and in reply to the message he said, " Well, I heard firing, and I was beginning to think it was time some of you lazy young fellows were coming to tell me what it was all about. Say to General Jackson that he knows just as well what to do with the enemy as I do."

After getting his corps under arms, and seeing the numbers in which the enemy was crossing, General Jackson suspected that this move was only a feint, intended to cover a move in some other direction. And such, indeed, proved to be the true state of the case, for General Stuart, whose cavalry pickets extended far up the Rappahannock, soon reported the movement of Federal troops, which showed that they would attempt to cross the Rappahannock farther up that stream, and some miles west of Fredericksburg.

Hooker's plan was as follows. The force crossing the river below Fredericksburg, and commanded by General Sedgwick, was designed to attract the attention of the Confederates, while with the rest of his forces Hooker would move rapidly along the northern bank of the Rappahannock, cross that stream at Kelly's Ford above its junction with the Rapidan, and, pushing across the country, cross the last-named stream at Ely and Germanna Fords, and move back in the direction of Fredericksburg, establishing and fortifying himself in the Wilderness, on General Lee's flank.

These movements he proceeded rapidly to execute. His men started on the march with eight days' rations in their haversacks, and the army was put in motion, the advance reaching Kelly's Ford on the evening of the 28th of April. On the 29th they reached Ely's and Germanna Fords, on the Rapidan.

In the mean time, General Stuart, being between the two rivers, in command of the small force of twenty-seven hundred cavalrymen, hung with these upon the flanks of the enemy, skirmishing with them until he found out their strength and the direction of their march, and then, crossing the Rapidan, he re-established his connections with General Lee. The main body of the Federal cavalry had already broken through the Confederate lines, and was gone, moving south, and evidently intent on a raid into the heart of the country.

So stood matters when General Jackson was summoned by General Early on the morning of the 29th to witness the Federals crossing the river below Fredericksburg. On the same morning the Federal forces crossed the Rapidan at Germanna and Ely Fords, and marched down towards Chancellorsville, which place is fifteen miles west of Fredericksburg.

General Lee, not aware of these movements, awaited the development of the enemy's plans, having stationed above Fredericksburg McLaws's and Anderson's divisions, the only two of Longstreet's corps which he had left with him. By the evening of the 29th, General Stuart sent him positive information of the enemy's movements. He at once sent Anderson to Chancellorsville. That general occupied the place that night, but hearing that the Federals were moving on it in large force, he prepared to withdraw in the morning.

Early in the morning of the 30th the Federal forces coming from the Rapidan marched towards Chancellorsville. Approaching that place, their skirmishers fell in with the rear-guard of Anderson, who had begun to withdraw at daylight in the direction of Fredericksburg, and took position at the junction of the Mine and Plank roads. On the evening of the 30th, General Hooker issued a general order congratulating his troops on the success of their movements, and moved his headquarters to Chancellorsville, where he took command in person, and where he was massing his troops.

McLaws was ordered at midnight by General Lee to move in the direction of Anderson and take position on his right. Jackson was ordered to move at daylight with three of his divisions in the same direction, leaving General Early to defend the works from Fredericksburg to Hamilton's Crossing.

McLaws arrived on Anderson's right at daylight. General Jackson set his column in motion at three o'clock in the morning, and thus escaped the notice of the enemy near Fredericksburg, who had tried to discover the movements of the Confederates by means of balloons, which they were continually sending up. Jackson reached Anderson by eight A.M. on the same morning, May 1, and at once ordered a general advance. Hooker, in the mean time, had ordered the same move on the part of his troops, and the Confederates accordingly had advanced but a short distance on the old turnpike leading to Chancellorsville, when they met the Federal cavalry, which they drove in; but, the Federal troops soon appearing in full force, the Confederate skirmishers were in turn driven back, and both sides made their dispositions for battle. The Federals stoutly resisted General Jackson's advance, until, by a move ordered by him, their flank was threatened, when they began a precipitate retreat. The victorious Confederates pushed after them as they went back to the position from which they had advanced in the morning, and followed them closely to their breastworks, which were from half a mile to one mile from Chancellorsville. The strength of the enemy's position there General Lee thus describes:

"Here the enemy had assumed a position of great natural strength, surrounded on all sides by a dense forest, filled with a tangled undergrowth, in the midst of which breastworks of logs had been constructed, with trees felled in front, so as to form an almost impenetrable abatis. His artillery swept the few narrow roads by which the position could be approached from the front, and commanded the adjacent woods."

As soon as the strength of the enemy's position was ascertained, it became apparent that to attack them there would be a useless waste of life; and accordingly nothing more than skirmishing was done along the line at the close of this day, Friday, May 1.

On the left of the plank road, just where it was crossed by the Confederate line, rose a small hill, its summit covered by a group of pine-trees, whose fallen leaves, together with the dry sedge on the ground, formed an inviting spot for a bivouac. Here Lee and Jackson bivouacked with their respective staffs on the night of Friday, May 1. Here the two generals sat beneath the pine-trees, through which the wind sighed, while the moon shone down in full splendor on places whose solitude forty-eight hours before had been broken only

MEETING OF GENERALS LEE AND JACKSON BEFORE CHANCELLORSVILLE. (Page 304.)

by the song of the whippoorwill or the cry of the owl, but which were now alive with soldiers, many of whom were sleeping their last earthly sleep, for with the morrow the musket and the cannon would again begin their work of destruction. The two generals felt that they were on the eve of great events, and the gravity of the situation rested in all its weight upon them. What was to be done? The situation of affairs was indeed serious. Lee's army was diminished one-third by the absence of Longstreet and two of his divisions. The Federal general Averill had broken through the Confederate lines with his well-trained and fine body of cavalry, and was moving rapidly southwards, evidently bent on an extensive raid, and on cutting off, if possible, Lee's communications with Richmond. Early was obliged to be kept at Fredericksburg and to present a bold front with his seven thousand men to Sedgwick in order to conceal Jackson's departure. This left but forty-three thousand men with whom to confront Hooker's overwhelming force in his magnificent position. The strength of this last at Chancellorsville—which consisted of but one brick house—has already been described. From this point on his left Hooker's line ran back west parallel to the plank road to the vicinity of Wilderness Church, two miles distant. The Eleventh Corps, commanded by Howard, held the right. The whole of this line ran through an almost impenetrable forest of scrubby oak and pine, which is fitly termed "the Wilderness." Once in its depths, it was difficult to find a way out, and more difficult still to know what was going on at a distance of even a hundred yards.

The encounter of the day which had just ended made it manifest that Hooker could not be dislodged from this position by an attack on his splendidly fortified left. Anxiously did the two Confederate leaders consult on that memorable night as to the next move to be made, —a move on which they felt that the fate of their armies hung. The presence of Jackson and his forces on Hooker's front could not long be concealed from the Federal general, and with each hour he was adding strength to his position and numbers to his already overwhelming force. He must be attacked, and at once, or all would be lost for the Confederates. Both generals felt this; and, in view of Hooker's almost impregnable position on his left, General Lee had already ordered his cavalry to reconnoitre the Federal right and see what could be done there. The vigilant Stuart soon accomplished this reconnoissance, and joined Generals Lee and Jackson during the night in their bivouac under the pine-trees. He reported that Hooker had ninety thousand men massed around Chancellorsville, and had his line fortified on the east, south, and southwest, but that on the west and northwest it was unprotected by fortifications, while the absence of Averill with the Federal cavalry rendered it particularly exposed to a flank attack. Here, then, was found what Lee and Jackson were so anxiously looking for,—a weak point in the enemy's lines; and they prepared to pounce upon it with all the swiftness and ferocity with which the eagle falls from the clouds on its unsuspecting prey.

It having been agreed to attack the Federals on their right, the two generals sought repose after the fatigues and anxieties of the day. General Jackson, unmindful of everything save the great events so soon to follow, had left his quarters in the morning without his blanket or overcoat. He therefore lay down at the foot of a pine-tree, to encounter without covering the heavy dews and the dampness of the night air. His adjutant, Colonel Pendleton, seeing this, offered and pressed him to take his overcoat, but the general politely though positively declined it. Young Pendleton then took from the coat its large cape and spread it over his general. Jackson waited until Pendleton was asleep, when, rising, he took the cape and silently and tenderly spread it over the prostrate form of his adjutant, after which he once more lay down at the foot of the tree. He awoke after an hour or two, pierced by the cold and chilled to the bone. This was his last bivouac.

" When his chaplain awoke in the morning, before the dawn of day, he perceived a little fire kindled under the trees, and General Jackson sitting by it upon a box, such as was used to contain biscuit for the soldiers. The general knew that his former pastoral labors had led him to this region, and desired to learn something from him about its by-roads. He therefore requested him to sit beside him on the box, and, when the other declined to incommode him by so doing, made room for him, and repeated, 'Come, sit down; I wish to talk with you.' As he took his seat, he perceived that Jackson was shuddering with cold, and was embracing the little blaze with expressions of great enjoyment. He then proceeded to state that the enemy were in great force at Chancellorsville in a fortified position, and that to dislodge them by a front attack would cost a fearful loss of life. He wished to know whether he was acquainted with any way by which their flank might be turned, either on the right or the left." *

---

* Dabney's Life of Jackson, pp. 675, 676.

After some further conversation with his chaplain about the roads, General Jackson at daybreak dispatched two of his staff to find out if there was a road by which he might swiftly and secretly pass round the flank of Hooker's army.

"The needed information was soon obtained. Seated upon two cracker-boxes, the débris of an issue of Federal rations the day before, the Confederate leaders held their consultation. With a map before him, General Jackson suggested an entire circuit of the right of the opposing army, and that the attack be made on its rear. Lee inquired with what force he would do this. Jackson replied, 'With my whole corps, present.' Lee then asked what would be left to him with which to resist an advance of the enemy towards Fredericksburg. 'The divisions of Anderson and McLaws,' said Jackson. For a moment Lee reflected on the audacity of this plan in the face of Hooker's superior numbers. With less than forty-two thousand muskets he was in the presence of sixty thousand. To divide his army into two parts and place the whole Federal force between them was extremely hazardous. But it was impossible to attack the Federal position in front without terrible loss. The very boldness of the proposed movement, if executed with secrecy and dispatch, was an earnest of success. Jackson was directed to carry out the plan." *

He had ascertained that by sweeping around in front of Hooker's line and round his right he would, after a circuit of fifteen miles, reach the old turnpike road at a point several miles west of Hooker's right, whence he could fall upon his flank and rear. General Lee's con-

---

* Battle-Field of Virginia—Chancellorsville, pp. 41, 42.

sent to this plan being given, orders for the march were immediately issued, and the whole corps was soon in motion, Rodes, commanding D. H. Hill's division, leading the march. By sunrise General Jackson appeared at the head of his column at Catherine Furnace, a mile and a half distant from the place where he had spent the night. The proprietor of the furnace urged him to stop and breakfast, but, declining his hospitality, he busied himself in pushing forward the advance of his troops.

Meanwhile, General Hooker, as had been determined upon the night before, was awaiting in his lines the Confederate attack. Some of his scouts, mounted in the tops of the highest trees southeast of Chancellorsville, caught a glimpse of Jackson's corps as it was passing the furnace. They immediately reported this movement of the Confederate forces to General Hooker, who was at the time examining in person his position. He at once suspected its object, and, on his return to headquarters at nine in the morning, he sent orders to his officers commanding on the right to be on their guard. He hoped, however, that this move on the part of the Confederates was in reality a retreat; and when finally the column disappeared, moving southward, this hope seemed confirmed. A Federal force was sent out to harass the rear of what was considered the retreating Confederates. A Georgia regiment which had been left by General Jackson to guard the outlet of a road by which the enemy could attack was captured by the Federals, and they were preparing to follow in full force when he was already beyond their reach.

General Lee, on his part, by the active movement of troops, and continual skirmishing with the enemy on their left, completely blinded General Hooker as to the real move on his right. Thus, while the enemy's feebly-roused suspicions were lulled to rest, the thunderbolt of war had been fairly launched, and was soon to burst upon the foe. The great captain was acting up to the Jackson motto, "swift by land and sea," and through dense forests and over unfrequented roads was thundering along with his veteran legions through brier and brake to accomplish one of the most brilliant moves that have ever adorned the annals of war. Often his column had to swerve still farther to the left, to avoid the enemy's pickets. His movements for the most part were concealed from the enemy by the dense forest through which he moved, and by Stuart's cavalry, who scoured the country between his column and the Federal lines. He marched southwest a few miles beyond Catherine Furnace, and then turned towards the northwest, marching on 'n that direction at a rapid, steady gait. His men, quickly finding that they were engaged in one of his brilliant flank movements, stepped forward with enthusiasm. So rapid was the advance that often the men had to break into a double-quick to close up the column. Across the enemy's front they marched swiftly, and bearing now to the right they approached his right flank. At last, by three o'clock in the afternoon, the head of the column struck the old turnpike, which ran directly west from the enemy's position at Chancellorsville. Jackson had marched fifteen miles; he had turned the enemy's flank without being discovered, and was now six miles from Chancellorsville, facing the enemy from the west, while General Lee confronted them on the east. The bright beams of the morning sun shone on the backs of his soldiers when he began the day's march, but now its slanting rays towards the decline of the day rested on their backs and played around their bright bayonets as, on striking the turnpike, they wheeled to the right and were ready to rush down upon the unsuspecting foe at Chancellorsville. While the Federals were preparing to pursue him from the furnace, he was ready to fall like a thunderbolt upon their flank and rear. Every precaution was taken to conceal the presence of his troops. Orders were given in a low tone, not a gun was fired, and it was forbidden to cheer the general as he passed down the column. He now addressed to General Lee his last official note, as follows:

"Near three P.M., May 2, 1863.

"GENERAL,—The enemy has made a stand at Chancellor's, which is about two miles from Chancellorsville. I hope so soon as practicable to attack.

"I trust that an ever-kind Providence will bless us with success.

"Respectfully,
"T. J. JACKSON, Lieutenant-General.
"General ROBERT E. LEE.

"P. S.—The leading division is up, and the next two appear to be well closed. T. J. J."

After riding down the turnpike and making a reconnoissance, General Jackson formed his line of battle. He formed his corps into three parallel lines, crossing the turnpike and facing the east. Rodes's division formed the first line, Colston's the second, and A. P. Hill's the third. Two pieces of Stuart's artillery were to move down the turnpike, which formed the centre of his lines. For two hours officers commanding and their aides were busy in giving and carrying orders from one part of the corps to another. Swiftly and silently did they gallop from point to point, until at length three lines were in battle-array and ready at the word of command to plunge into the dense forest in front of them, —a forest so dense and tangled that in rushing through it the soldiers had their clothes almost torn from their bodies.

The situation of the unsuspecting enemy upon whom they were so soon to burst like a tornado was as follows:

"The Eleventh Corps (Howard's) held the right of the Federal army. The works thrown up for its protection were parallel to the plank and turnpike roads, and faced southwardly. Steinwehr's division held the left of these works, joining Sickles; Schurz held the centre, and Devens the right. Devens's position was west of the intersection of the plank and turnpike roads, near Talley's House. The mass of his force occupied the works parallel to the road, which were formed by deepening the ditch on the side of the road, by earthworks thrown up hastily in the field, by timbers from the log out-buildings, and rails from the fences in the vicinity. But a portion of one of his brigades on the extreme right was thrown across the pike facing westwardly. These last were protected by but very slight works and an abatis. Two pieces of artillery were placed on the pike with these troops. These were the only preparations to meet the flank movement of Jackson.

"Just before six o'clock Jackson gave the order to advance. As swiftly as the brushwood would permit, the lines moved forward. The forest was full of game, which, startled from their hiding-places by the unusual presence of man, ran in numbers to and over the Federal lines. Deer leaped over the works at Talley's, and dashed into the wood behind. The Federal troops had in most cases their arms stacked, and were eating supper. All danger was thought to be over for the night.

"The startled game gave the first intimation of Jackson's approach. But so little was it suspected or believed that the suggestion was treated as a jest. Presently the bugles were heard through which orders were passed along the Confederate lines. This excited still more remark. Ere it had been long discussed, however, there came the sound of a few straggling shots from the skirmishers, then a mighty cheer, and in a moment more Jackson was upon them. A terrible volley from his line of battle was poured among the Union troops ere they could recover from their surprise. Those in line returned a scattered fire; others seized their arms and attempted to form. Officers tried to steady their men and lead them to meet the attack. All was in vain. Rodes rushed over the artillery and infantry of Devens's division, which were in position across the turnpike. The mass of Devens's division, at Talley's, taken in the rear by the Confederate fire, broke and rushed at once to the rear in the wildest disorder. The position at Talley's, which was high and commanding, thus fell with hardly any serious resistance. Five pieces of artillery are taken in the works, and a large number of prisoners. The Confederate line does not stop for a moment, but with increasing enthusiasm continues to rush on. Schurz's division does not stay to receive the attack, but joins at once in the rout. On, on pushes Rodes, closely followed by Colston and Hill. Here and there a Federal regiment takes position, fires a few rounds, and then, as the Confederate masses come up, is scattered to the winds, leaving half its numbers wounded and dying on the field. Like a tornado the Confederate lines pass over the ground, breaking, crushing, crumbling Howard's corps. Artillery, wagons, ambulances, are driven in frantic panic to the rear, and double the confusion. The rout is utter and hopeless. The mass of pursuers and pursued roll on until the position of Melzi Chancellor's is reached. Here a strong line of works had been constructed across the road, which, having a shallow ditch, could be made to face in either direction.

"During the time occupied in the dispersion of Devens's and Schurz's divisions, Steinwehr had rapidly changed front and thrown Buschbeck's brigade into these works. The other brigade of his division had been sent to support Sickles. Some of Schurz's men rally on Buschbeck, and for a short time the Confederate advance is arrested. But Jackson cannot long be held back. Colston's division has eagerly pressed on, and is already commingled with Rodes's. Together they charge with a yell; and in a few moments the works are taken. Pell-mell now rush the Eleventh Corps, the last semblance of organization gone, through the forest, towards Chancellorsville. Onward sweep the Confederates in hot pursuit. The arms, knapsacks, and accoutrements of the fugitives fill the woods. Artillery-carriages are to be seen overturned in the narrow roads, or hopelessly jammed in the impenetrable jungle. The wounded and dying, with their groans, fill the forest on every side. The day is rapidly drawing to a close; night comes to add confusion to the scene. It had been impossible in the broad daylight, owing to the intricacy of the forest, to prevent a commingling of regiments and brigades along the Confederate lines. The confusion thus produced is greatly increased by the darkness. In a brushwood so dense that it is impossible, under favorable circumstances, to see thirty yards in any direction, companies, regiments, brigades, become inextricably intermixed. Colston's division, forming the second line, has already become merged with Rodes's. Both move on in one confused mass. The right of the Confederate line soon reaches an abatis which has been felled to protect the approach to some works on the opposite heights. The troops, already disordered, become still more so among the felled timber. Behind this abatis some troops and artillery have been gathered to make a stand. Rodes finds it impossible to push farther until the lines can be reformed. The right is first halted, and then the whole Confederate line. Rodes sends word at once to Jackson requesting that the third line (A. P. Hill's division) be sent forward to take the advance until the first and second can be re-formed.

" While this was being done, there was a lull in the storm of battle. Jackson had paused for a time in his pursuit; Hooker was attempting to stop and re-form his flying legions." *

All during this magnificent charge Jackson was the impersonation of military enthusiasm. Onward he dashed at the head of his conquering column, as much carried away by the brilliant success of his move as the most thoughtless soldier in the ranks. " Forward !" " Press on !" were his answers to every question. As cheer after cheer burst from the Confederate line, and one by one the enemy's strongholds fell into their hands, the flush which reddened his cheek and the fire of his eyes showed how deeply he was moved by the scene which his master-spirit had, as it were, conjured up in the heart of that

---

* Battle-Fields of Virginia.

dense forest, whose wilds had so rarely been trodden by the foot of man. Never had he been seen to abandon himself so entirely to the enthusiasm of the moment as he did on this his last field of battle. Never before, while still dashing ahead in this wild, sweeping charge, had his hand been seen so often raised as his soul lifted itself up to God in thankful prayer. His most sanguine hopes had been realized. He had flanked the enemy's line, driven back his legions in hopeless confusion, and with scarcely any resistance pressed forward two or three miles into his lines. But Jackson knew much had yet to be done before the victory could be complete. He felt that all depended on the first successful blow being followed up rapidly by others. He saw, then, with bitter regret, the disorder into which the first line had almost necessarily fallen. The men had now marched twenty miles, and fought over three miles of ground, and they almost involuntarily halted and broke up into groups, as if the work of the day were done. An important work from which the enemy had just fled lay in front of them. At any moment it might be re-occupied by the foe. Jackson felt that precious moments were being lost. He sent messenger after messenger to different officers, ordering them to get their men back into ranks and press forward. His staff was scattered over the whole field, urging the troops forward. A young colonel of the line who came to report to him at this time that the work just mentioned was lying unguarded on his front, found him almost without a staff, and riding along the lines near the road, trying to get them into order. "Men, get into line! get into line!" he was saying. "Whose regiment is this? Colonel, get your men instantly into line!" Turning to the colonel who had just reported to him, he said, "Find General Rodes, and tell him to occupy that barricade at once with his troops." He then added, "I need your help for a time; this disorder must be corrected. As you go along the right, tell the troops, from me, to get into line and preserve their order."

After thus endeavoring to restore order to his lines, and while waiting for A. P. Hill, whom he had ordered to be hurried forward, Jackson rode along the turnpike to make a reconnoissance. He found the enemy, as he had expected, advancing, and, ere Rodes's men had fully occupied the barricade, a strong line of fresh troops, sent forward by Hooker, came in sight. Jackson meanwhile had advanced a hundred yards beyond his line of battle. Accompanied as he was by a portion of his staff, several other officers, and a number of couriers, the party might have been taken by friend or foe for a squadron of cavalry. He had ridden some distance beyond the pickets, and was near the Van West house, when one of the party said to him, "General, you should not expose yourself so much." "There is no danger," he replied; "the enemy is routed. Go back and tell General Hill to press on." He soon became aware of how close he was to the Federal lines by the advance of their pickets, and he at once turned his horse's head, and the whole party rode back to the Confederate troops. On both sides the skirmishers were firing, and Jackson's escort was mistaken for a body of Federal cavalry and received a volley from the Confederate line of battle. This fire told with cruel effect, several of the party falling from their saddles, some wounded, others killed. The general escaped, and, now mindful of the danger of his position, turned into the thicket on his left and advanced towards his own troops. By a strange fatality, however, his party was for the second time taken for the enemy, and was fired upon by a brigade south of the road, and not more than thirty or forty yards off. This time the general was struck, and received three balls, one in the right hand and two in the right arm, one of which shattered the bone and cut the artery about two inches below the shoulder. Half of his escort, including Captain Boswell, of his staff, fell, killed or wounded. Their horses dashed off wildly through the woods. Jackson's, terrified by the fire, wheeled and dashed madly forward with his wounded and almost powerless rider towards the enemy's lines. While thus carried through the dense thicket, the brushwood and overhanging limbs struck him, and a bough which knocked off his cap almost unhorsed him as it bore him backwards. His bridle-hand was powerless, but, gathering up the reins with his mangled right, he made a desperate effort, stopped the terrified animal, and turned him back to his own lines. Captain Wilbourne, one of his escort, and Wynn, his assistant, ran up to him as he reined up his horse on the plank road near the spot where he had received the fatal fire, and stood gazing at his troops as if dumfounded at what they had done. The firing had ceased, but around him were lying the dead and wounded, while their horses, dashing riderless and terrified through the woods, added to the confusion and horrors of the scene. On reaching the general, young Wilbourne seized his bridle and asked anxiously if he were much hurt. He answered that he believed his arm was broken, and he wished he would assist him to dismount; but the next moment, attempting to move the shattered limb, he fell fainting from his horse into Captain Wilbourne's arms. Quickly disengaging the general's feet from his stirrups, Captain Wilbourne and Wynn bore him into the woods a few yards north of the turnpike. Wynn ran off for a surgeon and ambulance, while Wilbourne, supporting the wounded man's head on his bosom, hastened to strip the sleeve from the crushed arm as the blood flowed steadily down to the wrist. He had nothing but a penknife with which to rip off the sleeve, and, seeing just then General A. P. Hill and part of his staff ride by, he called to him for aid. General Hill threw himself from his horse and took the general's body in his arms. His aide, Major Leigh, also dismounting, the three succeeded in getting at the wound and staunching the blood.

Just at this moment Jackson's aides, Lieutenants Smith and Morrison, came up. Young Morrison, his brother-in-law, could not restrain his emotion when he saw his condition. Amid all his suffering the general did not utter a complaint. "I believe my arm is broken, and it gives me severe pain," he said, in reply to a question. "Are you hurt elsewhere, general?" he was asked. "Yes; in my right arm." "Shall it be bound up?" "No," he replied; "it is a trifle." When asked how he had received his wounds, he said, calmly, "All my wounds were undoubtedly from my own men." He asked for Dr. McGuire, and was told that he was busily engaged in the rear. "Then I wish you to get me a skillful surgeon," he said to young Wilbourne. While lying on General Hill's breast, that commander ordered that the men should not be told who he was. The general opened his eyes, and, looking steadily at his aides, Morrison and Smith, said, "Tell them simply you have a Confederate officer."

General Hill was asked where a surgeon could be most quickly found. He said that Dr. Barr was close by.

He was at once summoned, and on his arrival Jackson whispered to Hill, " Is he a skillful surgeon?" When General Hill replied that he stood well with his brigade, and was only wanted to staunch the wound, Jackson replied, " Very good." But Dr. Barr found the blood had ceased to flow, and he did not apply the tourniquet he had in his hand. Just at this moment, when the hemorrhage had stopped and his arm had been placed in a sling, as the general lay silent and suffering in the arms of his friends, two Federal skirmishers, with their muskets cocked, approached within a few feet of the kneeling group. General Hill, with admirable self-possession, instantly told his orderlies to rise and demand their surrender. The orderlies quickly obeyed, and the men, amazed and confounded, at once laid down their arms. Lieutenant Morrison, fearing from the approach of these two men that the enemy might be close at hand, advanced into the road to reconnoitre. He found his fears realized, for by the light of the moon he saw a short distance off the black mouth of a field-piece pointed towards him, and heard distinctly the orders given by the officers to the cannoneers. He ran back to the little group in the woods kneeling around their wounded chief, and, reporting that the enemy were planting cannon in the road, said the general must be instantly removed. General Hill was now forced to leave for his own post. He sprang into his saddle, dashed off, and was a few minutes later struck down at the head of his column and borne, wounded and stunned, from the field. Captain Wilbourne had gone back in search of an ambulance, but none had as yet come up, and no time was to be lost in removing the general. His attendants proposed to bear him from the field in their arms, but he said he could walk to the rear if assisted. He was accordingly placed on his feet, and, leaning on the shoulders of Major Leigh and Lieutenant Smith, he moved slowly out into the road and towards his own troops. A litter having been brought up from the rear, the wounded man was being placed on it, when suddenly a volley of canister-shot was fired up the road by the enemy, and, passing over the heads of the group, cleared the road of everything else that was upon it. The general's horse broke from the person who was leading it, and dashed panic-stricken into the Confederate lines. Jackson's aides, Morrison and Smith, and two soldiers, bore the litter. But they had advanced only a few steps when a second volley again swept the road. One of the soldiers was struck, and fell severely wounded. Major Leigh sprang forward and caught the litter as it fell with him, or the general would have been thrown from it. They were now compelled to set the litter down. Scarcely was this done when a storm of lead and canister swept down the road and crashed through the trees on each side. This was more than flesh and blood could stand. The party bearing the wounded hero fled to the woods, Major Leigh and young Smith and Morrison alone clinging to him. Beneath this deadly shower the general lay in the road, with his feet extended towards the enemy. On one side of him was stretched Lieutenant Smith, on the other Major Leigh. With their arms thrown lovingly around their chief they sought to protect with their own bodies his prostrate form and shield it from the missiles now hurtling around them. More than once the balls plowed up the earth beside them and covered them with dust. The wounded man, conscious of the perils of the position, struggled violently as if to rise, but the strong arms of

o*

young Smith held him pinned to the earth, as he exclaimed, "General, you must lie still; it will cost you your life if you rise." For several minutes they remained thus prostrate beneath this fiery ordeal, every one of the four expecting each minute to be his last. But the enemy's fire at length subsided, and they were left untouched.

Another effort was now made to get the general to the rear. The four rose to their feet, and in the uncertain light of the moon moved along the edge of the road, —the general leaning heavily upon the brave, strong young arms thrown lovingly around him, and painfully dragging himself and being dragged along. They moved to one side, to avoid being recognized by the troops as pressing forward they hurried on to the front. Finding that in spite of this precaution the wounded chief was recognized, they turned still farther to the right into the woods. Here they fell upon the Confederate line of battle held by Pender's brigade of A. P. Hill's division. The men for the most part were lying down, to avoid the enemy's artillery fire. As the little party moved in the dim moonlight through and over them, the repeated question was, "Whom have you there?" To which the calm and invariable reply was, "A Confederate officer." Some endeavored to get a view of the wounded man's face, and in spite of Captain Wilbourne's efforts to conceal it they recognized him, and exclaimed, with horror, "Great God! it is General Jackson!" The news now ran rapidly along the lines, but the soldiers were quieted by the belief that Jackson's wounds were slight. General Pender, whose quick eye had almost instantly recognized the general, approached him, and, after expressing his sorrow at seeing him wounded, said to him, "The

"You must hold your ground, General Pender; you must hold your ground, sir!" was Jackson's last order.

(Page 323.)

troops have suffered severely from the enemy's artillery, and are somewhat disorganized; I fear we cannot maintain our position." For a moment the old battle look returned to Jackson's pale face, and the battle fire flashed from his eyes, as, raising his head and speaking in his habitual quick tones, he said, "You must hold your ground, General Pender; you must hold your ground, sir!" With this order his career as a general ended.

The little party now again moved on. The general, exhausted by fatigue and suffering, asked to be allowed to sit down and rest; but he was still too near the enemy to admit of this, and he was placed on a litter. Litter-bearers being procured after some delay, he was now borne rapidly towards the rear. As the party hurried rapidly through the dense and tangled thicket, the general's clothes were torn and his face scratched by the brushwood through which they passed. On they moved, thinking only of getting their wounded chief to a place of safety, when suddenly one of the litter-bearers caught his foot in a vine, stumbled, and fell. The general fell heavily, striking the ground with his wounded shoulder. For the first time, he groaned. His attendants caught him up in their arms, and as young Smith laid his head on his breast and found the blood again flowing, he feared he might be expiring. "General, are you much hurt?" he inquired. "No, Mr. Smith; don't trouble yourself about me," was the reply. He was again placed on the litter, and the party, turning from the wood, bore him half a mile under a heavy fire to the rear, where they were met by Dr. McGuire with an ambulance. Kneeling beside him, the doctor said, "I hope you are not badly hurt, general?" Feebly, but calmly, he replied, "I am badly injured, doctor; I fear I am dying;" and after a pause he added, "I am glad you have come; I think the wound in my shoulder is still bleeding." His clothes were found wet with his blood, which, as he surmised, was still flowing. His cold hands and clammy skin, and the deathly pallor of his countenance, betrayed the intensity of his suffering. Yet not a groan or a murmur escaped from him. Only these signs, together with the rigidity of his features, a wrinkled brow, and lips so tightly compressed that the impression of the teeth was shown through them, showed how great were his sufferings.

The hemorrhage was soon stopped, and after the general had taken some whisky he was placed in the ambulance, which set out for the field infirmary at the Wilderness Tavern. In the ambulance was Jackson's chief of artillery, the gallant Colonel Crutchfield, whose promotion, as we have seen, he had pressed so earnestly, and who now lay suffering from a serious wound, just received, in the leg. The general expressed his sympathy for him. Dr. McGuire sat in the front part of the ambulance, with his finger on the artery from which the general's blood had flowed, to arrest the bleeding should it again begin. The night was dark, and by the light of torches the ambulance moved slowly and carefully forward. Once Colonel Crutchfield groaned, when Jackson at once ordered the ambulance to be stopped, and asked if something could not be done to relieve Colonel Crutchfield. He had previously put his right hand on Dr. McGuire's head, and, pulling it down, whispered in his ear and asked if Colonel Crutchfield was dangerously wounded. When answered, "No; only painfully hurt," he said, "I am glad it is no worse." A few moments later, Colonel Crutchfield put the same whispered question about the general to the doctor, and when told that he was very seriously wounded, he groaned, and cried out, "Oh, my God!" It was this groan and cry which the general mistook for an expression of physical suffering, and which induced him to order the ambulance to be stopped. The ambulance finally reached the hospital in safety, and the general was carefully taken from it and placed on a bed in a tent which had been put up for him.

CHAPTER XVII.

DEATH AND BURIAL.

THE following incident, too curious and too authentic to be omitted from a life of Jackson, must be given before we turn again to the field of battle or to the dying man's couch.

In 1852, while going up the Mississippi River, Jackson made the acquaintance of a gentleman, Mr. Revere, who was afterwards a major in the United States army during the war. In a conversation with this gentleman one day during their trip up the Mississippi, the subject turning from nautical astronomy to astrology, Mr. Revere saw the great interest which Jackson took in it, and, on parting with him at the end of their journey, gave him the necessary data for calculating a horoscope. A short time afterwards, Mr. Revere received a letter from Jackson inclosing a scheme of their nativities, from which it appeared that their destinies would run in parallel lines, and that somewhere about the first days of May, 1863, they would both be exposed to great danger. The letter and its prophecy were soon both forgotten by Mr. Revere. At the battle of Chancellorsville he commanded a brigade, and while inspecting his picket line saw a party of horsemen approaching from the direction of the Confederate lines. I leave him to relate what followed:

"The foremost horseman detached himself from the main body, which halted not far from us, and, riding

cautiously nearer, seemed to try to pierce the gloom.
He was so close to us that the soldier nearest me leveled
his rifle for a shot at him; but I forbade him, as I did
not wish to have our position revealed, and it would
have been useless to kill the man, whom I judged to be
a staff-officer making a reconnoissance. Having completed his observations, this person rejoined the group in
his rear, and all returned at a gallop. The clatter of
hoofs soon ceased to be audible; and the silence of the
night was unbroken save by the melancholy cries of the
whippoorwill, when the horizon was lighted up by a
sudden flash in the direction of the enemy, succeeded by
the well-known rattle of a volley of musketry from at
least a battalion. A second volley quickly followed the
first; and I heard cries in the same direction. Fearing
that some of our troops might be in that locality, and
that there was danger of our firing upon friends, I left
my orderly and rode towards the Confederate lines. A
riderless horse dashed past me, and I reined up in the
presence of a group of several persons gathered round a
man lying on the ground apparently badly wounded. I
saw at once that these were Confederate officers; but, reflecting that I was well armed and mounted, and that I
had on the great-coat of a private soldier, such as was
worn by both parties, I sat still, regarding the group in
silence, but prepared to use either my spurs or sabre as
occasion might demand. The silence was broken by one
of the Confederates, who appeared to regard me with
astonishment; then, speaking in a tone of authority, he
ordered me to 'ride up there and see what troops those
were,' indicating the rebel position. I instantly made a
gesture of assent, and rode slowly in the direction indicated until out of sight of the group; then made

a circuit round it and returned within my lines. Just as I had answered the challenge of our picket, the section of our artillery posted on the plank road began firing; and I could plainly hear the grape crashing through the trees near the spot occupied by the group of Confederate officers." *

In an account of how Jackson received his wound, the " Richmond Enquirer" of May 13, 1863, says,—

" The turnpike was utterly deserted, with the exception of Captains Wilbourne and Wynn; but, in the skirting of the thicket on the left, some person was observed by the side of the wood, sitting his horse motionless and silent. The unknown individual was clad in a dark dress which strongly resembled the Federal uniform; but it seemed impossible that he could have penetrated to that spot without being discovered; and what followed seemed to prove that he belonged to the Confederates. Captain Wilbourne directed him to ride up there and see what troops those were,—the men who fired on Jackson; and the stranger rode slowly in the direction pointed out, but never returned with any answer."

Before again turning to Jackson, the progress and conclusion of the battle of Chancellorsville must be given. When Jackson fell, and General Hill, also, disabled by a wound, left the field, it was decided by Jackson's adjutant and the generals of the corps to offer its command to General Stuart. Brigadier-General Rodes was indeed the senior officer of the corps; but, General Stuart being the only major-general on the field, and

---

* Atlantic Monthly, January, 1873.

being better known throughout the army, General Rodes gracefully waived his claims to the command.

As soon as it was decided to offer it to General Stuart, Captain Wilbourne was sent to General Lee to report the state of affairs to him and to ask for further orders. Captain Hotchkiss accompanied Captain Wilbourne, and after a hard ride the two young officers arrived on Sunday morning before daybreak at a cluster of pines east of Chancellorsville, where General Lee was lying upon the ground beneath a thick pine-tree. On reporting themselves to his chief of staff, they were at once summoned to report to the general in person. There, beneath the stars that were disappearing before the rapidly-approaching light of the early dawn, he listened eagerly to the tale of Jackson's swift and noiseless march, of the rapidity with which his troops were formed into line when they found themselves actually in the enemy's rear, and of the magnificent charge which followed. But when they told him of Jackson's wound, he exclaimed, with ill-suppressed emotion, "Ah, any victory is dearly bought which deprives us of the services of Jackson, even for a short time." On hearing that General Stuart had been chosen to command Jackson's corps for that day, he confirmed the choice. He was then told that Jackson had said "the enemy should be pressed in the morning." "Those people shall be pressed immediately," he replied, as he rose; and a few minutes later the noble chief was in the saddle and off to arrange his troops for the movements of that eventful day.

But to return to Jackson's corps. The fall of its leader and the approach of night arrested its further advance—already checked by the enemy—on Saturday night. During that night Hooker formed a new front on his right with the troops of Sickles and Berry, the Eleventh Corps being for the time *hors du combat.* Reynolds's corps, having been summoned from Fredericksburg, where it had been acting under Sedgwick's command, was now near at hand. Sedgwick was still left with a powerful force—twenty thousand men—at Fredericksburg. It was most desirable for the Confederates to keep Reynolds's fine corps out of the fight the next day (Sunday).

This had been thought of by Jackson, and one of his last orders was for a movement of a regiment by which he hoped to throw Reynolds off his guard and check his further advance. Just before receiving his fatal wound, he ordered General Pender to send him a regiment for a special service. General Pender accordingly sent him the 16th North Carolina, Colonel McElroy. This officer received orders to go with a squadron of cavalry to Ely's Ford, where, he was told, he would find a corps of Federal troops encamped. There he was to approach as near as possible, and, at a given signal, to fire three volleys at them, amid loud cheering. The orders were promptly obeyed by Colonel McElroy, who, after this strange move, was back on the field of battle by three o'clock in the morning. Later in the day he had reason to believe that the corps he had attacked under cover of the night was Reynolds's, and that this attack had been designed to check his advance, and had been successful. Be this as it may, Reynolds's corps was not in the fight on Sunday morning.

The attack on the enemy was begun early on Sunday morning by General Stuart on the west and General Lee on the south and east of the enemy's position. Stuart moved his force somewhat to the right, and in his

advance recovered the vantage-ground lost during the
confusion which followed Jackson's fall the night before.
He led the corps rapidly through a belt of woods, from
which they emerged to see a second line of works on the
crest of a long declivity. Realizing the bloody task
that was before them, men and officers saw that there
was not a minute to lose in carrying these works. When
the gallant Stuart gave the order, in clear, ringing tones,
"Charge! and remember Jackson!" the air was rent
with shouts as this battle-cry was caught from their
leader's lips and re-echoed along the whole line. The
men of the Stonewall Brigade were conspicuous for their
valor. The Federals fought well, and made a stout resistance to the impetuous onslaught of the Confederates.
Stuart's left flank was thrown into confusion by a gallant
attack made on it by the enemy, but, being reinforced,
continued its advance, and the Federal line was pushed
steadily back until it found cover under a second line of
intrenchments. These had been thrown up on Saturday
night, and covered the road leading to United States
Ford over the Rappahannock. Hooker's efforts during
the battle seem to have been directed more to getting his
army into this second line than to resisting successfully
the Confederate attack. His brigadiers saw this with
dismay, and tried in vain to counteract with desperate
fighting his bad generalship.

Sedgwick received orders from Hooker at midnight,
Saturday, to march at once to his aid. He immediately
put his corps in motion, his command being stationed on
the south bank of the Rappahannock, three miles below
Fredericksburg. The Confederate force left to defend
that town consisted of Early's division and Barksdale's
brigade. As Sedgwick advanced, the Confederates fell

back before him, making no further show of resistance than very spirited skirmishing. Before the dawn of day, Sedgwick occupied Fredericksburg, but the force sent out by him as an advance was repulsed. The main body of his troops, coming up and finding the heights occupied by the Confederates, assailed and carried them with great gallantry. The Confederates fell back in full retreat, and, the plank road leading to Chancellorsville being open, Sedgwick moved along it without delay. Thus, while General Lee was hurling his forces against Hooker, the sound of Early's guns in his rear informed him of the disaster which had befallen this brave officer, and warned him of the perils of his own situation. Not hesitating for a moment, he wheeled a part of his force confronting Hooker right around, and sent them off at full speed to reinforce Early and arrest Sedgwick's advance. The two columns met about half-way between Chancellorsville and Fredericksburg, and at once joined in battle. A temporary advantage was gained by Sedgwick in the beginning of the encounter, but was followed by a repulse, and steadily he was pushed back until night put an end to the conflict. The day was now won for the Confederates: Hooker was driven back into his second line of works, and Sedgwick was checked in his march to his relief. Worn out by two days' incessant fighting, marching, and countermarching, covered with dust, and begrimed with the smoke of battle, but with victory perching on the banners which they had so proudly borne aloft, the Confederates sank to rest, arms in hand, on the field of battle. So ended this memorable Sabbath in the early days of May.

The next day, the 4th, at six o'clock in the evening, the Confederates renewed their attack on Sedgwick.

That gallant officer made a stubborn resistance to the violent attack of the Confederates; but in vain. He was pushed steadily back, and withdrew his force, under cover of the night, to the north bank of the Rappahannock.

General Lee on the 5th collected his shattered forces together, determining to renew the attack on Hooker the next day. But when the morning of the 6th dawned, Hooker was on the north side of the Rappahannock, having carried his army across safely during the night, leaving behind him his wounded, fourteen pieces of artillery, seventeen standards, and twenty thousand stand of arms. The reports from the two opposing armies make the Confederate loss a little over ten thousand men, that of the Federals a little over seventeen thousand.

So ended the spring campaign of 1863.

Several remarks made by Jackson during those last memorable days of his life, not found in the account of his death, which I shall quote, must be given here. In speaking of his flank movement against Hooker, he said, "Our movement yesterday was a great success; I think the most successful military movement of my life. But I expect to receive far more credit for it than I deserve. Most men will think that I had planned it all from the first; but it was not so. I simply took advantage of circumstances as they were presented to me in the providence of God. I feel that his hand led me; let us give Him all the glory." At his request, his chaplain came every morning at ten o'clock and read the Bible and had prayers. More than once on these occasions he assured the chaplain that he was ready and willing to die, but that he did not think his time had yet come, as he felt sure his heavenly Father had a work for him to accomplish in the defense of his beloved country. Asserting that the Bible gives rules for every profession, he asked one of his aides, smiling, "Can you tell me where the Bible gives generals a model for their official reports of battles?" The young officer laughed, and answered in the negative. "Nevertheless," said Jackson, "there are such. Look, for instance, at the narrative of Joshua's battle with the Amalekites; there you have one. It has clearness, brevity, fairness, modesty; and it traces the victory to its right source,—the blessing of God."

In speaking of the persons whom the Saviour healed, he expressed the belief that they never had a return of the same disease, and, after a pause, as if thinking of his own case, exclaimed, "Oh for infinite power!" To his little daughter he clung as long as consciousness lasted. Having sent for her once, his eyes were riveted on the door until it was opened and she appeared, when, with a countenance radiant with delight, he exclaimed, "Little darling!" and had her placed on the bed beside him, caressing her and playing with her as much as his feeble condition would allow. When his opinion of Hooker's plan of campaign was asked by some one, he said, "It was, in the main, a good conception, sir; an excellent plan. But he should not have sent away his cavalry; that was his great blunder. It was that which enabled me to turn him without his being aware of it, and to take him by his rear. Had he kept his cavalry with him, his plan would have been a very good one."

The day (Sunday) on which Jackson died, Lee, with his staff and lieutenants grouped around him, attended divine service at the headquarters of Jackson's corps. As soon as the chaplain made his appearance, the commander-in-chief advanced to meet him, and asked in anxious tones after Jackson. When told that there was scarcely a hope of his recovery, he exclaimed, in a tone almost of bitterness, "Surely General Jackson must recover. God will not take him from us, now that we need him so much. Surely he will be spared to us, in answer to the many prayers which are offered for him." And later he added, "When you return, I trust you will find him better. When a suitable occasion offers, give him my love, and tell him that I wrestled in prayer for him last night as I never prayed, I believe, for myself." His voice trembled with the deep emotion which he now turned away to conceal. Several days before, when Jackson's condition was considered more alarming than had been anticipated, General Lee had refused to believe that there could be any danger of losing him, and said to a gentleman who was going to visit Jackson, "Give him my affectionate regards, and tell him to make haste and get well, and come back to me as soon as he can. He has lost his left arm, but I have lost my right arm."

Certainly there is something exceedingly touching in the impossibility which it seemed to be for Lee to realize that Jackson would die and be torn from him at the time of all others when he most needed him. And the bitterness of his cry when that realization was at last forced on him! that lonely midnight wrestling in prayer that he might be saved! Was it foresight? Did the dim reality of the gloomy future dawn on his great soul? Was he startled at the thought of the lonely agony and sorrow in store for him, which the dying man alone could have shared with him, when, starting with his little army on that long declivity of disaster and misfortune, he saw the sorrowful way ending only in destruction? But not even the keen military instinct, the energy, and the splendid courage of his great lieutenant, had they been spared to him, could have altered the stern decrees of fate. And in Jackson's fall, untimely as it may seem, we must recognize the loving-kindness of that heavenly Father in whose love he trusted so unwaveringly,—the love which spared him the bitterness of that cup which the noble commander-in-chief was to drain to the dregs. Yet how he longed to live, how little the fires of ambition were burnt out in him, is clearly revealed by that exclamation, "Oh for infinite power!" as the possibility of death forced itself on him.

To the pen of an eye-witness I shall now leave the description of the closing scene of this noble life, taking up the thread of the story where it was dropped at the close of the last chapter:

"Two hours and a half after reaching the hospital it was found that sufficient reaction had taken place to warrant an examination. At two o'clock Sunday morning, Surgeons Black, Wall, and Coleman being present, Dr. McGuire informed him that chloroform would be given him and his wound examined. He told him that amputation would probably be required, and asked, if it was found necessary, should it be done at once. He replied, promptly, 'Yes, certainly, Dr. McGuire; do for me whatever you think best.' Chloroform was then administered, and as he began to feel its effects, and its relief to the pain he was suffering, he exclaimed, 'What an infinite blessing!' and continued to repeat the word 'blessing' until he became insensible. The round ball, such as is used for the smooth-bore Springfield muskets, which had lodged under the skin on the back of his right hand, was extracted first. It had entered the palm about the middle of the hand, and had fractured two of the bones. The left arm was then amputated about two inches below the shoulder, very rapidly, and with slight loss of blood. There were two wounds in this arm. The first and most serious was about three inches below the shoulder-joint, dividing the main artery and fracturing the bone. The second was several inches in length, a ball having entered the forearm an inch below the elbow and come out upon the opposite side just above the wrist. Throughout the whole of the operation, and until all the dressings were applied, he continued insensible. About half-past three o'clock, Colonel (then Major) Pendleton, the assistant adjutant-general, arrived at the hospital and asked to see General Jackson. At first the surgeon declined to permit an interview; but the colonel urged that the safety of the army and the success of the cause might depend on his seeing him. When he entered the tent, the general said, ' Well, major, I am glad to see you ; I thought you were killed.' Pendleton briefly explained the condition of affairs, gave Stuart's message, and asked what should be done. General Jackson was at once interested, and asked, in his quick, rapid way, several questions. When they were answered, he remained silent for a moment, evidently trying to think ; he contracted his brow, set his mouth, and for some moments was obviously endeavoring to concentrate his thoughts. For a moment it was believed he had succeeded ; his nostrils dilated, and his eye flashed its old fire ; but it was only for a moment. His face relaxed again, and presently he answered, very feebly and sadly, ' I don't know ; I can't tell. Say to General Stuart he must do what he thinks best.' Soon after this he slept for several hours, and seemed to be doing well.

"The next morning he was free from pain, and expressed himself sanguine of recovery. He sent his aide-de-camp, Morrison, to inform his wife of his injury, and to bring her at once to see him. The following note was read to him that morning by Lieutenant Smith:

"'GENERAL,—I have just received your note informing me that you were wounded. I cannot express my regret at the occurrence. Could I have directed events, I should have chosen, for the good of the country, to have been disabled in your stead.

"'I congratulate you upon the victory which is due to your skill and energy.

"'Most truly yours,

"'(Signed)   R. E. LEE, General.'

"He said, 'General Lee should give the praise to God.' About ten o'clock his right side began to pain him so much that he asked to have it examined. He said he had injured it in falling from the litter the night before, and he believed he had struck it against a stone or the stump of a sapling. No evidence of injury could be discovered by examining; the skin was not broken or bruised, and the lung was performing, as far as could be told, its proper functions. Some simple application was recommended, in the belief that the pain would soon disappear.

"At this time the battle was raging fearfully, and the sound of the cannon and musketry could be distinctly heard at the hospital. The general's attention was attracted to it from the first, and when the noise was at its height, and indicated how fiercely the combat was being carried on, he directed all of his attendants except

Captain Smith to return to the battle-field and attend to their different duties. By eight o'clock Sunday night the pain in his side had disappeared, and in all respects he seemed doing well. He inquired minutely about the battle, and different troops engaged, and his face would light up with enthusiasm and interest when told how this brigade acted, or that officer displayed conspicuous courage, and his head gave the peculiar shake from side to side, and he uttered his usual 'Good! good!' with unwonted energy, when the gallant behavior of the Stonewall Brigade was alluded to. He said, 'The men of that brigade will some day be proud to say to their children, "I was one of the Stonewall Brigade!"' He disclaimed any right of his own to the name Stonewall. 'It belongs to the brigade, and not to me.' This night he slept well, and was free from pain. A message was received from General Lee the next morning directing the removal of the general to Guinea's Station as soon as his wound would justify it, as there was some danger of capture by the enemy, who were threatening to cross at Ely's Ford. In the mean time, to protect the hospital, some troops were sent to this point.

"The general objected to being moved if in the opinion of the surgeon it would do him any injury. He said he had no objection to staying in a tent, and would prefer it, if his wife, when she came, could find lodgings in a neighboring house. 'And if the enemy do come,' he added, 'I am not afraid of them; I have always been kind to their wounded, and I am sure they will be kind to me.' General Lee sent word again late this evening that he must be moved, if possible; and preparations were made to leave next morning. Dr. McGuire was directed to accompany him, and to remain with him, and his duties with the corps as medical director were turned over to the surgeon next in rank. General Jackson had previously declined to permit Dr. McGuire to go with him to Guinea's Station, because complaints had been so frequently made of generals when wounded carrying with them surgeons belonging to their command. When informed of the order of the commanding general, he said, 'General Lee has always been very kind to me, and I thank him.'

"Very early Tuesday morning he was placed in an ambulance and started for Guinea's Station, and about eight o'clock that evening he arrived at Chandler's house, where he remained till he died. Captain Hotchkiss, with a party of pioneers, was sent in front to clear the road of wood, stones, etc., and to order the wagons out of the track to let the ambulance pass. The rough teamsters sometimes refused to move their loaded wagons out of the way for an ambulance until told that it contained Jackson, and then with all possible speed they gave the way, and stood with hats off and weeping as he passed by. At Spottsylvania Court-House, and along the whole route, men and women rushed to the ambulance, bringing all the poor delicacies they had, and with tearful eyes they blessed him and prayed for his recovery. He bore the journey well, and was cheerful throughout the day. He talked freely about the late battle, and among other things said that he had intended to cut the enemy off from United States Ford, and, taking a position between them and the river, oblige them to attack him; and he added, with a smile, 'My men sometimes fail to drive the Yankees from a position, but they always fail to drive us.' He spoke of Rodes, and spoke in high terms of his magnificent behavior on the field of battle Saturday evening. He hoped he would be promoted. He thought promotions for gallantry should be made at once upon the field, and not delayed. If made very early, on the field, they would be the greatest incentives to gallantry in others. He spoke of Colonel Willis, who commanded the skirmishers of Rodes's division, praised him very highly, and referred to the deaths of Paxton and Boswell very feelingly. He alluded to them as men of great promise and merit. The day was quite warm, and at one time he suffered from slight nausea. At his suggestion, a wet towel was put over his stomach, and he expressed great relief from it. After he arrived at Chandler's house he ate some bread and tea with evident relish, and slept well throughout the entire night. Wednesday he was thought to be doing remarkably well. He ate heartily, for one in his condition, and was uniformly cheerful. He expressed great satisfaction when told his wounds were doing remarkably well, and asked the surgeon if he could tell from their appearance how long he would probably be kept from the field. Conversing with Captain Smith a few moments afterwards, he alluded to his wounds, and said, 'Many would regard them as a great misfortune. I regard them as one of the blessings of my life.' Captain Smith remarked, 'All things work together for good to those that love God.' 'Yes,' he answered; 'that's it, that's it.' At Dr. McGuire's request, Dr. Morrison came to-day, and remained with him. About one o'clock Thursday morning he directed his servant Jim to apply a wet towel to his stomach, to relieve an attack of nausea with which he was suffering. The servant asked permission to first consult Dr. McGuire, who was sleeping in the room next to the general. Knowing that the doctor had slept none for nearly three entire nights, he refused to allow the servant to disturb him, and desired his chaplain, the Rev. Mr. Lacy, to give him a towel. About daylight the doctor was aroused, and informed that the general was suffering great pain. An examination disclosed pneumonia. It was doubtless attributable to the fall from the litter the night he was wounded. The general himself believed it was due to this cause. The disease came on too soon after the application of wet cloths to admit of the supposition, once believed, that it was induced by them. Some effusion of blood in his chest was probably produced by the fall referred to, and the shock and the loss of blood prevented any ill effects until reaction had been well established, and then inflammation and pneumonia ensued.

"Towards the evening of this day (Friday) he became better, and hopes were again entertained of his recovery. Mrs. Jackson arrived to-day, and nursed him faithfully to the end. She was a devoted wife and earnest Christian, and endeared all to her by her great gentleness and kindness. Mrs. Dr. Hoge, of Richmond, came and remained with her. The general's joy at the presence of his wife and child was very great, and for him he was unusually demonstrative. Noticing the sadness of his wife, he said to her, tenderly, 'I know you would gladly give your life for me, but I am perfectly resigned. Do not be sad; I hope I may recover. Pray for me, but always remember in your prayers to use the petition, "Thy will be done"' Friday his wounds were again dressed, and found to be healing. The pain in his side had disappeared; but he breathed with difficulty, and complained of a feeling of great exhaustion. When Dr. Breckenridge, who had been sent for in consultation, said he hoped that a blister which had been applied would afford him relief, he expressed his own confidence in it, and in his final recovery. On Saturday, Dr. Tucker, from Richmond, arrived in obedience to a telegram, and all that human skill could devise was done to stay the hand of death. He suffered no pain to-day, and his breathing was less difficult, but he was evidently hourly growing weaker. When his child was brought to him to-day, he played with it for some time, frequently caressing it and calling it his 'little comforter.' At one time he raised his wounded hand over its head, and, closing his eyes, was for some time silently engaged in prayer. He said to Dr. McGuire, 'I see from the number of physicians that you think my condition dangerous; but I thank God, if it is his will, that I am ready to go.'

"About daylight on Sunday morning Mrs. Jackson informed him that his recovery was very doubtful, and that it was better he should be prepared for the worst. He was silent for a moment, and then said, 'It will be infinite gain to be translated to heaven.' He advised his wife, in the event of his death, to return to her father's house, and added, 'You have a kind and good father, but there is no one so kind and good as your heavenly Father.' He still expressed a hope of his recovery, but requested, if he should die, to be buried at Lexington, in the Valley of Virginia.

"His exhaustion increased so rapidly that, at eleven o'clock, Mrs. Jackson knelt by his bed and told him that before the sun went down he would be with his Saviour. He replied, 'Oh, no; you are frightened, my child; death is not so near. I may yet get well.' She fell over on the bed, weeping bitterly, and told him again that the physicians said there was no hope. After a moment's pause, he asked her to call Dr. McGuire, who was standing in the anteroom, and said to him, as he entered, 'Doctor, Anna informs me that you have told her I am to die to-day: is it so?' When he was answered in the affirmative, he turned his eyes to the ceiling and gazed for a moment or two as if in intense thought, and then replied, 'Very good, very good; it is all right.' He then tried to comfort his almost heart-broken wife, and told her he had a good deal to say to her, but was too weak. Colonel Pendleton came into the room about one o'clock, and he asked him, 'Who is preaching at headquarters to-day?' When told that the whole army was praying for him, he replied, 'Thank God; they are very kind.' He said, 'It is the Lord's day; my wish is fulfilled. I have always desired to die on Sunday.'

"His mind now began to fail and wander, and he frequently talked as if in command upon the field, giving orders in his old way. Then the scene shifted, and he was now at the mess-table with members of his staff; now with his wife and child; now at prayers with his military family. Occasionally intervals of the return of his mind would appear, and during one of them he was offered some brandy-and-water, but he declined it, saying, 'It will only delay my departure, and do no good. I want to preserve my mind, if possible, to the last.' About half-past one he was told he had but two hours to live, and he answered again, feebly, but very firmly, 'Very good; it is all right.' A few minutes before he died, he cried out, in his delirium, 'Order A. P. Hill to prepare for action; pass the infantry to the front rapidly; tell Major Hawks——' then stopped, leaving the sentence unfinished. Presently a smile of ineffable sweetness spread itself over his pale face, and he said, quietly and with an expression as of relief, 'Let us cross over the river and rest under the shade of the trees.' And then, without pain or the least struggle, his spirit passed from earth to the God who gave it."*

Thus, in the fortieth year of his age† (born 1824, died 1863), died General Jackson. The next day the following General Order was issued by the commander-in-chief of the army:

"HEADQUARTERS ARMY OF NORTHERN VIRGINIA.

"GENERAL ORDER No. 61.

"With deep grief the commanding general announces to the army the death of Lieutenant-General T. J. Jackson, who expired on the 10th instant, at quarter-past three P.M. The daring skill and energy of this great and good soldier, by the decree of an all-wise Providence, are now lost to us. But, while we mourn his death, we feel that his spirit still lives, and will inspire the whole army with his indomitable courage and unshaken confidence in God as our hope and strength. Let his name be a watch-word to his corps, who have followed him to victory on so many fields. Let his officers and soldiers emulate his invincible determination to do everything in the defense of our loved country.

"R. E. LEE, General."

---

*This account of Jackson's death is written by Dr. McGuire, and taken from the Battle-Fields of Virginia, the excellent contribution to the history of the war between the States from which I have already quoted largely.

† "Thomas was born in Clarksburg, January 21, 1824. The early death of his parents and dispersion of the little family obliterated the record of the exact date, so that General Jackson himself was unable to fix it with certainty."—*Dabney's Life of Jackson,* p. 9.

1*

It is impossible to describe the grief caused by Jackson's death. The news of it reached Richmond about nightfall, and spread the deepest gloom and depression over the whole city. Now were fully realized the spell under which his strange and brilliant career held captive the imagination of men, and the strength of that devotion with which his splendid deeds bound the hearts of his countrymen to him. In camp the feeling was, if possible, deeper still, and the stern soldiers who had been hardened by two years of the horrors and hardships of war moved about silently and sadly, as if in the chamber of death itself.

The great Captain's remains were shrouded by his staff on Sunday night; the torn coat in which he had been wounded was replaced by a citizen's coat often worn by him, and his whole figure was wrapped in his military overcoat. A plain wooden coffin was procured, and in that his body was first laid; but some embalmers who were sent by the Governor with a metallic case arrived that same night, and his remains were by them finally prepared for the grave.

During the last moments of his life, while his mind was wandering, some one near asked him where he wished to be buried. Charlotte, North Carolina, as being the future home of Mrs. Jackson, was suggested; but, evidently not being able to keep his mind on the subject, he thought Charlottesville, Virginia, was meant. When Lexington was mentioned as a suitable place, he nodded assent, but showed, even if he understood what he was doing, no preference for that village as his final resting-place. But there it was decided he should be buried.

A committee of citizens and prominent men sent by

the Governor to escort his remains to Richmond started, accompanied by his staff, with them for that city on Monday morning. The time for the arrival of the train was uncertain; but long before the earliest hour at which it was possible for it to arrive, the population of the city, all ages and sexes mingled together, was seen wending its way to the point on Broad Street where it was known the train would stop. For hours they waited; but in vain: there was no sign of the approaching train. The morning hours of this lovely May day passed; the warm rays of the noonday sun drove the crowd to the shady side of the street, but could not scatter that sadly expectant throng, which gradually surged onwards in the direction in which the train would come. He whom they had fondly dreamt of one day welcoming with shouts of applause, and of bearing in triumph through the beautiful streets of their beautiful city, was indeed near at hand, and nature seemed to have assumed her loveliest garb to welcome him, for never had brighter skies overarched that devoted city, never had the freshness of spring and the purity of the atmosphere made so brilliant the green foliage and lovely flowers which adorn her streets as on that memorable day. He was indeed coming, but not in the pageant of war, not amid the pæans of victory and the shouts of applause which mark the victor's entrance into the saved city; not in life, but in death,— a death which he did not welcome and did not dread. With what chastened hearts did his countrymen then watch for him! with feelings how awed, yet how deep and tender, did they strain their eyes to get the first glimpse of his approach! and how meet that they should in a long watch, with every voice hushed into a whisper, give him this silent yet touching homage of devotion!

Suddenly the solemn silence was broken by the loud toll of a bell which resounded through the air. It was known to be the signal of the entrance of the funeral cortége into the city; and yet the train which was to bring it had not arrived. In a few minutes all was explained to the expectant yet startled crowd. Warned of the throng which was awaiting its arrival, the officers with the body stopped the train a mile out of town. Mrs. Jackson and the lady friends accompanying her were placed in a carriage and driven rapidly to the Governor's house, while the hearse in attendance received the general's remains, and with the little cortége attending them slowly entered the city. The first stroke of the bell had brought to their feet all those who were not already on the street, and silently the doors of the houses were opened as their inmates poured out to take part in this welcome to the nation's mighty dead. Every avenue leading to the street along which the procession moved was thronged; the eager civilian and the maimed soldier toiling along on his crutch were seen hurrying forward to the same goal. The profound silence amid so much motion was impressive in the extreme, and the effect was heightened by the solemn toll of the bell, which at regular intervals startled the still air. As the procession, passing down Grace Street, reached the Capitol Square, the gates were thrown open, and the cortége entered and passed directly down the avenue to the Governor's mansion. The crowd, aware that this Square would be the halting-place, had already swarmed over its beautiful grounds, and men were seen clinging to the sides of the Capitol, thronging the steps and pedestals of the Washington monument, and hanging from the trunks and limbs of the trees, eager to catch a glimpse of all that was earthly of him whose spirit had passed beyond the skies.

The people, restless in their grief, and anxious to give some further display of feeling, seized the occasion of the transfer of the general's remains from the Governor's mansion to the Capitol to do this. On the morning of the 12th, therefore, this solemn pageant took place. In it participated the Government officials, from the highest to the lowest, military men of every rank, from the lieutenant-general to the private, and citizens regardless of age, sex, or condition. All business was suspended, and a Sabbath-like stillness reigned through the streets of the city. The tolling of the bells was the first summons to the Square; but long before the appointed hour —ten o'clock—thousands of the citizens, among whom were hundreds of ladies and children, had assembled there in solemn silence. At the gate stood the hearse, draped in mourning, with four white horses attached to it. In the Governor's mansion, in an elevated position in the centre of the reception-room, was the metallic case containing the body. It was enveloped in the Confederate flag, and covered with bouquets and wreaths of flowers which had been sent as tributes of love and patriotic devotion. Around were assembled a few friends, many officers and officials of high rank, and the pallbearers, the last being six major- and brigadier-generals in full uniform. At eleven o'clock the coffin was borne from the house to the hearse, the vast concourse instinctively uncovering when it appeared.

The line of procession was formed, and moved forward slowly, as the band played the "Dead March in Saul," and the firing of the signal-gun on the Square announced to the thousands who could not get within sight of the

P*

line that it was in motion. Slowly the long procession wound through the streets of the city, all the sidewalks thronged with the populace and soldiery, and everywhere heads lowered and voices subdued, the measured beat of the drum and march of the procession alone being heard. Immediately behind the hearse, the war-steed of the dead hero, with his war-trappings upon him, was led; across the vacant saddle was thrown his master's military overcoat; in the stirrups, with feet reversed, were his boots. Next came members of the " Old Stonewall Brigade," who attracted much sympathetic notice, moving as they did with slow steps and downcast looks, as if each were following the corpse of a father. While the procession moved along, the bells were tolled and the guns fired until the head of the line appeared at the gate of the Square. At the western entrance of the Capitol the hearse stopped, and the coffin was taken out and borne up the steps into the hall of the House of Representatives as the band played a low dirge. In front of the Speaker's chair an altar had been erected, on which the coffin was laid. The superstitious had noticed with dismay that the coffin in the hearse was covered with the first Confederate flag which had been made upon the model selected a few weeks before by the Confederate Congress. It was considered ominous that its first use should be to envelop the body of the nation's darling. The same flag was wrapped around it in the Capitol. After the remains were placed in the Capitol, the cortége and military dispersed, but not so the people. They lingered still around the Capitol. What further honors could they now pay the mighty dead? What privilege did they still claim?—The dear and sacred one of looking on the face of the dead Jackson. As silently as they had followed his bier through the streets of their city, they now began to throng into the Capitol and file through the silent hall of death. At the door stood a sentinel with drawn sword, to keep the rush from being too great. Gentle women, and grave, stern men, passed in through the door, gazed for a moment on the dear face, and then sadly left the hall, many in tears, through a second entrance. One look, though it sufficed not, was all that could be obtained by each visitor, the throng behind pressing the visitor forward, the features of the mighty warrior in death's repose graven upon the tablets of the memory of all. Children of tender years, maiden and youth, who had never seen "Stonewall" Jackson living, crowded in, full of the parental injunction to look upon the features of "Stonewall" Jackson dead. What a memory these youthful minds bore away, to be recalled when their children's children speak of him in after-years! It is estimated that fully twenty thousand persons viewed the body thus lying in state; and the number would have been greater had the arrangements been better.

"The face of the dead displayed the same inimitable lines of firmness, with the long, slightly aquiline nose and high forehead, of marble whiteness; but the cheeks presented a deep pallor. The eyelids were firmly closed, the mouth natural, and the whole contour of the face composed, the full beard and moustache remaining. The body was dressed in a full citizen's suit. The doors of the hall were kept open to visitors until nine o'clock in the evening, when they were closed, and Richmond took her farewell of 'Stonewall' Jackson."*

---

* See Richmond Examiner, May 13, 1863, for the whole of this description—in quotation-marks as well as without—of the honors paid the dead hero by Richmond on the 12th of May.

Just as the sentinel was closing the doors, a one-armed soldier appeared, but was denied admittance, as the hour had arrived when it was ordered they should be closed. With flashing eyes, the soldier pointed to his empty sleeve, and said, "By this arm which I lost for my country I demand the privilege of seeing my general once more!"

The next day, May 13, Jackson's faithful body-guard, his staff, left Richmond for Lexington, by Charlottesville and Lynchburg. At almost every station flowers were sent into the car to be placed on the great man's coffin; and no tribute that love and admiration could suggest was omitted along the whole route. Arrived in Lexington, the remains were placed in Jackson's old lecture-room, and there guarded by the cadets during the night. On the morrow they were borne to the village church, where a simple and touching service for the dead was held over them by the dead warrior's beloved pastor. From thence they were borne, amid a weeping throng, to the village burying-ground, where they still lie.

The day the funeral cortége left Richmond, the "Examiner," in an editorial sketch of Jackson, said,—

"All the poor honors that Virginia, sorely pressed, could afford her most glorious and beloved son, having been offered to his mortal part in this Capitol, the funeral cortége of the famous Jackson left it yesterday morning on the long road to Lexington, in the Valley of Virginia. It was the last wish of the dead man to be buried there, amid the scenes familiar to his eyes through his manhood, obscure and unrecorded, but perhaps filled with recollections to him not less affecting than those connected with the brief but crowded period passed upon a grander stage. This desire, expressed at such a time,

demanded and has received unhesitating compliance.
Yet many regret that his remains will not rest in another
spot. Near this city is a hill crowned by secular oaks,
washed by the waters of the river, identified with what
is great in the State's history from the days of Elizabeth
to the present hour, which has been well selected as the
place of natural honor for the illustrious dead of Virginia. There sleep Monroe and Tyler. We have neither
a Westminster nor a Pantheon, but all would wish to see
the best that we could give conferred on Jackson. Here-
after Virginia will build for him a stately tomb, and
strike a medal to secure the memory of his name beyond
the reach of accident, if accident were possible. But it
is not possible; nor is a monument necessary to cause the
story of this man's life to last when bronze shall have
corroded and marble crumbled. Such expressions of a
nation's gratitude are not to be reproved or checked; but
they serve the giver, not the receiver, when thus worthy.

> " ' What needs our hero for his honored bones
> The labor of an age in piléd stones
> Or that his hallowed reliques should be hid
> Under a star-y pointing pyramid?
> Dear son of memory, great heir of fame,
> What need'st thou such weak witness of thy name?'

. . . "At Lexington the cadets had but little par-
itality for the taciturn professor. At one time his life
was threatened by a cadet dismissed from the Institute,
the wild boy actually going to the extremity of lying in
wait for him on the road leading from the Institute to
the village. As Jackson, in his accustomed walk to the
village, approached the spot where his enemy awaited
him, a bystander called out to him of his danger. 'Let
the assassin murder, if he will,' replied the professor, as

he walked in the most unconcerned manner towards the young man, who slunk abashed from his path. . . .

"The accounts of General Jackson's appearance are varied. Many could see nothing great in his form or face; but those are they that hold to the stage idea of a hero. . . . But experienced observers of men do not hesitate to declare that they have recognized him among a crowd of other officers as the only man there who could be Jackson. He was a muscular man, six feet high, of a clear, white complexion, blue-gray eyes, sharp aquiline nose; a prominent chin, set on a powerful and well-curved jaw. The skull was magnificent in size and shape; the forehead both broad and high, and balanced by a long, deep mass behind and above the ear."

Thus ends the record of the remarkable career of this most remarkable man. It is impossible to study his life without being struck by the useful lesson which it offers to mankind. To the young aspirant for fame; to the youth, thirsting for knowledge and struggling in poverty to secure an education; to all, in short, who are striving to make headway against a sea of troubles in their walk through life, what encouragement it offers, what lessons in patient perseverance! And in that exalted perfection of faith which no earthly cloud could dim, but which to the uncomprehending was only fanaticism, how highly blessed he was among his fellow-men! how many earthly treasures could have been dispensed with as long as this heaven-born gift was his,—this simple faith which in the midst of the darkest hour of trial revealed to him the hidden joys of the unknown world whose hallowed radiance illumined his pathway through life.

Born and reared in obscurity, passing through a child-hood marked in its earliest stages by trials which might have crushed a less buoyant spirit, he struggled on until in his admission to West Point he had the much-coveted opportunity of securing an education. From that time until he left Lexington at the head of a company of boys to enter the service of the Confederate States—save that short, brilliant period in Mexico—his life was uneventful. That he was good, that he was brave, that he was industrious, his acquaintances all knew. In the sunshine of his bright temper his family basked, while the warmth of his affections and his tender caressing manner in that sacred circle knit their hearts to his by ties too strong to be broken even by death. His intimate friends found in him a judgment so strong, so clear, and so just that his advice was oftener sought and oftener followed than that of any other. But to the world he was a fanatic in religion; in society he was considered a dull man; and to the students in his lecture-room he was a conscientious but uninteresting teacher. Yet it was during the silence of those voiceless years that the man was formed who in the brief space of two years was to have a career so brilliant as to leave his name enrolled among the great ones of the earth.

In secret and in silence the busy little insects of the deep toil for centuries, unseen by the world, when suddenly the fruit of their labors appears in the beautiful island which rises in the midst of a waste of waters. Beneath the cover of her dull winter garb the secret influences of nature are at work, until under the enchanting influences of a spring sun she bursts through her shroud and appears in a beauty so varied and so brilliant as to dazzle the eyes of her worshipers. And so it is with the great man. The calmest and most unknown period of his life is the great preparation-time. From the hour when Jackson, as a youth full of ambition and of aspirations for the future, inscribed in his diary the words, " You can be what you choose to be," to the hour of his death, he was never neglectful either of acquiring knowledge or of discharging the duties of life. He knew how to prize the little moments which make up the sum of life; how to seize the little opportunities of doing good which strengthen virtue in a man's soul and lead to noble deeds and generous sacrifices; how to strengthen his mind by daily study.

When the hour then came to summon him forth into the arena where honor and fame were to be won, he was not found wanting, but ready armed and equipped for the fray. A man of indomitable will, untiring energy, and endowed with personal courage to as high a degree as it is ever vouchsafed to the sons of men, he could indeed be whatever he chose to be. Devotion to duty was the star which guided him through life; and how many great names does not the world owe to this same devotion! It bore Washington through the trials of the cruel winter at Valley Forge; it sustained Lee in the bitter agony of the hour of surrender at Appomattox; and it sent Jackson forth from his lecture-room an unknown man, and found him at the end of two short years laid in state in this same room as a dead warrior, but one whose deeds in that short and brilliant period had made his name immortal.

Happy the nation that is fruitful in great men, and happier still when to those great men she can point as models of every manly and Christian virtue, and, as she inscribes their names in history, feels sure that they are as pure as they are brilliant!   Virginia, who has been so justly reproached for lagging behind amid such progress as this century has witnessed in science, art, and literature, may be pardoned for believing that in the simplicity of life and of manners which characterizes her people, and in her decried civilization, there must be some secret power, some potent influence for good, which could produce the man that in the war of Independence made the name of Washington peerless among those of the great leaders in that immortal struggle, and which, before the first centennial of the nation was ushered in, finds her emerging from the fiery ordeal of civil war with her household gods, indeed, lying shivered around her, but with unstained honor, and pure hands inscribing on her banners beside the name of this, her great first-born in glory, the no less loved, no less honored, and no less brilliant names of Lee and Jackson.

CHAPTER XVIII.

CONCLUSION.

Soon after Jackson's death, a number of his admirers in England formed an association whose aim was to have a bronze statue of the great Captain made. For this purpose a sum of four thousand guineas was raised, and the order for the statue given to the distinguished Foley. It was intended to present the statue to the Confederacy, with the stipulation that it was to be placed in Richmond. Mr. Foley immediately began the work of modeling, but the further execution of the work was delayed by the interference of other orders. In the mean time, the Confederacy fell, and the statue remained in embryo for several years. It was not cast in bronze until 1874, and was later offered to the State of Virginia in the following letter to the Governor:

"Arklow House, Connaught Place,
London, March 2, 1875.

"Sir,—When the news reached England of the death of General T. J. Jackson (so well known as 'Stonewall Jackson'), a subscription was spontaneously organized in this country among persons who admired the character of that truly great man, to procure a statue of him which they might present to his native country as a tribute of English sympathy and admiration.

"The work was intrusted to a-most distinguished
358

STATUE ERECTED AT RICHMOND, VIRGINIA, OCTOBER 26, 1875.

(Page 358.)

artist (the late Mr. J. H. Foley, R.A.), and, although its progress was delayed by the ill health of the sculptor and by his conscientious desire for the accuracy of the portrait, and latterly by his death, it has been brought to a successful conclusion in the form of a standing statue of heroic size, cast in bronze. It is a very noble work of art, and, it is hoped and believed, a faithful likeness.

"As representing the subscribers, it is now my pleasurable duty to ask you whether the State of Virginia will accept this memorial of its distinguished son, and tribute of English sympathy, and would guarantee its erection in some conspicuous spot in Richmond. If the answer is favorable, I would take the necessary steps to forward the statue to its destination. It is the privilege of members of our Royal Academy of Arts that the works of a deceased Academician may be contributed to the exhibition immediately succeeding the death. It is considered due alike to the artist and the subject that the English people should have the opportunity of seeing the statue before it leaves this country forever.

"The annual exhibition of the Academy closes about the beginning of August; after which date no delay need take place in forwarding the statue to Virginia.

"I have the honor to remain, sir, your faithful and obedient servant,

"A. J. B. Beresford Hope,
"M. P. for University of Cambridge."

In communicating Mr. Hope's letter to the General Assembly, the Governor said,—

"It is not doubted that the General Assembly will promptly and appropriately recognize the munificence which offers such an honor to Virginia, and will make whatever appropriation may be sufficient to receive the statue and erect it on a suitable pedestal.

" It revives no animosities of the past, it wounds the sensibilities of no good man of whatever party or section, to honor and revere the memory of Jackson. All the world knows that the earth beneath which his body lies covers the ashes of a patriot and hero whose greatness shed lustre on the age in which he lived. His example belongs to mankind, and his deeds and virtues will be cherished by all the coming generations of the great American republic as among the proudest memories of a common glory. Many others are now the objects of higher honors and louder praises. But when the accidents of fortune and success shall no longer determine the value of principles and achievements, when the names of others now more applauded shall have been swept into oblivion by the hand of time, the memory of Stonewall Jackson, like that of his great commander, will continue to grow brighter as the centuries pass into history."

On receiving this message from the Governor, with the letter accompanying it, the General Assembly passed the following preamble and resolutions:

" The Governor having transmitted to the General Assembly a communication from A. J. B. Beresford Hope, Esq., Member of Parliament for the University of Cambridge, tendering to this Commonwealth, on behalf of himself and other English subjects, a bronze statue of heroic size, by Foley, of the late General Thomas J. Jackson :

" 1. Resolved, by the Senate and House of Delegates, That Virginia, acknowledging with profound sensibility this generous manifestation of English sympathy by her people and admiration for her heroic son, very gratefully accepts the offering.

" 2. That the statue be erected on a pedestal worthy of the work, on some conspicuous spot within the grounds of the Capitol, to be preserved and cherished by the people of Virginia as a memorial of its distinguished subject and of the noble sympathies of its honored donors.

" 3. That the Governor be requested to give public notice, by proclamation, of the day on which the statue will be uncovered, so that the people may assemble to do honor to the event.

" 4. That A. J. B. Beresford Hope be invited to attend on the occasion as a guest of the State, and that he be tendered by the Governor the hospitalities of Virginia.

" 5. That the Governor be requested to communicate the above resolutions to Mr. Beresford Hope, and express to him and his associates the grateful acknowledgments of the people of Virginia.

" 6. That his Excellency the Governor; Captain J. L. Eubank, Chairman of the Senate Committee; General W. B. Taliaferro, Chairman of the House Committee; and General Jubal A. Early, be, and are hereby, appointed a board of commissioners, who shall be charged with the duty of receiving the statue, disbursing such appropriation as may be made therefor, and making all arrangements and contracts necessary to carry into effect the foregoing resolutions."

On the same day the General Assembly appropriated ten thousand dollars to defray the expenses of receiving and erecting the statue.

The statue arrived in Richmond September 22, and was at once taken in charge by a detail of the First Regiment Virginia Volunteers, and guarded until the evening of the next day, September 23. It was then placed on a wagon, ready to be moved up-town to its destination. But it was not the intention either of the authorities or of the citizens that the statue should pass through the streets of the city with only a small military guard. All the volunteer companies turned out, and, followed by a procession of citizens in carriages and on foot, they moved down the streets of the city to the spot where the statue was found resting on a wagon, to which was attached a long rope. This was seized by several hundred men, and the statue of the great Captain was drawn through the streets of the city by the loving arms of his countrymen. They drew the wagon with the greatest ease, and it was gratifying to see among those who were at the rope Confederate veterans and Union officers in the late war mingled together, the animosities of the past being lost in the presence of this touching tribute to the memory of the mighty dead. The streets were thronged,—men, women, and children of all ranks being out to join in the procession. A little girl of five years old was seen moving quietly beside her father, who marched along with the men at the rope.

When the head of the procession entered the Capitol Square, the concourse already there was found to be very great. The statue was drawn to the foot of the western steps of the Capitol. There the military were drawn up in line, and ordered to "Halt! Front face! Present arms!" Then followed a profound silence, and the officer in command of the military delivered the statue formally to the Governor, who received it with an appropriate speech.

The 26th of October was appointed as the day for the inauguration of the statue, and when it came a throng such as had not been seen since the days of the war was found in the city. People from all parts of the country —North, South, East, West—came to be present, and when the beautiful October day was ushered in it found the city bright with flags and floral and artistic decorations which had been made by loving hands, and an air of such a gala-day as had not been often witnessed in the eventful history of that devoted city. A procession, composed of ex-Confederate officers and soldiers, citizens, visitors, and the dignitaries of the State, made the tour of the city, with bands playing, banners flying, and beneath triumphal arches. Private houses were decorated, public buildings tastefully festooned with flags, and everything done to add to the brilliancy of the scene. In the Capitol Square the statue stood veiled on its handsome pedestal, and thither the steps of all were directed.

When the procession entered the Square, the ceremonies were opened by prayer from a minister who knelt at the speaker's stand, which was wound about with the United States flag. Then followed the Governor's graceful and cordial speech of welcome, and Rev. Dr. Hoge's finished oration, which being ended, the statue was unveiled amid salvos of artillery and shouts of applause.

THE END.